The Chocolate Set

A Swedish Journey

by Fredda J. Burton

Note for Librarians: a cataloguing record for this book that includes Dewey Decimal Classification and US Library of Congress numbers is available from the Library and Archives of Canada. The complete cataloguing record can be obtained from their online database at:

www.collectionscanada.ca/amicus/index-e.html

ISBN 1-4120-5030-8

Printed in Victoria, BC, Canada

TRAFFORD

Offices in Canada, USA, Ireland, UK and Spain

This book was published *on-demand* in cooperation with Trafford Publishing. On-demand publishing is a unique process and service of making a book available for retail sale to the public taking advantage of on-demand manufacturing and Internet marketing. On-demand publishing includes promotions, retail sales, manufacturing, order fulfilment, accounting and collecting royalties on behalf of the author.

Book sales for North America and international:

Trafford Publishing, 6E–2333 Government St.,

Victoria, BC v8t 4p4 CANADA

phone 250 383 6864 (toll-free 1 888 232 4444)

fax 250 383 6804; email to orders@trafford.com

Book sales in Europe:

Trafford Publishing (uk) Ltd., Enterprise House, Wistaston Road Business Centre, Wistaston Road, Crewe, Cheshire cw2 7rp UNITED KINGDOM

phone 01270 251 396 (local rate 0845 230 9601)

facsimile 01270 254 983; orders.uk@trafford.com

Order online at:

www.trafford.com/robots/04-2839.html

10 9 8 7 6 5 4 3 2

FOR THOSE WHO LIVED IT

Acknowledgements

The author wishes to acknowledge the support and encouragement of:

    Kent Haruf, Beth Lordan, Ricardo Cruz, H. Arnold Barton, Betsy George, Bill Ransom, and most particularly, my husband, Theodore A. Burton.

Introduction

I call this book 'heritage retrieval.' None of it is true, and, yet, all of it is true. The names and the people are composites and outright fictions; the place names and customs are real. The events and stories grew from my grandmother, Hilma Hanson's fertile imagination and our collective subconscious. The name of the ship, *Charlotta*, is meant as a tribute to Vilhelm Moberg and his 1951 book *"The Emigrants."*

This book started life as a short story written for one of Kent Haruf's classes at Southern Illinois University. With time it took on a life of its own and grew into the short novel required for my M.F.A. degree. Friends and relatives who read it asked about the events that led the family into poverty in the first place and did Klara ever make the trip to America. Here is the answer.

When I moved to Port Angeles, Washington, I learned Scandinavian folk art from the small community of rosemalers and Swedish painters there. [Thank you, Mikki Borup, Barbara Claboe, Mary Dahl, Maryann McFarland, Myrtle Halko, Luella Hilby, Ann Nilsson, and Nancy Powers.] My illustrations grew from this as well as two trips to Sweden and many years of scientific and botanical illustration. *The Chocolate Set: A Swedish Journey* is the amalgamation of all these things.

Maria, Anna, and Erik Axel.

All is Vanity: 1901.

Sixteen year old Klara Larsson stood in the long line winding through the Great Hall of Ellis Island. Her ankle-length dress of homespun wool enveloped her thin body and smothered her in the summer heat. She had removed her fringed shawl and draped it over the box at her feet. When the line moved, she pushed the box along the smooth marble floor a few inches, inches that brought her closer to the customs inspectors, the medical examiners, and her new life in America. Though the hall was immense, it seemed close and airless because of the crowds of people lined up back and forth across the room. They were surrounded by their baggage: all their worldly possessions were contained in the shapeless bundles, baskets, padlocked trunks, leather-bound suitcases, and painted boxes spread at their feet.

Klara glanced down at her own box, her granmutter's bride box, small and shabby alongside some of the other heaps of luggage sprawled across the Great Hall. As Klara stared at the mass of people, she felt light-headed, dizzy. Her neck ached and her stomach hurt. Her thoughts seemed about to pound through her skull, escape to the open space below the tiled ceiling high overhead. Would the officials let her pass or would she be sent back. How was she going to manage the heavy box containing her only possessions except for the clothes she wore and the few things packed in the bag she carried over her shoulder. Would anyone be there to meet her at the dock. As the hour wore on those worries were replaced by the fear she would faint or vomit, there in public, in front of all those people. The noise, a babble of many voices and many languages overlaid with the clank of ceiling fans, the horns, bells, and whistles of the harbor vessels, the high-pitched moan of unseen machines, seemed to wash over the huddled families like invisible waves.

Now and then an official would call a family or a single man from the group to hurry them out a side door. The gaps their leaving made in the lines were quickly filled by those behind them. When the family just ahead was called out, Klara struggled her box across the gap, dragging, pushing, half lifting the burden of the clumsy thing, afraid of losing her place in line.

The gap closed, she sat down on her box to catch her breath. While she gasped for air and calmed herself, she noticed the family now in front of her. It consisted of a mother with four or five very young children, apparently traveling alone. The children were barefoot and wore clothes cut down from old adult clothing. They had no boxes or trunks, only lumpish gray bundles tied up with string and rags. Even the tiny children had a bundle to shepherd through the building, but it was the burden carried by the oldest, a girl of six or seven, that caught Klara's attention. The gray-faced, dirty child had been entrusted with a family heirloom, a large antique bowl.

A terrible wave of homesickness washed Klara when she saw the child struggling to keep the bowl, a bowl of thinnest porcelain safe. She

had it clasped tight to her skinny chest. When she had to walk forward to keep up with her mother, she craned her neck to see the floor where she was to step. Even to Klara's untrained, back country eye, the bowl was a treasure. The pattern of roses twined with gold-edged leaves was so much like the pattern on the chocolate set that graced the shelf above the stove back home in Sweden that Klara had to swallow the sobs that gathered in her throat.

A great tumble of thoughts beat through her mind. Flashes of broken cups, fallen trees, leering tramps, her own dear mother screaming at her, the mad babble of the asylum. Klara tried to clear her head and concentrate on getting through Ellis Island. She looked away from the tattered child with the fragile bowl and focused on the line of people farther ahead of her. They must be close to the examiners by now.

When Klara finally saw the end of the room, she nearly swooned. The line didn't end there. It made a sharp turn and wound up a long staircase to the second floor. At the head of the stairs she could see tables and many people, men dressed in suits with ties and stiff collars, doctors in their white coats carrying stethoscopes and notebooks, nurses dressed in white with starched caps.

While she was thinking about the difficulty of wrestling her box up those many steps, a tall young orderly, a black man, approached, checking name tags and asking questions. For a few minutes the waiting travelers roused themselves from their apathy; some pulled back in surprise, others crossed themselves. Klara was only mildly interested in the man's deep brown skin and tightly curled black hair because she had seen several Africans on the wharf in Kristiania.

The child with the rose painted bowl, however, seemed terrified. She's probably never seen a black person before, thought Klara. The little girl screamed, then jerked away when he tried to read her name tag. With a crash she tripped over the uneven hem of her long dress and fell. Though she tried to protect the bowl, it slipped from her weary fingers and crashed to the floor in a hundred pieces.

With the child's screams beating on her ears Klara fainted. Days later she would remember many hands lifting her to a gurney, bumping her along to another building, placing her on a bed with cool rough sheets, but mostly she let her mind wander back to her home, her grandfather, her parents and siblings. Remembered stories of the early years soothed and entertained her as she drifted in and out of the hectic sleep of fever.

Kungsängslilja
(Fritillaria meleagris)

The Early Years: 1859–85.

Stone Tears, Stone Hearts.

Erik Axel Norrling walked across his barley field until he came to the huge rock that marred the symmetry of the newly plowed soil. He or his hired workers had plowed around that rock for seven seasons, now. His father and grandfather had whipped their ox teams to the left, to the right of the gray rock. Other generations of Norrlings had hammered on it, rooted under it, from time before memory or, at least since the Crown had kept written land records.

Erik Axel slapped at the granite monster with his coiled whip.

"Damn rock. You get bigger every season."

He spoke aloud, but to himself. The spare, blond man cared little for history or record keeping. Though those early records showed the rock as a boundary point of the Norrling family estate in Norrbarke Parish in north central Sweden, his grandfather had enlarged the estate until the river now marked its southwestern boundary. Erik Axel felt that the useless rock stole valuable yards and inches of space that could be producing grain to sell at the mill in Smedjebacken.

He walked around the rock to gain a better feel for its size. In his mind he measured, calculated weight and angle. Not so tall that a man couldn't see over it, nor so broad that four men couldn't link arms around it, the rock appeared to sit shallow in the earth. Erik Axel leaned into the granite with his shoulder and thought he felt the rock shudder the tiniest bit. I'll have it gone by Mid-Summer's Eve, he thought.

His whistling drowned out the birdsong as he hurried into the stable yard. Behind him the stone cast a long shadow over the neat furrows rippling outward from its base.

~~~

With two of his indentured workers at his elbow Erik Axel

Norrling knelt in the dirt to examine the broken cultivator. Three of its iron teeth were broken and the frame twisted in his hands.

"How did this happen?"

With his back against the rock which was hot from the morning sun, he studied the two workers. If they were insects, he thought, one would be a fat honey bee, the other a sharp nosed wasp.

"Who is responsible?"

Oscar, slow and square, not very tall, said nothing, but shrugged in the direction of the rock.

Lars wiped his face on his shirt tail and stood with his cap in hand, certain he was being accused.

"Not me, sir. It was the rock. Caught the tines as I steered around it."

Oscar found his voice. "The rock, yes sir. Couldn't be helped."

"Clumsy fools. You keep the oxen in the furrow, then go back and till around the rock by hand. How many times do I have to tell you?"

"Slow work."

"Hand work is stoop labor. It breaks the back. Makes a man unfit for real work. Besides, it's not in my contract."

"What do you know about contracts?"

Erik Axel had heard rumors about labor agitators in the parish, but dismissed them as frivolous.

"I hold your indenture papers and that means I own you. Five years I own you."

When neither man answered, Erik Axel announced that he intended to remove the rock the following day.

"Get here early and wear your heaviest gloves."

~~~

At dawn the three men stood beside the rock. A team of oxen and two stout horses were tethered nearby, barely discernible in the morning fog. Erik Axel thumped the huge boulder with his walking stick.

"We'll use levers, thick ones. If we can get it started, the team can finish it off."

"Mighty big rock, sir. Maybe we should get more help," said Lars. "More hands will make light work."

"Don't try to squirm out of it."

"Oh, no sir. We could try burning it. Dig a pit underneath and set a slow fire. I hear that makes the rock brittle so you can smash it into smaller pieces."

"I want this rock gone, today."

Erik Axel hit the rock again, this time his blow fell inches from Lars's head.

"Get to work."

Without a word the second worker, Oscar Bengt, grabbed a shovel and began digging as close to the rock as he could. He was red-faced and sweating by the time he opened a groove in the rocky soil large enough for the end of the first lever. By the time Lars picked up his shovel, Oscar had his lever in place. He moved over to dig a another trench and set the second lever.

Lars leaned on his shovel and watched.

"Why can't we blast the rock loose? Blow it to smithereens? Els Johansson blasted stumps on his place last fall. Worked neat as a whistle."

Erik Axel didn't answer. Dynamite was expensive. And more than a little frightening. He was unwilling to admit his ignorance of its use. His father and grandfather had always cleared land by hand and that was good enough for him.

Oscar called to Lars to come and help him.

"Rock's a bad un. Too smooth to grip."

He used an iron pry bar to wedge one of the long poles farther under the edge of the stone.

"It's a heavy bugger."

He searched for a firm grip on the lever.

Lars inched up to the second lever and stood ready to put his considerable weight to ousting the rock.

"We could rig a collar on this thing and bust it out of here with a team of oxen."

"Damn you, Lars. Shut up and lean on that lever."

Only the straw-colored hair and red ears of Oscar showed above the edge of the rock as he struggled to wrench it free of the earth.

"Push."

"I am." Lars spat in the dust at his feet. "I am pushing."

The stone held firm, then its earthy bed gave a little. A dark line of newly exposed soil showed around the edge of the boulder. It moved almost imperceptibly.

Erik Axel leaped into the wagon bed to better see what was happening.

"Throw your weight on that lever," he screamed. "More. Push. Now."

Squat, broad-shouldered Oscar looked as if he would squeeze out of his sweat-blackened shirt if he pushed any harder. Lars had barely broken a sweat.

"Lars, get that lever deeper under the edge. Hurry."

Muffled crunching, groaning sounds came from the far side of the rock. Its weight was shifting onto the dry brush and loose stones at its base. Both Lars and Oscar were shouting now.

Erik Axel's voice, harsh with the effort of being heard, cut across the noise.

"Push harder. Get your shoulders into it. Quick now. You've almost got the bastard."

He leaned over the edge of the wagon bed, knuckles white from gripping the sideboard, face purple with strain.

"Push. Push now."

The boulder shifted again. For an instant it balanced on the edge of its ancient bed. It looked as if it would roll free, then Lars slipped. He lost his grip on his lever and it shot from under the rock.

"Look out. It's coming back on us."

He jumped away from the rock and scrambled to the wagon. When he turned to watch the rock, he saw that Oscar still had his weight thrown across his lever. His toes just touched the ground, one shoulder nearly brushing the rock.

Lars opened his mouth to scream a warning, but no sound came out.

Oscar, balanced on the pole with his legs wide apart, elbows braced, was jolted by the boulder's backward motion. He tried to let go of his lever, jump out of the boulder's path, but his shirt snagged on the rough pole. The huge granite boulder shuddered, the thick poles held its weight just long enough for him to jerk his shirt free. But before he could clamber from its path, the ends of the levers cracked and splintered to pieces under the stone.

The rock moved, slow and ponderous, back towards the earth. Only Oscar's lever saved his life. It threw him like a wild pony, threw him clear of the rock. He landed in the pile of levers, iron pry bars, harness, and ropes with a crash.

"Look what you've done."

Erik Axel hesitated there in his perch on the wagon, then leaped down and cracked Lars alongside the head with his stick and turned to Oscar.

"Get up. Up. Up."

Oscar lay there bloodied and unconscious until Erik Axel prodded him with his stick. He opened his eyes and struggled to obey, to get up. With a moan he fell back, his leg crumpled under him.

Erik Axel turned on Lars. Who else could be to blame for this catastrophe. Though workers had few rights and lived little better than the livestock, they still had monetary value to the landowner. Oscar was an especially valuable worker.

"Look what you've done. Lout. Idiot."

With shaking hands Lars helped Erik Axel lift the injured man into the wagon. Oscar thrashed and screamed, begged them to kill him, put him out of his misery.

"Take the oxen back to the stable, then meet us at the cottage." Erik Axel shook the reins and the horses picked their way back across the field to the road.

Oscar moaned the first few bumps, then fainted. On the road Erik Axel whipped the horses into an awkward lope. When he reached Fork Road, he hauled back on the reins and turned the team onto the narrow track that led to the worker's cottage on the far edge of his estate. Though the horses maintained a fast walk on the straight stretches, the many twists and steep grades at the stream crossings slowed the trip to a crawl. Oscar came to his senses occasionally, but the shock and pain overwhelmed him each time.

At the last grade Erik Axel urged the horses into a trot and they muscled the wagon up the slope and through the underbrush into a clearing. The thatch-roofed tenant cottage on the far side of the clearing looked small and worn under the majestic fir trees.

The team trotted up to the cottage door and stopped with their front hooves in the small dooryard garden. Before Erik Axel could climb down to summon Oscar's wife, the horses had plunged their steaming muzzles into the clumps of daisies and summer savory.

"Mrs. Bengt." He pounded on the door. "Anyone home?"

A thin woman, arms soapy to the elbow, opened the door. Several small children crowded around her, pulled at her apron, her skirt.

"What is it? What's wrong?"

Without waiting for answers, she pushed past Erik Axel and ran to the wagon. She screamed when she saw her husband motionless and bloodied.

"He's dead. Dead, oh God. Don't tell me he's dead."

She climbed into the wagon bed and prodded Oscar, then shook him.

"Think of the kiddels and the new babe. They need you," she wailed.

Oscar moaned and his eyelids flicked. He struggled to answer, to sit up, but managed only a garbled cry before he fainted.

Erik Axel pulled Mrs. Bengt from the wagon.

"Calm down, woman. You'll make things worse. Lars will be here soon to help. We need to get your husband inside."

Mrs. Bengt straightened up, wiped her hands on her apron, and looked Erik Axel in the eye.

"So sorry to be a trouble to you."

She turned and called to her oldest son, a boy of about ten who had been gathering sticks at the edge of the clearing.

"Go. Run for Mrs. Breen."

She waved him away from the wagon when he approached and tried to look at his father.

"Hurry."

Called Old Bone by most folk, Mrs. Breen was the first to be called to attend the very poor. She had no formal training, could neither read nor write, but she would come for a few potatoes, a loaf of bread, or a hot meal.

Just then, Lars rode into the yard on one of the half-broke carriage horses. He slid off the horse as it tossed its head and side-stepped across the yard. Clutching the reins, he edged up to the group of people by the wagon.

Erik Axel called the Bengt boy and asked him if he could ride a horse.

"Yes, sir. Of course, sir."

"Lars. Give the boy a leg up."

"The horse is rank, sir. Let me go."

Erik Axel ignored him and helped the boy straddle the tall horse. He handed up the reins and told him to take a firm grip, hold onto the mane, and keep the colt to a moderate canter.

The boy jammed his bare heels into the horse's sides and tore out of the clearing.

"Now, Lars, we need to get this fellow into the house."

With Mrs. Bengt to give directions, hold the door, shoo children out of the way, they soon had Oscar laid out on the children's bed. It was a bed that folded out from one of the long benches along the wall by the fireplace.

"Maybe we should have put him in the big bed," said Lars.

The adults slept in a cupboard bed built into the wall of the one room house. It was partitioned from view with curtains.

"No, the old bone setter needs room to work."

Erik Axel finally put words to their unspoken fear. Oscar probably had a badly broken leg and needed much repair.

Erik Axel sat down in the one comfortable chair in the sparely furnished room, the chair usually reserved for the head of the household. He had resigned himself to spending the rest of the day tending to the problem of his indentured worker.

"I'll put the kettle on," said Mrs. Bengt. "She'll be needing boiling water and you two could do with a strong cup of coffee."

"Can you brew something to ease Oscar's pain a bit, too?"

"I'll steep some wild cherry for him."

The root bark of the black cherry tree was reputed to be a strong sedative. It released hydrocyanic acid when soaked in warm, but not boiling, water, so women were apt to keep it around to ease the pain of childbirth.

"Add a few hop cones, if you have any."

Before sundown they heard the clatter of hooves in the dooryard. It was the boy and a mud-caked horse. For a minute they thought he had returned alone. Was Mrs. Breen out on another job. Or ailing, herself. Then they watched as a tiny bundle of rags detached itself from behind the boy and slide from the sweaty horse. Mrs. Breen had arrived.

"Where's me patient?" The old bone setter tottered to the door. She paused and called back to the boy, "Bring me stuff."

"I'll fetch it," said Lars. He was glad to be out of the dim house.

Mrs. Breen grasped the door frame with one skeleton thin hand and pulled herself over the stoop and into the house.

At Oscar's bedside she pulled back the worn quilt that covered him and demanded they cut the patient's trousers off. When Oscar protested such an insult to modesty, she threw the quilt over his head, removed a huge pair of shears from her bag, and cut a long swath up his pants leg. Mrs. Bengt got her own sewing scissors and helped finish the job.

Oscar's complaints quickly turned to moans which escalated to screams when Mrs. Breen began her examination. When her knobby fingers probed the swollen mass of his thigh, he passed out.

"Broke sure enough," she said.

"Can you help him?"

"I be wanting a strip of muslin or stout cotton. And hot water."

With instructions from Mrs. Bengt who sat by the hearth nursing her baby, Lars found the long strips of linen kept ready to carry a coffin from the house to a waiting wagon. He also brought the kettle from the stove.

Mrs. Breen first soaked the linen strip in hot water, then mixed up a lavish handful of powdered spike root and wild ginger. After some thought and another examination of her patient, she added dried yarrow to her concoction until she had a stiff paste.

"Come boys," she called to Erik Axel and Lars. "I be needing strong hands now."

"Perhaps Mrs. Bengt and the children should go outside?" suggested Erik Axel. He, himself, wanted to go outside, wanted to climb into his wagon and drive his team home to comfort, a good meal, and the forgetfulness of sleep.

"Send them out," said Mrs. Breen. She looked over at the huddle of children in the corner.

The oldest boy had the little children gathered around him. He was knifing jam onto pieces of bread and portioning it out amongst them. When he heard the conversation, he led them from the room.

Mrs. Breen instructed the two men to stand close by the bed. Lars was warned he must hold the patient still no matter how much he begged and struggled.

To Erik Axel she said, "Grip his ankle. Both hands. I say pull, you pull."

With the strip of linen threaded under Oscar's leg, she laid a thick layer of herb paste over the swelling and down onto his knee.

"Pull, now," she commanded. "Be quick about it."

Lars threw his full weight onto the patient's chest, while Erik Axel pulled. Oscar howled like a wild beast. Oblivious, Mrs. Breen wound the linen strip around his entire leg, pulling it just tight enough at each turn. After the fourth or fifth turn Oscar lost consciousness.

About the time Erik Axel thought his arms would give out, Mrs. Breen muttered, "All done."

Though known throughout the parish for her abilities, Mrs. Breen's bone-setting talents were barely up to such a complicated task. She admonished them to fetch Dr. Waldsson out from the parish seat, Smedjebacken, as soon as possible. Erik Axel dropped a silver *ore* and two coppers into her bag and escorted her to the door.

"Get in the wagon. You can ride as far as the Grangeburg Road."

~~~

Erik Axel returned with Dr. Waldsson late the next evening after chores. They found the children bundled together in the cupboard bed ready for sleep. Mrs. Bengt was kneeling by her husband's side with a spoon and a bowl of thin porridge.

The doctor slapped his case down on the table.

"Oat gruel. Good. Just the thing for the invalid."

Oscar looked up. His eyes were bloodshot and stubble shot with gray shadowed his face.

"Damn pap. Fry me some fat pork or stew up a mess of hare with turnips."

"He's interested in his food. That's a good sign." The doctor took the bowl and spoon from Mrs. Bengt and placed it on the table. "You can eat later."

He slid the blanket from Oscar's leg and examined Mrs. Breen's handiwork. With his fingers on Oscar's ankle he stared at the ceiling for a space of time, then demanded more light. Mrs. Bengt found a fat candle and lit it with an ember from the stove.

"Hold it just above my shoulder," said the doctor. "Right there. So the light hits his foot."

"How is he? Is it worse?"

"He has good color in his foot. He may live after all."

He checked the bandage that Mrs. Breen had applied. "Dry. That's good. The old girl does pretty fair work."

With the application of a splint to hold Oscar's swollen leg steady, the doctor said his job was done.

"He'll be a long time healing, though."

"Damn. I'll not have any work from him this season?" asked Erik

Axel.

He glared at the doctor and thought about the fee he would have to pay. Cash money was always in short supply and this year was no exception.

"Keep his bowels open. Use this for the pain." He pulled a bottle of white powder from his case. "A teaspoon of this in a little honey three or four times a day. Mind you don't give him too much."

"When do you think he'll be up and around?"

"And back to work?"

"Who can say. Not this season," said Doctor Waldsson. "This is a very grave injury. I'll send Mrs. Breen to change the wrapping in a few days. She can show you how to do it, then." He packed his bag and said he was ready to go.

Outside Erik Axel untied the horses and lifted the doctor's case up behind the seat of the light wagon. The two men climbed up behind the team and headed for town.

"How soon can he be moved?"

"Can you get by with day labor for the summer?"

"Lars is a poor stick. I meant to replace him at mid-summer."

"Best keep him on until after harvest. Oscar can go to relatives in town by then."

"With so many out of work you'd think I could find decent help."

"In my opinion it's too much strong drink that keeps them down."

"Have the farm workers been meeting again? Lars mentioned something about a protest."

"Damn shame the government abolished the guilds. Kept a man in his rightful place."

"Harvest time, you say?" Erik Axel hurried the team across a stretch of muddy road. "Guess that will do."

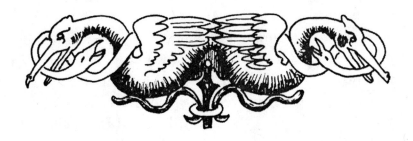

Bitter Harvest, Seeds of Hope.

Erik Axel climbed to a small knob of land where he could see his barley and oat fields stretching like ochre fingers through the green woodlands to the river. A chill in the air reminded him that winter was close. On his way back to the stable, he pulled a few stalks of barley. He ran his fingers through the rough bearded heads to dislodge a handful of grain. The plump kernels gleamed like gold nuggets in his palm. He prodded one with his thumb nail, then put a few in his mouth. Their flinty hardness dissolved to a sweet pulpy mass by the time he reached the stable door.

"Lars, hey, Lars," he shouted down the long ally way. "Sharpen the scythes and get the wagons ready."

Lars stumbled out of the empty stall near the tackroom. He had straw in his hair.

"Where you going?"

"I'll be back by supper time. Sweep the wagons and roll them out into the yard. Oil the harness and give the oxen an extra scoop of feed."

"Can't it wait?"

"Weather's about to change."

While he detailed work for Lars, he bridled a long legged roan mare and brushed her down. With more instructions to Lars he led the horse to the yard and dropped the harness over her back. With quick fingers he adjusted the breast strap and crupper, then backed her into the shafts of the two wheeled cart.

In Smedjebacken he drove to the market square and tied his horse to a tree. He walked past farmers with young goats and calves for sale, past the horse market with its long line of draft teams and sleek trotting horses, mares, foals, head tossing yearlings. When he reached the produce section, he paused to examine the wares displayed by giggling girls and bashful matrons. Crocks of summer jams and jelly, intricate stacks of brown eggs, mounds of lace work and knit caps seemed to draw his attention.

At one particular display of embroidered neck scarves he stopped and selected a linen piece with a snowflake pattern in black silk. When he paid the dark-haired girl, his hand lingered on hers a bit longer than necessary. He noted her smooth skin, red cheeks, and lively eyes.

He held the white scarf to his throat. "Your handiwork?"

"My name is Maria, Maria Lindbom."

"Very pretty."

From the livestock and booths filled with tempting goods he ambled past the mounds of used equipment and worn household goods. Next came the meat sellers, then the scrap dealers and a few old, black-clad women holding out a bunch of parsley or a few beads on a grimy string. At the very back of the market a crowd of men formed up into a ragged line when they saw Erik Axel coming towards them.

He walked down the line of men and examined several before he stepped back and faced them.

"You, with the red neck scarf, step forward."

The broad shouldered youngster grinned, tucked in his shirt tail, and hitched up his pants. Before he stepped forward he punched the dark man beside him.

"See, I told you."

"You ain't hired yet, boy."

Erik Axel tried to size up the young man. "What sort of work do you do?"

"Mining. Only work at Falun these days is underground."

"Falun? You're not local?"

Was the man on the run. Had he broken a work contract. Falun and its famed deep mine lay some ninety-five miles to the north. It would be just his luck to have the magistrate carry off one of his workers in the midst of harvest. Still, the lad looked strong and, besides, he only wanted him until the end of harvest.

The man misread Erik Axel's long silence and added, "I got to have sun and air. Tons of rock over head makes me right crazed."

"Family?"

"My name's Andor. No wife or kiddels if that's what you're asking."

"Be at my cart, the one with the roan mare, in an hour."

With a wave of his hand he indicated the direction of the road. He didn't bother to ask the man if he wanted farm work. He knew unemployed laborers were required to take any work offered. Any man without a job had only a few weeks to find employment before the sheriff could escort them to the parish line. Large groups of such vagrants flooded the roads.

Erik Axel continued to question the group of men he had pulled from the general mob. His tenant housing would serve a single man and a family man. The main house had not had a good cleaning since Oscar's accident and he was interested in a worker with a vigorous, willing wife in tow.

"You." He pointed to a stout man with neatly trimmed hair and clean shirt. "You have a wife?"

"I live at home. My mother is the baker's helper, sir."

"Damn," said Erik Axel. He waved the man away and motioned to a thin, dark man. A Finn or a Russian, he thought.

"Do you do farm work?"

"All me life. I can shoe a horse or an ox, too."

"Married?"

The dark man pointed to a large bruise on his cheek. "She has a real arm on her. Keeps me and the kiddels in line all right."

Erik Axel shook his head and the man slouched away.

He next questioned a broad shouldered teenager who insisted his brother be hired too. "We come together, or not at all. He needs me, sir. Can't speak a word. Works hard when I show him."

A stooped man with a fringe of wispy hair came next. He wore a battered cap and stood with his hands clasped behind his back.

"Married?"

"Twenty years to the same woman."

"Can you shock grain?"

"Did it all me life."

"Drive a team?"

"Of course." The man shifted his weight from one foot to the other.

"Take off your cap."

The man raised both hands to his head and fumbled with his cap. His fingers were bent and stiff from work and time and too many bitter cold mornings.

Erik Axel turned and walked back down the line.

"Anyone. Anyone who can shock grain and has a wife who can cook and clean, stand over this mark." He scraped a line in the dirt with his boot heel.

Only two stepped forward, a small flinty looking man and a blond fellow wearing trousers much too short for his long legs.

His interviews finished, Erik Axel gave the blond man directions to the estate and told him to move in as soon as possible.

On his way back through the market he hoped to catch a glimpse of dark-haired Maria. Her space was empty; she had already packed up her needlework and gone home.

~~~

Erik Axel gave the roan mare a pop with the whip the last quarter mile. She lifted her head, pricked her ears, and trotted up the lane past the main house to the stable yard. The new hired hand, the young man with the red neck scarf, rode in the back with his bundle of belongings on his lap, legs hanging out. He bounced from side to side, but managed to hang on.

Lars emerged from the open door.

"Lars, go help Oscar's family pack up their belongings. Take a wagon and team."

"Tomorrow would do just as well."

"You." With his whip he gestured at the man from Falun. "Drop your bundle in the stable room and go along with Lars."

Lars leaned against the stable wall and peered up at his boss who sat in the seat of the high-wheeled cart. "It's supper time."

"Move your own things into the stable room while you're about it."

"Name's Andor. Show me where to put my stuff."

"I'll meet you at the cottage." Erik Axel flicked the whip at the roan mare and drove out of the yard.

~~~

"Where can we go?" Oscar's wife sobbed loudly. Two small children hung on her skirts and added their wails to hers.

"The new worker and his family will be here before long." Erik Axel smacked his boot with his stick for emphasis and pushed past her into the dim house. He nearly forgot to duck his head at the low doorway.

He called back to her, "Lars is on his way. He'll help you pack and load the wagon."

While Mrs. Bengt summoned the older children from the woodlot where they were gathering sticks, Erik Axel spoke to Oscar.

"We start harvest tomorrow."

"I been expecting you."

"The new man will be here tonight or in the morning."

"Sorry I can't help."

"Here's a bit to tide you by until you're settled again."

He counted out a few silver *ore* and a handful of coppers. It was less than Oscar would have earned had he not been laid up, but more than nothing at all. Erik Axel had no obligation to pay him or let him stay on in the tenant house the past four months.

"Best put it away, man."

Shouts outside indicated that Lars and Andor, the Falun man, had arrived.

They carried the bedding from the cupboard bed out first. They arranged it in the wagon, then returned for Oscar.

"You can't move him," cried his wife. "It's too soon."

"Wrap his leg in the feather tick," instructed Erik Axel. "That's right. Bind it up tight."

"Lift," yelled Andor. He had Oscar's arm across his shoulder and he struggled to grasp Lars's hand to make a seat.

"No chance. Let me get a new grip."

Lars let go and Oscar fell back on the bed.

"Oh, please don't hurt him."

"Try again. Put your back into it, Lars."

Oscar gritted his teeth and the two men finally lifted him from the bed. With one of the children holding his injured leg steady and Mrs. Bengt helping they hoisted him into the wagon.

The hardest part of the moving job finished, they stowed the rest of the household goods around him. Quilts, clothing, the wooden bread kneading trough, an iron kettle, a few tools and dishes, the small store of food stuff and the baby's cradle.

The children rounded up the scruffy tan goat, the family's only livestock, and tied her behind the wagon. When the baby was secured in the cradle, Lars helped Mrs. Bengt to the wagon seat. She clutched a worn Bible, the only book the family owned.

Lars cracked the whip over the backs of the ox team and the wagon lurched into motion. The Falun man walked with the children alongside the loaded wagon as the oxen plodded out of the clearing. It would be early morning by the time the slow moving wagon reached the tiny village of Hagge. Once the wagon was unloaded, the two men were expected to turn around, drive back to the estate and work a fourteen hour day in the fields.

Bee Hives

Copper Coins and Golden Grain.

Home again, Erik Axel Norrling stabled the roan mare and checked on the other animals. The house and yard seemed unusually still in the wash of moonlight. He was loath to leave the warmth of the stable with its small sounds of life, the rhythmic breathing of the horses and oxen, the intermittent shuffle of hooves in straw, an occasional cough or snuffle. The manor house loomed dark and empty.

He walked across the yard, past the storehouse to stand in the open clearing where he could see the silver ribbon of the river. When he stood quiet, held his breath, he could hear small sounds from the roadway beyond the trees. As he listened, the rustling and murmuring grew into footsteps and voices.

He hurried to unlatch the gate for his new worker, Gubb Jansson.

"You found the way."

"Missed the turn at Hagge or we'd a been here sooner."

The new hand carried a large bundle across his shoulders. His wife seemed to have an equally large load and two small children held tight to her skirt.

"Good thing the moon is full."

"Where you be a wanting us, sir?"

"Tenant house is about a mile up and around that hill."

"Must be a big farm you got here."

Erik Axel's farm was one of the largest in the parish with open fields suitable for growing rye, barley, oats, and hay. In addition to the main house, the estate included a stable large enough to house a dozen horses and several teams of oxen, a cow barn, granary, distillery, well house, and numerous storage sheds. Over a steep hill, a rocky spine of land that extended to the river, stood the tenant cottage.

Erik Axel inherited the house and the surrounding land from his father who, in turn, had inherited the place from his father. Both his parents and his only brother had died in the cholera epidemic of 1834.

Erik Axel had been four that grim year of 1834. It had been especially bad in the city where 3000 died in a single month. The governor of Stockholm had drafted men from the poorhouse to dig their graves. A second plague in 1853 had taken Erik Axel's sister, the woman who had raised him. He had lived alone in the manor house some six years now.

"I'll show you the road to the cottage."

"Come along, Marta." To the tired children Gubb said, "Just a little farther, now."

"Let me get a lantern. The road goes through the forest."

"Don't suppose there be any land for sale hereabout?"

"The freehold around here is hard used. Most places have been divided as much as the law allows."

The Norrling farm was one of the few that had come through the century without division. The land had passed intact from one generation to the next without being broken up for the inheritance of many sons. In the same span of time neighboring farms had become smaller and smaller because each family had many sons and each son required a portion of the father's land until the land would no longer support the people living on it.

"You're lucky," said Gubb Jansson. He took the lantern and started down the road. "I'll bring it back in the morning."

"Work starts at sun up."

Erik Axel scowled at the new worker. Lucky, he thought. Lucky, because he had no kinfolk. Lucky because he was still unmarried and without sons. He looked at the empty house glowering in the moonlight and thought maybe he hated farming itself. Then he remembered the girl at the market and touched the white scarf he had tied around his neck.

Up before dawn Erik Axel made a quick trip to the small room at the end of the stable to be sure Lars and Andor would be up and ready for work. The door swung open with a touch. The straw filled bunks were empty and Andor's bundle slumped against the wall. The small table stood bare of anything except the gouged initials of previous tenants.

"Damn. The fools aren't back yet."

He kicked at the gray bundle on the floor. The cord binding it parted. The spare shirt and Sunday trousers unrolled to reveal a Bible and another small book. Curious, Erik Axel stooped to pick it up.

"*Description of the United States of North America*," he read aloud from the gold stamped spine of the narrow book. He flipped open the brown-speckled cover and glanced through the pages extolling natural wonders, free land, high paying jobs. It was an *Amerikas Book*. "Trash," he muttered. He tossed the book down and stalked out of the stable.

Gubb Jansson stood at the edge of the yard with the borrowed lantern in hand.

"Where do I start?"

"Those scoundrels, Lars and Andor, aren't back yet. Feed the oxen and horses."

Erik Axel returned to the house to scrounge himself some breakfast. He was surprised to find Mrs. Gubb there. She had a fire in the iron cookstove and water boiling for oat porridge. Chunks of horn bread and a pot of berry jam sat ready on the table and the sharp smell of new brewed coffee filled the air.

"Didn't know what you had, so I brought jam and bread from home."

"Looks good. It's been a while since anything was cooked in this house."

"Figured that from the looks of the pots."

~~~

Gubb and Erik Axel had two long rows of grain bound and shocked before Lars and Andor showed up. By noon the first wagon was loaded.

"I'll drive the load to the thrashing room." Erik Axel wiped the sweat from his face. "Come along, Gubb. You can unload, then eat."

"What about us?"

"Have the next row shocked and ready, then you can eat. Gubb will bring your dinner when he returns with the wagon."

Lars opened his mouth to protest, then thought better of it.

~~~

The harvest was one of the best in years. On the second day Erik Axel journeyed back to Smedjebacken and hired a man and his new bride, a strapping big woman who said she could work the fields as well as any man. Hiring themselves out at harvest time to pay the interest on a small inherited freehold, they thrashed and winnowed as fast as the others could bring it in from the fields. When there came a break in the thrashing, they hurried to the field to cut and shock the brittle grain.

On the fifth day of harvest Erik Axel returned to the rye field early. Gubb was bundling the shocked grain into a wagon perched on a side hill. His two small children, free from helping out at the house for the afternoon, scavenged loose grain. The married couple at the far side of the field looked like giant insects as they scurried along the row tying up grain.

"Where's Lars? And Andor?"

Gubb stopped work. "Don't know, boss. I've been working alone all morning."

"Damn. There's a wagon in the yard waiting to be unloaded."

"This one's ready to go, too."

Erik Axel climbed into the wagon and headed the oxen back to the barn.

In the yard he tethered them next to the pair already waiting, tossed them a mound of fodder, then went in search of Lars and Andor. In the stable he paused to listen. At first he heard only the small noises of animals at rest, the swish of a tail, the clunk of a shod hoof on the wooden floor, tiny snicking sounds that may have been a mouse hunting spilled grain. Then he heard a louder clunk and a low murmur of human voices.

He edged down the long aisle to the room occupied by Lars and Andor. When he listened at the door, he heard nothing. When he inched it open, he found the room empty. He could hear the murmur of voices, sharper now. The two workmen were outside, sitting with their backs to the warmth of the building, legs stretched out. A jug of *brannvin* sat between them. Erik Axel listened.

"We'd take a ship at Gothenburg."

"You say the pay is seven times as much?" asked Lars.

"And the food. All you could ever want. Better, too. Fat meat and gravy, white bread. No more salt herring. Think of the riches, the freedom."

"For anybody?"

"Everybody. Slaves, children, old folks, women. Even prisoners eat better than we do. And they have newspapers, games, music, soft beds, soft as clouds."

"Sure?"

"Sure enough. Books don't lie. It says right in the front that it's God's own truth." Andor reached for the *brannvin* jug.

"Money. We need money."

"Money? Don't you have some saved up? Working here all these years."

"Enough for the passage, tickets. Don't talk crazy."

Erik Axel jerked up the window and threw Andor's book out on the ground between the two plotters. He followed that with their spare clothing, boots, bedrolls, and tin cups. He plucked their Bibles from the shelf and tossed them out onto the small pile of possessions. Andor's book had lost the gold edging on its pages, many of which were bent and dog-eared, while the Bible Lars had received at confirmation was tight and unread.

"Go," roared Erik Axel. "Get off my property. Both of you. Get on with your trip to prosperity and freedom."

Lars reacted first. He stood, a little unsteady from the strong drink.

"But, boss, we were only resting a bit. The work was hard this morning."

"Work? What work? I should beat you purple, have you thrown into jail."

"Please, Mr. Norrling. We'll get back to the fields, now."

"No. You'll be marching down the road to Hagge. Ten minutes, no more."

He slammed the window shut and stalked out of the stable to the house.

When Lars and Andor staggered up from the stable, their possessions bundled and slung over their shoulders, Erik Axel was waiting for them at the gate. He handed each man a few copper coins.

"Your wages. More than you're worth."

~~~

With the extra work everyone quickly forgot about Lars and Andor. The clouds lay heavy in the sky and threatened rain or maybe even snow. They started their workday in the dark, labored several hours before breakfast, ate their noon meal in the fields, then dragged themselves out again after supper to work by torchlight.

~~~

Erik Axel woke. Had he heard something. He stretched under the warmth of the feather tick, then lay still to listen. Was that a footstep. Surely he had sent Mrs. Jansson and the girl home, though it had been late when they finished cleaning up after supper and making preparation for the next day. Probably a coal exploding in the cook stove. He pulled the covers over his head and dozed off.

The next sound brought him out of bed with a jerk. When his bare feet hit the cold floor something moved through the patch of moonlight on the wall. He squinted his eyes and tried to make out shapes in the dark room.

"Who's there?"

A loud crash answered.

Another shape slipped into the patch of moonlight and Erik Axel leaped to grapple with it. Something hit him alongside the head and he toppled to the floor.

The house was unusually cold when he came to his senses. Mrs. Jansson was standing over him, screaming. He tried to tell her she was making his head fill with pain, but no words formed on his tongue. The room swirled and he thought at first he had had too much *brannvin* the night before. No, it had been a work day. His muscles ached from yesterday's long stint in the fields. With a groan he remembered the noises in the night. There had been someone in the house.

Mrs. Jansson was still screaming, when Erik Axel realized he was lying on the floor in his night clothes. Gubb and the children entered the room. The children responded to their mother's screams and burst into tears.

"Go fetch water," said Gubb. He turned the children around and shoved them out the door. To his wife he demanded, "Stop that noise. Get the fire going

For Erik Axel the room stopped spinning and he managed to get up. With Gubb's help he staggered to the bed and sat down.

"What happened, man?" Gubb wrapped a quilt around his employer's shoulders.

"Someone must have broke in." He rubbed the side of his head. "Ouch. Must have hit me with something." He looked at the blood on his fingers.

"The door was wide open."

"Check the window. And the cabinet near the fireplace."

"Window's broke. Looks like they stove in the door of the cabinet, too."

"The locked box. Do you see it?"

"Smashed to pieces."

"Robbers."

"We could hunt them down. Get the sheriff."

The idea tempted Erik Axel, but the urgency of the harvest pulled hard.

"There wasn't that much cash in the strong box," he argued, more to convince himself, than anyone else. He gritted his teeth at the thought of the thieves holding his money, counting it, fondling it.

One of the children came running into the room. "See what I found. Outside, by the broken window."

He held up a rumpled book, a thin book with mottled brown covers. It was the *Amerikas Book*.

With shaking hands Erik Axel took the book from the child.

"They won't need it now. They have their passage money."

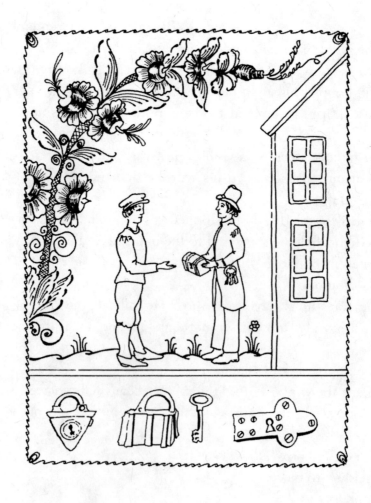

A Courting Spoon and a Yarn Doll.

When they had the storage granaries filled to the rafters, they hauled the surplus grain to the mill at Hagge to be ground into flour. The less mature grain made a flour that had to be used quickly before it spoiled.

"I can bake it into *thin brod* and horn bread," offered Mrs. Jansson. "It will keep all winter."

"Get one of the neighbor girls to help."

So when she wasn't sorting, scrubbing, chopping, peeling, boiling, and frying for the workers, her children, and Erik Axel, Marta baked bread enough to last into the New Year. Not leavened light bread, but stacks and stacks of flat unleavened *thin brod* and wheel size rounds of rye stamped through with a cow horn so it could hang on poles suspended from the ceiling. While the girl stirred and kneaded, Mrs. Jansson measured ingredients, shaped the dough, nursed the fire to just right temperature, and kept her own two children hustling for wood and water.

Though his head still ached and he often felt dizzy and disoriented from the blow he had received from the robbers, Erik Axel drove the oxen to and from the fields and loaded sheaves of grain alongside Gubb. He kept the *Amerika Book* in his pocket as a reminder of unfinished business. When his frustration and anger surfaced, he would reach for the book and squeeze it relentlessly. As the granaries filled and the winter bread baked, the book became more and more tattered and creased.

Then, on the third Saturday of harvest, Erik Axel called the workers together.

"No work tomorrow."

"Sunday off? All day?"

"No work till Monday."

Usually a worker had only a few Sundays a year to themselves and a Sunday off during harvest was a treat.

"The oxen are weary," he said. "The weather has cleared. Maybe winter will hold off awhile."

Indeed, it had turned off much warmer than usual after that first threat of winter.

"Church. Can we go?" Mrs. Jansson looked at her husband.

"Sure thing. We could go this evening. Visit your mother."

"Take one of the carts and the roan mare," said Erik Axel. He was feeling generous.

In the morning he fed the livestock himself, then saddled a horse. As he rode along the dirt road towards Hagge he tried to decide what to do. Church would give him a chance to see the dark-haired girl, Maria. He had not seen her since the market before harvest and winter would be upon them soon enough. The crumpled book in his pocket reminded him of other unfinished business.

~~~

"Morning sheriff."

"What can I do for you, Mr. Norrling?" The sheriff filled the door, unshaven and barefoot.

"Sorry to bother you so early, but I wanted to see you before church."

The sheriff waited for Erik Axel to explain. A rich and influential member of his jurisdiction demanded his attention no matter the day or hour.

"You know my worker Lars, Lars Smelsson?"

"What has the rascal done?"

"Run off, along with a workman from Falun."

"You want me to hunt down a couple of contract breakers?"

"They smashed a window, broke into my house."

"Vandalism. Probably drunk. Do you supply your workers with alcohol as part of their wage?"

"They knocked me out and stole money." Erik Axel pulled the *Amerika Book* from his pocket. "They dropped this."

"I'll send a message to the magistrate in Gothenburg. They can keep an eye out for them."

~~~

When the last cart load of grain groaned off to the mill and the cooking and baking were finished, the hired couple returned to their bit of land with a part of their interest payment earned. The scullery maid was let go and Mrs. Jansson returned to the tenant cottage to birth her third child. Her husband Gubb settled into a routine of caring for the livestock, repairing tools, and getting the buildings ready for winter. Erik Axel had the manor house to himself again.

A loud rapping on the door broke the silence.

"What is it? Stop your noise and come in."

His voice was harsh and raspy. He barely raised his eyes from the bit of wood he was carving.

"Yes, Gubb. What do you want?"

The broad young man stood in the doorway, his cap held in both hands, his face red. "Sir, please, sir. I've finished in the cow barn."

"So?" Erik Axel placed his carving on the table. "Do I have to tell you everything?"

"No, sir. I mean Yes, sir. I don't know. Sir. It's payday, sir. Please, my wife says the baby needs a tonic. And the loom needs a bit of fixing."

Gubb twirled his cap and shifted from one foot to the other. It was the first time he had actually had to ask for his pay.

"Money, I should've guessed."

Erik Axel wiped his knife on his trousers and got up. He walked across the large room and reached a metal-bound box from a shelf. With a large key he produced from a leather pouch at his waist, he unlocked the box and counted out six copper coins, then added an extra one *ore* coin.

"There, seven *ore*, six more than you're worth." He pressed the coins into the hired man's palm. "Check with the sheriff while you're in town. See if he has any word about the robbers."

"I can take the bent harrow to the smith, too."

"Ride the bay mare and have her shod at the same time."

"Sharp caulks or plain?"

"See if the smith has any of those new ones. The kind you can screw the caulks in when the road gets icy."

He gave Gubb more money and the man left. Erik Axel went back to his carving. "Almost finished," he muttered to himself. He held the wooden spoon to the light, then blew the wood chips and sawdust from the new cuts of his carving.

"Almost finished. I hope Maria likes it."

He bent his head over the wide-handled spoon with its open-work pattern of hearts and flowers to etch some fine veining onto the leaves.

A year ago Erik Axel had decided to approach the dark haired girl when his courting spoon was finished. His carving had become increasingly more elaborate over the past months. This was the seventh spoon he had carved. He had hurled the first six into the fire because of some small defect.

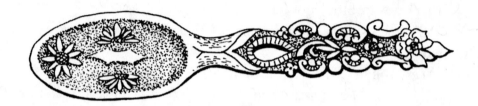

According to custom he would wear the spoon in his breast pocket or button hole, handle end showing, to indicate his interest in the woman. If he was lucky, she would encourage him by giving him a tiny doll braided from colored yarn. The more daring young men would collect a number of these dolls and pin them to their hats. A courting proverb inched through his mind, *I give you thread in return for a spoon.* It was the promise of the woman's labor of spinning, weaving, sewing enjoined with the man's responsibility to provide food and shelter.

Erik Axel was twenty-six years old and weary of living alone. He knew he could put off the exchange no longer. He would call on Maria Katrina's father sometime this week.

On Tuesday he dressed in his Sunday shirt and black wool trousers. The courting spoon poked out of his breast pocket. It glowed with several coats of rubbed beeswax. In the stable he selected a matched pair of mahogany bay mares.

"Hitch them to the new spring wagon."

"Will you be gone long?"

"Bring them to the house when you're ready."

Erik Axel threw a mohair shawl on the seat and stepped up behind the team. He pulled on his gloves and took the reins from Gubb.

"Good luck, boss."

As he drove through the forest, he imagined how he would approach Mr. Rundbak. He would speak of his large farm and successful harvest, tell of his family lineage and the service his parent and grandparent had rendered the crown in times of war.

At Hagge he pulled up the team and sat fiddling with the reins. He slipped the carved spoon from his pocket and studied its smooth curves. What if it's not good enough, he wondered. What if I'm not accepted. He shook the reins and turned the horses back towards home, then remembered Maria's dark eyes and long hair, her creamy skin and laughing voice. He turned the horses again, towards Smedjebacken and Maria, and hoped no one noticed his indecision.

"Good Afternoon." Erik Axel stood in the Rundbak's dooryard, hat in hand.

"Why Mr. Norrling. How long has it been?" Mrs. Rundbak stepped back into the room to allow Erik Axel entrance. "The mister is in the garden. I tell him you're here."

She called to Maria. "Company. Put the kettle back on the stove."

As Erik Axel was ushered into the little front room reserved for visitors, he caught a glimpse into the main room. Dishes and coffee cups still littered the table. His good timing pleased him. Earlier, they would have felt obliged to ask him to join them, later, they would have been back to work, Mr. Rundbak at his clerical duties, his wife and daughter at their housework.

Mr. Rundbak joined him and before many minutes had passed, Maria brought coffee and an overflowing plate of cookies.

"Nice weather for October." Mr. Rundbak dunked his cookie in his coffee.

"Warmest I can remember."

"Good harvest?"

"Best in years."

"I hear you had some trouble out there."

"Nothing much."

"Have they caught the thieves yet?"

"Sheriff had word they may be on their way to Gothenburg."

"What's the world coming to," murmured Mrs. Rundbak.

"You'll be wanting some time with the daughter, I expect."

"Please. If it meets with your approval, that is."

"She's a good girl," said Mrs. Rundbak. "Our youngest. Her sisters have found work in the city."

Maria blushed, but said nothing.

"The son has a place of his own over towards Ludvika."

"And two sweet children."

Maria smiled at her mother. "They're little brats. Spoiled through and through."

"I thought we might go for a drive. The weather is still quite fine."

Mr. Rundbak excused himself to return to work.

"Get your coat, Maria."

Outside Erik Axel led Maria to his new spring wagon.

"Let me give you a hand up."

Maria smiled with her red lips, her smooth cheeks, her eyes. "Thank you, sir."

"You're welcome."

"What a fine team, Mr. Norrling," she said. "I don't believe I've ever seen horses like this before."

She held her hand out to Erik Axel and he helped her into the wagon. He tossed the plush lap robe over her knees and took up his place behind the team.

"I'm glad you like them. They're German breds. I had them

brought over from Hanover along with a young stallion."

When Erik Axel dropped Maria at her gate a few hours later, he wore her yarn doll on his hat. Maria held the carved spoon and avowed once again that it was the finest she had ever seen.

Erik Axel whistled to the mares and turned for home. By the time he reached Long Meadow he was trying to decide if he had enough *brannvin* brewed to take care of the wedding guests. He barely heard the pound of hoofs as another team drew abreast.

"Beat you to the bridge." A round faced youngster leaned from the seat of a side-slat wagon and pointed to Erik Axel's team.

"Ten *ore* says you can't," he shouted back.

Crown of Silver, Crown of Thorn.

Erik Axel played with the ten *ore* coins the rest of the way home. He clinked them together in his pocket, pulled them out to toss them in the air and catch them again. He whistled until his lips were dry.

At home he placed his winnings in a perfect line along the edge of the mantel before crawling into bed.

~~~

Though Erik Axel had hoped for a Christmas wedding, a hard winter with howling storms and deep snow kept everyone captive on their farmsteads and in their homes. By spring most of the parish were ready for a celebration and involved themselves in the preparations.

Maria's mother pulled and straightened the folds of her daughter's heavy skirt. "Are you sure you want to walk all that way?"

Mr. Rundbak paused in his instructions to the fiddlers and spoke to his wife. "Why shouldn't she walk to the church? You did."

"Stop fussing, Mama. Where is Mr. Norrling, anyway?" She broke away from her mother's hands and looked around the crowded yard.

Bride and groom planned to make the traditional walk from the bride's house on one side of town to the church on the hill above Smedjebacken.

"Here he is. In the knick of time." The crowd of musicians, attendants, and relatives clapped and cheered when Erik Axel drove up and tossed the reins of his team to one of the boys standing nearby.

"Can't start without me," he answered. He elbowed his way through the crowd to stand facing Maria.

"I have your *brudbalte*."

He drew the silver bride's belt from its velvet case and held it up to the crowd with both hands. With a flourish he fastened it around Maria's waist. More like a girdle or a short skirt, the silver medallions separated with thick silver beads draped over her hips and hung nearly to her knees in front.

"Ooh. It's so heavy." Maria adjusted the belt and allowed her fingers to trace the raised pattern of its ornate fastener.

Maria's father stepped forward. "And here's your neck piece." He, too, held his contribution up to the crowd before placing a silver pendant with many crisscrossing chains around her throat.

"Now for the crown."

Erik Axel retrieved a bundled object from the wagon. The crowd watched as he unwrapped the crown. Which one had he chosen? This silver headgear was rented from the church and served as a symbol of the groom's financial status. He held up the crown which dripped with hammered hearts, leaves, and winged angel heads. He had rented the heaviest, most elaborate crown in the church collection. The crowd cheered and clapped. The youngsters whistled and made a few rude noises before they were shushed by their elders.

"Let the procession begin."

"Groom goes first."

"With the fiddlers. And Maria's grandfather."

Someone helped an old man to his feet. He had been sitting unnoticed on the bench by the door.

Maria, her attendants, and her mother followed the first group to the footpath that wound through the forest from the bride's home to the road up the hill to the church.

The fiddlers struck up a funeral march for the first few steps and the crowd laughed and jeered, thumped the groom on the back. Someone passed a flask. Most of the men and a few of the more daring women had a swig.

"Mama, they're spoiling things," Maria whispered. "Make them stop."

"Are you feeling all right? You look pale."

Maria ignored her mother's question, hitched her skirt above her ankles, and continued her walk.

At the end of the level forest path they entered a neighborhood of small houses, storage buildings, and stables. They could see the church steeple pointing the hill above them.

When the party paused so a fiddler could tighten a string on his instrument, Maria asked her mother for a handkerchief.

"Let me take that crown for a minute."

"It's giving me the headache," said Maria. She wiped her damp forehead and stood breathing deeply.

Erik Axel looked around. He had never been in this part of town before. The sod-roofed houses were close together as if helping each other stand against the elements. Chickens and small children scrabbled in the bare dirt by the road. A few bent and battered men and women sat propped against the house fronts to catch the rays of spring sunshine.

When one of the men raised his head and waved his cane in greeting, Erik Axel didn't recognize him.

"Oscar, Oscar Bengt. Remember me, boss?"

"Hello, Oscar. I'm on my way to be married."

"I can see that."

"How are you these days?"

"Poorly. The Missus takes in washing. The boys are indentured to a farmer over towards Ludvika. Don't see them but once a year."

Erik Axel asked the age of the boys, but Oscar's answer was lost as the fiddlers struck up a polka. That oldest boy couldn't have been more than twelve. he thought. Maybe I should send them a few bushels of grain.

Maria and her mother hurried to get her crown back in place before the procession moved on up the street.

"Hurry, Mama."

"Stand still."

"That's good enough."

"Wait. You have a smudge." She spit on her handkerchief and scrubbed vigorously at a small spot on Maria's cheek.

"They're leaving." Maria had to run a few steps to regain her place.

The road turned sharply steep as they left the poor section of town. As they walked, slightly bent to lean into the slope, they passed houses with white washed fences and flagstone entrance paths. At a sharp bend in the path a small child ran from a yard past the fiddlers and the knot of men leading the way. She stopped in front of Maria, out of breath, eyes wide.

She thrust a double fistful of daffodils at Maria. "For you, lady."

Maria accepted the daffodils from the bright child with her halo of white blonde hair.

"Thank you."

When Maria thought she could walk no farther, she reached the stone wall that held the graveyard tight to the hillside just below the church. She leaned against the cool rock and shut her eyes. Her cheek against the old stone, she tried to calm her racing heart, gather her strength. She could hear the shuffle of feet as the rest of the party climbed the steps above her. She could hear the church doors creak open, the first tentative clang of the steeple bell, the murmur of voices, a lone bird in a fir tree high above.

This is my day, she thought. Don't let anything spoil it.

Close to fainting Maria lurched up the steps and entered the old church. The main aisle seemed longer than she remembered. Her friends and schoolmates filled the rear pews. Her kin, brother and sister-in-law, sisters home from the city, cousins, aunts and uncles, watched from the front pews. Maria reached up and straightened her crown, then paced slowly up the aisle to stand red-faced and sweating before the altar for her vows.

The minister rose from his throne-like chair to the left of the altar and stepped to a small podium nearby. In a voice mellowed by years in the pulpit he spoke the old and hallowed words. "Dearly beloved," he began.

Maria sighed, took a deep breath, and stared at a spot on the floor a few feet to the left of the minister.

Erik Axel straightened his tie, inspected the ceiling, glanced at his bride. Who is this woman, he wondered. What have I done?

A noise at the rear of the church caught everyone's attention. Heads turned, eyes searched out the offenders in the dim light.

A small knot of girls sat in the rear pew with their heads together. Their fit of giggles had grown and over-flowed.

The minister paused, cleared his throat for silence.

The young women paid no attention. Several of them, dressed in the latest full crinolines imported from London, their hair up for, perhaps the first time, continued to whispered and snicker.

Maria turned to see what disturbance interrupted her wedding. She recognized the girls as a group a few years younger, girls known for their independent views. Why, they were even reputed to have attended a suffrage meeting at Ludvika.

The girls were eyeing the bridegroom. Perhaps they wished they had caught his fancy, or perhaps it was only the bit of strong drink they had dared to sample.

The rest of the congregation turned their attention to Maria. As she faced them, she seemed miserable, a weary bride with her drooping head and teetering crown. Long strands of dark hair had escaped her upswept hair-do and what was she thinking with that pitiful handful of daffodils. Was she ill or, worse, pregnant.

The minister coughed for silence again, then rapped on the podium.

Maria stared at the giggling girls. They think they're so fine with their fashionable skirts sticking out in the aisles. They're probably wearing colored undies, too. All the rage on the continent, girls had been dying their unmentionables pink or puce or even scarlet for months.

Green, she thought. I'll imagine they're wearing green petticoats. And bust improvers. Maria almost laughed out loud with the thought.

She stiffened and pulled her shoulders back, arched her neck and raised her head to steady the crown. With a wicked grin she sniffed and poked her nose in the air. The silver crown, which had looked so heavy, suddenly seemed light as a feather. She caressed the ornate belt at her waist. No one could miss the fact that she wore enough silver around her hips to pay for six span of choice oxen. She lifted her daffodils to her audience and with a flourish, turned to the minister and asked him to continue the service.

The minister attacked the short service with gusto, short at Erik Axel's request. He seemed to dwell on the command to Maria to "honor and obey" her husband, but only the new husband seemed to notice.

"You may kiss the bride."

Erik Axel gave Maria a peck of a kiss on the forehead, then lifted the crown from her head and placed it on the altar. He took her white hand in his sinewy tanned one and walked her back up the aisle. When they reached the last pew, the pew of the giggling girls, Maria stopped as if to address them. Instead she tossed the wilting daffodils in their direction and turned back to her husband.

They walked out into the watery spring sunshine, out of the church, past the tidy back-to-back rows of tombstones to the meadow that lay next door. A tent had been erected there on the newly mowed grass for the wedding feast.

Wine into Tears.

"Oh. It's beautiful," cried Maria. "When did you do all this?"

Erik Axel gestured towards a crew of aproned ladies standing off to one side. "I hired it done. For you."

"The flowers. It's way too early for daisies. And look, roses, and forest fern."

"I ordered the roses sent from Stockholm. The ferns came from the woods where we drove that first day."

"Red and white and green. It's beautiful."

They walked through an arch of flowers to the rows of white-clad tables. The first table held the sweets provided by the bride's mother.

Twenty marriage cakes marched down the center of the table. These cakes were made by stacking layers and layers of the thinnest white flour bread spread with two fingers of pure butter. Between each layer of bread and butter the cooks had added white sugar, cream, soft cheese, and honey. It was a recipe borrowed from the Norwegians who considered white bread the mark of good living.

Maria ran to the next table.

"Oh, it looks wonderful."

"I hope it's a strong table."

"Don't be silly. It's beautiful. Someone has the artist's touch."

The three tables holding the salty and sour dishes were, indeed, beautiful. The platters and bowls were laid out in a symmetrical series of spirals. Platters of new potatoes in butter, smoked eel, fillet of herring in sour cream, and dry-cured mutton sliced paper thin, wound their way through a surfeit of pickled beets, salmon pudding, liver paste, red cod roe, and eggs in a dozen guises.

"Food enough for an army," said Maria.

"Come see my contribution." Erik Axel had walked on ahead to the groom's table of sweets.

"My heavens. What are they?" Maria put her hand on her husband's arm. "They're huge."

The cakes looked like three fir trees decorated for Christmas. Flowers and fruit, raisins, currents, dried apple and candied orange slices nestled in whorls of colored icing on every branching layer.

"*Spettekaka*. Spit cake. I had them sent from parish Skane."

"Skane? So far?" Skane was a county in the far south of Sweden.

"Custom made. I ordered them when I traveled there to the iron works."

"Iron works? There is an iron works at Ludvika. Why go so far?"

"There was a race meet, too. Trotting horses."

"They must have large ovens in the south."

"No. They make them over an open fire, in the fireplace, on a special spit."

"That's why they're called *spettekaka?*"

Each spit cake required seven dozen eggs and stood almost four feet high. To prepare such a monstrosity the egg yolks were beaten together with pounds and pounds of powdered sugar. When the mixture was thick and creamy, a little flour and the beaten egg whites were folded into the batter.

This arduous feat of stirring was only the prelude to the labor of cooking this cake. A slow fire would be kindled in the fireplace and a cone-shaped iron spit cleaned, greased, and heated. The huge pan of cake batter would then be dripped slowly onto the rotating spit. The layers of batter would cook and dry on the spit and new layers would be added for hours on end until all the batter was used and the tree shaped cake was finished. After it was removed from the spit, it was allowed to cool, then it was decorated with flowers and colored icing.

"How do they taste?"

"Who knows. Most people keep them around for ages and ages just to look at."

Maria pulled herself away from the spit cakes. "What's this? More sweets?"

"We'll be dead of the tooth ache before all this is eaten."

As if three *spettekaka* and twenty bride's cakes weren't enough, or perhaps in the spirit of competition, Maria's siblings had commissioned the local bakery to produce enough *ostkaka* or molded cheese cake to sway the back of a sturdy table. Cream, eggs, sugar, and almonds made up the recipe for this rich affair.

"Come look at this, Maria" Erik Axel led his new bride to the edge of the meadow where meat was roasting on spits over an open fire.

"A whole pig, mutton, and a goat. My heavens."

Two boys with smudges of ash on their faces grinned up at Maria. They had been turning the spits all morning and had high expectations of a tasty meal for their efforts.

"And this," shouted Erik Axel.

He gestured towards the dozen barrels of beer and a trio of oak casks of *brannvin* lined up under a canvas awning, then walked over to draw a glass of the clear drink.

He raised the glass to the drink barrel. "A toast to Eva De la Garie, potato scientist."

"Why toast this Eva person? Who is she?" asked Maria.

"Ah. Only the first woman member of Sweden's Royal Academy of Science. In 1748 she discovered that the potato could be distilled into *brannvin*."

Home stills had sprung up all over the country and even the church brewed and sold strong drink to enrich its coffers. It had not been too many years since alcohol consumption had topped out at forty-four quarts per capita, forty-four quarts of liqueur for every man, woman, and child in the country. A temperance movement had slowed this sloshing down of spirits and government controls had slowed the proliferation of stills and personal breweries, but *brannvin* was still used to dispel the dark gloom of long winters.

"Is that all we have to wash down the food? What will the children drink?" asked Maria.

"I think there are pitchers of lemon sugar here somewhere. And, of course, there's coffee."

"I think we're being summoned for the wedding toast."

Erik Axel escorted Maria back to the table where the *spettekaka* glittered in the sun. The marriage bowl had been filled with red wine and placed on a cloth embroidered with a scene from the wedding feast at Cana.

The onlookers chanted, "Drink. Drink."

Erik Axel raised the two-handled tankard to the crowd, then offered one handle to Maria.

"To my wife."

The couple lifted the tankard and sipped in unison. Erik Axel drew deeper, pulled a bit at the cup, causing a little wine to trickle from Maria's lips onto the bodice of her gown where it left a small dark stain.

The father of the bride offered his toast to the long and fruitful union of the couple. This was followed by speeches and toasts from brothers, uncles, and schoolmates, sisters, aunts, teachers, even the giggling girls. When the marriage tankard was emptied, it was replaced by individual tankards of beer.

"Enough toasting," cried Erik Axel. He wiped his mouth on his sleeve and discarded his tankard.

"To the food."

"Thank God," murmured Maria. Her head was spinning from the wine. She looked around for her mother and found her seated with the older ladies.

"Can you take this for me?" Maria unfastened the silver belt and placed it in her mother's care.

An aunt spoke up. "Have you told Maria? About the marriage night? You know."

"Now, Gussie. She'll learn soon enough."

Maria bent and hugged her mother. "It's all right. Don't worry about me."

~~~

Some of the revelers were already dancing by the time Maria found a plate and a quiet place to eat. She thought she was ravenous, but managed to choke down only a few bites before Erik Axel called her to dance.

"Come, Maria. They're waiting for us."

"Is my hair straight? Should I get my silver belt?"

He grasped her arm and hustled her to a level area of hard packed earth. Torches and oil lamps vied with the light from a bonfire nearby. They were greeted with clapping and raised glasses of *brannvin*.

The quick steps of wedding dance made Maria's head spin and her stomach lurch, but she leaned on Erik Axel's arm and managed to hold on to the end. The crowd cheered when the dance ended, but Maria didn't hear them. She slipped away into the darkness to be sick.

When she returned to the party, she found Erik Axel engaged in a heated argument with a neighbor.

"You think that nag of yours is worth two silvers?" Erik Axel shook his fist at the short, sturdy man facing him.

"Blukka can out trot any horse in the parish."

"My money says he can't."

Maria tugged at her husband's sleeve, but he seemed not to notice.

"Sunday afternoon on the Hagge Road. Any horse of yours against my Blukka. Two out of three heats." The man turned and stalked away.

"But that's tomorrow," said Maria.

With his clenched fists thrust into his pockets Erik Axel watched the man retreat through the crowd.

"You're not going, are you?"

Erik Axel stood silent for a minute, then headed for the *brannvin* table. He nearly knocked Maria down before he realized she was standing at his side.

~~~

It was midnight before the wedded couple managed to sneak away from the party. Maria huddled on the wagon seat with a heavy lap robe pulled up around her throat. The spring nights were cold and she was stiff with fatigue and trepidation.

Erik Axel whipped up the team and headed for home.

"Cold?"

"A little."

"Won't be long now. I left instructions for Mrs. Jansson. She'll have the house warm."

"You have a house keeper?"

"Not really. She's the wife of the stableman."

The house seemed dark when they drove into the yard, but as a young man emerged from the shadows to take the horses by the bridle, Maria saw a faint glow of light at the window.

Erik Axel threw off the lap robe, handed her down from the high seat, and bowed her through the front door. The warmth of the house rose to meet her.

"You can wash up here." Erik Axel gestured to a towel and pitcher on a nearby table. "I'll go to the stable. Give you a little time for whatever it is you ladies do."

Maria looked around, then went to the doorway of the bedroom. Two closet beds took up the wall space opposite and a bench bed and trundle occupied the rest of the room, a room meant for a large family.

"Which bed?"

"The one with the blue and white curtain. Mrs. Jansson made it up fresh yesterday."

"Thank you, Mr. Norrling."

Maria hung her shawl on a peg and looked around. Yes. There was her trunk and her basket of everyday clothing. Her brush, comb, and mirror greeted her from a small table with an ornate baroque mirror. Her mother must have helped move her belongings this morning. Or was it yesterday morning?

Maria unhooked her silver necklace and laid it next to her hair brush, then sat down to unlace her shoes. She fumbled the many tiny buttons on her bodice open and removed her skirt. Her own plain muslin undergarments reminded her of the giggling girls at the church and she smiled for the first time since entering her new home.

When Erik Axel entered the dark room, Maria pulled the covers up around her chin. She had been close to sleep, but now her heart was racing. She listened as her husband thunked his shoes to the floor, then rustled his shirt and trousers off.

"Should I snuff the lamp?" he asked.

"Please. At least this first time." Maria's voice was a bare whisper.

"I could take the other bed. It is late and you've had a long day."

"No. It's all right." Maria's voice was firm. She flipped the cover back and scrunched closer to the wall to make room.

When Erik Axel pulled the bed curtain closed, the darkness was complete. He seemed to bring an aura of chill air with him.

"You're so cold," said Maria. She pulled the quilt up around his shoulders and reached her warm feet to his icy toes.

"So warm." He reached for Maria, cupped his left hand to her smooth shoulder.

"No nightgown?"

"Not tonight, Mr. Norrling."

He let out a long breath, warm on her neck, then wormed his right arm under her body. When he drew her close, she tried to relax, to melt into the curve of his body.

He pulled away from her. "Drats. Let me shed this nightshirt." Cold air flooded the warm bedcloset.

Maria shivered. She could hear Erik Axel shrug out of his night shirt. She remembered her shoes on the floor and called a warning to him, but too late to prevent his stumbling.

"Damn," he barked. "What dumbkoft left shoes out?"

"I'm so sorry." Maria was out of bed and kneeling on the cold floor beside him. "Are you hurt?"

"Get back in bed." He stood up and pulled Maria with him. You'll catch cold."

Maria burst into tears and scrambled back into bed.

"Now what's wrong? I'm the one with the sore toe and bruised shin."

Maria lay face down, her head pillowed on her bare arms. He drew the quilt up over her shoulders and crawled in beside her.

"Maria , Maria, don't be so silly. It's been a long day."

"You don't have to shout at me."

"I'll didn't think."

He turned her towards him and stroked her long hair, calmed her like he would a young horse. When her shuddering tears finally stopped, he kissed her, wiped her cheeks with the edge of the quilt.

"Silly goose."

Their coupling was swift, not unlike the awkward mating of mare and stallion. With a sigh Erik Axel clambered to his side of the bed and fell asleep.

Maria listened to his deep breathing turn to snores. She fought the urge to get up, to claw her way out of the closed space of the bedcloset, as long as possible. When she finally inched from under the covers and crawled over her husband, she felt uneasy, a bit guilty. He snorted a little, threw his arm over the covers, but didn't awake. Maria pulled the curtain closed and found her shawl to wrap around her bare shoulders. She tip-toed across the plank floor to the window where the moon threw a square of bright light through the diamond panes.

"Moon, are you shining on my old home?" she whispered.

The sigh of a breeze against the window told her the moon saw everything.

She sent a question through the rippled glass. "Mama. How do you bear it?"

It is the way of the ages, replied moon. It is your life stone to carry.

"My pain is hot, my tears are like the cry of the bewildered crane."

Return to your warm bed, sister. Your spring is at hand.

Evening Comes Bitter.

Maria woke with a start. Beside her Erik Axel was pulling free of the bed clothes. A great swirl of banging and clanging filled the air.

"What is it?" she shouted at her husband who was up and already jamming his legs into his pants.

"I don't know. It's still dark."

By the time Maria had pulled on her dressing gown, voices filled the front room. When she peered around the edge of the open door, she saw the younger segment of the wedding party. Her brother, sisters, several school friends had joined her husband's cronies and a few neighbors for the soiree.

"Here she is," called one of the young men.

"Have a little drink, Maria."

Someone with an old squeeze box burst in the door followed by three girls so tipsy they could barely stand. Wheezy music drowned out the conversation.

Erik Axel took Maria by the arm and whispered in her ear.

"Our guests could use some refreshment. Put the coffee on and see if Mrs. Jansson left sweets in the pantry."

"But it's three in the morning."

"They haven't been to bed yet."

Wrapped in her dressing gown, eyes red, hair down around her shoulders, Maria served her guests strong coffee and plates of cookies. Then, while she slumped on a stool by the cold fireplace, they pushed back the benches and danced. When they demanded alcohol, she shook her head and told them the party was over.

"Oh, shoot. It's early."

"Sun's not up yet."

"Dance in the dawn, dance all your life."

"You'll dance yourself right into the poor house."

By the time the revelers seemed ready to call it a night, Erik Axel was engaged in a heated conversation with the wagoneer who had driven the women of the party out from town.

"Are you sure it was Lars Smelsson?" He grasped the driver's shirt front to keep his attention from wandering. "Was he with another fellow? Young, tall, very pale with a scar next to his mouth?"

"Alone, I'm sure he was alone."

"Look, man. This is important. Where did you see this Lars?"

"Like I said, I saw him when I makes my route to Gothenburg."

"So you saw him in the city?"

"No, man. At the crossing where they're building the railroad bridge."

"On the road? Traveling?"

"No. Working. On the railroad. Terrible hard work."

"I don't believe it. I never had an honest days work from that scoundrel."

"Believe me or not. It's God's truth."

Erik Axel was still shouting questions at the wagon driver when Maria edged the revelers out the door.

They went back to bed, but slept little before the sound of roosters announced the dawn. Maria was still braiding her hair when Gubb Jansson and his wife trooped up the path from the tenant cottage to begin work.

Mrs. Jansson propped her swaddled baby on a bench and hurried to lay a fire. Before Maria had finished dressing, the mess from the soiree was cleaned up and thick slices of ham sizzled on the cook stove and coffee filled the house with its promising aroma.

"You bout ready for breakfast?" called Mrs. Jansson. She stirred the oat porridge with vigor.

Erik Axel filled his bowl from the pot on the stove, added milk and jam, then ate while he paced back and forth.

"I'm off to town, Maria," said Erik Axel. "Do you need anything?"

"Can I come along? It would be easier."

"It would be a dull day for you. Stay home and unpack your things."

"I could visit my mother and get my silver belt."

"Not this time. I have business."

"Aren't you taking the big wagon?" Maria peered over her husband's shoulder. Her gaze rested on the light, two-wheeled gig and the tall Hanoverian stallion tied to the front gate. "Seems a bit of a waste to use such a good horse to haul supplies."

"You forget I need to meet neighbor Dalsson's challenge. He'll be waiting with his horse, Blukka."

"Oh, yes. The fellow at the party."

"I may drive a ways down the Gothenburg Road. See if anyone has word of that thief, Lars Smelsson."

"Be careful."

"Don't trouble yourself, Maria." He grabbed his hat and gloves. "Eat your breakfast, then have Mrs. Jansson show you where things are kept." He hurried out.

~~~

"Don't fret, dearie. There's plenty to be done here."

"But it's supposed to be our first whole day together." Maria was close to tears.

"That's a man for you. Always into something."

Mrs. Jansson poured herself a cup of coffee and settled down at the table. She mended a gray sock stretched tight over a china egg while she talked.

Maria spooned sugar over her oat porridge, then stirred some into her coffee.

"How do you get to know someone if they won't stop and talk?"

"Might as well talk to the wind, as talk to a man."

Maria spent the morning walking about the old house. Except for the kitchen and a corner of the bedroom, the rooms seemed bare and unused, the cupboards and closets a jumble of items. The shelves and woodwork were dusted, but still lacked the luster that results from well applied elbow grease.

When she looked into the many cupboards and storage chests in the spare room, she found quantities of house linen, throws, table covers, wall hangings, sheets. The fine, tight material was yellowed with age though it was stored with sachets of lavender and layered with paper. She reached down an embroidered cloth and held it to the light to better see the weave and pattern.

"Mrs. Jansson, do you know who made this?"

"Mr. Norrling's grandmother was quite the weaver. It may be her work."

"Where should I put my things?"

Maria, like most girls, had spent long winter evenings with her head bent over a piece of embroidery or weaving until she had a marriage chest overflowing with towels, pillow covers, and underwear.

"Well, if it were me, I'd pack up these old things and hide them away in the storeroom."

"This table cloth is too beautiful to hide away."

"Made by another woman's hand. This is your house now."

When they finished packing away the past, Mrs. Jansson called her husband to carry the trunks and boxes to a storage room.

Maria signed and sat down by the fire with another cup of coffee. "I feel like a weight has lifted off my shoulders, Mrs. Jansson."

"Now you have space for your own pretties."

"Clean and new."

"Better finish your coffee. I'll get the keys."

"Keys?"

"To the outbuildings. This long silver one opens the distillery and the little bronze one, the tack room. The rusty key opens the lean-to behind the house." Mrs. Jansson sorted through the fat ring of keys.

"Stop, stop. Let me try those, then you can tell me about the others."

"Mr. Norrling keeps everything locked up since the robbery."

Maria inspected the lean-to first. It was full to the rafters with barrels, boxes, and sacks. Burlap bags of flour and cut oats, crocks of vinegar, pickled cabbage and beets, barrels of salt fish, hard crackers, fine weave sacks of sugar and salt.

While she secured the lock, she made a mental note to ask her husband why he kept such a mountain of stuff on hand.

The out buildings were next. She spent scant attention on the chicken coops and hen houses. The sweet acrid smell of the confined birds nearly made her sick. She peeked in at the calves and baby goats. When she met up with Gubb, she asked him about the cows and adult goats. He told her they had been taken to the summer pasture in the hills. Only a few fresh cows were on hand so there would be milk for the household and the young animals.

"My wife does the milking most mornings."

"This morning?"

"I milked and fed. No trouble. She's straining up the milk now, and skimming the cream from yesterday's take."

~~~

The tool room astounded her because its neat rows of hammers, awls, mallets, rasps were such a contrast to the disarray of the house. She double-checked the lock before she moved on to the tack room.

She found the tackroom door open. The sweet aroma of saddle soap and linseed oil engulfed her as she entered. Smooth-grained English leather, halters, headstalls, reins, saddles, single harness, double harness, traces, cruppers, blinders, and decorative rosettes hung from every surface. Maria leaned across a half-size flat saddle displayed on a crossbuck in the center of the room and breathed deeply.

Gubb interrupted her day dreaming. "There's time to see the horses before the Missus calls us to eat."

"I thought you would be busy in the fields."

"I should be plowing, but it's too wet."

"What if Mr. Norrling finds this Lars fellow? What will he do?"

"I'd hang him up by the heels. Beat him black and blue."

Mrs. Jansson appeared around the corner of the stable. "You and how many of your friends?"

Gubb snorted, sputtered, but didn't argue his prowess with his wife.

"See. He worked with that ruffian. Knows when he's over matched."

Maria followed the couple into the house. What would happen if Mr. Norrling found Lars, she wondered.

They sat down to eat the meal of boiled potatoes, cabbage, and salt fish. Gubb broke the silence.

"Does he have a pistol?"

Maria mashed her potatoes with her fork, but didn't eat.

"Does who have a pistol?"

Mrs. Jansson looked up from the baby on her lap. "Did he unlock the gun room this morning?"

"All I know is he wanted the fastest horse."

~~~

Maria spent the afternoon unpacking and arranging her things. As the sun swung lower, she walked to the front window more and more frequently. Several times she went outside to peer down the lane.

"I'll be going now," said Mrs. Jansson. "Time to do up supper for Gubb. There's a stew on the stove for you and the Mister. Table's set.

Bread is in the warming oven."

"Thank you, Mrs. Jansson."

~~~

It was full dark before the noise of hooves on the loose stone of the yard brought Maria's pacing to a halt. The stew sat congealed on the cold stove and the bread had gone from soft freshness to hard crusted staleness.

She ran to fling open the door. "Are you all right."

"You should have seen Dalsson's face when we trotted past him at the half mile stone. He was absolutely purple."

He tossed his coat on the bench and sat to wrench off his muddy boots.

"What's for supper?"

"Mrs. Jansson went home hours ago."

"That Blukka looked like a plow horse." He pulled on dry boots, then demonstrated how he had whipped by his opponent. "Ten lengths at least, maybe more at the oak tree."

"What about Lars? Did you see him?"

Erik Axel fingered his hair back from his forehead and looked around. "Have you let the fire go out?"

"The thief, did you find Lars, the thief?"

"Get the fire started while I see if the boy has the horse walked cool.

In addition to the Janssons, Erik Axel had an indentured boy of about fourteen to run errands and work with the horses. He lived in the small room in the stable left vacant by Lars and the Falun man.

Maria turned her back on her husband and began slamming kindling into the iron stove. Her tears wet the first match. She struck a second and finally willed a flame from the dry wood.

While they ate supper, Maria suffered through a blow-by-blow account of Blukka's every mistake and her husband's prowess at handling the reins, urging the Hanoverian stallion forward at just the right moment.

"How could a race last so long?" she asked when Erik Axel paused to jam a slice of buttered bread into his mouth.

"Best two out of three heats, then Willie Willisson came along and we had to have another go."

"Did you even get to town?"

"Dalsson's going to send his two best mares to our stallion in the spring."

"And Lars, the thief? Any news?"

"The Gothenburg road is closed at the first gorge. They're building the bridge so the railroad can cross."

"And Lars is working there."

"Just think. When the bridge is finished, the railroad will run through to Ludvika."

Maria, who had never been out of the parish, had no idea why her husband was so excited at the thought of a rail line running from the inland farms and mines to the coast.

~~~

Not until the fire had been banked, the oil lamp turned down, did Erik Axel think to ask Maria how her day had gone.

The Soft Shape of Spring, The Sharp Edge of Trouble.

While spring's tender green burst through the brown and gray of winter, Maria busied herself with renewing the old manor house. She polished the diamond-shaped panes of lead glass in the windows to let in the sun. She scrubbed, then varnished the beams of the open ceiling until they glowed amber. With Mrs. Jansson's help she washed and ironed embroidered curtains she found in one of the chests, then hung them at each window.

"Don't that look pretty." Mrs. Jansson sat down to rest her feet.

"Clean window and new curtains really brightens up the room," agreed Maria.

"Them crown poles need new hangings."

"It's the soot from the fire."

"That, and old age. I expect those things been hanging there since Moses was a baby."

The crown poles hung from the open rafters at select intervals to mark off the different sections of the main room. To have divided the kitchen, the eating area, the entrance way, the work space from the rest of the house with a solid wall would have prevented heat from circulating freely. So, in place of walls, long, narrow boards called *kronstang* were suspended a few inches from the ceiling, cross-wise of the rafters, then dressed with short, decorative curtains or woven hangings.

The crown poles in the Norrling house were elaborately carved, perhaps by Erik Axel's grandfather or great grandfather. Between the carved poles hung thin poles of peeled birch. These were used for hanging up clothes and bedding, bread and tools. In due time a cradle would hang from the crown pole nearest Marie's work place.

"I saw some thick weave linen in one of the storerooms," said Maria. "We could work it up into hangings."

"It would be good to have hand work for the long evenings next winter."

"By next spring all the old hangings could be replaced."

As the days lengthened, Maria blackened the cast iron stoves with a mixture of lard and soot. Polished them with arm numbing vigor. Erik Axel complained about the stink, but said little about the renovation of his house.

When the air turned warm, Maria and Mrs. Jansson dragged the heavy mattresses into the yard and turned out the old straw.

"We need fresh straw," said Maria.

"I'll have Gubb fetch some." Mrs. Jansson wiped the dust from her forehead. "You'll be wanting lye water to scrub out the bed closets."

When the cleaning and mattress stuffing was finished, Maria installed the bed linens and quilts from her bridal chest. Tired, but filled with a sense of pride, she stood in the doorway to survey the results of her labor.

The quilts glowed in the late afternoon rays of the sun through the bedroom window. With her mother's help she had pieced them in the long evenings of her teenage years, then shut them away in her marriage trunk. The bed she shared with her husband was covered with the formal, precisely patterned wedding ring quilt with its staid pattern of blue and white.

The second bed had the crazy quilt, a riot of colors and shapes cut from every imaginable kind of fabric: wool, taffeta, alpaca, linen, satin, hopsacking, velvet. Bits of lace, antique tatting, corners cut from worn, but well-loved handkerchiefs, embroidered flowers, ribbons, and ornamental buttons added to the rich surface. In the sunlight the quilt bloomed cadmium yellow, rose, pale blue, emerald, forest green, cobalt, and purple.

"A cover fit for a king," said Mrs. Jansson.

Maria didn't answer, but smiled and hugged herself, invaded with joy for the first time since she had come to live in the old manor house.

When the earth warmed, she planted flowers in the empty beds on either side of the front door. Daisies, hollyhock, tiny, ground-hugging moss roses, fierce goldenrod, and sweet alyssum. As she planted, she planned her fall planting of tulip, hyacinth, crocus, and daffodil. She had snipped, transplanted, and borrowed seed from her mother's garden for the summer garden, but the bulbs, she decided, must be bought at the market in town.

"I could go to town with you this morning," she said to Erik Axel. They sat at the long table drinking a last cup of breakfast coffee. "I'd get tulip bulbs, daffodils, and thread."

"I may be there until late."

"My mother expects me to visit soon."

"Have Gubb drive you."

"He's busy with field work."

"Drive yourself. Take the trap and old Gruie."

Maria had no argument for that and didn't answer. Her husband's trips away from home disturbed her. She was convinced Erik Axel drove the Hanoverian stallion to town more and more frequently. Sometimes he offered an excuse. He had forgotten the coffee, he must order a new grate for the iron cook stove in the laborer's cottage, his boots needed laces. A trip for the purpose of returning a borrowed awl, his fourth trip in as many days, had forced her to break her silence the day before.

"Why all these trips?"

"Just business."

"Can't you take one of the mares? This horse seems tired." The horse had indeed looked unusually gaunt in the flank that morning and sunken hollows appeared above his eyes.

"The horse is fine. The mares are too slow."

"I hardly see you, Mr. Norrling. You missed supper again last night."

"I stopped by Dalsson's place. He thought his mare was ready."

"Ready? Oh, you mean...."

"So she'll bring a foal in the spring you silly goose."

"Does this happen often? Other mares, I mean, not the same one."

"Often enough Tend to your own knitting, Maria."

Erik Axel had given her a quick hug before he left. Today he only pecked her cheek as he hurried out the door.

"Have fun picking out your flower bulbs. Get some red ones. My mother always liked red flowers."

Maria closed the door and walked to the stove to pour herself another cup of coffee.

She was still thinking about Erik Axel's comment about red flowers when there was a knock at the door.

"Speak of the devil. We were just talking about you, Gubb. What can I do for you?"

"Has the mister said anything about hiring on more help?"

"Did he say he would?"

"I can't manage the cultivating by myself."

"You could take the day and see if you could find some workers in town."

"That's not the way things are done, Missus."

"Take the young mare. The one you're breaking in. It will do her good."

"Yes, Missus."

"And Gubb, harness old Gruie to the trap and tie him out front for me. Please."

"Yes, Missus."

"If Mr. Norrling finds fault, send him to me."

Maria closed the door and found the nearest chair. Her knees were shaking and her head pounded. "What have I done." Her voice echoed in the empty room. She didn't move until she heard the chitter of hooves and the rattle of steel rimmed wheels pass the window.

Maria saw little of her husband the rest of the week. He came late to supper, only grunted assent when she told him about the new hired man. She didn't mention her own trip to the market.

"You'll need to take care of the new man's wages. There's money in the copper-bound box on the shelf."

"Is it locked?"

Erik Axel handed her a small key. "It's extra. Keep it."

"How much do I pay?"

"Six *ore*. That's about three *skilling* if you're thinking in the old currency."

Maria wasn't used to thinking in any currency since her father handled all the money at home. A few coppers to buy ribbons or candy was the extent of her education in economics. She had traded eggs and a pair of knitted mittens for the flower bulbs.

That the government had totally revamped the currency system of Sweden in 1855 meant nothing to her. Before the reform two major currencies had been in use. The old *riksdaler-banko* which was divided into forty-eight *skilling* was eliminated and the more popular *riksgalds* was replaced by the *riksdaler* which was divided into one hundred *ore*. This made commerce in the city and internationally much easier, but for Maria it meant a nightmare of worry when payday arrived.

Erik Axel was about to drive out of the yard when Maria stopped him.

"Mr. Norrling, the workers expect to be paid this morning."

"You have the key. Take care of it."

"I can't. Please do it."

"I'll be late. Don't wait supper."

~~~

When she lifted down the cash box, it seemed much lighter than before. After she counted out three stacks of copper coins, the box was nearly empty.

"Is that correct?" she asked the new hand.

"Yes, Missus. Six coppers." He held up six fingers.

"And you?" She pushed three coppers across the table to the stable boy.

The boy shoved the money into his waist bag and backed out of the room.

"You may have mixed the *skilling* with the *ore*," said Gubb.

"No matter. It's done." She pressed the remaining coins into his hand, then added three extra. "For the wife," she told him.

Gubb smiled. "She'll be surprised. Thank you."

~~~

By mid-summer it became apparent the spring planting had not gone well. The sowing was sparse and long empty spaces marred the fields of barley, rye and oats.

"I did what I could," said Gubb. "One man can't work that much ground."

"The barns are foul with manure. Why?" Erik Axel punched the air with his fist. "That stuff should have been strewn on the fields by now."

"I'll get on it now, Boss," said the new hand who had been standing off to one side with the frightened stable boy behind him.

"See that you do." He slapped his boot with his whip and turned away. He missed the raised eyebrows and mouthed complaints of the workers.

Maria, standing at the open window, saw it all. How can he not see his fault in the poor seeding, she wondered. She felt a pang of guilt about the dirty barns and the wasted manure, though. Why hadn't she thought to order it done. It wouldn't happen again.

A few days later, another problem came to light.

"I demand the return of the stud fee, Mr. Norrling." Bent over her sewing inside, Maria could hear the heated exchange. "And compensation for the foal I won't be getting in the spring."

"Be patient, Johan. Your mare is old." Erik Axel tried to talk his way out of the confrontation. "Bring her back and we'll try again."

"You know damn well it's too late in the season. I can't have the mare heavy in foal when I need her to plow."

"I'll loan you a team of oxen. You should know better than to plow with your horses."

"She won't be showing to the stallion this time of year. No, it's money I want or I'll be calling on the magistrate."

Erik Axel stalked into the house and reached down the metal-bound box.

"Damn. It's nearly empty." He slammed the lid down and shouted for Maria.

"What have you done with the money?"

"There was only a few coppers. Barely enough to pay the workers."

He stared at Maria, then noticed her trembling lip, the glisten of tears yet unshed.

"No matter." He went into the storeroom and emerged with another strong box. This one had two locks. Erik Axel shielded the box from view with his body when he opened it.

He counted out several silver coins for the man waiting in the yard.

A few days later another man stood at the door with a similar story. He, too, left with his stud fee and compensation.

Before long Erik Axel had paid out compensation to most of the farmers whose mares the stallion had serviced that spring, though some were clearly lying about the condition of their mares. When Maria asked him what was wrong, he told her it was nothing but a few jealous neighbors trying to get back at him, nothing to trouble her pretty head about.

A few days later Erik Axel left on a three-day trip to the iron works at Borlange.

~~~

"Mrs. Jansson. Come here." Maria's voice held a note of panic.

"Yes, Missus. What is it?"

"My silver belt, my wedding belt. It's gone."

"Are you sure you had it here?"

"Yes, yes. I got it from Mother the last time I visited."

"I don't remember seeing it."

"I put it in my wedding box. I'm sure of it."

"Let's look. Maybe you only intended to put it there."

Frantic, Maria began throwing scarves, gloves, stockings out of her chests to the floor. The chests and trunks emptied, they searched the house over and over without success.

"What could I have done with it?" She felt sick with anxiety and guilt, afraid she had been mistaken or that she had somehow mislaid the heavy belt.

"Maybe it's been stolen."

"Impossible. No one has been here except you and me."

"And the Mister."

"Mrs. Jansson. You don't think he took it?"

"It's very valuable."

Maria thought about the debacle with the stallion and the empty money chest.

"Surely not. He'd have told me."

But by the time her husband returned, Maria no longer blamed herself; she was certain Erik Axel had taken the silver belt.

"Where is my silver belt? What have you done?" She had been crying, her nose was red, her eyes swollen.

"I'm sorry, Maria. I should have told you." He tried to soothe her, but she pulled away. "I locked it up for safe keeping."

Maria did not press her husband on the matter, but she wore her silver necklace on her next visit home and asked her father to lock it in his strong box. Her father placed the necklace in its flannel bag in his safe and turned the key.

"Your husband is spending freely these days, isn't he?"

"I fear so, Father," she answered. "Could you speak to him?"

"It would do no good, Maria. It's in his blood."

He refused to explain his meaning to his daughter, but he clearly knew something.

He Multiplied Horses to Himself.

Several months later a man rode into the Norrling yard leading a tall gray horse with a tail so long it brushed the fall leaves blowing across the ground.

"Hello. Anybody home," he called.

"It's my cousin, Andrew," said Erik Axel.

He dropped his fork, grabbed his coat, and sprinted out to greet the visitor. Maria wrapped her cloak around her shoulders and followed him into the yard.

"Good to see you, Andrew."

"And you, cousin."

"This is my wife, Maria."

At a loss for what to call this stranger, Maria smiled and nodded.

"Erik, you scoundrel. How's married life treating you?"

"Fine. How was the journey?"

Erik Axel didn't wait for an answer. He was examining the gray horse. He ran his hands down the animal's slender legs, picked up his feet, pried his mouth open to see his teeth.

"What an odd looking horse," said Maria.

Erik Axel was so intent on the silver horse, he ignored her.

Maria tried again. "Such skinny legs and tiny ears. I don't think you'll get much work out of him."

"He's not a work horse," said Andrew. "He's a Russian trotter, an Orlov. One of the fastest horses on the continent."

"You brought him from the continent?"

"He was a real handful the first week. Took six men to load him on the boat."

"What a lot of bother over a horse."

Andrew smiled his agreement and handed the lead rope to Erik Axel.

"He's your problem now, cousin."

"How fast is he?" asked Erik Axel. He stood back as far as the lead rope allowed to better see the horse.

"He's the best I could get for the money you sent, cousin. Use him in good health."

"You bought this horse?" Maria stared at her husband.

Before she could say more, Cousin Andrew untied a wooden box from the back of his saddle and presented it to Maria with a bow.

"A little wedding present straight from Prussia. I didn't spend all my time at the horse fair when I was in Danzig."

"Take it inside and open it, Maria. We'll tend to the horses and come in later."

Erik Axel seemed relieved at the distraction, but could not take his eyes from the gray trotter.

Cousin Andrew said, "Be careful when you unpack that box. It's very delicate and has several pieces."

Maria carried the wooden crate into the house and put it on the table. Tears welled in her eyes, but she set the box on the table with great care. Just last week her husband had complained about how hard up they were with the poor harvest and lack of ready cash. Why, he had chided her about asking for a new gown and wrapper. Even complained about the bill from the shoemaker.

She spoke aloud to herself, "He must have traded my silver belt for that horse. How could he."

She tried hard not to blink so the tears would not over-flow and run down her cheeks. While she untied the cord holding the lid on the box, the silver horse reared and raged in her mind. With the lid off, Maria began picking through the packing material, scooping it out onto the table until the first piece of the wedding present appeared.

The fragile gold rim of a cup showed through the layers of wood curls, smooth and delicate next to the rough shavings. Seven more tall slender cups followed the first one, then the *piece de resistance*, the stately chocolate pitcher, itself.

The two men came in while Maria was examining the markings on the bottom of the pitcher.

"It's all the rage on the continent, Mrs. Norrling," said Andrew. "Hot chocolate has practically replaced tea in some circles."

"Where're your manners, Maria," Erik Axel interrupted. "Andrew has had a long ride."

"Sorry, I'll go put the coffee on." She placed the fragile pot on the table and went to the stove.

While the silver horse trampled the silver belt in Maria's mind, she filled the teapot with water. She jammed a couple of fast burning sticks of pine into the cook stove and set the coffee water to heating. The porcelain chocolate set that had emerged from the wooden crate could not, would not replace her beautiful silver belt, symbol of her husband's love and commitment. She stamped her foot and slammed the cupboard door shut with unnecessary force.

How did he do this, she wondered. Then she remembered Erik Axel's trip to Borlange. He must have sent the money to Andrew along with instructions to purchase the horse and deliver him. Wiping her eyes on her apron, Maria hurried to the pantry to load a serving plate with the obligatory seven kinds of cookie.

While Andrew and her husband talked, Maria polished the tall chocolate pot and its matching cups with their odd, stilt-like feet. Her hands moved woodenly, puppet-like as she placed each piece on the kitchen shelf with the other good china. She hardly looked at the thin, rose-decorated porcelain.

"That horse will trot the legs off anything in the parish," said Eric Axel.

"How does the barley crop shape up this year?"

"Young Sarensson got him an English horse a couple of years back. I didn't get to match with him before the horse popped a splint, but his foals will be on the roads come spring."

"I heard about a new kind of barley on the continent. Heads out early. Short stemmed and cold resistant. You might want to try it here."

Cousin Andrew held his cup for more coffee.

"Do you think this gray has raced?"

"Didn't think to ask. The barley is called Stromburg. I could get seed on my next trip."

"How often do you travel to Danzig?" said Maria. She was beginning to feel a bit sorry for Andrew.

"Work keeps me abroad most of the time. Better to ask me how often I'm home."

"How exciting."

"Meetings with crusty old churchmen, reading through tons of dreary papers. Very exciting."

"Are you a minister?"

"Administrator, overseer, messenger boy. Speaking of which, I need to be going. I have an appointment in Smedjebacken yet tonight and another in Ludvika tomorrow."

"I'll see you out."

Erik Axel tossed Andrew his coat, then disappeared out the door.

Andrew turned to Maria and said, "Good Day and good luck."

"Thank you for the chocolate set. What kind of barley did you say?"

"Stromburg," he called back as he followed Erik Axel out the door.

~~~

Maria hurried her supper preparations, sure that Erik Axel would be in at any minute. The pea soup with a fat ham bone was bubbling on the stove and the bread nearly warmed, when she heard the trap clatter through the yard. She reached the window in time to see her husband whip up the silver horse and disappear through the gate to the road.

That night Maria refused her husband's attentions and slept alone under the jewel-colored crazy quilt. In the clutches of night she realized something was different with her, something transcending her feelings of betrayal, transcending silver belts and fast horses, even her husband's love. Maria knew beyond all doubt that she was with child. Near dawn she drifted into sleep, her hands folded across her belly.

~~~

"Good Morning, Mr. Norrling." Maria had dark circles under her eyes.

Erik Axel sat down at the table. "Sorry I was so late last night."

She placed the pan of oat porridge on the iron trivet and went to the box outside the kitchen door for the jug of milk.

"Heavy frost this morning," she said when she returned.

"Did it freeze hard? I want to take the new horse out on the road today."

"Winter's taking its time this year."

Maria sat down and spooned a small mound of porridge into her bowl. She hadn't poured her milk before Erik Axel scraped his bowl clean and jumped up.

"Have Gubb haul the last of the rye to the mill."

"Wait. We need to talk."

"Talk?"

"We...I...am that way. We're going to have a baby."

"What? Are you sure? How did that happen?"

"It didn't just happen, silly. You're going to be a father."

"I'm going to have a son. How about that." He hugged Maria and kissed the top of her head, then bolted for the door. "When?" he called over his shoulder.

Maria answered, "In the spring," but knew he was too far away to hear her.

~~~

That afternoon it began to rain, a hard, pelting rain. Erik Axel drove the into the yard while Gubb and the stable boy were bringing the last of the livestock into the barn. Maria, intent on getting the chickens under cover, paid no attention to him.

He unhitched the silver horse in the wide isle of the barn and rubbed him dry before turning him into the box stall next to the harness room. He left the wet, tangled harness next to the muddy cart and went to help with the chickens.

"You shouldn't be out in this weather," he said to Maria.

"It's going to snow. I can feel it."

"How many more of these creatures?"

"Six, I think. The rest are safe."

"Get to the house. The boy can help me find them."

"He doesn't know their roosts."

The chickens, used to living outside in the summer, all had favorite places in the woods around the yard. The cold, dark day had sent them to roost early. Maria plucked another hen from her sleeping perch in a small alder tree and hurried her to the barn.

By evening the wind raged with cold fury. Maria picked at her supper, then pulled her shawl closer and went to sit by the fire.

"Go to bed," said Erik Axel. "I'll bring a warmer for your feet."

"The hens. Will they be all right?"

"Here's your flannel gown. Change here where it's warm."

"I should have dried the poor things."

"Get into bed."

By morning ice coated each branch and twig. The yard and the forest had become a crystal fantasy land.

"Come look, Maria. It's beautiful."

Erik Axel stood at the front window peering out across the yard.

When he heard no answer, he went back to the bedroom. Maria huddled under a mound of covers.

"Are you all right?"

He peeled back the quilts and put his hand on Maria's forehead.

"You're burning up."

"I'm all right." Maria tried to climb out f bed, but fell back with the effort. "Later. I'll get up later. Let me rest, now."

"I'll get Mrs. Jansson."

~~~

"So, You've a bit of fever." Mrs. Jansson smoothed the pillow case and brushed Maria's long, damp back from her face. "My oldest is down with it, too. Change in the weather, I expect."

Erik Axel hovered at her elbow.

"Do you think I should go for the doctor?"

"Not yet. Make some tea. Nice and strong."

~~~

When Maria's fever had not broken by early afternoon, Mrs. Jansson pulled Erik Axel aside.

"Do you know Edward Lof?"

"I've heard he's back in the parish."

"With a new wife, from over the mountains."

"Old Lof got himself a foreign wife. So?"

"She's said to have the healing touch."

Erik Axel paced around the room, picked a piece of unfinished embroidery from a chair, then dropped it on the side table.

"Enough gossip. I'm going for the doctor."

"Matilda Lof is closer."

"Old Doc Siergel has always taken care of the family."

"The Haroldsson's had her when the mister got the lung fever."

Erik Axel stopped his pacing. "The roads must be treacherous."

"Gubb can go afoot through the forest. They'll be here by supper."

~~~

Mrs. Lof burst into the room. Her long scarves, thick shawl, tall felt boots, and many bags made her seem huge. She dropped one bundle near the stove and consigned the others to Erik Axel.

"Take care with that. Put it gentle on the table."

She shucked off her shawl, a gray knit affair, and looked for a hook to hang it on.

As she unwrapped herself, she seemed to shrink. Expecting an old woman, Erik Axel went to help her. He stepped back when Mrs. Lof pulled off her last scarf to reveal black curls, rosy red cheeks, and bright blue eyes.

"Are you Mrs. Lof?"

"You be expecting different?"

"Yes, No. I don't know."

"Even kings and queens be babies once, you know."

"My apologies."

"Where's me patient?"

Erik Axel led her to the bedroom.

Mrs. Lof threw back the curtains surrounding the bed cupboard, then stripped the quilts from her patient.

"Open the window," she demanded. "Fresh air. A basin of cool water."

When Mrs. Lof placed cold compresses on Maria's head and chest, Erik Axel protested.

"You'll kill her."

"Do you have a dram of white wine? Fetch it. And a clean glass."

Mrs. Lof divided the wine into two portions, added a fine powder from her bag to one of them.

"What's that?"

"Piss-a-Bed. It draws the heat. Have your lady cool in no time."

"Dandelion? Are you mad?"

The quick little woman had Maria down the dose in a few quick gulps, then drank the leftover wine herself. She continued changing the compresses until Maria's fever abated. Her work finished, she put on her coat and wrapped the many scarves around her head.

"What now?" said Erik Axel.

"Broth and a little milk sop. She'll be frisky as a pup in a day or two."

"And your payment? A peck of rye flour, perhaps?"

"Cash only. Six *ore*. Mind you fetch your hired man to see me home, too."

Pride Cometh Before the Fall.

In the preparations for Christmas Maria brushed aside her bout of fever. She still had a cough and tired easily, but the memory of Mrs. Lof's visit dimmed. Cold and icy roads kept Erik Axel closer to home, too, and that pleased her. He spent the evenings near the fireplace carving, while Maria sewed tiny flannel gowns and wrappers.

"Could we invite your cousin, Andrew, for Christmas dinner?"

"The roads are terrible. Worse than I can remember."

"My sisters are coming from Stockholm, so my parents can't come for dinner."

"Andrew's in Augsberg or London or someplace."

"How about Mr. and Mrs. Lof? They are neighbors."

"I'll not sit at the same table as that bastard."

"She seemed nice. You did call her when I was sick."

"That was different."

"How about Gubb and Mrs. Jansson?"

"You can't have the help to dinner. They'll have a pair of ducks and the afternoon off. More than enough."

Maria bent her head and dabbed her tears with the corner of the flannel shirt she was embroidering with a winding trace of blue flowers. Mrs. Lof had predicted the baby would be a boy.

Erik Axel cast aside the tankard he was carving and stood up.

"I need to check on the horses."

~~~

The fire died down and the oil lamps flickered their need for attention. Outside the wind blathered icy twigs against the roof. Maria tucked her needle through the edge of the small flannel shirt and laid it aside. She folded her hands across her swelling stomach.

"Good evening little babe. You're so lucky to be safe inside."

The child in her womb leaped and danced under her ribs. His silent voice answered her tear stained tone with laughter.

"We will run glad over meadows and flowers," he said.

"How can that be? The ice is thick, the rivers are frozen and still."

"True. The leaves lay faded white on the meadow, blown by every storm."

"I fear the ice will stay forever."

"The ice will break like roaring thunder. We'll stand together on the bank and watch the silver cranes dance."

~~~

In early spring Maria birthed her first baby, a howling red son she named Matthew. Mrs. Lof made a brief visit, summoned by the anxious father. She applied a vile ointment to the umbilical and tightened the baby's belly band, then proclaimed mother and baby hale and healthy. With a wave of her hand and a heavier purse she departed.

"He's so beautiful." Maria held the baby as if he would shatter at any moment.

"Red. Why is he so red?"

"Don't be silly."

"I suppose you need a girl to help out now?"

A few weeks later Erik Axel decided to go to the Port of Gothenburg for a shipment of seed grain. The last railroad bridge was not yet finished, so it was a long overland journey.

"Can't you send Gubb?"

"I'll be gone several days, maybe a week."

"Can't the freight office in Ludvika handle it?"

"You'll be fine."

~~~

Maria spent the long week cleaning winter's debris from her flower beds, playing with Matthew, and instructing the hired girl in the art of ironing.

She held up a shirt with a hard crease marring its front.

"So? You call this ironed?"

"Sorry, Missus."

"Didn't your mother teach you anything?"

Maria flung the shirt at the girl. "Wash it and do it over. Right this time."

"The Mister hired me to help with the baby."

"You're not fit to scrub the hearth." Maria up-ended the ironing basket onto the floor. "See that this is finished by supper."

~~~

When Erik Axel returned, he had a second Orlov trotter haltered to the tail gate of the wagon. He stood in the yard and called for Maria to join him.

"Come see."

"I can see him quite well from here." Marie bit her lip and twisted her hanky into a shapeless rag.

"Not the best part. Hurry up."

"What is it?"

Erik Axel brushed the horse's mane aside and pointed out the brand on the horse's neck, a mark in the shape of a crown.

"What does it mean?"

"He's from the royal stud."

~~~

When the spring planting was finished, Erik Axel urged Maria and baby Matthew to accompany him to a race meet one afternoon.

"Fresh air, a change of scenery. It will do you good."

"Go on by yourself."

"You can show off your new frock. Everyone from Smedjebacken and Hagge will be there."

"I don't know."

Erik Axel held Matthew up to the ceiling. "Show off this little winner, too."

~~~

The morning of the race meet swept in, sweet and clear. The hired girl packed a lunch of cold sausages, beet relish, and white bread. Erik Axel secured a crock of cold beer and another of new pressed apple cider in a wicker basket behind the seat of the two wheeled gig.

Inside, Maria dressed the baby in one outfit after another. A wide collared sailor suit lay on the floor near a red jumper. She pulled an embroidered sweater over his head.

"He'll roast in that thing," said Erik Axel.

He plucked the red-faced baby from his wife's lap and removed the woolly sweater. Baby Matthew howled and gagged.

"Get his cotton shirt, the yellow one. And the matching cap and those silly things for his feet."

He walked the baby up and down the room, alternately jigging him above his head, then rocking him in his arms. By the time Maria brought the shirt and booties, Matthew was quiet. Erik Axel nodded towards the bench.

"I'll dress him, Maria. Get yourself ready."

~~~

The Norrling family made a charming picture as they made their way along the Grange burg highway. The crowds of people gathered along the level stretch of the road chosen for the races couldn't help but notice Maria's new frock cut in the latest style or Matthew's canary yellow cap and booties.

Though she held her head high and smiled, Maria felt anxious, close to panic. She tried to puzzle out the cause of her uneasiness. Was it the silver horse tied to the back of the gig tossing his foamy sweat slick head against the lead rope. Or the crowds of rowdy young men pressing around to assess the animal's chances. Maybe it was just nerves. She felt so strange these days, ever since baby Matthew's birth, like she could start weeping and never stop.

The birthing had been easier than she had expected. The horror stories told by her mother and girl friends had not materialized. Though she experienced no unusual difficulties, Erik Axel had brought Mrs. Lof to help her through her confinement. Even through her pain and utter exhaustion, she felt a warm happiness at his concern.

She was surprised at how quickly people had accepted Mrs. Lof, her being a newcomer to the parish and a foreigner from Norway at that. People were suspicious at first, but they welcomed her as midwife and healer. Maybe it was because the parish was without a doctor at the moment and because women were much more inclined to call for another woman to attend them. Though young, Matilda Lof was already an imposing woman with her knit bag filled with dried herbs and strange tinctures and ointments.

~~~

"Here's a good place, Maria. Right on the start and finish line."

Erik Axel stopped the horse under a spreading tree and climbed down.

"Let me help you."

He lifted Maria over the high wheel and set her down, baby and all.

"It's very pretty. Thank you."

Maria spread a quilt on the grass for the baby and returned to the gig for the basket.

"Will you take lunch with us, Mr. Norrling?"

"I'll be busy with the horse. Don't wait for me."

He unhitched the heavy Swedish-bred horse that had drawn the gig to the race meet, led him across the small meadow and tied him to a tree. He smiled down at his young son as he passed by to return to the gig. He bridled the Orlov trotter and backed the trembling gray horse between the traces and harnessed him to the empty gig. Without a backward glance he climbed up behind the trotter and bumped over the grass to the road.

Horses and rigs of all shapes and sizes were matched up, two-by-two. They seemed to trot miles of preliminary heats along the three mile loop of dirt road. The beaten horses were matched with other losers, the winners stood waiting to trot against another winner in a seemingly endless tangle of two horse heats.

Maria cheered Erik Axel and the gray Orlov when they won three heats. When no one challenged them for a fourth race, she thought her husband might join her to share the picnic lunch. She stood up and waved, but was disappointed when he ignored her to lead the horse to a quiet spot away from the crowd.

She watched him unhook the horse from the gig, loosen the noseband on the bridle and slip the bit from the horse's mouth. With a rag he washed the animal's poll and face, let him have a little water, then tossed a sheet over his sweaty back and flanks. He had walked the gray up and back down the field just once when a commotion at the starting line drew Maria's attention.

She checked to be sure baby Matthew was asleep on the blanket, then moved to a better vantage point. A light spring wagon with two men sped along the road towards the race course. Just before they reached the level section, the chestnut horse was pulled to a stop and the man dressed in rough workman's clothing jumped out to merge with the crowd.

The crowd converged on the wagon driven by a tall white-haired man. He tipped his hat to them and drove the chestnut horse to the starting line. Some of the men yelled to Erik Axel.

"Here's a match for you."

"Bring that gray flyer."

"Show him."

Maria recognized the man as Deacon Lof, the midwife's husband. His horse was a rib-thin, deep-chested stallion with a pendulous lower lip and white rimmed eyes. Deacon Lof stood up so the crowd could hear him.

"Here's your new champion."

"That nag?"

"How about you, Jarlsson? I'll match with that sorrel mare of yours."

"She's done for the day."

Erik Axel heard the challenge. He backed his horse into the shafts, reins, crupper, and surcingle flapping and dragging. One of the young men ran to help him with the harness. Erik Axel jumped into the gig and whipped up the gray stallion. The horse reared, nearly upsetting the cart before he trotted to the starting line.

Erik Axel was shouting at Mr. Lof, though the two men were only feet apart. The two horses walled their eyes at each other and pawed at the dirt.

"Damn English nag. He looks like a starved cow."

Mr. Lof adjusted his neck scarf and pulled on his gloves. "You may as well concede now."

"Never."

"A little wager, perhaps."

Maria missed the rest of the conversation. She watched her husband hand a large quantity of *riksdalers* to a bystander, a man in a suit, soft tie, and top hat. When Mr. Lof entrusted a similar amount of money with the man, Maria knew he was a betting agent . Was her husband wagering all that money on a horse and a tired horse at that? Couldn't the stubborn fool see that the silver horse was black with sweat, breathing in great gasps, while Mr. Lof 's horse was cool and rested.

Maria stumbled back to the blanket, the bright spring day a blur through her tears. She flopped down by baby Matthew and pulled him close, but her sobs could not blot out the shouts of the crowd, the whip cracks, the pounding hooves on the hard road. The truth cracked her heart to bits. It wasn't the racing or the love of fine horses that captivated her husband, it was the wagers on the outcome.

~~~

Maria sat stiff and silent on the ride home until Erik Axel asked if she had seen the man with Deacon Lof.

"Only from a distance."

"I thought he might be Lars the thief, but I never got a good look at him."

   "What would Mr. Lof be doing with someone like that?"

Trial by Fire.

Pale morning light filtered through the thick diamond panes of the front windows. A migrating flock of warblers settled in the holly bush by the door and filled the air with their rich song. Wrapped in a woolly shawl, Maria sat by the fireplace nursing baby Matthew.

"Where are you off to this morning?" she asked.

"A fire again? It's nearly May."

"Is the planting finished?"

"Don't wait dinner. I'm going to see Deacon Lof."

"Do you have to?"

"If he's harboring that thief...."

"You'll do what?"

Erik Axel didn't answer. When he returned home that evening, he slammed a small pouch of silver coin onto the table.

"The bastard thinks he can buy me off."

"He gave you money?"

"Restitution. To get Lars off the hook."

"Can he do that?"

"Um, yes. He had a judge in Ludvika prepare the order."

~~~

The stable of trotting horses had increased to five by the time Maria announced her second pregnancy. A new stone barn being built to shelter the Orlov trotters was chin high when Maria went into labor.

This birth was harder and Erik Axel sent for Mrs. Lof reluctantly and late. Matilda Lof stayed barely long enough to guide the new baby into the world. On her way out she showed Selma, the hired girl, how to brew a medicinal tea and cook up the barley water gruel recommended for the sick and feeble. Maria lay abed several weeks, too weak to care for herself or her family.

By the time she was up and around again, the new baby, named

Daniel, was well used to a diet of goat's milk and thin oat porridge.

"You might try nursing him, Missus." Selma thrust the baby into Maria's arms.

"He's so pale." Maria took the baby and held him at arm's length.

"You're just used to that black-headed Matty. This one's gonna be fair like the Mister."

Daniel screwed up his face and started crying. Maria tried to soothe the baby, but his cries turned to hiccupy screams. She handed him back to Selma.

"Take him. He must be hungry or something."

"He has a temper, that's sure."

By Mid-Summer Eve Maria felt better except for a persistent, deep cough. If only it would warm up, she thought. What a strange summer. She walked up and down her flower boarder searching for blooms suitable to cut for a bouquet, but even the hardy daisies drooped on stunted stems.

She wandered across the yard to the cow barn. The cows and goats would be driven to the *langfabod* or summer pasture in a few weeks. The farm's cleared land was too valuable to use for pasture or hay, so the livestock, guided and cared for by hired girls, trekked some forty miles to summer pasture in the hills.

Maria felt a pang of envy when she thought about the free life of the herder girls. They would live together in a log hut, cook their meals over an open fire, roam the meadows with the cows by day, take turns with the milking and cheese making with no one to dictate when to wake or when to sleep. Because she grew up in town where her mother bought milk and cheese from the market, Maria had never gone to the far pasture in summer.

"Need something, Missus?"

"Oh, Gubb. You startled me."

"It's feeding time." He gestured at the stalled cattle."

"They seem restless."

"They can smell the green grass, what little there is."

That evening Maria sat by the window with her embroidery spread on her knee. Baby Daniel had been fed, swaddled, and now slept in the cradle suspended from the beam at her side. Selma, the hired girl, was wrestling Matthew into the tin tub for his bath. Eric Axel was eating a late cold supper, his back to the women and babies.

Between mouthfuls of bread and cold mutton, he voiced his

concerns aloud.

"We're getting low on feed."

"Can't you buy more?"

"Everyone's got the same problem."

"Maybe the cattle should go to the far pasture early this year."

"Dalsson said the same, yesterday. He told his daughter to get ready."

"Can she take our animals, too?"

"Too many for one girl."

"You're not thinking of sending Selma?"

"Who else?"

"I need her here."

They settled on sending the young goats, calves, and heifers with the Dalsson girl. The mature cows, who were fresh and required milking, would remain in the home barn until after the Mid Summer Eve celebration. Since the forest path to the summer pasture wound through the Norrling farm, the cows could join the trek at the usual time. This would require little out-of-pocket expense since the Dalsson girl would be paid only, a few ore extra. The girls were usually paid a small share of the butter and cheese they made at the camp.

~~~

The Mid Summer Eve celebration began with a community gathering the day before to decorate the Maypole. Originally celebrated on May first, it was a custom brought to the region by German immigrants. When they discovered the countryside still locked in winter's grasp, they moved it to midsummer.

The pole, a tall spruce spar with two short cross arms, dominated the village green at Hagge year around, a reminder of good times. The men and boys would lay it out on the ground for the girls to garb with flowers and greens. The feast day itself was an all day party with games, drinking, bonfires, and the winding of the May pole. The dancing usually lasted long into the night.

"No horse races," thought Maria. She accepted another tiny sandwich spread with smoked salmon pate.

"A sip of wine?" Erik Axel held their shared tankard to her lips.

"Do you think the children are all right?"

"Gubb and his Missus looked in on them before they came."

"Selma can be so silly."

They danced a quick stepping round where they circled the May pole until Maria dropped out with a stitch in her side. Erik Axel joined her on the blanket and they grappled like two puppies in the darkness. Near midnight another young couple rousted them out to share a plate of fat sausages and *flatbrod*.

"Beer. Sausages demand beer."

"Bring me some, too," said Maria.

"And me."

"Me too."

"I'll bring a bucket. Hold on." Erik Axel waved his tankard and ran across the meadow to the food tables where a barrel of beer sat waiting.

When he straightened up from the barrel spigot, he saw a red glow flare into the night sky. He dropped his half-filled tankard and ran through the crowd of men and boys near the food table.

"Fire. Fire on the horizon."

"Where?"

"I see it."

"Get to the wagons. Quick."

"What is it?" Maria had found Erik Axel in the sudden crush of excited partiers.

"Fire." He pointed to the orange glow above the tree tops.

"It may be our house. Run."

Erik Axel stripped the harness from his horse and leaped astride. Along with the more sober revelers he tore off across the field, jumped the stream, and galloped down Hagge road.

Maria watched him disappear through the trees. My babies, she thought. Why did I leave them. She ran along the cart track ankle deep in dust. What a fool, that Selma. Probably forgot to open the chimney damper. She imagined Daniel and Matthew dead and in their coffins. She tried to run faster, but her shoes slogged off in the ruts and tripped her. On her knees she tried to catch her breath. A scream formed deep beneath her breast bone and fought her in-drawn breath.

A high wheeled cart pulled up beside her.

"Get in, Maria. Hurry."

Maria clambered to her feet and leaned against the side of the cart, willing her trembling knees to support her. Someone reached down and helped her up.

By the time they reached the turnoff to the Norrling farm, the orange glow had defined itself into raging flames. Maria, on the verge of fainting, urged the driver to whip up his horse, faster, faster, but a clog of carts and tethered horses soon brought them to a stop. The air thickened with bitter smoke, shouts, and popping embers.

As Maria struggled through the crowd, she dodged loose cattle and men leading frightened horses. When she reached the huge fir tree at the corner of the yard, she could see the flames eating the remains of the cow barn. To her great relief the house stood untouched.

While she caught her breath, she watched some of the men struggle to lead the horses from the stable whose thatch roof was beginning to smolder. A group of men and boys hauled water from the river, while others passed it up to a pair of men on the roof.

"Here, Missus," Selma yelled to Maria. "The babes are safe."

"Thank God."

Maria ran to embrace baby Daniel in Selma's arms. Matthew, thumb in mouth, clung to the girl's skirt. "Let's take them inside."

Dawn came quickly and with it the revelation of the havoc left by the fire. Only the stone foundation of the cow barn remained. Smoking piles marked the fodder bins, a line of charred mounds the bodies of cattle dead in their stalls.

The surviving animals wandered aimlessly in the woods, their low moaning cries indicating their need of food and milking. Two of the big animals were badly injured and the men prepared to kill and butcher them to save the meat.

The roof of the new stone horse stable had collapsed from the weight of the water poured on it, but all of the horses had been led to safety. Unfortunately, one of the young horses had pulled free of his rescuer and ran headlong back into the flames. He stood shivering from the shock of his injuries while someone hunted up a pistol to put him out of his misery.

It was a much reduced herd of cows that joined the trek to the long pasture from the Norrling farm that summer. Fewer cows meant less butter and cheese. Young stock that would normally be sold in the fall had to be held to replace the milkers lost in the fire. Money would be in short supply for some time.

"Matthew needs shoes."

"Can't he make do with his old ones?"

"Look at him, Mr. Norrling. He's growing fast."

"Fire the girl, Selma. Dalsson will take her on."

"What about my fall outfits?"

"The new cow barn has to be finished before winter."

"I've had the fitting. The material's ordered."

"I've set up a small distillery. We'll save the cost of beer and *brannvin*."

"Can't you sell some of the horses?"

"If you had let Selma take the cows to the *langfabod*, we wouldn't be in this mess."

Maria burst into tears and ran from the room. She threw herself down on the bed with the crazy quilt and pulled the doors of the bed closet shut with a crash. As she sobbed in the darkness, she resolved to cancel the order for her new gowns and rework her old ones.

She would dismiss Selma and do the cooking and rough work herself. Everyone would see her poor red hands and broken nails and know what a sacrifice she was making. She would serve Erik Axel's homemade beer and *brannvin* at every meal and never again put white bread from boughten flour on the table.

Trying to invent even more ways to economize, Maria fell asleep.

Erik Axel said nothing about Maria's capitulation. He tossed Selma's bundle of possessions into the wagon and drove her to the Dalsson farm. The small wage Maria had paid Mrs. Jansson, wife of the tenant worker Gubb, was stopped. Young Matthew went barefoot until winter, when Erik Axel finally relented and bought him a pair of the cheapest shoes at the fall market. Only the horses continued to eat the best of oats and sweet hay, groomed and bedded by a man whose only job was their care.

Rising Hope, Clouds of Doubt.

In late February of 1865, nine months past the Mid-Summer Eve fire, two years after Daniel's birth, Erik Axel and Maria's daughter was born. They named her Anna. She was a long, pinch-faced baby with Maria's dark hair. It was an easy birth attended only by Mrs. Jansson, wife of the hired man, Gubb.

The 1860 law that made the distillation of grain into brannvin illegal had finally reached Norrbarke parish and Erik Axel was busy moving his still to a less obvious place in the woods. The Kristiania to Karlstad telegraph was complete and the reform of the Riksdag made some five percent of the population eligible to vote.

The family's financial situation improved once more. Maria was too busy to question the reason. Perhaps it was the pair of winning horses which Erik Axel drove to victory nearly every weekend.

"Mamma, come see," said Matthew. "Pappa has a new sled."

"Put your mittens on."

"Hurry, hurry."

"Calm down. He's not going anywhere."

Maria felt a small dig of excitement, herself, and some of her son's worry that Erik Axel might vanish down the road before they could get out the door. He had been gone for three days this time, a special trip to Ludvika for a superior variety of oats for the racing horses.

Matthew tore across the yard. Maria followed more slowly. She noted the two men unloading the farm wagon her husband had driven to the city. A stack of boxes and grain sacks showed their progress. A single horse and the new sled were tethered out of the way, while Erik Axel unhitched the team from the freight wagon and stripped off their harness. She recognized one of the horses in the team, but decided the other one belonged to the men who had driven the wagon.

"Papa, Papa, did you bring me something?"

"All this," Maria indicated the pile of goods with her hand. "Can we afford so much?"

"The boys missed Christmas. Don't waste time with worry."

He paid the men, who stood fidgeting beside the empty wagon. They climbed astride the spare horse and cantered away.

Maria walked across the yard to exam the new sled with its dark green and gold paint.

"It's so small."

"Too small for passengers," said Erik Axel. "Very light, very fast. The horse barely knows he's pulling anything."

"Is it safe?"

"They're using it in England, America, too."

Maria ran her fingers over the smooth enameled wood, traced the up-curved runners that nearly met at the front.

"When the ice goes, you can replace the runners with wheels." He showed her the large, thin-spoked wheels.

"Two?"

"The gig sits close to the horse, so it's quite stable"

"Better hope he's not a kicker." Maria had lost interest and wandered around poking at the bundles and boxes stacked around the yard.

Erik Axel grabbed Matthew. "Go get you brother."

"Then we get our present?"

"You bettcha."

While Matthew and Daniel watched, their pappa unwrapped a red patent leather harness and a small cart of bright yellow.

"Now, go fetch Bucky, while I put the wheels on this thing."

The boys tore off to the barn and were back dragging a reluctant goat before Erik Axel had the last wheel tight.

"Here, Pappa. I can drive."

"Let's get the harness on the beast first."

Completely over powered, Bucky submitted to the red harness. Matthew and his little brother were soon bumping around the yard behind the high stepping goat.

Maria clapped and cheered their progress until a coughing fit drove her inside. Erik Axel followed her.

"It's nothing. Just the cold air."

The cough that had nagged Maria since the birth of her youngest son had worsened with each succeeding winter. Though she tried to conceal it, she often felt weak and feverish.

Then, a few days after the arrival of the goat cart, baby Anna, fell sick. When, her fever held on and various home remedies brought her no relief, Erik Axel sent the hired man for the doctor in Smedjebacken.

~~~

"Will she be all right?" said Maria.

The doctor had finished his examination and seemed prepared to leave.

"Stop your fretting, Mrs. Norrling. I'll leave some powders and a tonic for her."

The doctor, a young man new in his practice, laid a paper packet and a bottle on the table.

"An atypical case. I think she's about to break out in a rash, so don't be alarmed. Her fever will pass then."

"Measles? Do you think she has the measles?"

Maria was greatly relieved. This was something she understood, something she could deal with.

"How long?"

"Hard to say. A few hours, maybe."

He watched Maria intently. She felt he had not taken his eyes off her since he came into the room.

"When did you see a doctor, last, Mrs. Norrling?"

"It's nothing. Only a little cough."

He took her hands and turned them palm up, then felt of the soft places below her jaw. Finally he listened to her chest with his stethoscope.

"I suggest you see a doctor in Borlange. Someone with more experience with these things."

"What is it? What sort of things?"

"I can recommend a good man there. Here, I'll write his name for you."

The young doctor wrote a name on a scrap of paper and handed it to Erik Axel who stood staring at it.

"He's all right, a regular fellow."

Maria sat down by the cradle and pulled the coverlet up around baby Anna's face. She crossed her arms over her chest to hide her shaking hands and leaned back in the chair. The doctor's voice mingled with the deeper questioning tones of her husband's voice flowed over her, unintelligible, words unformed, drowned in the roar of her own heart beat. Poor baby. And what about Matthew and silly little Daniel, she thought. What will become of you if I die.

"Crooks, the whole lot of you are crooks. Out for the money."

Erik Axel spoke harshly for the first time since the doctor's arrival. His rough tones penetrated Maria's dazed mind. She jumped to her feet.

"Where are my manners. Doctor, will you take a cup of coffee with us?"

"I should be getting back."

"It would be no trouble. It's all ready." And, indeed, the house carried the rich aroma of new ground coffee gently brewed.

Maria hurried to the kitchen, pausing to lift the embroidered cloth covering the table laid with the best china and silver. She plucked up the tall chocolate pot and carried it to the stove where she filled it with coffee. The chocolate set had sat unused in the corner cabinet ever since its journey from the continent with cousin Andrew. One excuse after another had filled Maria's mind when she thought to use it. Today had seemed perfect, a visitor unlikely to complain about the tiny cups, nor apt to compare the table furnishings to his own. And using the pot for something less exotic than chocolate. What would people think.

Erik Axel raised his eyebrows when Maria passed him one of the pinch-handled cups, but kept silent. The many-layered cake and butter cookies were above reproach. Maria had made good use of the supplies he had brought from town.

When the plates were empty, the doctor stood up , thanked Maria for her hospitality, and reminded her to make an appointment to see the specialist in the city. Erik Axel gave him the agreed upon fee and escorted him out to his horse.

~~~

Before the first tiny purple harebells thought to push through the snow, Maria pushed the idea of a visit to the doctor out of her mind. Her fever had abated about the same time that baby Anna recovered from her bout of measles. Perhaps her fear energized her, perhaps it was the better food and respite from the labor of scrubbing floors, hauling wood into the house, tending the fires, standing over the laundry pots. So sure spring would take care of her coughing spells, she convinced her husband not to worry about it.

The bitter cold of winter had let up enough to make traveling easier. The snow-packed roads and frozen rivers made traveling by sleigh fast and fairly comfortable. The smith was kept busy hammering out horseshoes with sharp ice-calks.

A series of parties, a last fling before the beginning of Lent, were being held at the various farms and estates around the countryside. The mailman with his narrow wagon was kept busy delivering invitations.

"Was that the post?" Maria looked up from her sewing.

"Just party invitations."

"Can we go? At least to one?"

"And show off your new gown? Why not."

The party was a blur of bright lights, dancing, chatter with friends. The food was good and endless, the drink strong and the house warm. Out of breath after two dances, Maria giggled and flirted on the sidelines until Erik Axel joined her.

"It's getting late."

"One more drink."

"One more and I'll have to carry you home."

They thanked their host and left. The cold midnight air sucked them from the warm house into the darkness. Maria was coughing by the time she climbed into the sleigh.

Erik Axel shook the reins over the haunches of the gray Orlov stallion and guided him onto the road. The night air was sharp, but not bitterly cold. A full moon reflecting off the snow cast the landscape in high relief.

They traveled in silence through the village of Hagge. As they neared the mill stream bridge, they could hear shouts and rapid hoof beats in the distance. Closer to the narrow span, they could see a light carriage driven by a young man approach the far side. A second man lounged on the seat beside the driver, his face obscured in the shadows. By the time the Orlov's front hooves thunked the bridge planks, they could make out the lank form of Oscar Lof's chestnut thoroughbred.

"Who is that driving Lof's horse?"

"His hired hand, no doubt."

"And that rough looking fellow beside him?"

"Too dark to tell. He seems familiar."

"They're not pulling up. We better back up."

"We have the right away."

The horses were quickly nose-to-nose on the narrow bridge.

Below, open water, runoff water from the local mine, cascaded over a high weir with a roar. Spray blasted the carriages and froze to the bridge planks.

"Evenin, Sir, Missus."

Lof's driver saluted with his whip, but did not bother to tip his hat or remove the cigar from his lip.

"Mind movin that nag aside? I gotta get this rig to Mr. Lof. He don't like to be kept waiting."

"Mind your manners, boy."

Erik Axel shook the reins and his horse stepped forward on the bridge until he stood pressed against the Lof stallion. The chestnut's thin skin twitched as if he was covered with biting flies, his eyes rolled to white, and his nostrils flared. The gray Orlov stood brick still.

"Back up, boy. Back your rig out of the way."

"For you? I'll not give way for the likes of you."

The man sitting in the shadows leaned forward and grabbed the whip from the driver. He stood up and cracked the chestnut horse across the haunches. The tall stallion seemed a wraith against the night sky as he reared and skittered on the icy bridge.

Erik Axel stood up to better see the man confronting him.

"Lars? Is that you, Lars Smelsson?"

His voice rose to a scream and added to the noise of the horses and the rushing water below. Drowned out a small whimper from Maria.

"You thief. Let us pass."

"What's it to you? My master owns you," sneered the youth.

He took the cigar from between his teeth and spat in the snow at the edge of the bridge. Bending forward, he jeered and slapped the rein ends across his horse's back.

"He owns you, Mr. Lof do, and you know it."

He spat towards Erik Axel, then smacked the horse again. Refusing to push forward, the chestnut stood spraddle-legged on the bridge with rolling eyes and great swathes of foam swinging from his lips.

"Back off, boy, before that slick-footed horse of yours falls on the ice. Mr. Lof's not going to be happy to hear you been mistreating his horse."

Lars reached over, cuffed the youth on the ear, and grabbed the reins.

"Now we see who backs up."

He seemed to forget the gray horse blocking his path. He reversed his whip and clubbed the chestnut with the heavy handle end until the frantic animal began to rear and plunge against the Norrling horse facing him on the narrow bridge.

With a realization of the danger from the desperate horse, Erik Axel motioned to his wife.

"Get down, Maria. Move off the bridge. Quick, now."

"Can't you just back off?"

The answer was obvious, so Maria climbed out of the sleigh and inched back along the bridge rail. After she reached the safety of a broad tree just off the verge of the road, she turned to see the chestnut horse twisting and jerking in his traces.

The gray horse, restless with the close quarters, pawed the ice, tossed his head and nipped at the other stallion. The driver raised the whip with both hands and brought it down on his horse's flank with his full strength. The horse leaped forward, crashed into the solid gray, then slipped on the ice and went down under his sharp-shod hooves.

As the chestnut stallion struggled to get to his feet, he tangled in the Orlov's harness. Both horses were struggling now, kicking, pushing, fighting each other and the tangle of confining harness. The wood of the carriage and sleigh shafts splintered under the kicks of both horses, but Lars continued to clout the chestnut with the whip, raising great dark welts across the horse's back and sides.

With a bellow so loud nearby householders could hear it, Erik Axel jumped from the sleigh and pulled Lars from his perch on the high seat to the ground. Only when he noticed blood staining the snowy road around the struggling animals did he stop beating the man. When Erik Axel let go, Lars stumbled off the bridge into the woods.

The cowering youth thought to follow, but Erik Axel grabbed him.

"Don't make things worse for yourself. Get your knife."

Without regard to the danger of the flailing hooves, they worked to cut the horses free of the wrecked vehicles, the tangled harness. It was too late. The Lof's Thoroughbred kicked a few more times, but it was only involuntary reflex. The chestnut horse was dead. His blood pumped out on the icy bridge from a deep gash made by the ice cleats on the gray horse's shoes. The sharp calk had caught the downed horse inside the forearm where the artery lay close to the surface.

The gray horse fared a little better. The repeated kicks from the chestnut had battered his forelegs bloody, but bone and tendon still held.

A crowd had gathered by the time Erik Axel got his horse unharnessed and out of the traces. Someone threw a blanket over the trembling, bleeding animal. Someone else brought a team and dragged the dead horse away, pushed the damaged carriage off the bridge.

It was only after he arranged for a stall for his injured horse at a nearby stable that Erik Axel finally remembered his wife. He found a local man to care for the injured horse, then borrowed a rig and team to take Maria home. She huddled silent under the fur robe on the trip home. Once there, the blessed warmth of the house overcame her, almost before she could take off her gown, unlace her stays. The maid unbuttoned her shoes and brushed out her long hair. Feverish and racked by deep coughs, Maria climbed into bed, but not to sleep. Watching the nightmare scene of the bridge play out on the backs of her eyelids, she was afraid to let herself drift off until morning light. One thought bothered her more than everything else. What had that boy meant by Mr. Lof owning them? She must ask her husband.

Cast Down with the Stones.

Oscar Lof and Erik Axel Norrling stood before the magistrate to hear the settlement of the case. The two men seemed cut from the same cloth, though Mr. Lof was several years younger than Erik Axel. They were of average height, well fed, dressed in their Sunday suits of black wool, hands smooth and uncalloused, gentlemen both.

The magistrate called for silence and began the proceedings.

"I have taken your complaint under the strict advisement of the law, Mr. Oscar Lof, and I find in your favor." He turned to Mr. Norrling and said, "I order you to pay the full amount owed."

"I can't, not right now, sir."

Erik Axel ran his finger around the inside of his collar, then yanked a linen handkerchief from his pocket to wipe his forehead.

The magistrate leaned back in his chair and turned to Mr. Lof.

"Are you willing to wait, Mr. Lof?"

"I can wait no longer."

"I have good prospects. The fall harvest...."

"He has had two extensions already."

"I'm the one who should be bringing suit. His hired man injured my horse and damaged my vehicle."

"I have need of my money now."

"Then I must hand down an order of foreclosure, Mr. Norrling."

The magistrate yawned and sipped from a glass of water on the high bench in front of him.. This work of handing down foreclosures was happening more and more often these days. Hard times seem to follow close on the heels of government meddling, he thought. Distilling *brannvin* from grain was now illegal, so the price of grain was rock bottom. Farmers were standing in food lines and these damn foreclosures kept coming.

"Since you cannot repay the note held by Mr. Lof, you must vacate the property securing that note. I order you to hand it over before the week's end."

He banged his gavel down three times to make the pronouncement official. The sound of doom and failure. Erik Axel Norrling seemed surprised by the ruling. How could this happen.

"Sir, my family has owned this land for hundreds of years."

"No matter."

"What will I do? Where can I go?"

"You should of thought about that when you put your property in jeopardy."

The magistrate signaled his clerk to step forward.

"See that Mr. Norrling complies with this order."

Just as the magistrate was about to leave the room, Mr. Lof spoke up.

"Can you amend the order? I would let Mr. Norrling keep the workers' cottage."

The magistrate paused. "I don't know. This dividing of land has to stop."

"The farm is a double homestead. Comprised of thirty-two sixteenths. It's not been divided in a hundred years."

How curious, thought the magistrate. This Mr. Lof seems concerned about his adversary. Strange, indeed.

"His wife is poorly and there are three children. I plan to release his hired hands and build new quarters closer to the main house. The cottage is too isolated to suit me. I like to keep an eye on things."

"Yes, Sir," said Erik Axel. "My farm is larger than a double because of the river and the lay of the land."

"Can you leave him a sixteenth, then? Three acres to go with the cottage?"

"I don't know about that, sir. It wasn't my intention."

"Well, perhaps, you should make it your intention. It is against the law to divide the land into parcels smaller than a sixteenth."

"I guess the parcel between the ridge and the river is about a sixteenth. He can keep that. It will support a cow and a work team."

~~~

By the time he pulled into the yard, Erik Axel was shaking. His trembling hands transmitted to the horse who tossed his head, walled his eyes, and chawed the iron bit until gobs of foam whitened his neck. Erik

Axel didn't notice. He threw down the reins and stumbled into the house.

"My house, by damn," he yelled. "I was born in this house."

Maria came running, her hair undone, hands white with flour.

"What's wrong?"

"Wrong? Everything is wrong. They're killing me."

He picked up a heavy chair and crashed it into the wall.

"Stop, stop it. Talk to me." She clutched his arm, tried to lead him to a bench near the door.

"We have to leave."

He pulled away and grabbed a Venetian glass vase, one of Maria's recent purchases. The green glass reflected a roll of kaleidoscope colors across the room. He raised it overhead and dashed it to the floor in a shatter of knife-sharp shards.

"What are you doing?"

Maria dropped to her knees, crawled across the floor gathering up the fragments. While Erik Axel ranted on and on, she sat in the ashes of the hearth trying to piece the broken vase back together.

"I couldn't make the payment. Old Lof had me up before the judge. Do you understand?"

Maria didn't answer, gave no sign that she heard him. Ash mingled with the flour on her hands.

"Lof foreclosed. He's taken everything."

Maria looked up, wiped her hand across her cheek.

"He owns us."

"What?"

Maria's fingers continued to fit the bits of broken glass this way and that as if they had a mind of their own.

"He owns us. That's what the driver said that night on the bridge."

"The bastard. He wants us out by week's end."

"Can't you sell the horses?"

"Oh, God. He owns the horses now."

"I'm so sorry."

Maria's fingers slipped and the sharp edge drew blood, but she hardly noticed as it mixed with the ash and flour on her hands.

By the Rivers of Babylon We Wept.

While the boys played with baby Anna on the floor, Maria packed the household goods they would take with them. The cast iron kettle and griddle, the *aebilskiver* pan with its cup-shaped hollows, a set of everyday plates and cups, her embroidered tablecloths, the knives and forks.

"The good silver. I can't find the good silver. Matty. Go fetch Pappa."

When Erik Axel came in, Maria asked him about the silver.

"I sold it. Months ago."

"You.... What?"

"You didn't even notice."

"It belonged to my grandmother."

"Don't bother to look for the tea service, either."

"How could you?"

"No great loss. The preacher won't be calling." He picked up an armload of bundles and stalked out.

Their clothes and bedding were already packed and loaded. A few chairs, a long bench, the rag rug, the loom and spinning wheel that had belonged to Erik Axel's great grandmother stood by the door, waiting.

Thank God it's warm, thought Maria. Would the boys miss their goat and cart, the pony that had joined their menagerie short weeks ago. Only Matthew seemed old enough to really care and he was being quite brave about the whole thing.

At the noise of wheels on the graveled yard Maria went to look out the window. She saw her husband holding the halters of the team of work mares he had been allowed to keep, animals he had bred and raised. He seemed to be arguing with Mr. Lof there in the yard. She pulled the window open so she could hear the conversation.

"I appreciate that you're doing me a favor, Mr. Lof."

Erik Axel didn't seem very humble despite his words. He continued to speak.

"You won't be out anything. Let me breed them to the Orlov stallion before I go."

The animal he referred to was the same one that had been injured on the bridge just before Lent. Recovered enough to service mares, but not to race or even be put to harness, the trotting horse had passed to the ownership of Mr. Lof at the foreclosure hearing.

"It's the principle, Mr. Norrling."

Mr. Lof stood looking at his new property.

"You can put them to the Hanoverian stallion. Next spring you'll have a couple of foals suitable for all around work."

"You can keep the milk cow and the two goats you granted me. Just look the other way when I put the mares to the trotting stallion."

"Give up, man. Your racing days are over."

Maria felt sick. Her husband was offering to trade away food and future. How would they live without a cow. Without a work team to coax the rocky fields by the river to produce grain. How did he think he would feed his children.

~~~

Maria had only ventured the distance to the tenant house once before. It had been a day in high summer when a riot of flowers and velvety grass gave the cottage a pretty, rustic air. She had come to deliver the traditional basket of food to the hired man's wife and new baby. Leery of entering a strange house, she had handed the basket to the child who answered her knock. She saw nothing of the inside of the house and the stale, rank odor wafting past the urchin in the doorway made her grateful no one invited her in.

This time it was barely spring when the wagon labored up the muddy track to the cottage that would be their new home. When the team stopped in the muddy yard, no flowers drew the eye from the sagging door, the tiny window panes, cracked and black with soot and grime. Maria gasped at the sight of the low-roofed cottage built under the edge of the hill. Erik Axel cursed his ex-tenants for their sloppy ways.

No grass or flowers disguised the muddy yard or blocked the view of the sprawling garbage heap. A hard winter had left the half-round logs of the walls rough and shabby with the wadded chinking spilling out from between them. A melting pile of ochre-colored ice marked the spot where the recently evicted family had dumped their chamber pots through the winter. The sweet spring breeze couldn't cover or carry off the stink.

Maria let her gaze move to the roof. Made of layers of birch bark laid over a base of peeled poles, then covered with earth, the roof should have had a thick intertwining of grass and roots to hold out moisture and serve as insulation. Here, the bark sheets were rotted gray and the sparse growth of new spring grass sprouting on the roof would do little to keep the house secure. She burst into tears.

Five year old Matthew climbed down from the wagon and ran to explore, but Daniel, three, climbed onto his mother's lap beside little Anna. He turned his face to her bosom and sobbed. Anna added her wailing to their tears. Maria hugged them tight and rocked back and forth on the narrow wagon seat.

"Hush, Maria. And make the children shut up."

Erik Axel jumped down and started unloading the wagon.

"Don't just sit there. Time's wasting. I need to make another trip before dark."

Maria handed Daniel down, then climbed down herself, awkward with baby Anna on her hip. She walked across the yard to inspect the house. Dirt and piles of trash around the door and on the floor inside made it slow going. The two rooms were dark and airless, the sharp, rank odor of rotting potatoes made her cover her nose. She called back to Erik Axel.

"Don't bring anything inside, yet. I need to clean out the trash. Scrub the floors."

Her voice rasped with weariness and frustration. She looked around for a clean place to put baby Anna.

"I'll pile the things in the yard," said Erik Axel. "This door will need work when I get back. I can cut new hinges from scrap leather."

While her husband was off for another load, Maria settled Anna with the two boys in a dry corner of the yard. With a firm warning to the boys she rolled up her sleeves and went to work.

She pulled the old straw from the cupboard bed in the corner of the room that would be their bedroom. The room on the other side of the entrance vestibule was smaller and smelled of damp, of mildew and mold, from the leaky roof. She would deal with it later. For now it could serve as a store room.

By the time she had the flea infested straw, the rotting potatoes and moldy sacks of flour, coffee, and sugar piled in the yard, Erik Axel drove up with the second load.

"Can you burn this rubbish?" she said. "I need water, too."

"I'll put the team up, first."

He unhitched the mares and led them towards the shed across the yard from the house. It was a crude open-sided lean-to meant for sheltering a few goats.

Maria watched her husband make the horses comfortable, then picked up the bucket and walked to the open well to dip her own water. As she lugged the heavy bucket to the house, she saw that Erik Axel was nailing a long rail between the uprights of the shed to hang the harness on. When he finished, he would probably brush the horses, haul water for them, find them clean hay.

She struggled over the high board at the door sill, resigned to fetching her own water. Stepping over the high sill, designed to keep out blowing snow in winter, she banged her head on the low door frame.

"Blasted house must be made for trolls," she said.

Putting down the bucket, she went back outside for a breath of fresh air and to stretch her aching back. With her hands on her hips she leaned back to watch the clouds float past the tips of the tall pines, the same clouds that looked down on her old home. Much relieved with her short rest, she sat on the step a moment to watch the children playing in the corner of the yard. Guilt rising in her chest, she called them to her.

"Matthew, Daniel, take Anna to your father, then come here."

When they returned, she said, "It's time you learned to work."

She showed them how to pick up trash scattered around the yard and throw it on the garbage heap; satisfied that the two boys would keep busy for awhile and Anna was looked after, she went inside to her cleaning.

Maria was on her hands and knees scrubbing the wide floor boards, when Erik Axel came in from the stable with baby Anna in his arms.

"Have you put her cradle up yet, Maria?"

Weary and drawn, her lips a hard line of strain in her pale face, she looked up at her husband. Tears welled up in her eyes again. The floor which had looked black, now seemed almost white as new lumber. The room smelled of pine and lye soap. Before she had started on the floor, she had shoveled a year's accumulation of ash from the fireplace and carried it, a bucket full at a time, to the garbage heap outside. From the looks of their gray-dusted shirts, the boys must have helped with this task, also.

"Would you split some wood, so we can have a hot supper," she said to Erik Axel. "I still need to scrub the table and benches."

He sat Anna down on the damp floor and disappeared out the door. He returned a minute later with a wooden crate.

"I brought the chocolate set," he said. "You must have forgotten it in the confusion."

He placed the wooden crate on the table, then disappeared out the door. Maria stared at box that held the chocolate set and loosed her held-in tears, let them spasm her tired body until she fell on the floor. Over the sound of her sobbing the ring of the ax on seasoned wood began and seemed to go on and on until it drowned out her weeping, dried her sorrow to dust. She placed the crate holding the chocolate set on the highest shelf of the storeroom and vowed to never look at it again.

By the time Erik Axel had the wood box filled, Maria managed to dry her tears and find a clean apron in the chaos of her belongings.

"What's for dinner?"

"The children had bread and jam."

She gestured toward the low end of the table where the jam pot with it's curlicue lid and little claw feet stood guard over a litter of crumbs and dirty plates.

"Can't you get a fire going? The wood is dry and I've split kindling."

"Have you found the skillet. Or the coffee pot?"

"There's more stuff outside. I wonder who made this table."

"Whoever built the house. It's anchored into the wall," said Maria.

"Must have been a big tree."

"Large families, many children."

The slab of wood that formed the table jutted out from the wall at a level suitable for adults, then stepped down to a comfortable height for smaller and smaller children. The top of the table was polished smooth by years of use and many coats of varnish, but the under side was a rough whorl of knots and bark.

Bed time in the one room house provided new challenges.

"There's only one bed closet. Are the children to sleep with us?"

"There's probably a trundle. Or a bench bed."

Since Maria had to stitch up a ticking for the straw for either, the boys shared the closet bed with their parents the first few nights. The Norrling family quickly learned that poverty meant the loss of privacy.

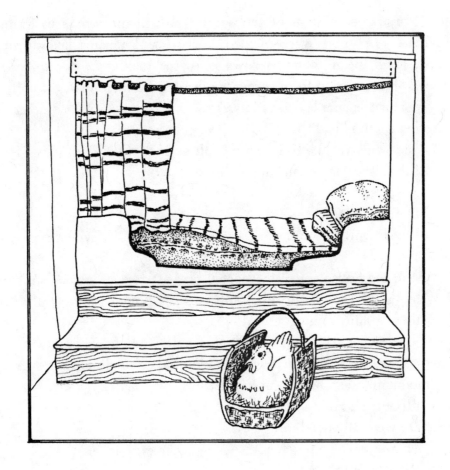

~~~

Maria had little time to brood over her changed status. Everywhere she looked, work appeared. The little house stubbornly held on to the stink and filth of its succession of tenants over the past hundred years. With only two small windows in front and it back dug into the breast of the hill, ventilation was difficult. Maria had been so used to flinging open the windows to let the spring breezes, even the bluster of approaching storms, scour the air of the house clean, that she felt defeated by this stagnation.

After the first weeks of airing and scrubbing, Maria abandoned her housework for the garden. While Erik Axel coaxed a meager crop of oats and barley from the rocky fields, she planted beets, cabbage, turnips, kale, and carrots. She taught the boys how to tell the difference between good plants and bad, to weed and hoe. When they finished in the garden, they were sent to the fields to pick up rocks.

As summer ground on into fall, Maria learned to make cheese and butter. She grated mounds of cabbage to layer in the crocks to ferment into kraut. The beets were pickled, carrots and turnips laid down in sawdust, green beans hung in rows from the ceiling to dry to leather hardness. She struggled to preserve the fish her husband brought up from the river. Horrific smells from the various crocks and barrels told her that yet another method had failed.

"Did you layer the fish with the salt like I told you?"

"I'm sorry. Maybe pickling will work."

"My grandfather salted fish every year."

"Did he eat it?"

"It was good. I'll make some drying racks. Maybe drying will help."

Soon the house and yard sported great strings of silver fish drying to brown. Erik Axel built small smoky fires under some of the fish, turning them a shiny orange.

Then, when the first cold nights yellowed the grass, Erik Axel decided to take the team and wagon and join other small holders on a trek to the mountain meadows to cut hay.

"I'll only be gone a couple of weeks."

"Do we really need more hay?"

"There won't be much grain. We got the crop in late."

"What about the roof?"

"I'll stop by your brother's place on the way back. Maybe he'll be willing to come help with the roof and put up a proper outhouse at the same time."

"He could stay with my folks in town."

"He'll be glad to have a chance to visit. He hasn't even seen baby Anna."

"I could stay with my folks for a few days, while you're busy with the roof."

The thought of a respite from work stirred joy in Maria's heart even as Erik Axel whipped up the team and headed for the mountain meadows.

Wind of Change, Water of Weeping.

In the long days of waiting Maria kept her knitting bag close at hand. She soon had a pile of mittens, scarves, and socks beside her chair. She tried to teach Matthew to knit, but soon gave up and used the boys' out-stretched hands to size the dozens of children's mittens flowing from her clicking needles.

Three weeks later Erik Axel returned with a towering load of hay on the wagon and dragging a second load on a flat bottomed sledge.

"That should get us through the winter as long as old man Loft gives us our share of the grain harvest."

Since the Norrlings had already prepared the fields and provided seed grain before the foreclosure, they were entitled to a portion of the harvest. The law was scrupulous in such matters.

Maria held the sweet grass to her face.

"Finally. Something that smells good."

"I left your brother in town. Said he wasn't about to blister his hands pitching hay. Says he'll drive out this afternoon to get you."

"I'm ready. I just need to get Anna dressed."

"He intends to ride out each day, so you can catch up on old times in the evenings."

~~~

At her parents' house baby Anna was the center of attention. Much relieved, Maria had no trouble slipping out to the market to display her knitting for sale each morning. Busy with her project, she barely noticed changes in her mother. She thought her slow pace and bent back, her difficulties holding her knife and fork were no more than the usual aches from a change in the weather, the cold induced rheumatism she had complained about since Maria's childhood.

By the weekend she had sold every last mitten. Just in time, too, she thought. Erik Axel had promised to come for her today.

Money in hand, she hurried past the tempting food stalls to the livestock section of the market. After much comparing and haggling, Maria selected a crate of young hens, hens just past their egg producing peak. The seller, a wrinkled crone with one front tooth, added a tough old rooster to seal the deal.

"You'll be glad to have Old Spur when these biddies turn broody. Raise you up some chicks for next spring."

"Thank you."

"You hear bout the plague over Ludvika way?"

"Plague? What sort of plague?" At first Maria thought the old woman was muttering about some chicken disease going around.

"Them as gets it bout cough their lungs out before they pass on."

"Old folks?"

"Not so much. Youngsters, workmen, milkmaids."

"Well, Ludvika is far away."

"Ever been?"

"My husband goes there on business now and then."

Or did, she thought. Would he ever have any concerns beyond picking rocks and cutting hay again. Would any of us.

By the time Erik Axel came to take her back to the cottage, she had forgotten the conversation about plagues and sickness, forgotten her niggling worry about her mother. She displayed her crate of chickens as if they were some rare breed of fowl and told anyone who would listen how she knitted and sold mittens for their purchase.

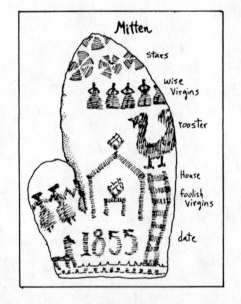

Erik Axel smiled at her pride and loaded the crate into the wagon.

"Your brother is a good worker."

"Did you get the roof fixed?"

"Of course. Put up an outhouse, hinged the front door, and put walls on the lean-to. It's a good, tight stable, now."

"I wish he could stay longer. We had a good time singing the old songs after supper."

"Did he say anything about leaving?"

"Leaving? He left for his own farm this morning."

"No. Leave Sweden, emigrate to Amerika."

"What?"

"He's not happy."

Later that evening Maria heard her husband digging through the trunks and boxes in the storeroom. He emerged with a tattered book in hand.

The *"Amerika Book,"* he said.

Maria looked puzzled.

He continued, "That's its name. Mostly propaganda put out by land agents or, maybe, the shipping companies."

"Is that what my brother is reading?"

"He thinks he can get free land in America. Said something about a new homestead act."

"He has land, almost seventy acres."

"He says he can have twice that, and the same for his wife and each child. Nearly five hundred acres."

"For free? I don't believe it."

~~~

The next morning a strong wind howled out of the north. Though it was not yet cold enough to coat the countryside with frost, it chilled to the bone. The grain and whatever vegetables still remaining in the fields had to be harvested immediately.

Maria swaddled little Anna tight and tied her into bed. She hated the thought of leaving the toddler alone in the house while she worked in the fields, but it was too cold for her outside. She dressed Matthew and Daniel as warmly as she dared and put them to work picking the last crop of beans, digging the potatoes and carrots, sweeping off the thrashing stone.

Just as picking and digging was new work for the boys, so was field work for Maria. Walk behind Erik Axel as he cut the grain with a scythe, stoop over the bundles of grain, grasp the rough stalks, tie them into bundles. Walk, stoop, grab, tie, over and over. It was a great relief to move on to collecting and loading the bundles onto the wagon. Her back and legs ached so much, she was staggering by the time she returned to the house to fix dinner.

She could hear little Anna before she reached the clearing. Her hiccupy, wheezy cries demanded attention. With no thought to her own sore back and torn hands she ran to the child sitting in the dirt and scooped her up, held her close.

"Matthew. Why is the baby out here?"

"She wouldn't stop crying. I untied her."

"It's too cold for her."

"She wanted to come out."

"Get Daniel and wash up."

Though the fire had smoldered out hours ago, the house felt warm for the first few minutes, then a dank chill seeped through their clothing. Maria tried to hold the child over her shoulder and lay a fire at the same time, gave up and plunked Anna down on the floor.

With the fire roaring the room warmed quickly and the coffee pot jiggled on the back of the grate. The raw September air was quickly forgotten. Maria set about washing Anna's dirty face and hands.

"You even have dirt in your ears, baby girl. And in your hair."

She held the child on her lap and worked the clumps of soil loose, brushed the fine locks clean, scrubbed her tender neck and ears. Finally, she found a clean shirt for squirming Anna and let her loose.

"Stay clean, now."

She could hear Erik Axel in the yard calling to the boys. Bread and cheese, jam, herring, and pickled cabbage would have to do, she thought. There's no time to cook. She hurried to set the table before he got his boots off. His harsh voice interrupted her.

"There's no warm water."

"The fire was out."

"Can't you boys be trusted to keep the fire up?"

"I think I forgot to tell them."

They ate in silence. Only little Anna chirped and giggled, while she ate her bread and jam with messy gusto."

"She'll be talking soon," said Maria. She offered a morsel of fish to Anna.

"Fish," she said slowly. "Fish, Anna."

~~~

The cottage seemed even smaller after the days outside with the harvest and thrashing. It was hard to believe the building had been intended as a home for two families. With the long dark evenings of winter looming, Maria wondered how she could live in this tiny place, so hard to keep warm with air so close it seemed to have passed through the lungs of generations.

After the first hard freeze, but before the first winter storm, the roads were at their best. Maria's father paid a visit.

"Pappa. What a surprise."

"Is your husband home?"

"He's setting nets at the river. I could send Matty."

"No. I wish to speak to you alone."

"Come in. Have a cup of coffee. How is Mamma?"

Mr. Rundbak followed his daughter inside. If the rude cottage offended him, he gave no clue. He sat down at the table and placed a flannel sack in front of him.

"I can leave this with you, now, daughter."

He opened the sack and slid Maria's silver bridal necklace out onto the table. The silver, though nearly black with tarnish, sparked like a living thing against the rough wood.

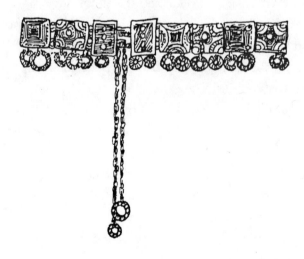

"Oh. I had forgotten how beautiful it was."

"If ever you needed it, the time is now."

"What can I do with it? Trade it to some itinerant peddler for a pound of coffee and a length of Chinese silk?"

Maria reached out to touch the antique silver, but quickly withdrew her hand. If she touched it, she felt she would never let it go.

"Mr. Norrling would find it and trade it for a horse."

"I guess I could take it along to Stockholm. Rich people there."

"The city? Are you leaving?"

"The house is sold. We take the train tomorrow."

"What will you do in the city?"

"You forget. Your sisters are there." He closed the bag. "Maybe it would be easier to sell it there."

"Maybe so, Father."

Maria could think of nothing else to say. She was empty. It was as if she stood on the edge of a great pit. The security of having her parents near, the nest egg of the silver necklace, it was all ashes, false hope.

"Goodbye, then. I'll send the money as soon as possible."

~~~

She heard nothing from her parents through the bitter months of winter. Every report, every bit of gossip fueled her worried imaginings. One neighbor had heard through a distant cousin that long lines formed on the streets of Stockholm early each morning. Lines of men, women, children, babies, all hoping for a little bread, a few potatoes, a job, a room or even a corner to call home.

"How can they live?" Maria asked the neighbor.

"I hear bodies are stacked like firewood in the city morgues."

"The cold. How can they stand outside in this cold."

After the visitor had gone on his way, Maria slumped down by the fireplace and wept.

"I should have begged Pappa to stay."

"Don't be silly, Maria. They have money. And your sisters are there to show them around and find them a place to live."

Maria continued to fret about her parents, pestered every visitor for news, waited eagerly for the sporadic mail delivery. Finally, a letter arrived, addressed in the blotchy handwriting of her oldest sister.

Though she had waited for months, Maria couldn't bear to open the letter. She held it between thumb and forefinger at arm's length and walked slowly to the house. The letter lay unopened on the table when Erik Axel came in for supper.

"What's this?"

"I'm afraid," said Maria. "You open it."

"Silly goose. What's for supper?"

He sat down at the table and slit open the flimsy paper of the envelope. Maria stood watching, unaware that she was holding her breath.

His face told her the news was bad.

Dearest Sister, the letter began. *I am sorry to be the bearer of such bad news, but I must inform you that our parents, Hans and Matilda Rundbak, perished in the recent epidemic that ravaged the city. Officials say that overcrowding of the distinct in which they resided was a factor in the rapid spread of the contagion.* That certainly didn't sound like the words of her sister. She must have copied it from some letter or newspaper.

"There's more," said Erik Axel. "It says *the funeral is to be held on Tuesday.* Judging from the postmark, that would be the Tuesday before last."

"Where?"

"They fear spreading the epidemic. It may be cholera. They recruit gravediggers from the poorhouse."

Maria seemed not to understand. "I must go."

"To Stockholm? Impossible."

~~~

Maria wandered around the house for weeks afterwards. She would touch things, a chair carved by her father, the red painted tea box she had brought from home, a favorite picture of an idyllic glen, the quilts she had sewn with her mother. She packed a small trunk a dozen times, then unpacked it with weeping.

When she finally realized there was nothing to be done, she begged Erik Axel to write to her sisters.

"Why, Maria? What more can I say?"

"About my silver necklace."

"What can they know about that?"

"Pappa was to sell it for me."

Erik Axel wrote the letter and rode into town to send it on the first train. When no answer came, he sent another by registered post. A brief reply did not mention the silver necklace or any money intended for Maria. A third letter was returned unopened and Maria never heard from her sisters again.

Lost and Found, Lost Forever.

Spring brought quagmire fields and impassable roads with cycles of freeze, thaw, heavy rain, flooding, then freezing again. The crocus and snowbells lay flat, dead in the mud of the yard. The two work mares stood miserable in their stalls, gobs of icy mud grasping their tails. Hunger dimpled hollows in the soft tissues above their eyes and around their hip bones to contrast with their foal swollen bellies.

Erik Axel paced and stewed. The tools gleamed with oil, the plow share was bright with scouring, the sacks of seed grain lined the wall just inside the door. Only the weather refused to bend to his will.

"God, this place reeks."

"If only the sun would come out," said Maria. "It's so gray."

"Can't you dry things somewhere else?"

He grabbed a handful of socks and mittens from the rack over the stove and dashed them against the wall. The spill of damp material cascaded gray against the dark floor. The stink of wet wool swelled until it filled the room.

"Stop it." Maria gathered up the socks and mittens, fingered them smooth, and draped each one over the drying rack again.

"The seed should have been in the ground weeks ago." He grabbed his coat and headed for the door.

"There's no remedy for the weather."

"I'm going to check on the mares. With my luck they'll be dropping their foals just when I need them to plow."

"You've checked a dozen times today. If you'd stop mucking back and forth to the stable, there wouldn't be such a mountain of wet clothes in here."

Erik Axel called the boys from their job of picking over a jar of dry beans, sorting the good from the moldy.

"Let's go bring up that wood you loaded this morning."

"Can I drive the horse? Please, Pappa," said Matty.

"Me go too," announced little Anna.

"Can't you take her along?"

"No. Keep an eye on her until we're out of sight."

He hurried the boys outside before Anna could work herself into a tantrum.

Later that afternoon Maria realized the house was unusually quiet. Was little Anna still napping. She checked the bedcloset, but found the blue and white quilt smooth, undented by a small body. She checked the storeroom. The stacked boxes and trunks stared back at her, their layers of dust undisturbed. The stable, she thought, maybe she wandered out to visit the horses. Horse, she corrected herself. Erik Axel had taken the other mare to bring back the load of firewood.

With her scarf tight around her ears, her hands pulled up in her sleeves, she walked to the lean-to-stable. The horse stood quiet, one hind foot cocked, head drooping. The hens pecked and scratched in the straw, the old cow lay on her breast bone chewing her cud.

After the stable Maria checked the outhouse though she knew the little girl hated the stinking toilet, would not enter that rude door without a screaming protest. Then she heard the jingle of harness and was sure Erik Axel had relented and let the child ride the sled to the woods to pick up firewood.

She raced back up the path to the yard, then ran a little way along the road to meet the sled. The bay horse was a dark shape against the darker trees and sky by the time she found them.

"Is Anna all right?"

"What are you doing out here, Maria?"

"Anna? Where is she?"

"You goose. Where's your coat?"

Maria grabbed Matthew and demanded he produce his sister.

"She's not with us," he said. "Let go."

Erik Axel handed the reins to Daniel. "Come Matty. Let's help your mamma find Anna."

At full dark they gave up the search and stabled the horse who had stood in the yard harnessed to the loaded sled for hours. They stumbled through evening chores, ate bread and jam, a little soft cheese, then fell into bed, exhausted yet wide awake with anxious imaginings.

After a hasty breakfast they began a meticulous search for the lost child. As convinced as Maria was that Anna had tried to follow Erik Axel and the boys, Erik Axel was certain the child had hidden herself somewhere in the house or stable and fallen asleep. Bitter argument spiced the search.

By mid-day they decided to send Matty to the neighbors for help. Erik Axel bridled one of the mares and lifted the boy to her back.

"He can't manage that horse," said Maria.

"Don't fall off, Matty. You'll have to walk home."

He led them to the road, handed the reins up to Matty, then slapped the horse on the rump to get her moving.

While Matty and the big horse bumped away towards the nearest farm, Erik Axel and Maria stood in the gray drizzle.

"How could she get out of the house? Did you forget to latch the door?"

"She must have followed you."

"How? How could you?"

"We should search the woods again."

And again and again. Maria's head felt like wool. Her chest hurt and her feet blistered. She walked the rough ground to the woodcutting place for the tenth time. Her throat, hoarse from shouting her daughter's name, produced only tiny, bleating calls.

How foolish, she thought. If Anna came this way, she would have met up with the wood haulers. Look closely at the edges of the path. Maybe something frightened her. Maybe she's hiding. In several places Maria found disturbed soil, broken branches. When she brought Erik Axel to examine them, he convinced her that the horse had strayed from the path or the sled had slipped there.

"She's too small to leave much of a trail."

"Oh, dear God. She could be anywhere."

With the realization that Anna could crawl under the low hanging branches, Maria set her search lower to the ground. She took Daniel with her to inspect the dark caves formed by the dense fir branches, to crawl under leaning windfalls, and clamber into old sink holes. She promised the weary child toys, plump sausages, his favorite sweets, if only he found his baby sister.

"Maria. Maria."

She heard Erik Axel on the path, called Daniel to her side, and made her way through the brush to the path. A bit of hope leaped in her throat.

"Have you found her?"

"Matthew brought help. Your brother's here."

"Why? I don't understand."

He plucked Daniel from the path and lifted the tired boy to his shoulder.

"Come back to the house. You need to rest, eat."

Despite her worry and weariness, Maria knew that there was something ominous and out of kilter about her brother's presence in the neighborhood. He greeted her with his customary reserve, then took her in his arms and held her tight.

"Don't worry, Maria. Everything will be all right."

"What are you doing here?"

"We spent the night at Willborg's place. You remember him? Mother's cousin?"

"That's almost to Ludvika. Have you come all that way?"

"We're staying at Jansson's tonight."

"We?"

"The whole family. Hope to catch an early summer sailing from Gothenberg. They say a June crossing is the best."

"You're leaving? When were you going to tell me?"

"Now, Maria. Don't be angry. We have work in Minnesota, on a farm."

"How could you do this?"

"They tell me it looks like Sweden."

"Rocks and mud? You might as well stay."

"We need to find your child. We'll talk later."

~~~

In the end it was Anna who found herself. When the searchers gathered at the house for a brief rest, food and drink, they heard a scrabbling noise outside. When they rushed to investigate, little Anna toddled into the clearing. She had leaves in her hair and a ring of dirt around her mouth from sucking her dirty thumb.

"Baba eat. Baba eat."

Maria paid no attention to her daughter's request for food. Instead she gathered the child in her arms and carried her into the house, where she stripped off Anna's filthy clothes and scrubbed her until she howled. By the time she was fed and asleep in her parent's bed, twilight had enveloped the clearing.

Outside again, Maria's brother mounted his horse and said his good-byes. Maria stood next to her husband in the darkening yard. Her shoulders shook with silent tears.

"Don't cry. I'll write."

"It's so far away."

"Be happy for me, Maria. It's a chance for a new life."

"I'll never see you again."

"You can come visit. Maybe you and Erik Axel will decide to emigrate."

"The money. It must cost the earth for a ticket."

"I'll send you a ticket. When I get settled."

Maria turned away to hide her tears. She barely had the will or the strength to walk back into the house. Dear God, she thought. We haven't had Anna baptized. If the child hadn't made her way home, she could be burning in Hell right now. How can I survive the journey to the parish church. I haven't been to church in Smedjebacken since Daniel's baptism. Hell. Anna will go to Hell. And it will be all my fault. Overwhelmed, Maria fainted.

Erik Axel bent over her, pushed the damp hair back from her face.

"Is she all right?"

"I'll get her inside."

"Should I go for the doctor?"

"No. Be on your way. It's just strain and worry."

"If you say so. We do need to get going."

Maria's brother reined his horse around and trotted out of the yard. Amerika and a new life awaited him. He did not look back.

Rune Stone

Walking the Fine Line.

As spring struggled into summer, the mares dropped healthy foals and the old milk cow calved a tiny bull calf. The soil dried out enough to receive the seed grain and now a green haze covered the small patchwork of fields. Erik Axel and the boys walked the rocky verges between the plots daily. They rooted out errant weeds, plucked up stray rocks, and kept the hungry birds away.

Maria's spring garden had wilted, then died in an onslaught of gray mildew. She traded half of her newly hatched chicks for more seed and half a sack of sprouted potatoes. Now the side yard sported rows and rows of knee high potato plants. Each morning she scoured the rows picking beetles from the tender plants. Little Anna followed along behind to squash the bugs under the very bottom leaves. Their viscous juice stained her fingers black.

As the calendar edged into July, the spindly rye and short-stemmed oats headed out with less than a third the usual number of kernels. With little work to bind him to the home place Erik Axel along with Matty, took the team and wagon to the high pastures to cut hay. They returned on a cold, drizzly day two weeks later with a scant wagon load of meadow grass.

After greeting her husband and hugging Matty until he pulled away, Maria pulled a handful of grass from the wagon.

"The hay is damp."

"There wasn't enough sun to cure it properly."

"I thought the weather would be better in the mountains."

"It's bad everywhere. Cold, rain. They've canceled the Mid-Summer celebration at Hagge. The village green is nothing but mud."

"And the roads?"

"Look at the wagon."

He gestured towards the high wood-spoked wheels. Mud, dried

and fresh clogged them solid. Twigs and leaves added to the pack of earth that swelled the rims to twice their width.

Maria glanced down at Erik Axel's boots. They, too, were leaden with mud. When she looked up, she realized she had not really looked at her husband for months, now. How tired he seemed, deflated, gray and stooped.

"Let's spread the hay on the threshing floor. Maybe it will dry there."

"The boys can do that. I'll put the team up."

Daniel and Anna climbed onto the wagon, eager to help.

"Take your boots off. You'll dirty the hay," said Maria. "I'll get dinner on."

~~~

Two more trips to cut meadow grass brought smaller and smaller returns. Bundles of willow shoots supplemented the last load and each morning the children were sent out with sacks to gather whatever dry grass, bark, and edible twigs they could find. Erik Axel hovered over the stunted grain fields, railing at the birds and varmints, counting the days until he could harvest the crop.

Maria spent hours in her garden. Each day she would worm her fingers into the loose soil under the largest potato plant to check its progress. When the potatoes grew large as pullet eggs, she dug a few from each plant. She placed the new potatoes, boiled and buttered, before her family that night.

Erik Axel responded with a muttered comment about wasting their winter food, but still forked into his portion with relish.

"I wish we could eat this every day," said Matty.

"Have some more egg pie," said Maria.

The hens were laying and eggs were part of every meal. The egg and onion pie seemed bland and dull without the chunks of cured pork that usually flavored it.

"More tatties, Mamma," said little Anna.

"You've had your share," said Daniel.

Maria slid the potatoes from her own plate onto Anna's.

"Pass half to Daniel," she instructed Anna.

"No. No. I won't."

The little girl stuffed her mouth full, then grabbed her plate and ran from the room.

When Erik Axel rose to discipline the child, Maria caught his arm.

"Let her go. She doesn't understand."

"She needs to understand."

He glared down at Daniel who sat staring at his empty plate. With a groan he put his own plate in front of the boy and stalked out of the room.

~~~

When the threat of frost grew to certainty, the harvest began. The grain was cut and bundled, carried to the threshing floor in muslin sheets, quilts, flour sacks, anything to catch and preserve as much of the grain as possible. The children were put to the task of picking up spilled kernels and scrounging the fields for missed stalks and broken grain heads. The straw and chaff were saved. It would be chopped and added to the meager stash of hay in the barn.

In a short week the job was complete. Erik Axel stood counting the bags of oats, rye, and wheat piled in the corner of the threshing shed. Maria swept up the last bit of chaff.

"When we take it to the mill, I can start making bread for winter."

"Bread? There will be no trip to the mill this year."

"How can I make bread?"

"There's barely enough to plant next year's crop. And the *brannvin*. I need to set a batch to fermenting."

"No bread? How will we eat?"

"This is our seed grain, Maria. No bread."

"*Brannvin*? The children can't live on alcohol."

"What if one of us gets the toothache? Or chilblains?"

Maria turned away to hide her tears. She would harvest her potato crop and make potato *lefse*. The soft flat bread wouldn't store as well as that made from grain, but it would have to do.

~~~

By first snowfall rows and rows of the thin potato bread draped the drying poles in the corners and rafters of the house. Crocks of pickled cabbage and beets lined the storeroom. Eggs were sealed in kegs of water glass. The top shelf held Maria's pride: rows and rows of jam, jelly, and fruit syrup. For sugar she had traded eggs and the two dozen half-grown chicks her hens had hatched in the spring.

A sense of loss almost overwhelmed her when she handed her pretty chickens over to old Mrs. Pedersson in return for two ragged sacks of sugar, sugar lumpy and hard from years of storage. She wondered where the old woman had acquired the scarce commodity, but feared to ask. Sweets like jam and jelly seemed a luxury, but she feared the children would balk at eating dry *lefse* and lumpy oat porridge, sour cabbage and sulfurous eggs without a bite of sweet to feed their souls.

~~~

By Christmas more than half the crocks and kegs stood upside down, scrubbed and empty, on the storeroom floor. The little *lefse* remaining was brittle and edged with green mold. Though solid ice only rimmed the river and skimmed its deeper pools, Erik Axel decided to try fishing.

"Be careful," said Maria. "Stay off the ice."

"Get your boots, Matty."

"Can I come, too?" said Daniel.

"No."

"Not this time."

When they returned empty handed, Maria decided the last two hens would become Christmas dinner. The decision pained her. The hens, bought with her knitting, seemed like old friends. They had been cooped in a woven reed basket under the table the last few weeks because the stable held little protection from bitter cold or hungry predators.

"Before you take off your coat and boots can you do the hens?"

With only a gruff order for Matty to drag to coop from under the table, Erik Axel took the two hens by the feet and went outside. Daniel grabbed his coat and ran after him.

"Stay and get warm, Matty," said Maria. "How was it, fishing?"

"The ice kept breaking. I couldn't get my line in the deep water."

"It will be solid before long, then we'll have fish, fried crisp."

"I'm sick of cabbage and pickled beets."

~~~

Boiled with some of the seed barley, the last of the rubbery carrots, and a measure of salt, the chicken stew sent a marvelous odor through the house.

"When can we eat, Mamma?" said Matty and Daniel in chorus.

"If only we had bread," said Maria.

"A little real coffee would be good," said Erik Axel. "What is this swill?"

"And candy? Or apples?"

"Can't you trade something at the market? I have a broach. It's not silver, but it's pretty. Someone might like it to give as a present."

"I don't know. Everyone's in the same boat."

"Except the Lofs. Their store houses are full to bursting."

"They'll not be wanting any of our baubles."

~~~

Christmas morning the children lined up by the closet bed.

"Wake them up. Daniel," said Matty.

"You do it."

"Me." Anna ran forward and rapped on the wooden headboard.

"What do you ruffians want?" said Erik Axel.

He climbed out of bed with Maria close behind. The room was warm, the soup bubbled on the stove.

"We did it. For you."

The three children suddenly became shy. They pushed Anna to the front again.

"Here," she shouted. "Show them, Matty."

Matty presented his mother with a lumpy bundle, gray sacking tied with string. She nearly dropped it.

"It's so heavy. What is it?"

"Open it. Open it."

"Here." Matty pulled his mother to the table. "So it won't spill."

In the dusty wrapping lay a waxed bag of coffee beans, dark and fragrant with oil. Under the coffee was a half sack of flour, fine ground wheat, new and sweet without a trace of mold or weevil.

"Where did you get this, Matty?" said Erik Axel.

Daniel burst into tears and ran to his mother. Matty stuck his thumb in his mouth and stood dumb.

"I got," said Anna. She stood straight, almost belligerent, in the circle of stares.

"You? How?"

"They lifted me up. I got it." She pointed to her brothers.

"Where? Tell me. Now."

Matty found his tongue. "Lof's store barn. It's packed full. He'll never miss it."

"You stole it?" said Maria. "In the night?"

"Sort of. They can't use so much."

"And you took Anna along?"

"Me and Daniel are too big to squeeze through the little window at the top."

"The ventilation window? How in blazes did you get up there?"

"The door had a big lock," said Daniel. "We climbed the tree."

"And held Anna's feet so she could squiggle in."

"Cold," added Anna. "And I hurted my knee. See?" She pulled up her skirt to show off her scraped knee.

"She had to take off her coat to fit through the window."

"She pushed the sacks out, then we pulled the rope."

"Rope?"

"So we could get her out again."

"You rascals thought of everything. Let's grind these beans."

"Mr. Norrling. They stole. They used their sister. They could have killed her," said Maria.

"They didn't, so be still, Maria. Old Lof has flour out the ears. Rightly ours, too."

"They need to be punished. Take this stuff back to the Lofs."

Overcome with her own protest, Maria started coughing. With her handkerchief pressed to her mouth, she crossed the room to the water bucket to ladle herself a drink.

"Enough. Calm yourself, Maria," said Erik Axel. "Heat the oven and make us some bread. It's Christmas."

With a little sour milk, soda and salt, chicken fat skimmed from the stew, Maria turned the purloined flour into crusty loaves of bread. Slathered with cloudberry jam, the warm bread, fresh strong coffee, and meaty stew seemed a meal fit for the king. Even Erik Axel's announcement that the old milk cow was barren went without comment.

Pride Before Falling.

Before the New Year they butchered the old cow. The chance that she would breed and produce another calf was minuscule. Her last calf had been a spindly weed of an animal who failed to thrive. It had been sold as a weanling to pay the yearly head tax.

The meat was dry and stringy. Some of it Maria chopped fine, then boiled it with barley and dandelion root. She cut the rest in thin strips to dry smoke in the fireplace. The children could be seen at their chores with a strip hanging out their mouths, their jaws working the impossibly tough meat into digestible submission. When beggars came to the door, ragged, hungry, often toothless, they were given strips of the dry meat. Some of them cursed and threw the hard meat into the snow. Others complained they could get more sustenance from chewing bones.

One morning Maria opened the door to find four children digging through her garbage heap. They leaped up and stared at her with watery, sunken eyes. The oldest wiped her runny nose on her sleeve. The two young boys bowed politely and removed their ragged caps.

"Please, Mum," said the oldest. "Could we have the bones?"

Maria saw that they had picked the beef bones and fish heads from the molding pile of hair and hide scraps. Each child had a patched sack grasped in their mittened hands, but had made no move to put their spoils inside. She turned away to hide her tears. These starved urchins could be her own children.

The beggars mistook her gesture as rebuke.

"So sorry, Mum."

"We'll be going."

Maria turned back in astonishment. "It's two miles to the next farm."

They stopped, stood quietly.

"Come in and warm yourselves before you pick up the bones."

They followed her inside and huddled in front of the fire.

"Why do you beg here? The Lof's have enough for a hundred beggars on their refuse heap."

"The big farm up the road?" The girl poked her nose in the air and minced around holding a pinch of her ragged skirt between thumb and one finger. The boys snickered.

"They throwed rocks at us," said one.

"See, mum. Right here she hitted me." The boy displayed a fresh scrape on his forehead.

"That witch," said Maria.

She gave each child a strip of dried beef and a spoon of jam before she sent them on their way. What will happen to them, she wondered. What will happen to all of us.

By the end of February the crocks in the storeroom were empty, all the wilted, shriveled potatoes and carrots were gone, only a few dozen jars of jam and a little grain remained. With their father's blessing the children made another night-time foray to the Lof's store house. Their only reward was cold fingers and runny noses. The Lofs had discovered their loss and cut down the tree that gave thieves access to their goods.

In desperation they butchered the remaining goat.

"Better we eat her before she starves," said Erik Axel.

"The horses still have hay and willow shoots," argued Maria.

"We must get a crop this year."

"But, four horses?"

"The mares are old."

"They may be in foal. Sell the colts so we can eat."

"No."

~~~

When Maria went to the store room for some barley to cook with the goat meat, she realized the sacks of seed grain were nearly empty. With tears of anger she dipped out a double measure to add to the soup pot. Let him sell one of the colts to buy seed, she thought. The children have to eat.

As spring drew near, Maria, again, begged her husband to sell the yearling colts. A horse fair was being organized in a neighboring parish. The colts were well grown, tall and leggy, just the sort of animals that would sell promptly. Erik Axel refused, called the boys and went out to work up the ground for spring planting.

Through the long cold spring, they plowed and harrowed, picked rocks, piled rocks, cleared brush, cut trees, hauled stumps. The colts grew thinner as their diet changed from hay and grain supplemented by shoots and bark to mostly chaff and roots. The children looked more and more like the hoards of beggars scouring the countryside each day.

When the fields were ready, Erik Axel set about finding seed grain. With their few remaining items of value, a cameo brooch, a hand ax, his watch, he frequented the village market, neighboring farms, the blacksmith in Smedjebacken. If he had cash to approach old Lof, it would be better, a man-to-man transaction.

While their father tried to find seed, the children hired out to clear rocks from the neighbor's fields. When they had picked and stacked all the rocks small enough for them to carry in a easy radius of home, their father found them work with farms farther and farther away. Each week they were paid a few pennies, an egg or two, the scag ends of a curing of salt pork. The beggars who beat the roads into muddy paths with their restless feet did as well.

As the latest possible time for planting drew near, Erik Axel gave up trying to raise cash. Cap in hand, he went to Oscar Lof to beg for enough seed grain for planting.

"You have enough to plant the whole parish."

"Foresight, my boy, and planning."

"I only need a few bushels."

"Save enough in the good years and you'll never run short."

"You'll have it back at harvest with interest."

"Bring me that team of yearling colts and you can have seed and enough flour to see your family through till harvest."

"The colts are worth far more than a few sacks of flour."

"They're worth what you can get for them. These are hard times."

"A good harvest and we'll be on our feet."

"One colt and no flour."

"Just as collateral. If I can't return your seed two fold, you get the colt."

Mr. Lof agreed to the deal and specified the larger of the two colts.

Angry, but beaten, Erik Axel shook hands with Lof to seal it. If he could not return the seed grain with fair increase after the fall harvest, his bay colt would belong to Oscar Lof.

~~~

"You found seed," said Maria.

"Old Lof was stubborn, but he finally came around."

"The boys are fishing. Farmer Hansson sent them home at noon."

"Rock picking is probably over for the season. Everyone else is planting."

"It seems too cold for planting."

"Where's Anna?"

"With the boys. I can't keep her inside."

In a few weeks the planting was complete and shoots of new grain tentatively greened the fields. Still, the days did not warm with the usual spring breezes and the nights remained sharp. A cold rain settled in as if determined to outlast the plants waiting for the sun. Only Maria's cabbage, kale, and spring peas flourished in the cold, damp air.

When they could add greens to their diet of fish, it was a celebration, so Maria and Anna spent hours hunting wild lettuce, lamb's quarter, mint, and sorrel to add to the garden vegetables.

"Do you realize it's almost festival time?" said Maria.

"Mid-summer. Who would believe it," said Erik Axel. "The barley should be headed out by now."

"Will they have the dance on the green this year?"

"Have you noticed more adults in the crowds of beggars lately?"

"Maybe I could have new ribbons. New ribbons for Anna, too."

"The sheriff evicted the Bjorks yesterday."

"Don't you think she would look pretty with pink ribbons on her cap?"

"The oats are sparse. I think Lof gave me old seed."

"Could you haul another load of wood today?"

"Wood? We should be done with wood except for cooking by now."

"I thought I saw frost in the hollows near the river yesterday morning."

"Frost? Impossible. It's June."

But it was possible. A hard freeze laid the tender crops flat and black the next morning. Erik Axel led the bay colt to the Lof place and tied the young animal to the fence in front of the house.

Before he returned home he went into Hagge to send a letter to his cousin Andrew, a letter he had agonized over for most of the night.

My dear Cousin Andrew,

I take pen in hand because I have no where else to turn. The crop has failed, we have no money, no prospects, and little food. I fear the children will be walking the roads begging before long.

You once mentioned that rich people on the continent sometimes indenture children to work in their homes and that some even adopt them as their own. Is it possible to place my boys with a good family?

I await your reply.

Your Humble Relative,

Erik Axel Norrling

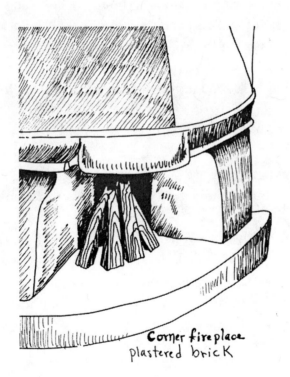

Corner fireplace
plastered brick

Lemon Drops Sweet, Lemon Drops Bitter.

Summer inched on with cold drizzle and low clouds nearly every day. With no field work to fill his days Erik Axel chopped wood and fished. Maria worked in her garden for hours each day. The outdoor work seemed to give her strength, calm her bouts of coughing. Then, in late August, a storm front stalled over the region. Cold rain and high winds beat the trees against the house, lashed anyone who ventured out, day after day.

Maria found Erik Axel in the store room searching for something.

"What do you need?"

"I'm going away for awhile."

"Where?"

"Ludvika. I here they are hiring at the mine."

She helped him bundle up a suit of clothes, a blanket, plate, and cup.

"How long will you be gone?"

"You'll be all right. The boys are big enough to get in wood. You have the garden and the fishing is good."

When the boys heard he was making the long journey to Ludvika to look for work, they begged to come along.

"You must stay to care for your mother and sister. And the horses."

"Ah, Pappa. I'm big enough to work," said Matty.

"Me, too," said Daniel.

When he returned a month later, he asked if they had heard from cousin Andrew, by any chance.

Puzzled, Maria said they had had no visitors, no messages. It had been a long, slow month.

"We gathered acorns," said Matty. He gestured to the baskets in the yard. "See."

"Be sure you leech the poison out of them."

"We got nuts and willow bark, too," said Daniel.

"Mamma says she can make bread with them."

"Famine bread," said Erik Axel. He pulled back his lips in disgust, then he smiled. "Look what I brought."

He led them into the house and dumped his bundle onto the table. He pulled out his dirty clothes and tossed them in the corner, then drew out some paper wrapped packages.

"Coffee." He handed the oily paper packet to Maria.

A larger sack contained wheat flour, a tiny box, lump sugar. He plunged his hand to the bottom of his bag.

"Ah. Nothing else. A *nisse* must have stolen it."

When he saw the disappointment in the children's faces, he looked again. This time he brought out a small parcel wrapped in white paper. When he untied the string, a sprawl of colored candies rolled out onto the table.

"Peppermints," yelled Matty.

"And horehound." Daniel grabbed one of the sugary candies.

"Here, Anna. Try one of these." Erik Axel handed her a bright yellow lemon drop.

"Candy? You buy candy while we eat famine bread." Tears snaked down Maria's gray cheeks. "How could you?"

"They paid us in credit at the company store."

"No wages? Will you go back?"

"Not until spring. Now hush, Maria. Let the children enjoy their candy."

Anna had stood watching this exchange between her parents with her lemon drops forgotten in her clenched fist. She accepted her father's words as permission to thrust one of the sugary treats into her mouth.

"Oh. Sour."

The child went to plucking the hard candy from her tongue until her pappa stopped her.

"Keep sucking. It will surprise you," he said.

A slow, spreading smile on Anna's face confirmed this. She reached for another of the yellow candies.

~~~

As fall deepened into winter, Erik Axel grew restless. He went about his work with an eye to the road, watching for something, someone. If he heard the noise of hooves, he would drop his ax or spade, slacken the rein on the colt he was breaking to harness, and watch the break in the trees where a visitor would first come into view. When no one appeared or it proved to be a neighbor, he would shrug and go back to work.

In the lengthening evenings he sat silent by the fire carving ale tankards with whorls of leaves and flowers.

"Why so many?" Maria asked one night. She was unraveling sweaters the boys had outgrown to knit new ones.

"Wedding cups," he said. "I can sell them at the Christmas fair at Smedjebacken."

"Some puzzle cups might sell, too."

"Yes. If I can find a good stout birch. A standing dead one so I don't have to wait for the wood to dry. Why don't you use that yarn for mittens?"

"The boys need sweaters, not mittens."

"To sell, I mean. You'd get several pairs of mittens from one sweater."

"And leave the boys without warm clothes?"

"What they need is a good home, a chance to go to school, make something of themselves." He stood up and hurled the tankard into the fire.

~~~

Maria was helping Daniel and Anna arrange a wreath of fir for the Advent candles. The clean, sharp smell of bruised needles filled the house.

"Where's Matty?" said Anna.

"He took his sled to the forest for a load of wood," said Maria.

"Where's Pappa?"

"Fixing a broken door hinge in the stable."

"Where's Daniel?"

"Right here, silly," giggled Daniel.

"Where's Mamma?"

"You ask too many questions."

Daniel ran to the window. "Somebody coming."

Maria saw that it was a wagon driven by a man in a fur coat and top hat. When he pulled up at the yard fence and climbed down, she realized it was cousin Andrew.

"It's your uncle Andrew. He must have rented a wagon in town"

Erik Axel hurried to meet him. Something about his eager

demeanor worried Maria. And what would Andrew be doing here this time of year, she wondered. Why do they stand talking in the yard, in the cold. Put up the team and come in, she urged silently. Everything would be all right if they would just come in, stomp their boots, take off their coats, sip a cup of coffee.

A tug on her sleeve reminded her of the children. Their big eyed stares surprised her.

"Can we go out and see Uncle Andrew?"

"Please, Mamma."

"Not now. Daniel. Get your coat and go help Matty with the wood. Hurry now."

Anna dropped the fir branch and ran to hide her face in her mother's skirt.

"Get your coat, Anna. We'll go see what's going on."

As she approached the men, she heard Andrew ask if the boys were ready to go. Her heart lurched and bumped when she heard her husband's answer.

"Their things are packed and waiting in the store room. I'll fetch the boys from the woods when you're ready to leave."

"You haven't told them, then?"

"No. I thought it best not to."

"Told them what?" Maria drew back and stared at Erik Axel. "What have you done now?"

"We can't feed the boys through the winter. Would you have them begging fish heads from the neighbors' garbage heaps?"

"But where…?"

Maria's voice was a thin croak. Tiny needles of pain jigged behind her eyes. She reached for Anna's hand, held it tight. The child whimpered, then pulled away and sat down in the dirt. Maria paid no attention. Why had she sent Daniel to the woods. She should have told him to run, to hide, to take Matty with him.

"Danzig. They will be well taken care of, Mrs. Norrling," said Andrew. "It's much better than sending them to be indentured in the copper mines."

"Now? Do they have to go now?"

Erik Axel tried to reason with his wife. "You would rather they starve and take us to the grave with them?"

"They'll be with a family in Danzig. They can go to school. Learn a trade."

"And when things get better, they can come back," said Erik Axel.

"So far away. I'll never see them again." Maria was shaking so hard she could barely stand. "How will we live?"

"I'll get their stuff. Are you sure you can't find a place for the girl?"

Erik Axel walked across the yard to the doorway. He seemed anxious for his visitor to be on his way with the boys. He stopped and called back to Andrew.

"Anna is strong and healthy."

"No. No girls, especially not one too young to work. Maybe when she's ten or eleven." Andrew looked at the nearly hysterical Maria. "Hold tight to little Anna, Mrs. Norrling. Take your consolation from her."

He lifted the little girl to her feet. Her doll, its porcelain face cracked and dirty, a leftover from the days of plenty, slipped from her arms. Andrew picked it up and handed it to her.

"Take her into the house, Mrs. Norrling."

He pressed the child close to her. He could see Erik Axel emerging from the store room with two small bundles of clothing.

"Oh, I almost forgot. I have a little present for you. For your anniversary."

Through her tears, Maria watched him retrieve a small parcel from the wagon, but made no move to take it when he held the box out to her.

"Take it, Anna. Go help your mamma open it."

Maria staggered across the yard behind the little girl. Anna lead the way with Andrew's gift clutched tight alongside her doll. Inside, Maria collapsed on the floor.

"Mamma, Mamma. Help me with the box."

When Maria failed to respond, Anna dropped the broken doll, then placed the box on the table. With searching fingers she peeled off the wrapping paper. She hesitated, waited for the expected reprimand, then pried the flimsy box apart. Inside she found wads of shredded wood fiber surrounding something smooth, pale. She worked her dirty fingers along the gold edges of the object until she had it free of the packing material.

"Oh. Pretty."

She grasped the figurine and stood it upright. A porcelain lady danced between her hands, cheeks tinged with ruby, eyes painted dark and mysterious.

"Come see, Mamma. It's soo pretty."

Maria did not respond. She lay on the floor and continued to sob, long hiccupy sobs punctuated with wails of grief. If she heard Anna's voice, she gave no sign.

"Come put the pretty lady on the shelf, Mamma."

When she heard no answer, no order not to touch, Anna pulled the figurine from the rough wood table, clutched it to her chest with both hands, and carried it to the trundle bed where she slept. Careful to check to see if her mother was watching, she pulled the trundle out a bit and laid the dancer on her pillow. Hearing a noise at the door, she yanked the quilt over the figurine and pushed the bed back in place.

"Maria, Maria. Supper ready yet?"

It was her pappa. Anna waited for her mother to get up and go about the task of putting supper on the table. When she didn't, Anna ran to the cupboard and began setting the table.

Finished with the table, she saw that the fire in the cookstove was only coals and embers. With great effort she lifted a thick piece of wood into the fire box, added a few pine cones, the box and packing from Andrew's present, then blew on it until trickles of flame licked up. Standing on a chair, she saw that the kettle was full. She pulled it to the middle of the stove top where a little of the water sloshed out. It hissed and popped. Anna toppled off the chair in surprise. She looked around to see if her mother had noticed, but no scolding words, no slaps, no cuff to the ear happened.

By the time Erik Axel came back in for supper, she had bread and jam, hot coffee, and leftover fish soup on the table.

"Maria? What's going on here?"

"She won't get up," said Anna.

"Stop this nonsense, Maria. Wash your face and come to the table."

Anna remembered she hadn't washed and ran to the basin. By the time she had finished, her father was already eating. She slid the bench out from under the end of the table and joined him. Maria sat across from her, face streaked with dirt, hair in tangles, eyes unfocused, staring at her plate.

"Where's Matty? And Daniel?"

"They went with Andrew. It's just us now."

"Why?"

"So they can go to school."

"What's wrong with Mamma?"

"Eat your soup."

That night Anna moved her quilt and pillow from the trundle bed to the pull out bench bed the boys had shared. When no one was looking, she moved the porcelain dancer, too.

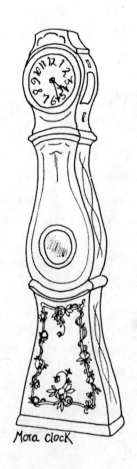

Mora Clock

Stone Soup, Stone Soul.

That winter was hard beyond description. The Norrlings, along with many other people in the parish, were forced to subsist on the barest of food and fuel. Starving children, blue with cold, wandered the countryside begging. Itinerant peddlers went house to house trying to sell wooden spoons, woven baskets, and even, family heirlooms. Peddlers and children, alike, sometimes fainted and froze to death along the roads.

The sheriff and his men were out in force almost daily picking up corpses. When they weren't collecting the dead, they were going from one poor home to another collecting goods for unpaid debts. These visits from the sheriff and his men became so common, they were added to the local lore. When a stranger approached a house, the children inside would sing a ditty about hiding their mittens to keep them from the sheriff.

Little Anna had nightmares where she imagined the sheriff pounding at the door. She feared he would demand she give up her dancing lady and kept her best mittens ready to offer instead.

Erik Axel and Anna scrounged the forest for anything that might be edible. They filled sacks with yellowed grass, willow twigs, wild nuts, seeds, rose hips, and dried berries. Stiff with cold, they carried the meager yield to the storeroom each day until a heavy, wet snow covered the ground knee deep.

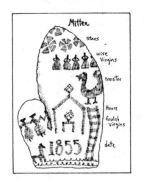

Maria lay abed hours past first light, then she would get up, wrap herself in a blanket and sit staring into the fire.

"We need to make bread, Mamma," said Anna. "Please come."

"You do it."

"How, Mamma?"

"Get the big bowl, the wooden one. Fill it half with chaff."

"Chaff? The animals eat chaff."

"Just do it. Find the cleaver, the flat-edged knife, and chop it fine."

Anna stood on the bench and worked the cleaver back and forth, up and down the sides of the bowl, over and over until the chaff was fine dust and her back ached.

"Now, the beechnuts."

"I'm tired, Mamma."

"You've only started."

When the tiny nuts were powder, Anna added a few cups of the precious flour, starter from the foaming, smelly crock, and then, water.

"Stir it. Use your hands. Put some muscle into it."

By Christmas Anna was adding dried mountain ash berries and heather seed to the brittle dough. When baked in the fireplace, the rough gray mess sent out a bitter odor.

One morning she found she had used up the supply of wild nuts and berries.

"Mamma, Mamma, no more berries.

Maria turned her face to the wall. "Use the acorns."

So Anna pounded the hard kernels and added them to a small amount of flour and water to make a flat cake. She tasted the dough and spit it out.

"Ooh. Bad. Can we really eat this?"

"Pigs eat it and survive."

Maria had forgotten the bitter tannin contained in the acorn. The nuts became edible only after it was leeched out, their hard fibers broken down. A pig could digest acorns, but a human could not.

After the family recovered from a week long bout of constipation and stomach cramps, Maria tried another way to keep hunger's hound from their door. She sent Erik Axel to gather the inner bark from the stand of pine trees below the house.

Anna pounded the stringy mass to a pulp, then boiled it with the half-rotted fish that Erik Axel brought in from his cache. Unable to buy salt to cure the summer fish catch, he had buried the baskets of silver fish in the earth in an attempt to preserve them. Before the weather turned cold enough to keep the fish, they had begun to ferment. The stink of the fish made it almost impossible to choke down, but the bark soup diluted the taste until it was bland and indifferent. Fresh fish would not be available until the ice on the river melted enough to cut through.

When they were alone in the house one day, Maria showed Anna a stash of round reddish fruits.

"These are special, for you."

"Rosehips."

"I sorted them from the stuff you harvested in the fall."

"The horses like them."

"It would be shameful to waste them on the horses."

She showed Anna how to boil a few of the rose hips into a sweet syrup.

"It's good."

"Eat it all. Chew the seeds."

"More, please."

"Next week. We have to make the rose hips last till spring."

The horses were being fed bark, twigs, branches, and turnip roots. Erik Axel tramped the woods and river bank hours a day searching for any vegetation that might have a morsel of sustenance in it. And night, after night Anna heard her parents arguing about the horses.

From her warm burrow under the quilts she listened to her mother beg Erik Axel to sell or trade the colt.

"You give away your own children. Sell the colt."

"Now, Maria. I explained all that."

"In the name of God, I beg you. We'll starve."

Anna didn't hear him answer and decided he had probably rolled over and gone to sleep. She patted the figurine in the bed beside her.

"Pretty lady," she whispered, then fell asleep.

~~~

In mid-January Maria started vomiting. She blamed the wretched diet, the rotted herring when her husband noticed. But when she fainted one afternoon, Anna ran to find her father in the stable.

"Pappa, Pappa. Come quick."

"What is it?"

"Mamma is on the floor. She won't wake up."

In the house Anna helped Erik Axel carry Maria to the bed and splash cold water on her cheeks, rub her wrists. Maria groaned, coughed, opened her eyes, then turned away.

"Go build up the fire, Anna."

While she tended the fire, Ann listened.

"How long has this been going on, Maria?"

"It's just the rough food. Your fish doesn't set well."

"How long, Maria?"

"I'm sorry," said Maria. She saw there was no way around the truth. "I'm that way again."

"That way? No." Erik Axel put his hands on her shoulders and shook her. "What are you saying?"

"You know. I'm that way, like with Anna." She burst into tears, great hiccuping tears.

"You're with child?" Erik Axel let go of her and she fell back against the pillows. "How could you let this happen?"

"Let it happen? Let it? What are you saying?"

"How could you?"

Their raised voices beating on her ears, Anna pulled out her bed and slid under the covers. In her need to hold the dancing lady close, she even forgot to take off her shoes.

"How could you?"

"How could you?"

The words hovered in the air when they sat down to their famine bread and fish gruel in the morning. The words echoed in the dark room when Erik Axel and Maria climbed into the cupboard bed at night. The words pounded in Anna's gut as she went about her chores. Though she didn't understand, she knew the only quiet place was under her quilts with the dancing lady.

Even that sanctuary was violated the morning Erik Axel raced into the house and jerked the quilt from the bench bed.

"No, Pappa," yelled Anna.

She scrambled to pull her pillow over her treasure. No one noticed.

"Hurry, Maria. I need warm water. And get the *brannvin* jug."

"Calm down. What's wrong now?"

Her dancing lady safe from view, Anna ran to get the kettle from the stove.

"It's hot, Pappa."

"Pour it in a bucket and add some cold until you can put your hand in it."

Maria stood in the center of the room, hands folded over her swelling stomach.

"It's those damned horses, isn't it?"

"The colt is down in his stall. Did you find the *brannvin*, Anna?"

"Empty, all gone."

"Empty? Ginger. Do we have any ginger? We have to try something."

They covered the shaking animal with Anna's quilt, dosed him with warm water and ginger, rubbed his trembling, twitching legs to no avail. The horse drew a few more rasping breaths, his chest lifted and heaved to reveal every rib, then he lay still.

Erik Axel stood up, Anna's quilt in his hand.

"It's ruined. I'm sorry."

"Don't worry, Pappa. I'll find another in the chest."

"Go do that. I have things to take care of here. Hurry, now."

While Erik Axel bled and butchered the dead colt in the stable yard, Maria railed at Anna, at thin air, at the unfairness of it all.

"How could you? How could you?"

Anna avoided her mother and edged around the room to the storage chest. In the chest she found the crazy quilt with its bits of crimson, cobalt, and gold. She looked to see if her mother was about to snatch it from her, but saw no glimmer of awareness in her eyes. Anna pulled the quilt from the trunk and carried it to her bed. A fit cover for her dancing lady.

 Maria's scream of injustice became her mantra. Eyes staring, white rimmed, racked by fits of coughing, she cursed the precious colt dead in the stable, cursed her stubborn husband, her innocent daughter, the very God that made them all.

"How could you?"

The words split the air as Anna boiled the bits of horse meat into stew. The words hung over the table as they forked up the strong flavored meat, drank the bullion.

"How could you?"

Maria's harsh words and simmering anger blighted the sweet air of spring even as it blew the fumes of rotting fish and bitter famine bread from the house.

"How could you?"

Erik Axel silently accused Maria each time he looked at her.

Maria, bone thin except for her swelling belly, crept about her chores. Except for her tirades against her husband and the coughing spells that came more and more often, she was tight lipped, silent. By Easter she was coughing up blood.

"Has your mother planted the spring garden, yet?"

"I'll get the seeds, Papa."

Anna ran to the storeroom and returned with the seed collected from last year's plants. They were sewn into small cloth bags to keep them dry and safe from mice.

"These are peas. Radishes. Garlic. I don't know these."

"Plant a row of each. We'll know soon enough."

"Is Mamma going to die? Like the colt?"

Erik Axel didn't answer his daughter's question. He pushed the matted hair back from her forehead.

"Get your mamma's hairbrush."

With awkward fingers he brushed Anna's hair and tied it back with a bit of ribbon.

"There. You need to do that every morning."

"Just like the horses's tails?"

"Just the same. Maybe your mamma can show you how to braid it."

"She mostly sleeps. Or stares into the fire."

"Tell her I'm going to see Oscar Lof about seed grain."

When Erik Axel returned with the wagon, Anna ran to meet him.

"Did you get it?"

"He must have had a change of heart. He threw in a sack of flour and some oats, too."

"For us?"

"Can you get them? The muslin sacks on top."

Anna climbed over the wheel and pushed the sacks to the ground.

"Boil up some oat porridge for your mamma. It'll do her good."

This time Mr. Lof had not demanded collateral or even payment. Perhaps his petitioner had demonstrated sufficient humility, perhaps he was in his cups or had some presentiment about the Norrling household, or maybe he just felt guilty because of the considerable profit he had gained from the strapping bay colt the previous season.

~~~

With storm clouds massed in the western sky Erik Axel worked through the dinner hour to get the last of the seed in the ground. Foot sore, weary, muzzles nearly touching the ground, the team plodded around the last field. Intent on his seeding, it took several minutes for Erik Axel to realize Anna was running beside the team screaming at him.

"Come quick, Pappa. Pappa, Pappa."

"It's not her time. Too early."

"She needs help. Please, Pappa."

~~~

Erik Axel escorted the midwife through the door and directed her to the bed in the corner, then turned to leave.

"You're not staying?" The old midwife sounded disapproving, sharp voiced.

"Anna, here, can fetch what you need."

"She's your wife."

She sighed and smacked her gums together when Erik Axel left the room without answering.

"Guess it's you and me, dearie. How long has she been like this?"

"It started last night," said Anna.

"Good God. Is the kettle on?"

"Boiling."

"Get a dish."

The woman took a handful of some dark mildewed substance from her bag and mashed it into the bowl with a cup of boiling water while Anna watched. A sharp odor, a combination of ripe fruit and decay, rose from the bowl.

"Will you make Mamma eat that?"

"Silly girl. It's the German Meddle fruit. To stop the baby coming."

The midwife stripped the covers from the suffering Maria, pulled up her night clothes, and applied the black paste to her belly. To no avail. Hours later Maria still writhed on the bed.

"Oh, there's blood," said Anna.

"We'll not save this baby. Probably dead before I got here."

The midwife directed Anna to make a strong tea from some of the dried herbs in her bag. Anna recognized the sage, and the sharp minty presence of penny royal, but the foul briony was new to her. Its loathsome smell made her stomach churn.

When the repulsive drink was held to Maria's lips, she swallowed a little, gagged and lay back on the pillow. The midwife held her head in the crook of her elbow and forced the rest of the dose down her throat.

"Poor Mamma. So tired."

"She needs to push the dead baby out."

Anna wiped her mother's face with a towel, brushed her hair back from her face.

"Cover her and build up the fire," said the midwife, "then fetch your father."

~~~

The midwife explained the situation to Erik Axel in a raspy whisper while Anna sat on her bed and rocked from side-to-side with her thumb in her mouth. The dancing lady peered up at her from under the crazy quilt.

"Do something." Erik Axel made no effort to keep his voice down.

"I've done all I know to do. It's out of my hands."

Anna pulled the quilt down and picked up the figurine, slid off her bed and padded around the room to where her mother lay. She climbed onto the covers beside her and slid the dancing lady against Maria's hot cheek.

"Mamma, Mamma. I'm sorry. Take her."

Maria moaned, opened her eyes, lifted her hand to Anna's hair.

"Poor baby."

Despite their efforts, Maria died that night, the dead child still in her belly. In the space on Maria's death certificate for cause of death it was written, *general decrepitude*. She was thirty-two.

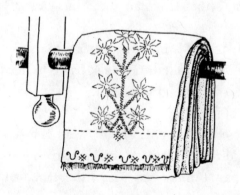

Out of the Past, Into Tomorrow.

Erik Axel and little Anna now lived alone in the house under the edge of the hill. Anna grew up quickly, while Erik Axel aged a dozen years a day. He spent his time away from the plowing, planting, and reaping, in building onto the homestead. He cut trees, sawed them into lumber, hammered up a granary, a storage building, a small cow barn at the end of the house. It was slow, slow work, but then, Erik Axel had more time than anything else.

Anything else, except rocks. After each spring thaw the earth heaved up a new crop. Without sons or wife to root out the stones, he had to clear the fields himself. He knew better than ask Anna to do the job, because she had the cooking and cleaning, soap-making, laundry, candle-making, gardening, sewing, weaving, and endless unnamed chores to jam her waking hours full.

To give him credit Erik Axel did manage to wrest a living from the poor piece of ground once the weather settled into a more normal pattern. After the fields were sown to oats and barley, rye and wheat, he would go to the mines northwest of Grangeburg to work underground. Three years of that damp, demanding pick and shovel work left him with swollen joints and a permanent stoop, but it brought in enough money to buy a pregnant sow, chickens, and a pair of goats.

Reserve Rights and Bridal Crowns.

In 1881, when Anna turned sixteen, Erik Axel deeded her the house and land. It was not a clear transfer of property, but rather the more common encumbered form of transfer. Erik Axel agreed to tender the property to Anna, but she, in turn, agreed to grant him reserve rights and take his last name. At this time in rural Sweden it was still customary for children to use their father's given name in the possessive for their last name. Until this legal change, Anna had used the name, Eriksdatter, Erik's daughter. Now she would be called Anna Norrling

Some people, friends and neighbors alike, thought Erik Axel too young at forty-three to be making such arrangements for his old age and believed he was giving up too easily. After all, he had had a fairly easy life until he was forced from the manor house to scrape and scrounge a living from the rocky soil. Others felt they knew the discouragement and bone-dead weariness that led him to this point. The alternative might well have been the poor farm in a few years.

The specter of the poor farm was a fearful one. The thought of living out one's days in the company of empty-eyed ancients, ex-prostitutes with God-knew what diseases, criminals, idiots, religious fanatics, and hopeless debtors struck terror in the breast of everyone. The poor farm with its flea infested buildings where people slept ten to a room, fought like animals for the thin blankets, and subsisted on a bowl of sop handed around once each day, would frighten anyone but the most wretched beggar.

The reserve right Erik Axel demanded was a room and board for the remainder of his life. This method of insuring one's security in old age often meant parents would build, or hire built, a small house nearby or an addition to the main house. For the very poor or the infirm it was a matter of moving into a spare room of the existing house. Since the Norrling house had no spare room and hoping for a suitable marriage for his daughter, Erik Axel opened a new door beside the fireplace and painstakingly dug himself a small, low-ceilinged room into the hillside behind the chimney. The room was warm, but dark and windowless.

As time went by, he enlarged and walled the room with the same rough-planed boards, hand-smoothed and whitewashed, that finished the rest of the house. He built a cupboard bed against the back of the fireplace, though his fingers were too stiff to do the finer work required for making doors for the bed. Anna loomed a pair of heavy black and white striped curtains to keep the cold air at bay. A straw tick and a feather bed, along with a rude chair, completed the furnishings of the room.

By the following summer he was no longer able to work in the mines because of a persistent cough and joints that swelled painfully in the damp of the underground. He still walked behind the plow, planted and fertilized the fields. He still cut and sheaved the ripe grain, butchered the fat piglets and billy goat kids, but more and more, it was Anna there behind the team with the heavy reins draped over her shoulders so she could keep both hands on the plow to steady it, give it weight so it wouldn't skip out of the furrow. More and more it was Anna in the killing pen wielding the long knife.

On sunny days Erik Axel would drag his chair outside and sit by the front door, smoking his pipe and carving crude wooden horses which he sold at the market in Hagge or Smedjebacken. Sometimes he would prowl the woods searching for wild mushrooms or herbs to treat his rheumatism. In particular he searched for a plant called monkshood or stormhat because its purple flowers were shaped like little pointed hoods or hats. Though the bitter herb was commonly used to treat fevers, he had heard it could be mixed as a liniment to numb the pain in his joints. When the days grew short and the weather bitter, he would spend his days napping or, when his pains subsided, painting odd, fanciful designs of flowers and twined leaves on the walls of his room. It was sixteen year old Anna who chopped the wood and carried the water, fed the animals and hauled the winter's accumulation of manure from the stable to the newly planted fields. With vigilance and hard work the small farmstead yielded a comfortable living for the two of them, but it was a delicate dance of man, beast, and nature.

~~~

Erik Axel sat by the open door to better see the knob of wood he whittled. To practiced eyes the carving was beginning to resemble a two handled cup, a toasting cup, perhaps. Many of the young people Anna's age were beginning the courting rituals. He no longer cared much for tradition, but he worried about Anna. It seemed important for her to marry soon. They had no other family.

"I noticed the Jacoby boy watching you at church."

"His nose is too big."

"He's a nice young man."

Anna stood with her back to her father. She had persuaded herself that a husband had little to offer. Why did she need a husband, when she could plow and butcher as well as any man?

"And he's shorter than me."

"Planting's done. Take a little time to fix yourself up for the Midsummer Eve festival."

"I don't have anything to wear, Pappa." She turned to face him. "And there's too much work here."

"Your mamma's marriage trunk is in the storeroom. Find something in there."

His dead wife, Maria, had brought an over-flowing bridal chest to their marriage, though Erik Axel had hardly noticed at the time. He had dismissed the fancy work, lace, and knitted coverlets as so much frippery.

Unlike the other girls her age, Anna's own marriage chest was nearly empty. Though Anna could spin and weave course cloth and sew basic clothing, she had never learned the finer arts of embroidery, cross-stitch, knitting, and lace making. Her bridal chest would contain only the plainest of bed covers, table cloths, scarves, and under garments. No fancy wall hangings or decorated linen towels, no bed ropes or chair covers had come from Anna's hardworking fingers. The proof of her industry, her domesticity had to be found elsewhere.

"I'd rather work in the fields," said Anna.

She wanted to divert her father from this talk of courting. It was one thing to talk to him about crops, about livestock, about labor unrest in the mines, but to speak of her secret dreams, her private hopes, that was unacceptable.

"I have no time for a beau."

"At least you could spend some time sewing a groom's shirt. You never know."

Anna didn't answer, didn't need to answer. The flush spreading up her neck and over her cheeks was her answer.

"You've already started your groom's shirt, haven't you?"

"Yes, Pappa."

She had secretly worked on a bridegroom's shirt all winter, while she day-dreamed about a prince in bright armor arriving on a tall horse. This vision of being handed up behind the stranger and riding away to a better place lightened the long winter days. She knew she could present her husband-to-be with a respectable shirt. She had selected the best of the flax to beat into fibers. The finished thread was as soft and fine as any she had made before. She wove it into long strips, then cut out the pieces. She made the shirt extra large since she had no idea of the size of the man who would wear it. The shirt had both collar and cuffs, carefully stitched with tiny, almost invisible stitches. The sleeves were long and full, the tail ample. She made up for her lack of embroidery skills by adding rows and rows of decorative stitches to the shirt-front and collar.

"Look through your mother's bride chest tomorrow. Let young Jacoby take you to the Midsummer party, if he wants." Erik Axel went back to his carving.

~~~

With her father away, at the market in Hagge or a union meeting in Grangeburg, Anna decided it was time to examine the old trunk in the storeroom. Worn and covered with dust, the wooden trunk had been there, unopened, longer than Anna could remember. With the brass key her father had given her, Anna forced the lock to move its rusty bowels. She opened the lid with more fear than anticipation. What ghosts of the past inhabited this old box?

By the time she had the contents of the box piled on the floor, Anna realized that anything of value had been removed, sold or bartered years ago, probably by her mother, herself. No silver ornaments, no fine embroidery or yellowed lace, no imported Moroccan leather girdles, shoes, or gloves. A few dried flowers turned to gray dust in her fingers. Childish drawings on cheap paper shredded when she touched them.

Most of the odds and ends of clothing seemed flimsy and old fashioned, but she found a white blouse with long puffed sleeves and a black skirt that could be refurbished. She would bleach the linen blouse, then starch and press it smooth. The skirt was of unfamiliar material, store bought. She would have to ask someone if she dare wash it.

After she placed the rest of the things back in the trunk, she noticed a box at the back of the shelf above. When she pulled it down, she saw that it was a crate with old wood shavings leaking out from between the slats. She carried it to the table and removed the lid. With care she unpacked the box. The shavings were filthy with droppings and she nearly quit in disgust when a dried mouse carcass fell out onto the table. Only the glimpse of a bright gold handle kept her from chucking the whole mess out into the yard. She lifted the delicate cup from the box and rubbed it on her apron.

When Erik Axel got home, Anna had the chocolate set washed and polished, the mess of packing material tossed on the rubbish heap. She had placed the tall pot and eight matching cups on one of her mother's embroidered cloths in the middle of the table.

"It's beautiful, Pappa."

He ignored her comment. "The underground workers at the Copper Mountain Mine are thinking about forming a union to fight the bosses. They're having a meeting next week."

Though no longer able to work, Erik Axel couldn't stay away from mine affairs. He had started meeting with some of the more disgruntled workers.

Anna was glad her father had something to occupy his time, but she had no interest in listening to him rant about injustice to the working man.

"Was it Mamma's? A wedding present?"

He finally looked at the chocolate set on the table.

"Andrew brought it. Said it was a chocolate set."

He squinted at the porcelain cups and matching pot, then sat down at his place at the table.

"Is supper ready?"

"Andrew? Who is Andrew?"

Anna laid the plates and utensils on the table, then went to the stove for the kettle.

"You don't remember him?" He tucked the white napkin under his chin and picked up his fork in anticipation. "My cousin, he died about ten years ago. You saw him when you were four or five."

"Why are the workers meeting?"

"Higher wages mostly. They want the owners to shore up the west tunnels and divert the water. Too many men are getting sick standing in water the whole shift."

"I could use it to serve tea." Anna hefted the tall pot. "I wonder how much it will hold."

"Your mother always liked tea."

"English tea. Maybe we can buy some at summer market."

"Damn nuisance. Put it away."

Reluctant to hide the set away from view, Anna placed it next to her dancing lady figurine on the highest shelf above the stove. These were always open shelves, the first thing a visitor would see when they entered the home. It was the place of honor where families displayed their prize possessions. More affluent households had shelves crammed with polished copper molds, hand-painted China plates, souvenir plaques and spoons sent from relatives in America, engraved glass tankards, and decorative tinware. With the discovery of the chocolate set, Anna had her badge of honor.

~~~

When the groom shirt was finished, Anna washed and starched it, ironed the linen to a high polish. Then, satisfied her work would hold up to public scrutiny, she draped it over one of the ceiling poles in plain view of anyone who might come calling.

The Jacoby boy did ask permission to escort Anna to the party. The Midsummer Eve festival was held in late June, a combination of the ancient celebration of summer solstice and the German May Day with its dancing round the May pole. When the German iron workers immigrated to Sweden, they quickly discovered May brought no flowers, no vegetation at all to decorate their May poles. And it was still too cold and dark to dance the night away. May Day was moved, merged with the summer solstice and a new celebration was born.

The evening started with games and food, but as the light changed to the silvery twilight that would last until sunup, the dancing started. At first it was the winding of the May pole with all the young people weaving in and out as they circled the pole. The long ribbons of blue and yellow wove an intricate pattern up the pole to the cross bar above. When the winding was complete, the dancers paired off and continued their dancing on the close-cropped grass of the surrounding meadow.

Anna found herself alone with Matteus Jacoby in a small clearing away from the others. The music was loud, the freedom exhilarating. Anna did not protest when the young man put his arms around her. When he kissed her, she kissed him back and wondered why she had wasted so much time working when she could have been dancing. Like two young animals they lost themselves in kissing, touching, exploring. It was not until the sun shone full on the damp grass that Anna came to her senses.

Immersed in long sessions about unionizing the mine, Erik Axel barely noticed Anna's uncharacteristic behavior. An over heard conversation alerted him to the fact that his daughter was spending more and more time cavorting around the countryside with various young men. When he asked her about it, she first denied it, then cried and said she was sorry, it wouldn't happen again. The situation escalated; Erik Axel found himself milking the cow and goats several mornings a week because Anna, out all night, was still not home in time to do it. It galled him to be doing women's work and he hoped none of his friends would find him crouched on the milking stool, his head pressed into the hot side of cow or nanny. The garden grew up in weeds and the pickling crocks remained empty. No beets, no cabbage, no parsnips or carrots had been put up for winter. With harvest near at hand he knew he must put a stop to her nonsense.

When he approached her the next day, he was surprised at Anna's appearance. She had braided her long dark hair and wound it over the top of her head in a coronet. That, and the dark circles under her eyes, gave her an uncanny resemblance to her mother, his dead wife, Maria. The resemblance ended with her physical presence. Where his wife had been yielding, obedient, seldom lifting her head to look him in the eye, Anna was developing an air of authority, defiant, pushy.

"Who were you out with last night?"

"Matteus Jacoby." Anna sounded tired "You saw him come for me with his father's gig."

"Has he declared his intentions?"

"Intentions? We were just having fun."

"That's two nights this week. People are beginning to talk."

"I won't marry him. He's a fool."

"Better to marry a fool than to burn. You're not tending to your chores either."

"I'm sick of cows." She set her jaw and stomped out of the room.

~~~

By November it was obvious that Anna's nocturnal activities had caught up with her. Though she had faithfully gulped down a cup of boiled hollyhock root tea each night, the bitter drink had not prevented conception. Anna was pregnant. She tried several herbal concoctions reputed to bring down her courses, her monthlies. She tried a tea made from the bark of the elder, then, more desperate, one from the shrub rosemary. This made her sweat and shake as if she had a terrible fever, but had no effect on her condition.

Weeks passed before she finally went to Mrs. Lof for a remedy. The midwife reluctantly gave Anna oil of yarrow and told to take ten drops in milk and go to bed. The drug gave her terrible cramps, followed by diarrhea, but Anna stayed pregnant.

When her father found out, he made every effort to force a marriage with Matteus Jacoby and, though Matteus was willing, Anna was not. Her situation was not unique and there was little shame in bearing a child out of wedlock. The boy's father put an end to his part of the problem by sending his son away to a military school. For Anna the resolution was far more painful.

As her pregnancy advanced, she became huge and clumsy. Though she was tall and thin, her belly expanded more than usual. Her ankles puffed up over her shoes, her cheeks grew round, her fingers swelled. Mrs. Lof explained it by saying Anna probably carried twins, so no one thought to consult the doctor in Smedjebacken. By December Anna could not manage the milking, so Erik Axel took over the care of the cow and goats. He soon decided to let them go dry for the season.

January found Anna almost unable to get out of bed or to rise from a chair. Her days were filled with slow trips from stove to table and back again as she tried to keep meals on the table. She could take little thought for her own appearance when she could barely drag her feet along. Her hair grew lank and dead looking, her teeth ached constantly as did her back and legs. She found some relief with frequent doses of her father's strong home-brewed liquor, *brannvin*. Through it all, Anna found herself with a growing desire for the baby in her womb.

The morning Erik Axel found his daughter still sitting in the chair by the stove where he had left her the night before, he hired a girl to help out. Her name was Britz Varm. With little money to pay out for wages he worked out a trade with the girl's parents. They were unlanded, indentured servants. Man and wife worked at menial labor for the Lof family and were amenable to any arrangement that relieved them of the burden of providing for another mouth. For the weeks Britz lived at the Norrling house there would be that much more food on her parents' plates.

Britz was expected to cook, clean, chop wood, lug water, and care for Anna until the baby's arrival. In return she was given room and board, a length of wool cloth woven by Anna, and Erik Axel's promise to paint a rose bud pattern on her bride's box. Ample wages for a girl of such low status.

~~~

With Mrs. Lof's help Anna delivered a son at the end of February. She named him Carl Gustav. He was a big, listless baby. Four days later Anna found him dead beside her in the bed when she awoke.

"Britz, come here. Now."

Anna's voice was choked and hiccupy. She climbed out of bed to stand on the ice cold floor. Her knees gave out and she elbowed herself up to lean over the still baby lying in the rumpled covers.

"Karl. Baby Karl. Wake up."

She grabbed the child with trembling hands and gave him a shake. Baby Karl did not respond.

"Britz. Britz. Where are you?"

"Comin missus. I'm comin."

The hired girl finally shook herself awake and got up from the bench bed across the room. She tottered over to Anna still dragging her feather tick.

"What's wrong?"

"It's Karl. He's so still. I don't think he's breathing." Anna took a deep breath and tried to concentrate on the baby. "What can we do?"

"I don know missus. Me mamma always thumps the little ones when theys havin trouble breathin."

Anna turned the baby over and slapped him on the back. Her hands felt disconnected from her body.

"Breathe, please breathe."

She lifted him to her face, laid him against her ear.

"I can't hear him."

Erik Axel shuffled into the room, his sparse gray hair sticking out in wild disarray.

"What's going on?"

"The baby. He not be breathin," said Britz. In a whisper she added, "He be dead, I'm thinkin."

Still kneeling on the floor Anna clutched the child tighter. She turned away from the hired girl to shield the child from the killing words in the air between them.

"Don't say that, Britz. He can't be."

Erik Axel bent down and tried to take the baby from her, but she screamed and collapsed on the cold floor. He craned his neck and looked at Britz.

"Build up the fire, girl. I'll deal with Anna."

~~~

The ground was frozen hard and deep and the roads were deemed barely passable. Since it was unclear if the church would even allow the unbaptized baby to be buried in consecrated ground, Anna and Erik Axel scraped out a space at the foot of one of the huge fir trees down the slope towards the river. Anna wrapped the baby boy in a towel and placed him in the shallow depression. Erik Axel piled stones around and over the body until he had a mound tall and wide enough to discourage animals.

Anna stood in the snow, her coat open to the bitter wind, her head bare. She felt nothing.

"I wish we had some flowers."

"Would do him no good."

Erik Axel rubbed his aching hands together and started back to the house. When Anna didn't follow, he called to her.

"I'll be along in a few minutes, Pappa," she said in answer.

The howl of the wind nearly drowned her words, but she made no move to pull her coat around her or cover her head with the wool shawl hanging down her back. When Anna was sure her father had, indeed, gone to the house, she turned back to the heap of stones under the guardian pine. The snow was busy covering their footprints, covering the harsh gashes where they had dug stones from the frozen dirt, covering the pain of life lost.

"I'm so sorry little baby. So, so sorry. This shouldn't have happened. You shouldn't have happened."

The dead baby mulled over his response. Should he forgive her of her guilt? Not the guilt of smothering him, rolling the covers over his face in her sleep, of course. That was an accident pure and simple. It happened all the time. Her crime was deeper. Bringing forth unwanted life, denying his father, that was the guilt.

As she stood at the grave, Anna prayed time would move backward far enough to obliterate this nuance of history. If she had stayed home sewing instead of going to the Midsummer festival, if she had told Matthew no or slapped his face at that first kiss, if she had hurled herself into the river that first day she realized her body was no longer her own. A new flood of tears rushed from her eyes as she thought of the difficult months she had carried this baby.

"It's not fair, not fair."

Then the words of an ancient song, a song said to belong to the Vikings, came to her remembrance. She stood straighter and murmured the words, a prayer, a benediction over the grave.

> Cattle die, kinsmen die;
> I will have to die, myself.
> One thing I know that never dies:
> The doom over each one's head.

~~~

Anna was older and wiser by the time another man came courting. No callow youth this suitor; Per Larsson was nearly as old as her father, a widower with two daughters. Erik Axel had met Per Larsson at one of the union meetings and brought him home. He and Anna found a kind of comfort in each other's company and he came often, to supper, to help with falling a dangerous tree leaning against the storeroom, to chat about union affairs.

Still, it was a long time before Anna agreed to marry Per. Almost two years. The wooden marker she had placed on the baby's grave had rotted and fallen over.

Even before Per Larsson began courting Anna, Britz Varm had married an odd young man with a growth on the side of his nose. Britz, the girl who had helped out during Anna's first confinement, had a child of her own that fall. She named her daughter Sofia. Anna thought that a pretension for someone living in an abandoned sheep shed on the edge of the Lof estate. Her husband, the young man with the growth on his nose, had died of cancer before the child was born. The small growth had spread until it had enveloped his entire face, spread until he could no longer eat or see, then spread some more and smothered him. Weeks before he died, Britz had moved out of the worker's house into the old sheep shed because she was afraid of marking the baby. She now lived on the charity of neighbors. Had it not been for the Lof's kindness, Britz and her baby, Sofia, would have been homeless beggars. Many things had happened in the space of time between Baby Karl's death and Anna's betrothal to Per Larsson.

~~~

The Norrling house became the Larsson house in the fall of 1884. Because Per was an out of work miner from Soderbarke parish, a man without land or home of his own, he moved in with Anna and her father, moved into the house under the rocky hill in Norrbarke parish near the village of Hagge. Though frail and gray by now, Erik Axel still crept from his room to sit outside the front door to soak up the sun, whittle a little, and keep an eye on the comings and goings of the household. The two-handled cup he had carved while Anna and Matteus Jacoby courted was the last of the fine work he was to do. The cup sat waiting on the shelf above the stove, one shelf down from the chocolate set and the dancing lady.

Per Larsson was a forty-one year old widower with two daughters, Sonja and Hulda, aged five and eight, when he married Anna. Per was a sturdy man of medium height, already stooped from his years in the copper mines. Puffy joints that swelled red with overwork gave indication of the arthritis that would eventually relegate him to the chair by the stove currently occupied by Anna's father.

Anna was as tall as Per, but so ramrod straight she gave the impression of being much taller than her new husband. She was clearly pregnant at the time of the wedding, which gave the pastor several sleepless nights debating in his mind the wisdom of letting Anna wear the traditional wedding crown on her walk down the aisle of the parish church. On the day of the ceremony he relented, though he still firmly believed the crown, symbol of the Holy Mother of God, should be worn only by the pure and unsullied woman.

Anna walked to the altar wearing the plainest of the parish collection of bridal crowns, an unadorned circle of silver with three connected triangular shields in front representing the Holy Trinity. Her husband wore his Sunday suit of black homespun wool, his only good suit, which with luck would serve for his burial suit as well. He carried a wooden spoon in his breast pocket with its carved handle showing prominently. This spoon was his only offering to the bride. She would place it in the pouch at her waist with her own spoon, a symbol of the joining of the two households.

At the brief party that followed the wedding, the bride and groom toasted each other with the two handled cup filled with home-made *brannvin*, danced a sedate turn around the reception hall, then went home. Their guests stayed on to dance and drink until the pickled herring and *tinbrod* ran out. Britz Varm and her nearly two-year-old daughter, Sofia, were not invited. Rumor had it, Britz supported child and drinking habit alike lying on her back for any man who came calling.

Though an "outsider," Per Larsson was well regarded in Norrbarke community because he had made an honest woman of Anna. No one took into account that he was some twenty years older than Anna and brought to the marriage only his name and two small daughters. Forty-one years old and already feeling the aching joints so characteristic of the men who labored underground in the cramped, low-ceiled mines, Per got work at the local mine before his marriage. His job was loading ore into the cars. The workers had failed in their attempt to get better conditions underground; hours were still excessive, water still puddled the deeper passages, wages barely covered living expenses.

The house under the hill was crowded. Anna and Per had the cupboard bed. Per's two little girls slept on the long bench across the room. The bench, itself, was fastened to the wall, but its seat lifted up to reveal a rolled straw mattress which pulled out at night. The covers and feather tick were stashed in the small storeroom by the front door in the daytime and had to be brought out each night. Erik Axel, of course, had his dugout room behind the fireplace.

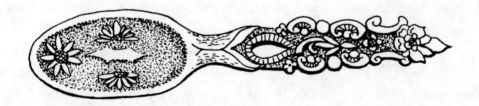

Klara, Perl of Great Price.

Per and Anna's baby was born without complications that January. They named her Klara Perl. Anna recovered quickly, except for the recurring tooth ache that had so distressed her during her previous pregnancy. It was not the aching of a single tooth. Her entire jaw pulsed with a deep throbbing pain. She had dosed herself with small nips from the *brannvin* keg when the pain gripped her the first time. With the return of the pain she took up the habit again.

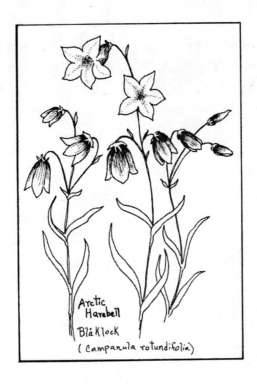

Arctic
Harebell

Blå Klock
(Campanula rotundifolia)

Unto The Third and Fourth Generation.

Five year old Klara knelt on the scrubbed pine floor and looked up at the shelf above her head. Her mist fine hair seemed a halo in the slanting light stabbing through the small window behind her. The light danced over the treasures that tempted her, just out of reach.

Sometimes her mother, Anna, brought down the dancing lady or the miniature tea set from far away China. She was allowed to play with the tiny tea cups and tea pot, the sugar bowl with a lid no bigger than her little fingernail under the watchful eye of Hulda, one of her older stepsisters, but it was the chocolate set that drew the child like a magnet.

Never did her mother offer to let her play with the majestic pot and its eight matching cups. Though Hulda was nearly grown-up at thirteen, even she wasn't allowed to dust the fragile set. Little Klara had been forbidden to touch it, though with her bright blue eyes and angel hair framing her face, it was hard to understand how anyone could deny her heart's desire.

Her granpappa had told her the story of the chocolate set often. The set, a stylish addition to any home in the middle of the nineteenth century, had twice been a wedding present. The first wedding was in 1860 when Klara's granpappa, Erik Axel Norrling married Maria Katrina Jonsdotter, prettiest girl in Norrbarke parish. His cousin, Andrew, a stiff, proper fellow who often traveled to Prussia on business for the State Church of Sweden, bought the chocolate set on one of his trips abroad. The chocolate set first graced Erik Axel's fine manor house, then for fifteen years it was packed away in the storage room. Klara's mother, Anna, had rescued it and placed the set on the rude shelf above the stove.

The Victorian era pitcher and its matching cups were much like a tea set except the cups stood tall and slender on tiny feet. The pot echoed the shape in its sweeping height. Hand painted roses of pink and garnet decorated pot and cups alike, and splashes of gold accented the feet, handles, and rims. In the dim light the chocolate set glowed like a precious jewel against the time-stained wood of the shelf that held it.

Whenever Klara looked at the fine pot or listened to Granpappa's story, she wondered what it would be like to drink chocolate. She had once tasted the waxy brown candy they called chocolate, but could not imagine sipping it from the delicate cup.

~~~

Though she wouldn't admit to believing in the old superstitions, Klara's mother, Anna, never allowed a fire in the fireplace or stove on Thursdays during the spring and summer months. No fire meant no bread baking on Thursdays, either. It was an old and primitive fear of blighting the year's grain harvest that prompted such drastic precautions. Instead of cooking and baking, Anna cleaned the wide planked floor on Thursdays.

She recruited the children to haul the benches, the cradle, the loom, and the big wooden churn out into the yard. Most of the furniture, such as the beds and the long table, were built into the house and couldn't be moved. She would send Klara and her siblings to their chores of taking the goats to pasture or picking weeds and stones from the garden patch, then, on her hands and knees, dragging a wooden bucket of water with a lump of lye soap, she would scrub the floor white, inch-by-inch.

Though she was only five, Klara was expected to tend the old nanny goat her mother milked each morning and evening so baby Kristina, Stina to everyone, could have a steady supply of milk. Barely able to tie a knot, Klara was supposed to move the goat from one grazing plot to another throughout the day and lug several buckets of water for the animal.

This day was particularly hard for Klara because it was the day the goat had to be tethered amongst the long grasses on the roof of the Larsson home. Though the house was built into the side of the hill, it was still a hard climb for a little child towing a reluctant goat. By the time the sun crossed its zenith Klara had wilted from her efforts to keep the water bucket filled and the goat content. She had eaten her lunch of bread and cheese hours ago and longed for supper time. Afternoons in summer seemed to last forever.

Klara stretched out on her back in the grass and watched the clouds flounce across the sky. She wondered why the summer sun used so much time for its daily trip. It was still high above the rocks when she was called to bed. In winter the sun sped through the day so quickly she was frightened at the swift fall of darkness. It was dark when she awoke and dark soon after lunch and the few hours of daylight were gray and dim with the sun barely above the horizon. Klara couldn't decide which was worse, too much daytime or hardly any at all.

Bucket in hand Anna crossed the yard and reached the three legged milking stool from the wall. Before she disappeared into the stable she called up to the roof where Klara shooed flies from the goat's back.

"Bring nanny to her stall, then wash up for supper, Klara."

"Ya, Mamma."

Klara led the animal down the steep roof and through the narrow door into the stable attached to one end of the house. The stalls where the livestock lived in the winter were built so they could be entered from the family's living quarters. In summer only the milk goat remained on the home place because older girls from all the neighboring farms drove the cows and goats to the common grazing land in the mountains to the west.

Klara's stepsisters, Hulda and Sonja, had already gone to the *langfabod*, or long pasture, this year. They had driven the family cow and several of the neighbor's cows to pasture. They would be given a small wage for the job which involved staying away from home a month or more. They, and other girls from the Hagge area, would sleep in rude shelters built several hundred years ago, milk the cows, turn the milk into soft whey-cheese, butter, and molded cheese. The farms were too small to use precious land close to home for grazing. A family with five children and a grandfather needed every bit of land it could muster to raise enough grain and potatoes for winter.

After dousing her hands, face, neck, and ears with the cold water in the basin next to the door, Klara dried herself on the coarse linen cloth that hung on a peg above the wash bench. The house was so quiet, she felt she must tip-toe across the clean floor. Baby Stina must be asleep, she thought. The summer emptiness of the house always surprised her. A clean cloth embroidered with daisies covered the plates and utensils already in place on the long table. One plate for Mamma, one for Pappa, one for Ivar who was picking potato beetles in the garden, and one for herself. Granpappa Erik Axel ate by himself in his back room. He said the children's voices made him tired.

Klara knew a ewer of *fruksoppa*, a cold fruit soup, and slices of black bread waited under the table cloth for the evening meal. Her mouth worked in anticipation of the crusty bread with a layer of sweet butter and maybe a spoonful of lingonberry preserves if her mamma could be persuaded to bring the crock down from the shelf.

Klara's attention was drawn to the jam crock on the shelf above the stove, then her gaze moved upward to the treasured chocolate set on the shelf just above the jam. The elegant cups with their gilt legs and curving handles tantalized her. Klara could imagine the delicate cups skipping about the room in a lively dance when everyone was in bed, asleep.

Mamma is long about her milking tonight, Klara thought. I could help by bringing down the jam crock.

Klara pulled the empty salt fish barrel over to the shelf with the thought that she could reach the crock if she stood on the cold stove. The iron stove was cold most of the week in the summer. Balanced on the stove, she was surprised that she could not only reach the jam crock, but also the chocolate set on the higher shelf.

With the precious chocolate pot and its delicate cups at eye level she forgot about lingonberry preserves and supper and all of her mamma's warnings. Klara reached out to the painted flowers on a forbidden cup. Her finger touched one of the tall slender cups just as her mamma's voice struck her.

"What are you doing, Klara? Get down this instant."

Startled, Klara jerked in alarm and tumbled from the stove. She bumped the shelf as she tried to catch herself. The chocolate pot teetered on its tiny feet, then settled back in place. Not so the cup. Klara had her finger on it when she reacted to her guilt and her mamma's voice. Klara knocked the cup off the shelf and it flew over her mamma's head to shatter on the floor.

Anna reached down and pulled the sobbing Klara to her feet. A quick look told her the child was more scared than hurt.

"You make me tired, Klara. Always into something."

"I'm sorry, Mamma. I didn't mean to." Klara rubbed the bump on her head. "I just wanted to help."

"Breaking things isn't much help."

Anna glared at Klara, her forehead furrowed, pale. She seemed too tired to hustle a willow switch to administer a whipping.

"You're not to touch these things, ever."

"I promise, Mamma."

Sisters Three.

Hulda threw down her basket of smelly, mold-covered lumps of stable dung, then pitched her sharpened stick into the bushes and threw herself down on the grass. It was spring and the turnips were just poking their tender green leaves up through the earth. The girls' job that morning was to carry the piles of manure from the stable and mix it with the dirt around the new plants.

"I hate it here," she declared. "I hate turnips; I hate this stinking manure; I hate the cows."

"Hate the cows? You can't hate the cows, especially the babies," said Sonja.

Twelve year old Sonja doted on animals, babies in particular. She loved the calves, the goat kids, the new hatched chicks, even her baby brother, Will. She was anxiously looking forward to the birth of a foal before summer.

Eight year old Klara went to Hulda, her oldest step-sister, and wrapped her arms around her shoulders.

"Do you hate me, too, Hulda? Hulda? Please don't."

Hulda wiped her hands on her skirt and pulled Klara onto her lap.

"I wish we could have some fun," mused Hulda.

"What would you do if you could choose?"

Klara laid her head against Hulda's shoulder.

"Anything? I'd have me a fine house, a board house, not logs, with flowers at the windows, lace curtains, a house in the city. And a handsome husband who would take me dancing every night. New dresses, shoes. Real store-bought dancing slippers, not homemade boots."

Klara sat up and faced her sister. "Husband? Dancing? How silly."

"What do you want, baby Klara?"

"A horse and carriage. A strong, fast horse I can drive and drive. I want to see the whole country."

Klara flung herself down on the grass and pretended to drive her dream horse, clucking to speed it on, jiggling the invisible reins, cracking her invisible whip.

"What a ninny. I'm sure it all looks the same."

Sonja ignored her sisters giggling on the grass and trudged on down the row, dumping some of the vile looking mixture from her basket around each small plant, but being very careful not to get it too close to the tender stems. When she had emptied her basket, she turned around and came back down the row with her pointed stick. At each plant she meticulously stirred the black muck into the soil until she reached the spot where her sisters sat on the grass. She looked at them a minute, then pitched her stick into the bushes, too.

"What can we do?"

Klara said, "We could go see Sofia, maybe go down to the river."

A few years older than Klara, Sofia lived on the Lof farm over the hill. She and her mother, Britz, subsisted on handouts and the little money Britz made hiring out to various neighbors when Mrs. Lof gave her time off.

"She's a baby," said Hulda.

"She's older than me and I'm not a baby."

"We're supposed to clean out the stable," Sonja said. "And work up the rest of the garden."

Klara stared up at the fluffy clouds. "Nobody would know. Pappa's at the mine."

"Mamma would know we were gone."

Sonja had started calling Anna Larsson, Mamma, immediately after her father had re-married, but then, she was only four at the time. Because Hulda had been seven, she found it harder to call a strange woman by the name she had always called her real mother. It had upset her father when she called her step-mother by her given name, so Hulda compromised by calling her nothing at all.

Klara got up and dumped her basket at the end of the row. She skipped back to her sisters.

"Mamma wouldn't notice. Her teeth are aching her. I saw her

sipping Granpappa's *brannvin*, rolling it around in her mouth. The *brannvin* always makes her sleepy."

Hulda got up and shook out her skirt. "Her teeth are always aching her these days."

"So, are we agreed? We'll go see Sofia?"

"Might as well. Sofia may be a dumb little brat, but you got to admit she thinks up some interesting romps."

"And there's nothing else to do."

Just before they got to the Lof farm, the girls left the road and made their way through the forest. The last person they wanted to run into was Mrs. Lof. When they reached the back of the Lof woodlot, they stopped to peer out through the underbrush. Sofia might be hoeing the cabbages or setting out onions, but no one was working in the garden plot except the strawman lolling on his pole threatening the crows.

They walked along the dirt path leading to the outhouse. They could hear voices and a pounding noise. Again they approached cautiously. To fall into adult hands meant a thrashing for sure. At home they were fairly safe from the strap or the willow switch because their father punished them only when Anna made a great fuss. To be found even mildly disobedient in some other jurisdiction, meant sure punishment. Mrs. Lof had whipped the three of them on more than one occasion and Sofia's mother had an equally heavy hand.

When Klara peeped through a gap in the pole fence, she could see a small hand holding a beater whopping the dust from a carpet thrown over a pole.

"It's Sofia," said Klara.

"Is she alone?" said Hulda. She stood a little behind Klara and Sonja, trying to see over the top of the fence.

"Foolish child, she's talking to herself."

Sonja walked boldly around the end of the fence. In the clearing stood Sofia with a rag tied around her head, covered with choking brown dust. She was not talking to herself, though, she was addressing a small dog perched on a stump. When Klara hallooed her, she dropped the beater and whirled around. Even through the coating of dust, Klara could see she had a black eye and new bruises on the side of her face.

"Oh, I be glad t' see ya," said Sofia. "Dis dust be a killin me. Me arm be 'bout t' fall off."

"We could go swimming, wash that dust away," said Hulda.

"And the stable stink." Sonja reached out to pet the little dog, rub his ears, and fondle his silky coat.

"Gotta tek care of t' doggie." Sofia wiped her face on her filthy apron. "I don need another hidin'."

"We'll take him along," said Hulda. Is he yours?"

"Na. He be t' missus's lap doggie."

"I'll watch him," said Sonja. She untied the bridle rein that served to keep the dog from running off and gathered the animal into her arms. "He's so little. What's his name."

"Bobo. Nasty runt he be."

The four girls headed for the river, giggling quietly until they were out of earshot of the house. By the time they reached the river they were laughing and teasing each other, oblivious to the world around them. In a quiet place beyond the mud flat where the cattle were driven for water, the girls stripped off their long dresses and petticoats. None of them wore shoes in spring and summer. Sonja wanted to let the little dog run free, but Sofia became so agitated at the idea, they tied him to a willow tree on the bank.

"Take off your head scarf, Sofia," said Hulda. "You're not beating rugs, now."

"Ruther not," said Sofia.

Naked except for her pantaloons and head scarf, she stood, pigeon-toed, on the bank before taking the plunge into the cold water. The ten-year-old was small for her age; her ribs and knobby breast bone showed through her pale skin, pale but for the bruises and long red welts across her back. With a sudden leap she plumed into the river.

The other girls followed. When the sting of cold wore off, the water felt soothing. The dirt and sweat and boredom of the morning's work rinsed away in the river's gentle current. After awhile Hulda and Sonja ducked their heads under to wash out their long blond hair.

"I wish we had soap. We could wash each other's hair and braid it up new."

When they had finished their own hair, the two older girls converged on Klara. They unpinned her braids and unplaited them. Then, with the vigor of the older tormenting the younger, they ducked her under and gave her hair and scalp a rubbing that made her head tingle. Finally, gasping for breath, she broke away from them and swam out into the deeper water. There, Klara rolled over on her back and taunted Hulda and Sonja, knowing they could not swim with enough confidence to venture after her.

With Klara out of reach, they grabbed Sofia. She fought back with surprising strength.

"Hey, stop that," said Hulda. "We only want to wash your hair. Get some of the stink off you."

"Lemme go. Don' want no washin'."

"Yank that rag off, Sonja," said Hulda.

Klara watched from a safe distance, treading water. Just as the girls got the scarf away from Sofia, the little dog began yapping, high pitched and frantic. Hulda and Sonja let go of Sofia and splashed to shore. Only Klara saw the reason for Sofia's fight to hang onto her scarf. The child had raw patches on the side of her head where the hair had been pulled out in clumps.

So interested in Sofia's wounded scalp, Klara almost missed the doings on shore. While she helped Sofia tie her scarf, she watched Sonja and Hulda scrambling to pull their dresses on over wet hair and skin. The little dog's yapping grew more and more shrill.

"What's wrong with the dog?" she asked Sofia.

"Dunno. You see anythin?"

"Two men coming along the path. With sacks."

"An black beards? Long hair?"

"Yes."

Sofia paled and fear tightened her mouth to a knot. She grabbed Klara around the waist and buried her head against her wet shoulder. They were standing in thigh-deep water by now.

Klara kept an eye on the approaching men, but she also saw her step-sisters sneak off through the bushes.

"Tis t' Ruski spies. I hear me ma tell there be spies about."

"That's silly. My pappa says they're Russian immigrants. They go around sharpening saws and things." Though Klara spoke firmly, her lip trembled and she wondered if Sofia was right.

"We'd better get out of here," said Klara. "They're coming this way."

"Gotta git outta here. Hurry," said Sofia. She seemed to have forgotten her nakedness.

Klara followed her. "They're wearing long black coats. Do you think they steal children?"

Sofia started wailing and sat down in the water.

"Thet's what me ma said."

Klara hauled her screaming playmate out of the water by one arm. It was too late to go down the bank for their clothes or the yapping dog. Sofia had on only her pantaloons, ragged and full of holes. Klara wore a sleeveless camisole as well as her patched pantaloons. Both girls dripped trails of water as they scrambled through the woods. By the time they were so out of breath they had to stop, the yapping dog could no longer be heard.

Sofia lay on her back gasping for air. "Oh. Oh, me side hurts."

Klara flopped down beside her friend. They were in a small glen surrounded by huge rocks and clumps of birch trees, a world apart.

"Can you hear them? Are they coming after us?"

"Don't ker. Cain't run no more." Sofia crossed her arms over her bare chest as awareness of her own nakedness overtook her.

"Ouch. Look at my feet. We musta run through a bramble patch." Klara was busy pulling thorns from her bleeding feet. Her legs were scratched and dirty.

Sofia rolled over and sat up. She re-tied her head scarf, then got to her feet.

"We gotta get back, Klara."

She was pulling at the ragged edge of her pantaloons with frantic fingers in an effort to haul them high enough to cover her chest. She succeeded only in ripping them more.

"T' doggie, we left t' doggie. T' Ruski's will steal him. Boil and et him. T' missus gonna kill me."

"What if the spies are still there?" Klara looked up at Sofia.

"Don care."

By the time Klara and Sofia found their way back to the swimming place, the sun was low on the horizon.

"I didn't know we had run so far. We've missed supper for sure."

"Where's t' doggie? Bobo. Bobo. Cum out ye dirty runt."

"Our clothes. Where are they?"

"Missus kill me sure. Doggie, here doggie."

"The Ruski spies probably stole them. Let's go. We'll be in big trouble if we don't get home."

"No. Got to find runt." Sofia took off up the river bank in the opposite direction.

"Come back, you booby."

Klara ran after her. They thrashed through the brush, hunting the missing dog until the sun slipped below the skyline. As the light faded, the temperature dropped and though it was springtime, the night was cold. Unsure of the way back, the two girls crawled under a fallen tree to wait for morning.

~~~

When Mr. Lof found them, they were huddled together, cold and frightened. He left Sofia with her mother, Britz, where her punishment was sure and immediate. Even before Mr. Lof led Klara from the yard, they could hear her screams. Without a backward glance, he found an old horse blanket and wrapped it around Klara.

"Now to get you home. Your pappa has been out all night looking for you."

He helped her into the wagon and whipped the horse into a trot. By the time Klara was deposited in her mother's arms, her teeth were chattering and her head ached.

After a dose of dried sword lily and willow bark steeped in a spoon of *brannvin*, she was put to bed. Chills and fever kept her tossing and sweating through the next several days. To her family it seemed that she lay abed a very long time, though Klara had little recollection of her illness. Her fine blond hair fell out and was growing in course and black by the time she was up and around again.

No trace of the little dog, Bobo, was ever found, but the story of dog-eating spies circulated through the parish for a long time.

We Walk Through The Valley.

Two years went by and the family living in the small house under the hill continued to grow. Klara now had three younger brothers, Ivar, James, and Will, in addition to her sister, Stina, and older stepsisters, Hulda and Sonja. Her granpappa, Erik Axel Norrling, still lived by himself in the dugout room behind the chimney. Though the rest of the family crammed into the main room of the house, no one ever considered allowing or demanding that some of the children share the room with their grandfather.

Nine in number, they lived and slept in one room, a room shared with stove and fireplace, table, benches, loom and churn, and in winter, shared with racks of drying bread, drying clothing, drying shoes, cooped chickens, the family dog, and various ailing calves or goatlets or lambs. Anna and Per claimed the cupboard bed, while the four girls shared the straw pallets they unrolled on the benches. The boys, Ivar and James, slept where they could, in the stable in warm weather, wedged in with the older girls as winter blew in. Will, the youngest, slept with his parents.

~~~

In mid-summer of 1894, Hulda and Sonja were away from home with the livestock at summer pasture. Because Hulda planned to leave for Stockholm in the fall, the two sisters were sharing a last mountain summer together. The rest of the children, Klara, Ivar, James, and even little Will, had outdoor chores enough to keep them busy from first light until dark.

Klara's mother, Anna, stood on the flat stone that served as a step at the front door and summoned Klara in from the garden.

"Klara, come here. Now."

"What, Mamma?"

"Come go with Granpappa. He wants to look for some herbs for his rheumatism. Help him over the rough spots."

She handed Klara a spading fork almost as tall as the eleven-year old girl.

"See that you're back in time for supper."

"Yes, Mamma," said Klara.

She was glad to get out of weeding beans and picking bugs off the potato plants. Her back ached and it was hours until lunch time. She watched Granpappa totter out of the house.

He looks like father time, himself, thought Klara. His beard and fringe of white hair hung to his waist. His face was dominated by dim blue eyes set in parchment skin under brows shaggy as a pony's forelock. He wore a black felt hat battered shapeless by the years and so loose it settled over his pendulous ears.

"Time's a wasting, child."

"I'm coming."

"Hurry up, hurry up."

Granpappa urged Klara to move faster, though he seemed to move in slow motion himself, picking up each foot extra high and selecting the right spot to place it before raising the other foot. He waggled his elbows and stabbed the ground with the burly stick he used to balance and support himself.

Klara took a firmer grip on the three-pronged spade and joined her granpappa on his trek across the farmyard to the woods beyond. How blue the sky looks when you can stand up straight, stretch your arms wide, and breathe the sweet air of the forest. So much better than stooping, stooping and smelling the stable muck used to fertilize the potatoes.

A short way into the woods, Klara stopped. She crouched on a cool bed of moss and fern.

"Is this it, Granpappa? This skinny plant with the pricky leaves?"

"Harump. Maybe so, maybe so. Does it have leaves growing opposite from each other?"

"Yes, Granpappa." Klara plucked one of the delicate plants and held it close to the old man's watery eyes.

"Drat it, child, I can't see it when you hold it so close."

He took her wrist between his rough fingers and moved the plant to arms length. He didn't try to take the plant from her with his swollen, bulbous-jointed grasp. He squinted his eyes and moved his head back and forth, trying to see the plant. Klara thought he looked like an old cow startled by an intruder. The animals always moved their heads like that.

"Does it have a flower yet?" he said. "It should have a white flower."

"No, but I'll look at the others. The plants growing in the sun may have flowers already."

Klara walked around the old tree to inspect the plants on the other side, then moved to an ancient oak just beyond. She was sure they had the right plant when she spied several white flowers peaking out at her. She snatched one up and ran back, surprised at how far she had strayed.

"Granpappa, where are you? Where are you?"

Klara looked in every direction. Am I in the right place, she wondered.

"Granpappa, come out. I'm here now."

Was he playing a game with her? She looked behind the row of saplings, then jerked back, embarrassed. Even the dog couldn't hide behind those slender trees.

She began running back and forth across the open place until she had covered every inch of it. Each time she returned to the moss bed where she had last seen her granpappa, she expected to see him standing there, huddled over his walking stick. Each time, she found no one.

Klara called, she ran, she looked behind every bush and tree in the clearing. She heard no answer, saw no trace. Afraid to venture farther into that particular part of the forest alone, she gave up and pounded up the path to the house.

Hours later, Klara's father and several neighbors returned to the house no more successful than Klara had been. She had led them to the spot she last saw Erik Axel, then returned home at her father's insistence.

Anna was pacing up and down the yard when she heard the men cross the farmyard. Per looked tired and his hands and forearms were scratched and dirty.

"Did you find him, Per?"

"No, Anna. I'm sorry. We've searched the whole area."

"Please do something."

"We've searched the woods and the slope below the barn. It's a puzzlement to me. He couldn't have gone very far. He can hardly walk."

"What are we going to do?"

"We need to eat. Send Ivar to tell Mrs. Lof that her husband and hired man are staying, then have him go to the Hansson place. We need more searchers."

When the men went out again, Anna, Klara, and Stina fed the chickens and horses, milked the one goat left on the homeplace, carried water, and chopped wood for the cook stove. Then, though it wasn't churning day, Anna poured the accumulation of cream into the big churn and set Klara to work. She, herself, sat down at the loom across the room and tried to finish the strip of cloth she had been weaving before Granpappa's disappearance.

Too young to really understand, but happy with the respite from hoeing, Stina, James, and Will played quietly in the corner. The room soon filled with the monotonous lubbing of the churn and the clack and snick of the shuttle, over and over in a mind-numbing chorus.

Stina, James, and Will were sound asleep on the straw pallet bed when Per returned. A shake of his head told them they had not found Granpappa yet.

"Maybe it would be of help if Klara came with us. Show us the place again."

"At least it's still light," said Anna.

Automatically she got up to find something for her husband to eat and to hunt up a sweater for Klara.

While Klara dressed, Per ate his butter smeared *thinbrod*.

"It's cool for a summer night," he said. "Come along, now, Klara."

Outside Mr. Lof bent down and spoke slowly and carefully to Klara.

"I want you to pretend I'm your granpappa and show us exactly where you went this afternoon, every step."

Klara thought this an odd thing to do, but squinted up her eyes with the effort to remember. With Mr. Lof at her side and the other searchers fanning out behind them, Klara walked slowly across the farmyard and down the path into the spruce forest.

"Are you sure you came this way?"

"Yes. See these broken places in the moss? It's where I started digging around looking for Granpappa's herbs."

"Started?"

"Granpappa said the plants were too small. He wanted big ones with flowers, so I left him to look on the other side."

"He was here when you left him?"

"Think hard, Klara. Did he say anything?"

At first, Klara just shook her head, then she looked at her father with sudden realization spreading over her face.

"Rushes, rushes to hold the poltice. He said we'd hunt rushes next."

"Rushes? Where do rushes grow around here?"

Mr. Lof was already heading for the low side of the clearing.

"The swampy place near the river," said Per. Excitement tinged his voice. "It's downhill, so he may have felt he didn't need Klara."

"Could he have walked that far?" Mr. Lof seemed to have forgotten Klara's presence.

"Probably thought he could. He's a stubborn old coot."

Per followed Mr. Lof to the edge of the forest before he thought to tend to Klara. He could barely see her in the dim light across the clearing. He walked back to her and pointed her in the right direction and gave her a firm shove.

"Go back to the house, child. Tell your mamma we search the path to the river now."

"Please, Pappa. Let me stay."

"Go. Your mother needs you."

"But, Pappa...."

~~~

Klara didn't know how long she had been asleep, when she heard voices outside. She opened the door of the cupboard bed, her parent's bed, where she had been sleeping. The light from a candle on the table did little to push back the darkness. At first, Klara thought the room empty except for the huddled shapes of the sleeping children on the straw pallet nearby, then she saw her mother standing, gray and alone, waiting by the door.

The silence of the room was barely violated by the small group of men stooping through the low door, their entrance made awkward by the long bundle they carried.

Klara watched the stillness of her mother's face shatter like the surface of a clear pool broken by a thrown stone. The waves of anguish moved across her features to draw her mouth into a trembling grimace, her eyes, her cheeks all pulled awry and the tears washed down into her silent scream.

As she knelt on the hard bed, Klara realized she was crying, too, and trembling so hard she thought she would never stop. It was all her fault. She should never have left Granpappa alone.

"Put him in the dugout room behind the fireplace," said Anna. "It's too late to make preparations tonight."

"Yes, Mum."

"What happened? Where did you find him."

Anna's voice was choked and soft. She followed the men to the doorway of the dugout room, then she whirled around and ran to her sewing basket.

"The lock of hair, I must cut a lock of hair."

She upset the basket, dropping buttons, scraps, and needles on the floor as she rummaged. Only when she found the scissors did she stop. She ran back to the bedroom, waving the shears.

The men ignored her until they finished arranging their burden on the bed. When they stepped back, Anna slipped one hand under her father's head and drew out a hank of hair from the back of his head. She cut it off and pushed past the men to the front room. They followed her, not wanting to stay in the presence of death any longer than necessary.

Mr. Lof picked up a strand of yarn from the spilled sewing basket.

"Let me help you with that, Mrs. Larsson."

He tied the yarn around the bundle of long gray hair and made a loop in it. It was the custom to hang the lock of hair on the door to warn people of the dead one inside.

"There. I'll hang it on the door on the way out."

"Thank you."

Anna went to her husband, stood by his side.

"What happened?"

"He didn't go far."

"No. We must have walked past him a dozen times."

"If the boy hadn't slipped down, we'd be searching still."

"You mean Ivar? Are you all right, Ivar?"

For the first time Anna noticed Ivar sitting by the door scrapping mud from his boots. She ran to him and reached for his hand, brushed his hair from his forehead.

"I'm fine, Mamma. It was a big old sink hole. Must have opened up after that rain last week." He pulled away from his mother's grasp. "I didn't actually fall into the hole."

"A shaft cave-in from the old Copper Mountain Mine, I expect."

"I'll send the hired girl over in the morning," said Mr. Lof. "With your grown girls off at the *langfabod* with the cows, your missus will need some help with the washing and laying out."

"One of my boys can go to the parish office tomorrow," said Mr. Hansson.

He touched his hat to Anna and backed out the door, almost tripping over the high board sill. Per followed him outside.

"Thanks for helping."

"Expect you'll want the burial as soon as possible."

~~~

While the women worked in the house, Per and Ivar built the coffin. A neat stack of planed boards had been set aside for this purpose some years earlier as was customary when there was an old one in the household. With Ivar to help measure and hold the pieces, while he drove the nails, the job was finished by noon.

Klara shuttled back and forth between the women working in the house and the yard where her father hammered the sweet pine boards together. The air seemed alive with the shrill of insects gathering nectar from the flowers and the sky domed blue over her head. How hard it is, she thought, to remember to feel sad. Why isn't it gray and rainy today?

"Now we must stain the box black and we'll be done for now," said Per.

He brought a crock of linseed oil down from a high shelf and motioned to Ivar.

"Find a clean stick to stir this and I'll add the soot."

With his father's help Ivar used a bit of rag for the messy job of coating the raw wood of the coffin.

"What a mess."

"We'll wipe off the residue and polish it a little after we eat."

"It looks ugly," said Klara.

Near tears, she watched the pale blond coffin turn black and ominous under her father's able direction. A pang of dread, the dread of grief and guilt, made her feel sick and ashamed.

"Not so good as if we had paint, but paint costs. The color will hold until it's in the ground. None to see it then, anyway." Per looked at Klara. "Why don't you go to the garden clearing and gather your apron full of flowers and ferns. We'll line the inside of the box and your granpappa will lie surrounded by the outdoors. It won't matter what the box looks like then."

"Yes. Yes, Pappa. I'll get daisies and purple loosestrife, goldenrod and anemones, and cattails. They'll look so pretty together."

Klara smiled and raced to gather the flowers. She finally a job she understood in the confusion of the day.

~~~

With the help of the Lof's hired girl, Anna and the younger children set the yeast rising for the funeral cakes and laid a fire to heat the oven. They heated the flat irons at the same time and pressed the dead man's suit, then their own best dresses. By the time Klara came in, they were ready to wash and dress Granpappa's body.

"Stina, mix the dough. We need to get Granpappa ready," said Anna. "Let James help."

"Can I help with the bread, Mamma?" said Klara.

"No. We need you to help with Granpappa. Carry the water basin to the back bedroom."

"Do I have to?"

Klara was suddenly frightened. She did not want to see a dead person. Her mother seemed not to hear. She was handing the hired girl a stack of towels and gathering Granpappa's shirt and suit coat in her arms. Klara sighed and followed the two women.

The laying out was both fascinating and horrible. Granpappa seemed far away. His body was so small and shriveled, so cold and waxy, it wasn't real, except for the eyes. He seemed to watch them as they worked.

By late afternoon Erik Axel Norrling's earthly shell was dressed in the suit he had worn at his confirmation fifty years ago. Split up the back to fit his matured body, the old fashioned suit gave the crumpled figure a rakish air it had never enjoyed in life. He rested in the bed of fern and flowers. Klara watched her mother place his hands on his sunken chest, crossed at the wrist. The hired girl combed his hair across his age-freckled forehead to cover the abraded spot on his temple where he had hit his head in his fall at the sink hole.

Anna closed the dead man's eyes with her thumbs, but when the lids wouldn't stay down, she sent Klara for a needle and thread. While she held the lids down, she directed Klara to put a stitch in each eyelid to keep them in place.

"I can't," said Klara. "I'll hurt him."

"Don't be silly. He can't feel anything." Anna was trembling and pale. She sat down on the stool by the door. "We'll try again in a minute."

"How do you know?" said Klara. "How do you know he can't feel anything?"

Anna got up and thumbed the dead man's eyelids down again.

"Now, Klara. Do it now."

The hired girl turned her head away as Klara whip-stitched her granpappa's eyelids shut.

Per came in and nailed the coffin lid in place. Now polished to a high shine, the wood grain glowed through the blackening.

"Get the funeral towels for your father, Klara," said Anna. She seemed determined to do everything correctly.

Klara reached the linen towels down from their customary place on the small shelf by the door. The long narrow strips of fabric were not really towels, rather, they were used to carry the coffin out of the house and, again, to let it down into the grave. Decorated with cross-stitch embroidered designs representing the tree of life, they always lay in readiness on a small shelf beside the door or hanging from the bed posts. When the coffin was carried from the house, it rested on three of the long linen strips, one at the head, one at the foot, and one in the middle.

Per and Ivar held the ends of the front strip, Anna and the hired girl handled the strip at the foot, while Klara and Stina balanced things in the middle.

They carried the coffin to the well house where it would wait until morning. This little outbuilding was barely large enough to hold the coffin's length cross-wise, but it was thought to be the coolest place in the farmstead. There, with the company of three fat white candles, Grandfather Norrling would spend the night. The next day he would make his last journey to the churchyard at Smedjebacken.

They sent the hired girl home with a basket of mushrooms and a round of bread as payment. When they got back to the house, Per and the boys cut and spread pine boughs on the floor and around the front stoop. Anna, Klara, and Stina set out a cold supper. Before they could sit down to eat, someone knocked on the door. Klara went to answer it.

"Come in," she said to the girl in the doorway. To her family she said, "It's Sofia, Britz's daughter."

"No, no, I just brung these pretties. Mrs. Lof, she sent 'em. From her garden, I think, or maybe she forced 'em. From bulbs, ya know.

Tuberoses, she names 'em. She knowed ya wouldn't have any. Only the best families have nice things."

Sofia thrust the mass of flowers into Klara's hands, turned around, and bolted down the path towards home. In her haste she allowed her ragged skirt to hike up past her knees, revealing her dirty feet, bare legs, and pantaloons gray with dirt or inefficient washing.

Klara shouted for her old chum to stop and supper with them, but Sofia gave no indication she heard the invitation.

"Take the flowers to the well house, Klara. Right now," said Per.

Too late. The thick cloying odor of the tuberoses had already permeated the air of the house. Not really roses, the stalks of small waxy flowers were synonymous with death and funerals. The heavy polluting scent of the white blossoms had been used to cover the stink of death for so long, it had become the smell of decay, itself. Klara hurried to the well house to place the flowers on the coffin.

~~~

Klara awoke the next morning with the sound of pounding rain in her ears. She hurried to wash and braid her hair anew. Already dressed, Anna wore her one good dress, a respectable black wool with a high collar and wrist tight sleeves puffed at the shoulder. She paced the floor by the window with jerky steps.

"What will we do?"

"We will do our best, Anna." Per appeared tired, his eyes squinty in the early morning light, his mouth drawn, thin-lipped. "This rain has most certainly turned the roads to mud, ankle-deep mud. The mare is only a few weeks past foaling, too."

"Maybe we could borrow a team from the Lofs or the Hanssons," said Ivar.

He, too, had on his Sunday suit, pant legs short, coat tight across his shoulders, worn shiny at the knees.

"Perhaps, but I surely hate beholding to either of them."

"Well, whose fault is it we don't have another horse to team with the mare?"

Ivar sounded angry, bitter beyond his years. He slicked back his hair at the cracked mirror over the wash basin and poked the comb into his back pocket.

"Hush, Ivar. It was an accident." Per sat down at the table. "We were lucky the Lof's didn't ask for recompense for the wagon."

Klara ladled out porridge into her father's bowl, then served her brothers. Lastly, she divided the remaining porridge between Stina and herself. Her mother refused to eat.

~~~

"Come along, Ivar," said Per. "We'll load the coffin, while the women clean up here."

Anna stood by the bed twisting her long string of jet beads around and around with fluttering hands, hands which seemed incapable of either purposeful action or stillness.

Ivar looked pale, almost sick, but he pushed his bowl aside and followed his father out of the house. Klara wondered if he felt that much grief at Granpappa's death or was it just the turmoil of preparation. She knew her brother thrived on routine and hated, almost feared change.

"Stop daydreaming, Klara. Get the basket of remembrance cakes and we'll be off."

~~~

We must be a strange spectacle, thought Klara. She tried to imagine the picture they made as they straggled and struggled along the road to Smedjebacken. A creaking wagon pulled by a sweat-soaked, muddy-legged mare with a bright bay foal leaping and bouncing at her thin ribs. Per and Anna Larsson sat together on the wagon box with their funeral black stifling them with woolen efficiency. Behind the wagon came the children carrying their shoes, the boys with their pant legs rolled high, the girls holding long skirts above the muck of the road. In the wagon the coffin lolled on a bed of wilted flowers, where its new coat of black stained everything it touched including the strips of linen used to lower it into the ground. With a sigh Klara realized she was thinking about scrubbing the linen strips back to their pristine whiteness instead of remembering her grandfather, dead in his coffin.

The tolling church bell announced the last part of the journey, the hardest part of the road, the uphill section to the church. The village called Smedjebacken, the smithy on the hill because the blacksmith's shop once stood on the high land now dominated by the church. The cemetery shared the hilltop with the church. Anyone, landlord or pauper, registered in the parish, Norrbarke parish, was entitled to burial in the church cemetery without charge.

Klara surveyed the small group of people gathered around the open grave. They were mostly old, very, very old. Did these men and women know her grandfather in his youth or did they just show up as mourners at every funeral? No flicker of recognition touched her as she watched them. Perhaps she had seen them at the sporadic Sunday services she had attended or the market in town.

The minister's voice put an end to her speculation. The coffin swayed on the linen strips just above the hole, held by Mr. Lof, Mr. Hansson, and several of the men of the community. They were ready to let it down into the ground. The minister asked for the shovel.

"Dust thou art and unto dust thou shalt return."

The minister shoveled up a small amount of earth and took a handful. He spilled the dirt over the coffin.

"But, Jesus, the Almighty God, will waken you on the last days."

With a second and third handful of earth, he repeated the words.

"Marvel not at this: for the hour is coming, in which all that are in the graves shall hear His voice, and shall come forth; they that have done good, unto the resurrection of life; and they that have done evil, unto the resurrection of damnation."

Klara cringed at the minister's emphasis on the words, evil and damnation.

The service over, the assembled people threw flowers onto the coffin as it was lowered into the ground. On leaving each adult took a remembrance cake from the baskets Stina and Ivar held. The cakes were stamped with a design symbolic of the tree of life.

~~~

The trip home was more funereal than the trip to the church yard and the burial service combined. The exhausted mare could barely haul the empty wagon along through the deep shadows of sundown. Her load consisted of the stained funeral towels, the empty cake baskets, and the family's shoes. Even the bay foal walked slowly along behind his dam.

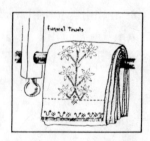

Part Two–Klara..1896–1900.

Mugwort, Horsetail, and Bay Tree Berries.

When Klara emerged into the full sun of the clearing, she stopped to catch a better grip on the edges of her apron without spilling the mass of flowers it contained. The Swedish countryside was in the full bloom of its brief summer and twelve-year old Klara Larsson stood on the threshold of her own blooming.

Sunlight filtered through the tall fir trees guarding the rutted path which wound from the river to the farmyard where a small house sat hard against the hillside. The young girl, barefoot and tender, picked her way around puddles and sharp stones as fast as she could without dropping her burden. Now and then, the breeze drifted the sound of hooves and iron clad wheels from the Grangeburg road to her ears, but Klara was too intent on her project to notice.

She burst in the door of the house, not yet tall enough to have to duck to miss hitting her head on the doorframe. Dark hair escaped from her tight braids and lay plastered to her skin. Skirt hiked high, face flushed with excitement, she thrust her armful of sweet columbine, field daisy, wild rose, and yellow butterweed towards her mother.

"Look, Mamma, the river bank is covered with flowers."

The flowers glowed in the dimmer light of the room, but the woman bending over a basin near the stove seemed not to notice.

Klara buried her face in the bouquet.

"They smell sooo sweet, Mamma."

Without waiting for an answer she poured her load of flowers out on the table and began rummaging through the pantry cupboard. She found an old enamel milk pitcher to hold her wealth of blooms and ran to fill it from the bucket outside the door.

"Don't they look pretty? I wish summer was forever."

She gave a drooping stem of wild rose a tweak to complete her arrangement in the center of the table.

"Clean up your mess, Klara."

Anna, spread her towel to dry over the edge of the shallow basin where she washed dishes, then sat down. Her movements were slow, heavy footed.

Even Klara could see her mother was uncomfortable, in pain.

"Will the baby come today, Mamma?"

Klara stooped to pick up the clots of leaves and dirt she had trailed across the floor from the front door. She could remember when three year old Will had been born. To her it had seemed a long and messy affair, so she was surprised when the adults said how quick and easy the birth had been. That was the first time she had been allowed to stay at a birthing. She was only seven when James was born and five when Stina came along; Ivar was before her memory. On those occasions her stepsister, Sonja, had led her to a neighbors or to the granary to play.

Klara wondered about Sonja. And Hulda, too. Her stepsisters were nearly grown now. Sonja, at sixteen, had left home just a few weeks ago. Hulda had gone three years before. She had boarded the train at Ludvika and traveled to the city. Being an honest, hard-working girl, not unattractive, she had immediately found work at the Grand Hotel. In April she had sent money to Sonja who quickly packed her belongings and caught the next train to Stockholm to join her. Now both girls worked as maids at the Grand, a first class hotel near the railroad station.

Klara was torn between her curiosity about the soon due baby and her desire to follow her stepsisters, to see the paved streets, the fancy carriages, the tall buildings, the ladies in fine clothing.

"Oh bother," Klara mumbled to herself. She had dropped a clot of mud on her skirt.

"Day dreaming, Klara? You're dropping more of those weeds than you're picking up. Get the broom and do it right."

"Yes, Mamma."

~~~

Early next morning Klara was shouted awake by her father, Per. His voice was rough with anxiety.

"Get up, Klara. Run to the Lof place. Ask Mrs. Lof if she'll come back with you. Hurry now."

When Klara returned with Mrs. Lof huffing and gasping for breath behind her, she could hear her mother's screams from across the yard. Mrs. Lof hurried into the house. Klara entered more timidly, fearful of what she would find. She placed Mrs. Lof's knitted bag on the table and went to stand beside her father.

"Please leave us, Mr. Larsson," said Mrs. Lof. "I'm sure you have chores."

"Will she be all right?"

"Take them with you."

She gestured at Ivar, Klara's younger brother. He sat in the shadows with the other children, biting his finger nails and plucking at stray threads in his britches. They leaped up to follow their father from the house.

Mrs. Lof studied the woman on the bed, noted her pallor, bluish lips, and sweat-beaded forehead, then drew back the heavy quilt that covered Anna to her chin.

"Feeling a chill are we, dearie? I'll have that kiddel out and howling before you know it."

She examined her patient quickly, before another contraction could tear through Anna. Her long experience as midwife told her trouble had a good foothold here. A woman with six confinements behind her was either a quick birthing or a long struggle fraught with danger. She pulled the bloody sheet from the bed.

"Get me some clean towels and a basin of water, Klara, then start these filthy rags to soaking."

While Klara ran to obey, Mrs. Lof made a more thorough examination.

"When did the pains start? Yesterday? And bleeding? Did you have bleeding yesterday, too? Off and on all week, you say. That's not good, but don't worry. I've not lost a patient since Mrs. Tolsson. Poor soul just wouldn't stop bleeding."

She took the basin from Klara, positioned the dry towels, and began wiping Anna's face and neck.

"Get her a clean handkerchief to bite down on when the next pain comes."

"Is it bad?"

Klara felt light-headed from anxiety and fear, from such a vigorous run to the neighbor's farm without breakfast, from the overwhelming presence of Mrs. Lof.

"Now what?"

Mrs. Lof peered up at Klara, seemed to see her for the first time.

"Get some food into your stomach, child. I don't need another patient to worry over."

Anna's arms and legs twitched and her body spasmed with new pain. As she opened her mouth to scream, Mrs. Lof inserted the folded handkerchief between her teeth.

"Bite on that, dearie. Push, now."

Klara nearly passed out watching Mrs. Lof hold her mother down. When the contraction had finished, Klara breathed out a great gasp of air.

"You can't be laboring with her, child. I need you to help."

"What should I do?"

"My bag has some packages of herbs. You need to boil a kettle of water, then I'll give you directions for making up the medicine."

Klara felt better with knowing she could do something. She ran to fill the kettle and soon had the water boiling. She chewed a little dry bread as she waited for it to boil.

"I have the water hot. Now what do I do?"

"Take a handful of mugwort, that's the dried leaves in the biggest packet, and about six drops of the pennyroyal oil. Put it in a china bowl and pour a cup of boiling water over it. After your mamma drinks it, she should have a contraction strong enough to pop the kiddel right out."

The decoction had a strong mint odor which grew stronger as Klara stirred it.

"It's too hot," said Klara. "Can I put some cold water with it?"

"No. We don't want to weaken it. She won't take much. A little sugar and a drop of milk is all right, though."

The pennyroyal curdled the milk, but Mrs. Lof urged Anna to drink it down. Satisfied, she let Anna lay back on the pillow.

"Now take a deep breath, dearie."

"Can't you give her something for the pain?"

"Tis pain that brings the baby."

Klara was shocked at the violent contraction the tea produced. She leaned against the wall and hugged herself. With her eyes squeezed shut she tried to imagine the fun she would have with the other girls at the *langfabod* in a few weeks. She bit her lower lip until the sharp taste of her own blood brought her back to the present.

As Anna's labor progressed, Klara found there was little she could do except wash out the sweat soaked cloths and endless wads of bloody rag Mrs. Lof dropped on the floor. At mid-day she carried bread, cheese, and salt fish outside for her father and the children. Mrs. Lof ate while she worked, oblivious of the pain and blood.

Near two o'clock Mrs. Lof told Klara to boil another kettle of water.

"This time we'll use the bay tree berries. It's the strongest medicine I know. Seven berries in a half cup of water. Make sure you count out the right number of berries."

"What will the berries do for Mamma?"

Klara felt sick, nauseous and dizzy, but she counted the berries over and over before she put them into the cup. I'm never, ever going to get married, she thought.

Mrs. Lof had to force the bay tree decoction through her patient's clenched teeth.

"Kill or cure time. Go outside, child. Gather a bundle of horsetail and a bunch of last year's cattail. I saw them growing along the low marshy place by the rhune stone. We'll need them to stop the bleeding."

Klara stood staring at Mrs. Lof, who repeated her instructions, louder and firmer this time.

"Tell your father to come in, too. Tell him I need his help."

"I can help."

Klara wanted to leave. More than anything, she wanted to be somewhere else, anywhere else, yet she stood staring at Mrs. Lof, trying not to look at her mother writhing on the bed.

"You're not strong enough. Send your father. Quick now."

Klara bolted for the door, unable to get out of the house fast enough now that she had her legs moving. At the granary she repeated Mrs. Lof's words to her father, then grabbed a basket from a shelf and ran down the path to the rhune stone.

She tried to blot the scene in the house from her mind by thrashing through the horsetail, trying to jam every single stalk she saw into her basket. She felt leaving just one of the odd plants would cause dire consequences. Maybe the one fragile stem she left behind would be the one that would make her mother well again. When her basket would hold no more, she pulled a mess of cattail. Some of the heads burst and filled the air with frizzy seed carriers.

When she reached the house, her basket heaped full, Mrs. Lof was waiting at the door.

"Land's sake, child. I don't need the whole patch."

The midwife had lost her calm demeanor. Her face was flushed and sweat beaded her broad forehead. She snatched the basket from Klara and turned to go back inside.

"Wait, Mrs. Lof. How is Mamma? Can I come in?"

Klara felt the panic rise up through her chest to set her thoughts reeling again.

"Has the baby come yet?"

"So many questions, when a body is in a hurry."

Mrs. Lof took Klara by the upper arm and pulled her into the house.

"Here, then. See for yourself."

She shoved Klara towards the bed where her mother lay, pale, eyes closed, but breathing in short shallow gasps. The swaddled baby, squinch-eyed and puffy-red, had been placed in the cradle near the head of the bed, where Per sat watching. He had sweated through his heavy work shirt, but whether it was from exertion or nervous fear, Klara couldn't tell.

Mrs. Lof said, "We make a poultice to get the bleeding stopped. Bruise the horsetail, then we'll boil them a little to soften them."

She demonstrated by scrunching a stalk along its length between her fingers, then tossing it into the simmering water on the stove.

"Hurry, child. Time is wasting."

Klara barely heard Mrs. Lof's order. She had to see the baby, touch its tiny puckery mouth and smooth cheek, be certain it lived by watching the swaddled chest move gently up and down.

"So little, it's so little. Is it a boy or a girl?"

"A girl and not so small either. Now get to work, child."

While the horsetail simmered on the stove, they stripped the soft heads from the cattails. Mrs. Lof soaked the soft mass in the juice from the horsetails and packed it tight between Anna's legs and wrapped her with a strip of cloth. With a practiced hand the midwife flipped the cover over the exhausted woman.

"Rest now. In a few days you'll be good as new."

She spent some time giving Per instructions, but Klara was too busy clucking to the baby to notice.

~~~

They named the new baby Astrid Marie, a name full of soaring promise. The first hours after her birth, she lay quiet in the old, hand-carved cradle. While Anna slept, Per brought the children to see the new baby.

"Quiet now. Just look. You can hold her later."

Stina, Ivar, and the younger children gathered around the cradle to watch the baby squinch her eyes and wave her hands back and forth.

"Lookie. She's swimming," said James.

"Is she supposed to be so wrinkly?" asked Ivar.

"Prunes. Her cheeks look like prunes," said James.

Two-year old Will, no longer baby of the family, ran around the room muttering prune baby, prune baby. When no one noticed, he puckered his lips, scrunched up his face, and crawled into the circle of his siblings. He flopped over on his back and began flailing his arms wildly. James fell down beside him and joined in.

"Stop it, you two."

"Yes, stop. Before you wake Mamma."

Per stepped in and grabbed the scuffling boys. He sat them down on the bench by the fireplace and admonished them to behave or else.

The baby whimpered a bit, then let out a fierce howl. Anna sat up, seemed to reach toward the screaming baby, then lay back and turned her face to the wall.

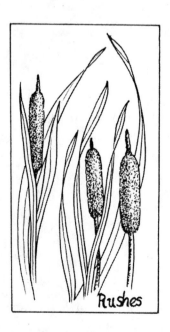

Rushes

Moochie, The Nisse Child.

The baby continued her howling. Per picked her up from the cradle and tried to place her at Anna's breast. Neither babe, nor mother took notice of one another. Klara took the child and paced the floor with her. The newborn stiffened her body and screamed harder.

"Why is she screaming?" asked Stina.

"Mrs. Lof said we could feed her goat milk." Klara put the infant back in the cradle.

"I'll heat it."

Klara and Stina took turns soaking a rag in warm milk and squeezing it into the baby's mouth.

"Why doesn't she suck, Klara?"

With milk rivualing down her arm, Stina tried to aim the stream into the puckery little mouth.

"Don't babies know how to suck when they're born? The baby goats always know how."

"I don't know, Stina. Maybe she's a little slow from having such a hard time being born."

"But she'll learn won't she? Won't she?"

Klara wiped up the ropy drool and tried again. Between screams she dabbled milk into the tiny mouth. Most of it burbled back out.

"Stroke her throat with your finger. Gently, now. Maybe it will help her swallow."

"It looks like she's chewing, but her mouth is all limp."

"Her tongue isn't helping either."

Klara slid her finger into the baby's mouth and held her tongue down before dabbing in the milk.

"She swallowed. I know she did."

"I'll try again," said Klara.

It was a slow process, but the girls managed to get a few spoons of milk into the baby before she fell asleep on Klara's shoulder. By taking turns holding the baby they managed to strip both her and the cradle. With dry bedding, and a new flannel wrap, the baby was back in her snug place.

"There. All done," said Klara. "Except for washing this stuff, that is."

"I think we should call her Moochie. At least until she learns to eat properly."

"Soon, I hope."

"Nighty, night, Moochie."

Klara and Stina argued briefly about washing the baby things immediately or in the morning. Klara won and they spent an hour sudsing the milk soaked flannel, binder, blanket, and quilt. Wrung out and draped over a line above the stove, they filled the close room with the heavy smell of souring milk.

"They should be dry by morning," said Klara.

~~~

Long before morning Moochie's screams jarred the household from their warm beds. When Anna did not respond, Klara roused Stina and they repeated the tedious feeding procedure. The girls got her fed and cleaned though Moochie fought them the whole time.

Anna was strong enough to be up cooking a little and taking care of herself at week's end, though she wasn't up to the heavy work. The scrubbing, laundry, carrying wood and water were too much for her. She ignored Moochie and seemed to have forgotten she had ever birthed the child.

When the girls weren't feeding or washing Moochie, they swaddled her and placed her in the cradle. At night Stina took her to bed with her in the dugout room behind the fireplace, Granpappa's old room.

The three boys shared one of the cupboard beds and Stina had the other. Klara slept on a bed that pulled out of one of the long benches in the main room, while her parents had the cupboard bed. A thin curtain pulled across the corner of the room gave them a measure of privacy.

This arrangement gave the household a measure of peace and allowed the girls to get on with their work, for a week or two. Then, on laundry day, while Stina hauled water from the well to fill the iron wash pots and Klara beat the loose dirt from a heap of work clothes, Moochie let out a scream that sent both girls running to the house.

"We just fed her," said Stina.

"Maybe something's poking her."

They lifted Moochie from the cradle, but could find nothing wrong. She was quiet while Stina held her, but screamed when she was put back in the cradle.

"Maybe she doesn't like being alone in the house."

"Let's take the cradle outside. We need to get the laundry going."

With Ivar's help they pulled the heavy cradle outside, but it didn't stop Moochie's screaming. Klara finally tucked the baby under her arm and went back to work.

"You can't carry her all the time," said Stina.

"Anything is better than screaming."

"How will we manage when you leave, Klara?" Stina was thinking about the summer trek to pasture with the goats.

~~~

Klara and Stina had proved to be good nurse maids. By the time Klara was ready to go to the *langfabod* Moochie was eating voraciously, grunting and drooling, but getting much of the goat's output of milk into her stomach.

"I wish I could go with you, Klara."

"Me too," said Ivar.

"Boys don't go, silly. You'd be teased forever."

"Better than listening to screaming Moochie."

"Maybe we can get Sofia to help out."

~~~

But, when she asked her father about having her friend over to help Stina with the baby, he chided her.

"What foolishness, Klara. We have no money to pay her wage."

"Three meals a day should be pay enough."

"Where would she sleep?"

"She could go home at night."

"Speak to her tomorrow. It's time the animals went to summer pasture."

~~~

Morning chores done, Klara slipped away from the house and made her way along the road to the Lof estate. Before she reached the looping drive to the house she turned onto a footpath worn deep by many feet. The path ran behind the cow barns and sheep sheds, past the manure piles and woodlots until it reached the muddy verge of the river where the cattle watered. The area also served as the estate's garbage heap, a great flotsam of cast off farm equipment, lumber, broken furniture, broken paving stones.

Had Klara been less distracted, she would have marveled over the fact that anyone could be rich enough to have such garbage. At her house everything was used and re-used ad infinititum. Forever and then once again for good measure.

She squinted her eyes against the glare from the water and found the low doorway of the sheep shed hidden amidst the junk. Was the flag out. Surely Missus Varm didn't have customers at this hour.

When Valter Varm died, the family had been evicted from the servant cottage behind the main house. Unable or unwilling to look for work elsewhere and pregnant with Sofia, Britz Varm had moved to the unused shed by the river. And there she stayed, eking out a living by lying on her back for anyone with pennies to pay.

~~~

Per tugged the reluctant goatlet from the stable. The animal's tiny hooves flailed at the hard packed dirt and he twisted in his halter until it seemed his slender neck would snap His mother, shut up in a stall, called and argued to no avail. She must remain at the homeplace to feed the always hungry Moochie. The kid soon joined the milk cow and her heifer calf waiting in the yard. Klara would have to lead the reluctant animal on her trek to the far pasture.

When Per looked up from tying the kid to the fence, he saw a thin girl with white-blond hair emerge from the forest. From a distance she looked like a fairy child, but as she ambled across the clearing her smudged cheeks and filthy dress became visible. Per nudged Ivar and the boy ran to the house.

"Sofia's here. Pappa says it's time."

Klara folded the last of the laundry. "Be good and help with Moochie while I'm gone."

"Pappa says to hurry up. He has work to do."

"Tell Sofia to come in."

"She stinks."

"What?"

Ivar pinched his nose and gagged.

"Bring her to the side yard. The wash water is still warm."

"Stina. James. We have another bit of laundry to do."

They wrestled Sofia into the laundry tub, clothes and all, and soaped her clean. When she finally stood on the grass with water streaming from her hair and skirt, Klara found her an old dress and helped her dry off on a length of toweling.

"I have to go. Stina will help you get those rats nests out of your hair."

~~~

With Sofia to help with the baby, the household would manage to survive Klara's absence. Though several years younger, Stina taught Sofia how to braid her hair and do it up in ropes and whorls over her ears. They altered another old dress Klara had left for her. Sofia was taller, but much thinner, so the finished dress had an up-to-date flair to it.

When Klara returned from the *langfabod* at the end of summer, she found Sofia much changed. The dirty urchin had become a presentable young woman.

"My, my," said Klara. "You look like you're about to go courting."

"Don't want no fella."

Klara walked Sofia as far as the Lof driveway.

"Maybe you could help out during harvest," said Klara.

"I be grateful for the work, mind you," said Sofia. "Cain't come."

"A sack of flour and two *ore*?"

"At baby tis a devil. *Nisse* brung her."

"There's no one else I can ask. Please, Sofia."

"You think I so poor I have to look after that shit eater?"

"It can't be that bad."

"The screamin worms inta my belly. She be takin my soul if I stay."

With that Sofia bent to grab a handful of dust. She tossed it over her shoulder in the direction of the Larsson house and took off running towards home.

The Far Pasture.

Klara felt totally alone standing in the road watching her friend disappear through the trees. The warm satisfied glow she had worn home from her weeks at the *langfabod* dissipated like mist on a hot tile. She sat down on a rock and tried to recapture it. What did she like best. The freedom, fresh air, fat sausages roasted over the open fire, and talk. The six girls talked through breakfast, during milking, on the way to the day pasture, while cooling and skimming the milk, setting the cheese, at bedtime.

Even the trip to the summer farm had been fun. When Sofia had arrived to help with Moochie, Klara, her things rolled into her quilt, gathered up the lead ropes of the cow and the newly weaned goat kid and walked down the woodland path to join the other girls. The cow's new calf and her yearling trailed along behind with the two nanny goats.

Only the fresh nanny, the mother of the kid who tugged and struggled at the end of Klara's lead rope, stayed on the homeplace to provide milk for Moochie.

When they reached the Lof place, their troop increased two fold with the addition of several sleek-coated milkers and a herd of black-faced goats. The Lofs did not send a girl to help, but they did pay generous wages.

Lindy, the oldest of the herders, a girl with a generous figure and huge hands, slapped the newcomers into line and they were underway again. Two more farm stops and they were into open country, country too steep and rocky to grow crops or pasture.

"A nice lot this year," said a tiny girl named Inge. She was so fair it seemed that sunlight would pass right through her.

"Gobs of milk from this bunch," said Lotte, a girl as dark as Inge was fair. Her long hair was braided tight and rolled into two buns over her ears. She grinned up at one of the boys on horseback escorting the herders.

"Sure you won't camp with us this year, Tomas?"

"Sleep with these stinkin cows? You must be daft. You'll have the smell of them on you til Christmas."

Tomas gestured to the other man and they turned their horses to catch up a stray yearling trying to head home. Their job was to keep the livestock on the path, protect the herd and the girls, and pack their gear to the far pasture. With every bit of tillable land on the estates and farms used for growing grain, the livestock had to be taken to the forest some thirty miles away. The herder girls would spend the summer with them in return for small wages and a share of the milk and cheese.

"He's cute," said Lindy.

"Tomas? He looks like a wart hog."

"Not Tomas. The other one."

"Arvid Lindblad? Stay away from him, Lindy."

Lotte joined the conversation. "They say his pappa is a womanizer from way back."

"I only said he was cute. Not that I wanted to marry him," said Lindy.

"Like father, like son."

Klara listened to the talk with one ear. She wanted to ask about this Arvid fellow because she had heard Sofia mention him, but the newly weaned goat kid demanded her attention.

"He's hungry," said Lotte.

"Arvid?"

"No, silly. Klara's goatlet."

"See if he'll suck old Saddie here. He'll wear your arm off by the time we get to the farm."

They put the hungry kid to the placid old nanny. He sucked greedily, then stood stoically while she licked his face clean. With a sigh of relief Klara slipped the rope from his neck. The pair trotted back to the herd and the journey continued.

"See. I told you it would work," said Lotte.

If only they could foster baby Moochie off like that, thought Klara.

The first night in the open air the girls barely slept. The young men camped on one side of the clearing, the girls on the other with the livestock between them.

"Is he looking this way?" said Lindy.

"Don't be such a block head," said Lotte. "He's got a girl."

"Six or seven of them," said Inge. "Go to sleep."

"It isn't even dark yet."

"Lindy's got a fellow."

"Gaga over a handsome face. Are you in love?"

"Lindy's in love."

Lindy threw her feather pillow at her tormentors.

~~~

The next day's trek started at first light. The herders ate their bread and cheese as they moved the animals along. The animals kept to the path and moved briskly in the chill morning air, but by noon a sluggish pall seemed to envelope the group.

"The calves and kids need to rest and eat," said Inge. She spoke as much for herself as for the livestock.

"And drink. Are we near the watering place yet?" said Lotte.

Lindy, who had made the trek several times before, said she thought it was a mile or so, yet. She caught up with Arvid and walked at his stirrup for a few strides.

"Can you take Klara's goatlet on your horse? He's slowing us down."

"I'd rather take you."

"Don't tease."

"For you, anything."

He turned his horse and jogged back to pick up the weary animal.

Late in the afternoon of the third day they reached the *langfabod* with its sprawl of low dark buildings. A row of cattle sheds fronted on a small fenced meadow. A larger fenced hay field surrounded the buildings where the girls would live and work.

"Get the gate, Inge," shouted Lindy.

Inge ran ahead to pull the rails from the opening. The herd churned through to mill around a few minutes before dropping their heads to munch the knee high grass.

The animals secure, the girls hurried to the central building to direct the unloading of their supplies and start the fire in the open hearth.

"How old is this building, anyway?" said Klara. "It feels like a tomb."

"Hundreds and hundreds of years. There hasn't been heat in here for a year."

"Two years. We didn't use this camp last year," said Lindy.

The girls laid out their bedding on the low shelf built into the wall on one side of the room and their bowls, cheese presses, sieves, and buckets on the shelf on the other side. The center of the room was several steps below the level of the dirt floor to provide a cooler place for the milk. The building, itself, was constructed of split timbers, round side out. The roof was thatch and the sills and doors cedar.

"I asked the fellows to stay over. They can leave in the morning just as well."

"Where will they sleep?"

"In the cow shed. The animals can manage another night in the open."

"Speaking of cows. We better get on with the milking."

"Are the storage vats clean?"

"Of course not. Start scrubbing."

"It will take us a week to get caught up with all this milk. We should have dumped it in the forest."

"And throw out part of our wages?"

Two of the girls hauled the vats and kettles into the yard, while the other four went to separate the milkers from the yearlings. When they finished dividing the herd, they had twenty-eight cows and several dozen goats to be milked. The warm cow's milk was strained into the vats and set to cooling. By morning the cream would separate and the girls would skim it off to make butter.

"Oh my aching back," said Lotte.

"My poor fingers," said Klara. "I've never milked more than one cow before."

"You'll get used to it," said Lindy. "What can we fix for supper?"

"Did you invite the fellows?"

"Of course."

"Salt fish and hard tack. What a feast."

"Don't be so gloomy. We have rice. And cream."

"There's sugar and jam."

"*Ris* pudding. My favorite."

"Pancakes. We can make pancakes."

"I'll get the bacon frying," said Inge.

~~~

Despite her weariness, Klara had trouble sleeping that night. At moon rise she heard one of the other girls get up and tiptoe from the room. With equal caution Klara followed her outside and watched until she joined another shadowy figure at the edge of the forest. Lindy and Arvid. How could she, thought Klara.

She forgot Lindy's indiscretion in the hurry of the morning. Milking , unpacking, seeing the young men on their way. After a cold breakfast the girls churned the first batch of cream into butter and clabbered the leftover milk for cheese.

Klara relished the days when it was her turn to take the livestock to graze. She loved the freedom from the drudgery of pouring and heating milk, squeezing the whey from huge gobs of clabbered milk, dumping the milk solids into the cheese presses, freedom from cleaning, washing, scrubbing buckets, strainers, bowls, vats.

The stink of milk, fresh milk, sour milk, curdled milk, and clabbered milk mixed with the odor of fresh dung, stale dung, and cow breath threatened to smother her, so her days with the grazing animals in the meadow were like heaven. Some mornings she just stood at the edge of the clearing and breathed the pine air.

~~~

Klara looked up from her musings to see two little boys racing up the path.

"Will. James."

"Klara, Klara. Did you bring us a cheese? Stina said you'd bring a cheese."

"How is Mamma?"

"Is it in your bag?"

"Carry it to the house and we'll find out."

Klara picked up her bedroll and followed her brothers to the house where she helped them lift the heavy bag over the stoop.

Ivar grabbed the bag and hoisted it to the table. A dozen small soft cheeses rolled out before he pulled out a waxed round of cheese bigger than a platter and a foot thick.

"Now that's a real cheese," said Ivar.

"Can we eat it now?" said James.

"Not yet. By Christmas it will be aged enough," said Klara. "We'll have the soft cheese now."

In the background she could hear Stina pleading with Anna.

"Please take the baby for a little while."

"You can have your cheese later," said Anna.

Klara cut a section of cheese and sliced it thin. One plate for Mamma and one for Stina, she thought, then added a little extra to Stina's plate. Maybe Moochie would like a taste.

"Here's a sample, Mamma. The cheese came out extra good this year."

To Stina she said, "Bring the baby. We'll go outside and eat ours under the beech tree."

~~~

"She's gotten so heavy, Klara. I can barely manage her."

"Is she any better?"

"The cheese is good. Did you have fun?"

Klara sat with her back to the tree with Moochie on her lap. The baby lay quiet for a bit, then stiffened, flailed her fists, and began wheezing and grunting. Klara rocked and jiggled her, but Moochie only increased her agitated movements.

Stina leaned over and stuffed a tiny, tiny bite of cheese into her mouth.

"Babies don't eat cheese," said Klara.

"Better cheese than some of the things she eats."

Moochie was quiet as long as she had a morsel of cheese on her tongue, then she would swallow, grow stiff, and let out a scream.

"Hey, she's learned to swallow," said Klara.

"She tries to roll over and pull herself up, too. Mostly she screams."

"What about Mamma? Is she better?"

"She won't even look at Moochie."

Klara soon found that the baby would eat anything she could get in her mouth and no amount of rocking or cuddling would comfort her. She hated being held and would relax only when exhausted enough to sleep. When really frustrated, she flailed her fists and held her breath until her eyes rolled back and her body went limp.

~~~

As Moochie's second birthday approached, the girls found that watching the child was not enough. She had learned to run even before she crawled and habitually bolted for the forest when set loose. More and more often she spent her days tethered to a bed in the back room, her hands tied or wrapped in socks to keep her from eating her own waste or pulling out her hair.

What's to become of us, thought Klara. Even small problems threaten to send us to the poor house. We all need to work if we're to eat. This poor child keeps at least one of us from the fields and garden constantly. And, Mamma is most certainly with child again. How can she bear it all. How can we.

And what about the baby. What if it is like this last one, the *nisse* child, sent by the forest demons. She was sure the neighbors talked behind their hands about Moochie. What sin had the Larsson family committed to deserve such burden. Others shook their heads and said it was the capricious finger of fate and could happen to any of them. Then they spit on a rock and rolled it into the dust to keep that wind of chance from their own door stoop.

Sofia's Escape to the Promised Land.

"Mamma, Mamma, come quick." Klara appeared in the doorway and yelled at her mother sitting at the loom by the fireplace.

"Slow down, Klara," said Anna. "I can't leap up every time you call."

"It's Sofia. She's leaving. Forever."

Klara wiped her hands on her apron and smoothed her hair from her face. Red-faced and sweating from work or excitement, she backed out of the room with a plea for Anna to hurry.

"Nonsense, Klara. Get back to work. The wax will set up and you'll have to start over."

Klara had been outside dipping tallow candles, while her mother worked up a long spindle of wool. With a sigh Anna stood up and laid the shuttle aside. When she got outside, she understood what Klara had been talking about. Three wagons loaded with household goods, trunks, and people waited in the road. On the last seat of the third wagon, Sofia Varm sat, stiff and prim at the side of a young man. He held her arm in a possessive embrace.

Anna hurried to catch up with Klara who was running back to the wagons.

"Where are you going, Sofia?"

Klara stood in the road looking up at her friend. She had never seen Sofia dressed so nicely. Her long skirt was made of some bright store-bought material, cotton, perhaps, a real treat in a place where cotton was an imported commodity.

"Amerika. First to Karlstad in ta wagon. We finda ship in Kristiania. A gud big ship"

"How? How can you go? And who is this?"

Klara knew Sofia was among the poorest of the poor in the parish. Her mother, Britz Varm had recently died of syphilis after years of being known as the parish harlot. And who was this fellow hanging on Sofia's arm. Klara stared at him trying to remember where she had seen him before.

Sofia stiffened, pulled her shoulders back, and adjusted her hat a bit. It was a frothy thing with wide brim and feathers at the crown. An odd choice for several days travel in an open wagon.

"We be married this morning," said Sofia.

She smoothed the fabric of her flamboyant skirt and fingered the bit of lace outlining the waist. She looked up at the young man sitting beside her.

"Arvid takes care of me."

"Arvid? Arvid Lindblad?"

"That's right, lady. Arvid Lindblad, entrepreneur."

"I didn't recognize you without a goat under your arm," said Klara.

She looked at Sofia and wondered how much her friend had heard about her new husband. By reputation, he was a brawler, a hard drinker, a womanizer, known to start trouble even in church. Respectable girls avoided him.

"You should come, too, Klara."

Klara stood silent. No matter how much she wanted to go, she vowed it would not be like this.

~~~

They heard no more from Sofia until a letter came in the spring of the new century, almost two years after her departure. McKinley would soon be elected president in the United States; Queen Victoria ruled England. Neither would live to see another summer. On the home front the differences between Sweden and her subject country, Norway, were marching to the final dissolution of that unholy bond, a dissolution which would be finalized May 18, 1905.

Fair harvests and relatively mild winters also marked the time. Anna had lost one baby and birthed another in the interim. The fears that the new baby would be a *nisse* child were unfounded and the neighbors were content to relegate the unfortunate Moochie to the category of accident.

~~~

Gathered at the supper table, the family listened as Per read Sofia's letter again.

My Dearest Clara,

I have much to share with you. First, you will notice, I have learned to write. I'm not too good yet, but Arvid is helping me. Baby Lillian is starting to crawl. She is the most beautiful baby ever. New York is heaven. We have a flat all to ourselves. Two rooms. And the food! Meat every day--sausages as fat as your arm--pork chops--fresh fish. And fruit! Apples, bananas. Did you ever taste a banana, Clara? Clara--that's how your name is spelled here. And I'm now Sophia. Much more sophisticated. Learning English is slow work. Arvid takes to it quickly. He can speak and write English as good as he writes Svenska. He has made a good bit of money helping new immigrants find housing and jobs. Why am I writing after all this time, you ask? We are coming back for a visit. Arvid wants to recruit more emigrants and will be paid for each one who signs up. We hope to get his sister to return with us. Hired help are hard to keep. Everyone wants to work for themselves. We will wire you from Stockholm.

Your Friend Always,

Sophia Lindblad

"That don't sound like dumb old Sofy," said Ivar.

"Probably hired someone to write it. Even Arvid can barely spell his name."

"People can change. Learn things," said Stina. "Maybe they went to school in Amerika."

"They'd learn in English there, dummy."

Klara watched her father fold the letter and tuck it away. The boys showed some interest in the stamps covering half the envelope, but soon wandered off.

"When? When are they coming?"

"They'll wire us when they reach Stockholm," said Per.

"Soon, then. This very summer," said Klara.

"You'd best get the Hansson girl to take your place at *langfabod*."

So, instead of preparing to take the goats to the far pasture, Klara stayed home to ready things for Sofia's visit. As she scrubbed floors and aired feather beds, she imagined herself churning gallons of cream into butter, heating vats of clabbered milk into soft cheese, reveling in the freedom and fresh air. Perhaps this would have been the summer she met a nice young man, one of the village boys sent to bring back the finished butter and cheese. So romantic, she thought, what a silly goose to be daydreaming about a fellow hauling whey and skimmings to feed the pigs.

Strange to be making such a fuss for Sofia Varm, thought Klara.

Not Varm, Klara corrected herself; Sophia Lindblad was her name now. Sophia, daughter of the harlot, Britz Varm. Sophia, her childhood friend, Sophia, who had lived in a tumbled down sheep shed on the Lof estate over the ridge.

Klara tried to conjure her absent friend by thinking through all she could remember about her. She knew the stories about the death of Sophia's father of course and how, mother and baby daughter had been allowed to stay on in the old sheep shed and work for the Lof family.

Even at five or six, Sophia was expected to help with the laundry and garden, working eight and ten hour days. She earned a few *ore* a year, a few cast off pieces of clothing, and the scraps from the Lof family table. For girls like Sophia a cheap pair of shoes cost more than a half year's wages and new clothing was out of the question.

When she got the chance to emigrate by marrying Arvid Lindblad, Sophia did not hesitate though she knew of his affairs and petty crimes. Now, along with her husband, she was coming back to the old country for a visit and to show off her new baby.

Klara and Sophia had been in the same confirmation class at the Lutheran church in the valley, but they saw little of each other as they got older because Sophia was not allowed to attend school. With a jab of resentment in her heart, Klara wondered why she was still scrubbing and tending her younger siblings, while Sophia had gone off to adventures in the new world.

Visitors, *Aebleskivers*, and Dreams Galore.

Klara looked around the kitchen. The slab table was set and covered with a perfectly ironed linen cloth. The floor had been scrubbed white though it was only Monday. New loaves of rye bread cooled on the sill. The visitors from America would be arriving any minute and Klara wanted everything to be perfect.

Visitors this time of year, she thought. How strange. Everyone she knew labored from morning light until midnight darkness in the summer. The luxury of visiting came only in the slow cold days of winter.

The short season of growing and harvest demanded long hours of work in the fields and gardens so there would be enough to eat through the winter. Rye, oats, barley, and potatoes were maturing in the small upland fields. Cows and goats, fresh now, had been driven to the long pasture, the *langfabod*, by the older girls.

The work of preparing for visitors had kept Klara from the *langfabod*, but for now her disappointment was buried in the excitement of seeing her friend again.

~~~

"Mamma, may we use the chocolate set to serve the coffee?"

Klara wound her hands in her apron as she faced her mother. She felt like a child begging for a forbidden treat.

"It is a special occasion and the white porcelain would look so nice with the pansies I gathered for the center piece."

"They'll think you're putting on airs, daughter."

Anna placed a tray of butter cookies on the spotless table.

"You're dressed in your Sunday best and Granmutter's embroidered cloth is on the table. That's enough fancy for the likes of Arvid and Sophia."

Exasperated, Klara stamped her foot and turned away from her mother. Tears of frustration and weariness threatened to engulf her. Though many fifteen year old girls were planning their weddings, Klara felt like a child, controlled and put upon.

"Oh, Mamma. When will it ever be special enough to use the chocolate set?"

"All this pretty will be ashes when they see Moochie. Is she clean?"

"Yes, Mamma. Moochie is washed and fed. And Stina will have the baby asleep before long, too."

"What's to become of us, I don't know."

"I wish we had a room over the stable like the Lof's. We could put her there and the Lindblads wouldn't have to see her."

"You can't hide such things. You forget that Sophia helped out here the year Moochie was born."

"She was so frightened. Thought the *nisse* had stolen the baby and substituted one of their own."

"Arvid's father is Per's cousin, so he's kinfolk. No sense putting on airs for kin."

Strange, thought Klara. Back in his brawling days, before Arvid emigrated, her family would never consider declaring the Lindblads kin.

Anna finished the row of *fagelbo* by adding the last concentric ring of chopped lettuce to the raw egg yolks. In their flat bowls with rings of capers, diced anchovies, and bits of pickled beet the deep yellow egg yolks looked like a set of targets lined up on the table.

"I hope they still have a taste for country food."

"It'll be the best meal they've had since they left."

And certainly the best meal to grace this table in many a year, thought Klara. It seemed like they had eaten salt fish, beets, and boiled potatoes more times than not these past six years.

"Is it time to start the sausages frying?" she asked her mother.

"Go outside and listen for the wagon. I'll start the sausages."

Anna threw a handful of pine splints into the stove to make a quick, hot fire. Sweat beaded her temples as she forked the meat into the cast iron skillet.

Before the fat pork sausages had fried crisp, Per drove up the lane. He was alone in the high-sided wagon, but before Klara could reach him to ask about the Lindblads, a light buggy drawn by a matched pair of bay trotters pulled into the yard.

Klara barely recognized the young man driving the team. She had never seen this Arvid with wavy hair and waxed mustache. His tall hat and dark blue suit reminded her of the visiting speakers that sometimes came to the Lutheran church in Smedjebacken.

The woman seated next to this dashing gentleman wore a wide brimmed hat tied under her chin with a flowing sash of some thin gauzy stuff of pale pink which matched her long gown. She bore no resemblance to the Sophia who had told them all good-bye a few years ago. That Sophia had labored from dawn to dark caring for another woman's house and children and garden with never a minute to look to her own clothing and person. This Sophia looked like the lady of the manor.

"Klara. Don't stand there gawking," said Per.

He climbed down from the wagon where he was mobbed by the younger children.

"Ivar, take care of the horses."

Ivar, Klara's fourteen-year-old brother stepped to the horses' heads and held their bridles, while Arvid climbed from the buggy and turned to take the baby from his wife so she could gather her skirts and step down.

Arvid held the baby for all to see.

"This is Lillian."

"She's two, almost," said Sophia, "and already an American."

Anna joined them in the dooryard.

"What a healthy looking little one," said Anna. She reached for the baby. "Let me take her. You must be tired after that long ride from the train station."

Klara smiled at her mother's comment. She thought Lillian a homely child and knew her mother was comparing the red-faced, dark-haired infant to her own fair, blue-eyed babies.

"What sort of name is Lillian?" she asked.

Sophia shook out her skirt and removed her long gloves.

"A modern name. None of the old country for this baby," said Arvid. He mopped his face with a handkerchief. "We'll name the next one Sam."

"Arvid, what if it be a girl?" Sophia pouted and frowned up at her husband. "I wanna another girl. A sweet little girl."

She looks like a fish with her lower lip stuck out like that, thought Klara, but she smiled and said, "Come in and rest. Supper's nearly ready."

The young man squeezed his wife's arm. "Go on inside. I'll help the boy with the team. They're from Blom's Livery and he's pretty particular about his horses."

~~~

A brief disagreement erupted between Sophia and Anna over the best way to keep baby Lillian occupied while the adults had supper. Sophia was horrified when it was suggested the child be swaddled and placed in the cradle occupying the chimney corner. Anna's youngest lay quiet on the closet bed in the corner.

"Me baby's not one of them dead 'gyptians. I won't wrap her up."

"Nonsense. Everyone swaddles babies."

"At's for ta bad ones, always pulling over the flour bin or tumbling into the fire."

Sophia untied Lillian's bonnet strings and slipped the frilly affair from her daughter's head.

"Lillian's a smart one. Good, too."

"They can't hurt themselves if they're swaddled."

Anna took the pink bonnet and the tiny organdy jacket Sophia handed her, then added a retort about curious children filthifying their fine clothes.

"Clothes wash. She needs ta explore."

Sophia gave the child a wooden spoon and placed her on the floor away from the fireplace.

"She kin play about while we talk."

Just then the men came in from putting up the horses and washing up at the basin of cold water on the bench out front. Ivar, Will, and James followed them in, but were given a forkfuls of hot sausages and shooed out of the house. The younger children did not eat supper with the adults when there was company.

~~~

"Klara, pass the potatoes."

Anna had to repeat herself to get Klara's attention.

"Got your head in the clouds, daughter?"

"Probably thinking about going to America," said Arvid. He ladled gravy over his potatoes. "I told her she ought to come back with us. For a visit and to help Sophia when the new baby comes."

At the mention of baby everyone looked at Lillian, playing in the corner.

"I don't know what I'd be doing in such a far-off place," Klara mumbled.

She looked across the table and saw that Sophia was scowling at her. Wondering how she had managed to offend her visitor, Klara reached the bowl of pickled cabbage and forked some onto her plate, though she still had an ample portion of the sour vegetable. She peered into the near empty bowl.

"Should I fetch more from the larder, Mamma?"

"What you'd be doing in America is living easy, wearing fine clothes and steppin' out with the fellows."

Excited now, Arvid stuffed a whole sausage in his mouth and continued talking.

"I had to work like a slave when I lived here. When I was thirteen I got my food and ten cents a week working for the railroad, twelve hours a day, six days a week. I still lived at home and my mamma had to provide my clothes. That's no way for a man to live. Why, in New York they pay three dollars a day and a man only works half days on Saturday."

Per interrupted, "What about prices? You can't live with your mamma in New York."

"Why, a good hat cost two dollars, less than a day's wages. I'd have to work two months to buy a hat here. And shoes, talk about quality and price. Look at these."

Arvid stood up and planted one foot on the bench, pulling up his pant leg to show off his spit-polished patent leather oxfords.

"Tell me the truth now, can you even buy shoes like this here?"

By their silence the family conceded that Arvid had made his point. Klara had never seen shoes like Arvid's and had thought them a bit silly and impractical for a man. What sort of work did he do wearing such flimsy shoes? One trip through the manure deep yard to the storage shed would ruin them forever.

Though she ached with curiosity, Klara kept silent. With her step-sisters, Hulda and Sonja, working away from home, Klara, almost sixteen, was now the oldest child. Next in line came Ivar who was eating in the stable with his younger brothers. Eleven year old Stina was hiding out in the back room with Moochie. I'll be paying her favors for months, thought Klara.

As the meal progressed she could hear the boys playing in the yard. They would sleep in the granary if the visitors decided to stay the night. Usually they shared a bed in the back room behind the huge fireplace that dominated the house. The room Grandfather Erik Axel had dug out of the hillside was now the children's room. Being a boy, Ivar would join the adults when he turned fifteen and even be encouraged to voice his opinions on adult matters. As if he ever had an opinion of any value in his whole life, thought Klara. It's so unfair.

Arvid and Per continued to dominate the conversation throughout the meal. Arvid extolled the cheap, plentiful food and easy living of New York. Per countered with reminders of family ties and high moral standards of the Home Land.

Silent up to now, Sophia suddenly spoke up, interrupted the conversation of the men.

"You going ta ask her? Or you change your mind?"

"Ask what? Who am I to ask?" Arvid looked at his wife and frowned. "What are you talking about?"

"Your sis. To be going back with us."

Embarrassed, she dropped her fork and it skittered over the edge of the table.

"Now you be trying to talk Klara inta comin with us."

She made a show of picking up her fork, wiped it on her napkin and placed it just so alongside her plate.

When Arvid failed to answer, she continued, "Never mind. We doin what you think is right, Arvid."

Klara thought Sophia looked frightened. She must have been thinking about what Arvid had said at the beginning of the meal all this time. Maybe she wasn't used to contradicting her husband or maybe he didn't take kindly to his wife speaking out in public.

"Let me get you another fork," said Klara.

She got up and traded a clean fork for the dropped one.

"I'm sure Arvid means to ask his sister. He was just teasing me when he asked me to come along."

The dog sleeping in the corner by the fireplace suddenly sat up, ears pricked and a low growl rumbling in his throat. He crossed the room to the door in a couple of leaps and sent baby Lillian sprawling. She let out a terrific wail.

Arvid paid no mind to his daughter, but spoke sharply to his wife.

"Sophia, make that child hush. Now."

Sophia jumped up from the table and stooped to grab Lillian and press the sobbing child to her shoulder.

Per got up and let the dog out.

"He hears something in the woods. Probably just the neighbor's dogs or maybe a wolverine passing through. Nothing to worry about."

"How far is it to your parents' farm, Arvid?" asked Anna.

She seemed intent on changing the subject and diverting attention from the crying baby.

"I've not seen your father since he moved to Grangeburg. How long has it been?"

"Maybe you should emigrate, Mrs. Larsson."

Arvid helped himself to another fat sausage. His appetite was huge for such a skinny fellow and his manners belied his fancy clothes. Elbows on the table and a tiny bit of grease rolling off his chin, he continued to argue the wonders of America.

"See the world. After the first couple of years you'd even be able to afford a maid to do the rough work."

Anna got up to put wood on the fire. The summer night was cool, almost cold.

"You'll stay the night? We aired the beds just today. Shook out the straw mattresses and everything."

She took the child from Sophia and walked up and down the room to quiet her.

Sophia twisted her napkin with both hands.

"Please, Arvid."

"Are you sure it won't put you out? It'll be light for several more hours and we could make the drive yet tonight."

"No trouble."

"Maybe we should go, Arvid," said Sophia.

"Hush, Dumplin. She said the bed was ready."

The young man loosened his collar and slipped a pair of cigars from his inside coat pocket. He rolled one under his nose and breathed deeply, then offered the other to Per.

"Why don't we go outside for a smoke while the women clean up and get the baby off to sleep."

After the men had disappeared into the yard, Klara and Sophia opened the long bench at the wall and unfolded the mattress fitted inside. Klara usually slept on the folding straw tick, but tonight Anna and Per would sleep there so the Lindblads could have the cupboard bed across the room. Klara pulled the thin curtain that provided a measure of privacy. She would sleep with Stina and Moochie in the back room, displacing Ivar, James, and Will. The three boys were excited to be sleeping in the granary, an unexpected adventure.

Klara lay awake in the darkness after the house was quiet. She was so disappointed with the way the evening had gone. Their guests had made the house seem so shabby and mean. When Sophia had snagged her fine gown on the bench, Klara wanted to sink through the floor. Why hadn't she noticed that splintered place before? She had gone over everything so carefully in preparation for the Lindblads' visit. Sophia had been nice about it, saying it didn't really matter; it was an old gown, anyway. She had even given Klara a silk scarf, a pale green square with tiny white flowers.

The scarf was lying smooth against her cheek right now. So different from the fabric of the homespun wool night dress she always wore against the cold. Cold crept into the house year round even though the beds were built into small closet-like enclosures with doors or curtains the sleeper could pull shut to keep out drafts. The fire was banked to avoid the danger of torching the house and to be sure enough coals remained to renew the fire in the morning.

Tonight Klara wished she could throw her rough clothes in the fire and wrap herself in cotton lawn and Chinese silk. She'd be light as a dragonfly dancing over the water.

In her drowsing imagination she was flying, flying low over the waves, then swooping down to gather up something precious gleaming on the shore. Was it bits of gold and silver, polished stones. Or was it a cup from the chocolate set. Whatever it was, it always it slipped through her fingers and smashed on the rocks. Then her flying brought her to America, the Promised Land where everyone wore fine clothes and drank their tea from cups of real gold.

On waking she thought about the free land available to anyone who would use it. That was an amazing thing Mr. Lindblad had told them, free land, acres and acres, one-hundred and forty acres for each person who would settle there and build a house. Why a couple with a child could claim an enormous parcel of land. It sounded like a fortune to Klara whose father owned less than twenty acres of land, some of it a distance away on the mountain and accessible only in the summer months. Why hadn't the Lindblads claimed a farm by now? She had so many questions.

The sun was rising on another long day when Klara finally fell asleep again. The old black rooster soon rousted her awake. She tumbled out of bed by force of habit. After a quick wash in the cold water in the enamel basin on the shelf by the door she stoked the fire to a quick, hot burning. Coffee was soon boiling and the cast iron *aebleskiver* griddle hot enough to sizzle a drop of water.

She could hear the Lindblads stirring, so she knocked on the wall to be sure Stina was awake. She hoped that Stina would think to take care of Moochie. I must remember to slip her some breakfast as soon as possible. Maybe I can keep her quiet a few more hours. Everyone, including the babies, would gather around the long table at breakfast before the Lindblads left. Everyone except Moochie. Maybe by taking turns, she and Stina could keep her out of sight.

Per began the meal with bowed head and a brief grace. In more devout households something close to a full-length sermon would follow, but the Larssons attended church only on special occasions like Christmas, Easter, baptisms, confirmations, and burials. Klara got the meal going by passing pitchers of cream-topped milk and bowls oat gruel, hard packed brown sugar, a plate of pickled fish. Lingonberry and wild strawberries preserves, along with homemade syrup were already on the table waiting the hot *aebleskivers.*

Klara hovered over the stove to add the dollop of applesauce to the batter filled cups of the hot pan, then turn the half-done cakes with a knitting needle. It was all she could do to keep up with the appetites of the group around the long table. The apple-filled *aebleskivers* and hard-fried back bacon were something to be savored and remembered. She finally got a break and bolted for the back room to feed Moochie and let Stina join the others at the table.

When the meal was finished, Arvid and Ivar went out to harness the team, while Sophia got Lillian dressed in her frilly outfit, then packed their belongings for the rest of the journey.

"We'll be back through here in about a week." Arvid handed the sleepy Lillian to his wife seated in the buggy, then stepped up himself. He gathered the reins and wheeled the team around and clattered out of the yard to a chorus of good bye, God speed, and see you soon.

Leave Taking and Strong Drink.

Life shifted back to normal after the Lindblads' visit. Klara set Stina to cleaning up the breakfast dishes and putting the house to rights and hurried outside to help her mother with the laundry. Anna had the water heating and was shaving bits of soap into the iron wash tub from a bar of lye soap. Ivar and his father helped James and Will drive the milk goat and cow to pasture and stayed to fell a dead tree and work at levering a big rock from the edge of the hay field.

Stirring the heavy mass of shirts and underwear, Klara wished she could go with the children to watch over the livestock. The warm summer air would carry the tangy smell of spruce needles and she would lie on her back in the sweet grass watching the clouds. She remembered Sophia talking about her hired girl doing the laundry and the ironing. Sophia must have lots of time to play with Lillian, learn English, and sit over coffee chatting with new friends. She could see Sophia's hands so smooth and white holding a dainty fluted cup.

Anna stood waiting for Klara to dip out the first piece of clothing so she could drape it over the line.

"Klara, you're going to wear those shirts out with so much washing."

"Oh, Mamma."

"Whatever are you thinking about?"

"Sorry, Mamma."

Klara fished one of the soggy undervests from the nearly boiling water and wrung it out. No wonder her hands were always red and sore.

"Do you think Stina's old enough to help with this job?"

Anna spread a long petticoat over a bush and waited for the next piece.

"Stina has her hands full with Moochie and the baby. She's only eleven."

She took a closer look at Klara.

"Are you thinking about leaving? Going to America?"

"Mamma, I'm almost sixteen. Sonja left home to work in the city when she was sixteen."

Five days later the Lindblads returned, several days earlier than expected. Klara was in the yard beating the dust from the straw ticks she had hauled outside to air. Vermin such as fleas, lice, and bedbugs were a continual, almost overwhelming problem. She dropped her beater and tried to wipe the dust from her face.

"You're back already."

"We wore out our welcome," said Arvid. "Actually, the family needed to get to work."

And I'll bet you left in a hurry to get out of helping, thought Klara.

Tired from the long journey, the team didn't need restraining, so Klara helped Sophia by taking Lillian from her. With the child in her arms she turned to Arvid who slouched on the wagon seat.

"Where's your sister?"

"Hope it won't put you out if we stay the night. It wasn't very comfortable at my folks' place. Sophia had to sleep with the kiddels and I stayed with the haying crew in the barn."

Arvid looked around for someone to take the horses, then, seeing no one, he unhooked the double tree and led them into the barn himself.

With Lillian on one arm Klara motioned Sophia into the house.

"Sorry about the mess, but it was a nice day to air the beds. Mamma's making hard cheese with neighbor Hansson. She'll be back soon."

Sophia perked up a little once she was inside.

"It was awful, Klara."

"Was it a very long ride?"

"Mattie's pappa said she weren't to come with us." Sophia started to cry. "He said she have to take her brother's place on the farm."

"Why?"

Klara wondered if Sophia was crying for the luckless Mattie or for herself.

"Her brother run away to work in the city and now Mattie is working in the fields with the men. She so unhappy. She beg and beg to come with us. Her pappa whupped her good."

"You'll feel better after a rest, Sophia."

Klara guided her to the bed in the corner of the living room. She fluffed a quilt over the bare bed, and retreated with little Lillian on her hip. She would have rather put Sophia in the back room, but Moochie was tied to one of the beds.

"I'll take Lillian outside. Stina can keep an eye on her while she works in the garden."

By supper time Sophia was just awakening from a sound asleep. Arvid on the other hand seemed vigorous and ready to talk non-stop It was decided to have a small going away party and Ivar was dispatched to the close neighbors to invite them over.

Klara and Stina hustled around laying out bowls of sour cream, pickled beets, and plates of rye crisp. From the larder Klara brought three tall jars of *glasmastarsill*, glassblower's herring, a colorful layering of red onions, carrots, ginger root, horse-radish, and of course, raw herring, with vinegar and sugar pickling. Arvid and Per went to the storehouse for a half-barrel of homemade beer and a gallon of homemade *brannvin*, a hard liquor distilled from potatoes, flavored with spruce berries. The women started a kettle of pea soup cooking and set the table.

Always happy for an excuse to eat and dance, drink and tell tall stories, the house was soon full of people. Mrs. Lof was too much the lady of the manor to come to such poor doings, but her husband, Otto, son, and twin daughters were there. The new tenants of the Smaldag place, Emma and Lars Hansson came with their three teenage boys, as well as the itinerant farm hand, Hans Earlsson, who just happened to be in the neighborhood. The oil lamps lit up the center of the room, but as the evening progressed and darkness came, the corners remained pools of shadow.

When the party reached its peak, Arvid, full of herring and beer, decided to teach the group of Swedes a song about America. The little ditty had been set to the melody of a Lutheran hymn. He called it "*Skada at America*," "There We'll Find America." He sang the first verse in Swedish:

> *Broder vi ha langt at ga*
> *Over salte vatten*
> *Ok sa fins Amerika*
> *In vid andre stranden*

Then, in an attempt to teach the crowd some English or to show off his own fluency, he sang the same verse in English.

Brothers, it is far to go
Over salty waters;
There we'll find America,
On the other shore.

Satisfied with his success, he sang the chorus:

Skada at Amerika, Skada at Amerika,
Lige skal so longt ifron.

The young people quickly picked up the chorus, which they sang loudly when Arvid would point at them to indicate he was at the end of a verse. After a few rounds, Arvid decided to teach them the English version of the chorus. He lined a simplified version for them:

It's so bad America,
Wonderful America,
Should be so far away.

At the end of each chorus one of the men would toast Arvid with a solemn *skoal* and Arvid would down another shot of *brannvin*. Another rousing verse of the song would follow, each more ludicrous than the last.

America is where you find
Girls like pretty flowers.
If you decide you need a wife,
Four or five will offer.
From the ground and in the fields,
English money grows.

While Arvid was slowly and meticulously explaining this verse in the mother tongue, one of the men produced a bottle of imported whiskey. Arvid beamed when he saw the bottle.

"A proper toast we can drink now."

He turned and grabbed one of the stilt-legged chocolate cups from the high shelf by the stove. He held it out for his share. He looked absurd with his red face and big hands clutching at the fragile cup, but he finally got the slim gold handle pinched between his thumb and forefinger. He looked directly at Klara when he made his toast.

"To the beauties of the homeland, *skoal*."

Everyone present knew this was bad manners, an impertinence of the worst kind to toast the hostess or the unmarried daughter of the house, but no one would have even thought to reprove Arvid. He was the guest and no ordinary guest at that. He was a guest from across the sea.

Someone handed Klara a glass of the strong liquor. She looked around the crowded room for her parents, hoping one of them would intervene, speak up in hearty, jocular tones to tell Arvid the daughter of the house was much too young for strong drink and take the glass from her hand. It didn't happen.

She supposed her mother was in the store room for more salt fish and flat bread, her father breaking out the other half-keg of beer. She downed the liquor with good grace and was momentarily surprised that it slid down her throat without the choking fire of the home brewed *brannvin*.

Even the smallest child had experienced the raw taste of the home-distilled drink. It was spooned out to cure sore throats and winter chills, female complaints, the pain of sprains and strains, cracked heads, broken bones, and general misery.

After Arvid swallowed the contents of the tiny cup, he stared at Klara, then bowed and plunked his cup down on the table. A smattering of applause followed and Arvid began a slurred version of another verse.

When it rains, the birds do fall,
Ducks and chickens pour down.
Geese all fried, to eat by all,
The fork is in the drumstick.

While he was singing, Klara edged around the table to retrieve the precious cup before disaster could over take it. Just as she reached for it, Arvid plucked it up and dangled it in front of her face. His hand was so close she could see the ridges on his fingernails, smell the earthy musk of his tobacco.

"Looking for this?"

His voice was a whisper so only Klara heard him.

"Let me have the cup, Arvid."

She felt hot and a little dizzy. The harsh flickering light from the oil lamps made the faces around her bright masks against the shadows. Klara tried again to get her hands on the cup.

"It's very old and fragile. I'll get you something more suitable."

He leered at her. "I need fresh air."

Cup in hand, Arvid pushed past a group of men arguing the merits of rye over potato *brannvin*. Though it was illegal, nearly all these isolated households had a still and a beer brew-barrel somewhere on the premises.

"Come along, Klara. Keep watch over your precious cup."

Klara followed him into the yard. The cool air revived her a bit and she stopped to breathe deeply of the fragrant night air. She could hear murmured conversation coming from a discrete location under the spreading fir trees. Ivar and one of the Lof twins, no doubt, she thought with a pang of loneliness. Before her eyes had adjusted to the darkness she felt Arvid's hand on her shoulder. She jumped away in surprise, but Arvid was quicker.

He reached his hand around her waist and turned her to face him.

"How about a little smooch, kid?"

Klara struggled against his hands until she felt Arvid tap her cheek with the chocolate cup.

"Gimmie a kiss or I'll drop yer silly cup."

"How could you even think such a thing."

She struggled to get away, but he pulled her against him. The rough fabric of his suit smelled of sweat and cologne. Klara jerked her head back, away from him so she could breathe.

"What about Sophia, your wife? What would she think?"

"What about her? What she don't know, won't hurt her."

He nuzzled her neck with his wet mouth and tried to fumble one hand inside her blouse.

"Come on, kid."

Klara felt sick to her stomach. His stubble-rough chin rubbed across her face. The stink of alcohol and cigar thickened the air between them. She braced both hands against his chest and tried to push him away. Klara was a strong girl and nearly as tall as Arvid, but she couldn't force him away. A little signal of fear jumped in her chest when he grabbed both her wrists with one hand. The shot of whiskey she had downed earlier was bitter in her throat and she wondered if she was going to throw up.

"Please don't, Arvid."

He stepped back as far as he could without releasing Klara's hands.

"Not so high and mighty, now, are we."

Her coronet of braid had come loose and her blouse was untucked. He still held the cup in his free hand. With great care he turned her hands over and placed the cup in the nest of her palms.

"See, I'm not such a bad fellow after all."

With a quick move Arvid let go of her wrists and put one hand around her shoulders, the other he used to tip her face to his. He kissed her hard with his tongue forcing through her clenched teeth, then he pushed her away.

"That's just a sample, Klara. Wait'll you come to stay with us in New York."

"Never," she hissed at him.

She ran for the house. Now she knew why Sophia was so unhappy that Arvid's sister couldn't return with them to New York. She must know all about her husband's habits with women. Klara wanted to wash out her mouth, throw up, clean the rough filth from her soul, but instead she drew a deep breath and tidied her hair and blouse before she entered the house. Inside she washed the porcelain cup over and over, then polished it dry before replacing it on its shelf.

That night she dreamed of flying again, but this time she could see that the precious objects on the shore were cups, the porcelain cups from the chocolate set. A few were of solid gold; all of them slipped through her fingers to smash on the rocky beach.

Slaughter Soup.

Anna busied herself at the stove, where she hovered over a hot skillet and boiling coffee water. Gray dawn seeped into the close kitchen and shadowed the white washed walls.

"Call Pappa and the boys, Klara. Breakfast is nearly ready."

When Klara stooped through the doorway to the yard, the chill in the air surprised her. It feels like December instead of August, she thought. She glanced at the prim row of flowers under the window, expecting to find them black and wilted, or at least crusted with a white rime of frost. The flowers nodded and smiled back at her to her relief.

"Pappa. Ivar. Willie, James. Breakfast. Hurry, now."

Anna poured coffee while Klara helped the younger boys get washed up. Stina and Moochie were already settled on the bench nearest the wall. When Per came in, the boys scrambled to sit down.

"I hear the Lofs are cutting their rye already," said Anna.

"Too bad. This is such a promising crop."

The rye, barley, and oats needed another month to mature and dry if it was to grind into good flour or keep through the winter.

"Better safe, than sorry."

Per sipped the strong brewed coffee, then spooned tart lingonberries and cream over his butter-crisped pancakes. He seemed not to notice his food. The worry of early frost weighed on him, furrowed his brow, twitched the small muscles near his left eye.

"We need to make a trip to town before we think about harvesting."

"Maybe you could send Ivar this year." Anna got up to get the coffee pot. "He needs to learn to deal with the merchants sooner or later."

"We don't have much to trade this year. And I need to get the scythe repaired."

Most tools and household items were maintained and often made at home, but an occasional bit of ironwork had to be done by the village blacksmith. The importance of the iron worker could be seen in the name of the nearest town, *Smedjebacken*, the smithy on the hill.

Per tried to assemble the possibilities in his mind. The worry of it deepened the creases in his forehead. He picked at the edge of the table with work-thick fingers.

"Make a list of what we need."

"We're almost out of coffee and sugar," offered Klara.

She wondered why no one ever thought to send her for supplies. She was the oldest, old enough to work side-by-side with the men in the fields all day or spend hours over the wash tubs and scrub board.

"Salt would be good, too, if we can afford it."

How could we not afford salt, she thought. We need it to preserve the fish, pickle the cabbage and beets, to say nothing of the hams and bacon.

It was decided that Ivar and his father would make the trip to town. Anna and Klara would pack them a supper of cold sausage and hard tack with a jar of pickled cabbage. They could sleep in the wagon in *Smedjebacken* and be up early to get a good spot at the market.

In the meantime, much work remained. The veal calf and one of the sows would be butchered. Some of the forcemeat and fresh veal would be used as barter for the needed staples.

Thinking about the lifting and long hours of standing that would be involved in butchering, Klara vowed to work as hard as she could manage in an attempt to spare her mother some of the work ahead. Though she had no confirmation of it, she suspected her mother was pregnant again.

The red calf, a scant three months old, was killed that same day. One blow in the center of the forehead with Per's stout stick did the job. With a quick slice of his knife he slit the animal's jugular and hot blood foamed into the basin Klara held. Along with the calf's liver, heart, and kidneys, it would be used to make slaughter soup.

Klara sent James to the house with the basin and a stern warning to walk slowly and not spill a single drop. She helped her father spread the calf's hind legs wide apart and fasten them to an old single tree which had a long rope tied to the iron ring set in its center. With a backhand toss Per lobed the rope over a branch of a nearby tree. Though it wasn't necessary because of the small size of the calf, Ivar helped his father pull the animal up off the ground and wrap the rope around the tree trunk. Leaving Ivar to skin the animal, Klara and Per walked to the house for the gutting knife and hand saw, basins, and bowls to hold the organs and intestines.

Klara held her long skirt away from the ground with one hand and tried to tuck an errant lock of hair away from her face with the other.

"Will we cut our grain early, too, like the Lofs?"

She felt justified asking about early harvest because it would make weeks of extra work for the women of the household.

"The calf is small, three of the goats slipped their kids, and the old sow was empty this year. We can't take a chance with the grain."

Per rubbed his swollen hands together and paused to look at his daughter.

"I'm sorry. For the extra work. Maybe you should have gone with the Lindblads."

He turned away and continued up the path to the house.

Anna met them at the door with the tools wrapped in a clean cloth. "Where's Ivar?"

Per brushed past her to the pitcher of cool drinking water on the bench by the wash basin, where he helped himself to a long drink from the communal cup.

"I let him do the skinning by himself. He's getting good at it."

He washed his hands and dried them on the stiff towel that lay on the bench.

"Will you trade the hide this year?"

Anna stood in the doorway with the sun at her back. Klara thought her mother looked almost transparent in the hard morning light with her wispy hair spilling from the coil of braid at the nape of her neck.

Per wiped his mouth with the back of his hand and shook his head.

"The harness needs repair and James need boots. It would be better to have a thick cow hide or a piece of haunch leather from a horse hide, but the calf hide will have to do. It's time he passed those old shoes down to Will."

He picked up the basins and took the bundle of tools from Anna.

"Send Stina out to wash the gut in about a half hour."

Even processing a small veal calf was non-stop work for most of the day. After the animal was gutted, eleven-year old Stina had to carry the steaming, stinking mass of intestines to a place down stream from the shallow pool where the cows and goats watered. Here she emptied the intestines and rinsed them clean. They would be kept moist in a pan of salt water until it was time to use them to encase the various sausages made by the family.

When Stina finished with the gut, she went back to help Ivar scrape the hide clean of fat and bits of meat. Finished, the two of them spread the hide out on the grass and sprinkled it with salt, which they worked into both sides of the hide with their bare hands. Klara felt the sting of the salt in the many little cuts and scrapes on her own hands as she watched the two of them. She saw the tears well up in Stina's eyes and remembered other years, other butcherings when Stina's job had been her own.

The rubbed hide passed Per's inspection at last, so they rolled it up and placed it in the rack under the ceiling of the storage shed to cure.

The meat, itself, was hung in the cool, dark space dug between the back wall of the house and the hillside. Like a cave, the temperature in the narrow, dirt walled place stayed cool this time of year.

Few parts of the veal calf were considered inedible. Things like the spleen, gallbladder, and lungs were carried to the chickens by seven-year old Will. The frantic chickens almost knocked him down when he appeared in their midst with the entrails.

While the younger children attended to these chores, the kidneys, heart, and liver were washed, chopped fine, and added to a slow cooking pot which already contained potatoes and carrots. At just the right time little dumplings made with barley flour and blood would be added to the slaughter soup.

This dish, eaten with slices of sour rye bread, served as the main meal for several days after the butchering. The rest of the calf's blood would be used in the sausage making. The head, tail, and feet would be cleaned and cooked. The boiled head was sometimes made into a dish some euphemistically called mock turtle. It was a tedious concoction of meat and wine, which country families could seldom afford.

The Larssons followed the country custom of cooking the head, tail and feet until the gelatinous mess was soft enough to grind. The mess was added to the other trimmings to make head cheese.

When Klara ladled out the dark, rusty tasting slaughter soup to the children late that night, she decided to join them. She was too tired to sit through an adult meal with its on going conversation about work and more work.

She sat down by her sister, Stina. How can an eleven-year old look so old and weary, she thought. The little girl's blonde hair hung in stringy tails around her thin shoulders and her pale cheeks were smudged with grime. Her hands were red and scaly against the smooth skin of the baby she held on her lap.

With a stab of guilty pity Klara said, "Let me take the baby, Stina."

Stina handed the girl child over without complaint. Then she broke the wheel of rye flat bread into rough chunks and passed it around the table.

"Somebody needs to give this kiddel a name before winter," said Klara.

"She's almost a year old and we're still calling her Baby."

"Call her Lilly Bean, like Sophie's brat," suggested Will.

"Don't be silly."

"She's not been baptized yet," offered Ivar. "The babe will go to hell if it ain't been baptized."

He broke a large hunk of sour rye bread into his soup and began eating.

After she took her share of the bread, Klara broke off a small bit of it and soaked it in the soup before giving it to the child on her lap.

"Seems like we just had a baptizing."

Stina said, "That was Will and he's almost seven now."

Will giggled and stuffed his mouth full of the hard bread when he heard Stina talking about him. She tweaked the boy's ear and smoothed his rough straw-blonde hair back from his face.

"Show off. Don't put so much in your mouth at once."

"At least he has a name," offered James. "Papa says he's going to make me new boots."

Klara felt a warm surge of gratitude for her father. James worked hard when he was persuaded of the value of the job. He could be responsible far beyond his nine, almost ten years, though, lately, she thought he seemed preoccupied, almost defiant. Growing pains, perhaps. She knew his feet hurt in the old boots he wore because she had watched him trying to stretch them. Old boots, hand-me-downs, were often cut out at the toe to provide more room for growing feet, but having another boy right behind him in the succession of siblings had kept James from this option. Will could get several years of wear from the boots when James moved on to a bigger pair.

From thinking about her father tediously cutting and stitching James's new boots, she wondered how her mother would fare through another winter, and another pregnancy. Aloud she tried to excuse the neglect of the baby.

"Mamma's been too tired to be worrying about naming the little kiddel. We could think of a name. Not Lilly Bean. Then we could ask Mamma if it would suit her to use it for the baby."

Ivar put down his spoon for a moment. "Ask if we can take the babe to be baptized, too."

Of all the children Ivar was most worried about such matters. He was always asking questions about God and death and heaven.

There were seven children in the house, now that the two step-sisters, Hulda and Sonja, had moved to the city. Klara knew her mother had birthed another child, named Karl, before she married. He lived a few days and had been buried at the edge of the forest. After the birth of Moochie, Anna was long in recovering her health and most assumed she would have no more children. Caring for the peculiar child, Moochie, was a difficult chore for everyone. There was an unvoiced dread during Anna's next pregnancy. Would this child be a changeling, or worse, a monster? This was never spoken of and was only manifest by the fact that, now, a year later, the new child was still unnamed, unbaptized.

Seven children living and one dead meant that Anna had gone through eight pregnancies. This was not uncommon, but the number of surviving children was above average. Most families lost half of their offspring before their fourth birthday.

Klara roused herself from her musings. "Off to bed with you now."

She gave the baby to Stina, who left the room to bed the child in her parent's cupboard bed in the main room. They would keep the baby in with them when they came to bed or move her to the trundle. Klara washed and changed four-year old Moochie and put her down in Stina's bed in the dugout room she shared with the boys.

"We butcher the old sow tomorrow," she told them, while she swaddled Moochie.

James had been pummeling Will half-heartedly. He stopped and cheered.

"That means we'll get cracklins and pork chops. Ribs with sauerkraut. Boy, I can taste them already."

He let go of Will's shirt and the younger boy escaped to hide behind Klara.

Klara restrained James and gave him a token swat. "That old sow will be so tough it'll take you a week to chew through her chops."

She gathered up the dirty dishes. "Mostly we'll grind her for sausage and cure the hams and shoulders. Get some sleep now. You'll have to work extra hard tomorrow."

Kungsängslilja
(Fritillaria meleagris)

Head Cheese and Leaf Lard.

Per took a firmer grip on his stunning stick and opened the gate to the pig pen. He wore his oldest boots and a pair of bitches worn and ragged at the seams. A sharp bladed knife honed thin with many sharpenings stuck out of his belt.

Klara pulled the gate shut to keep the children from following. Ivar was especially eager to help.

"Please, Klara. I can stick it after Pappa stuns it."

"Hush. You'll spoil Pappa's aim or scare the pig."

Per dropped a handful of feed into the sow's trough, set his feet, and gripped the club with both hands. When the sow dropped her head, he swung the heavy stick and clouted her square in the forehead.

The heavy sow dropped to her knees, kicking and grunting her protest. Knife in hand, Per grabbed her by the snout and tried to pull her head up so he could cut her throat. The sow was too big to straddle, so he had to brace her weight against his thigh. When he plunged the knife into the soft spot under the animal's jaw to open the jugular vein, the blade caught on the thick bone and snapped.

Ivar pushed past Klara to grapple with the pig. The two, man and boy, managed to haggle the broken blade through the animal's jugular.

With its life blood gushing out the pig thrashed wildly. Klara gripped its ears and twisted with all her strength in a futile attempt to keep the animal from struggling. All hope of saving the blood disappeared. It shot everywhere except into the basin James held.

Will and Stina grabbed onto the pig's legs and managed to topple the nearly dead pig over on its side. They were covered in mud and manure, but still erupted into a fit of giggles.

Per yanked the broken knife from the carcass and stood up. He rubbed his back and tried to shake the kinks from his cramped muscles.

"Finally. She was a tough one."

Her executioners stood around her, smeared and panting for breath.

"Get one of the horses harnessed, Ivar. We need to drag her out of this mess."

Klara sent the children for water. "Clean yourself up some, too."

When Klara reached the house, Anna had a huge iron kettle of water heating on an open fire in the side yard.

She asked her mother if the water was hot yet.

"I'd better get the laundry water heating, too," said Anna.

"I'm a bit messy. The kiddels are worse."

"Is everyone all right?"

Klara dipped her hand into the water.

"Not quite boiling. Good."

The water had to be just the right temperature to loosen the pig's hair. Sacks made of course fabric would be soaked in the hot water and laid across the pig's side and hams. If the temperature was right, the bristly hair would lift off easily when it was scrapped. When the killed sow was completely free of hair and pearly white clean, she would be hoisted head down from the tree.

When the pig was clean, Per and the boys gutted the hog; Klara and her mother worked on the head until it was ready to be split lengthwise and boiled along with other parts that were impossible to bone out.

They removed the eyes, eardrums, and nasal passages and tossed them in the scrap pan that would go to the chickens. The flat, worn teeth were chipped out and the jowls removed to be cured with the bacon and hams. The tongue was boiled with the other parts, to be pickled later.

"Now for the ends," said Klara.

"I hate the ends," said Anna. "Especially the feet."

"Too bad we can't pitch them to the dog."

"Waste not, want not."

They continued their tedious work of removing the hair from the ears, tail, and feet. The feet were particularly difficult to clean because the horny toenails and dewclaws had to be pulled off and the glands between the toes cut out.

"All done. Throw this mess into the pot with the head."

"Did you do the skin yet?"

Squares of skin were sewed up in muslin bags and added to the pot to provide a gelatinous base for the head cheese. The whole mess would boil for hours, then it would be set in the spring house to cool. The skin would be removed and the meat separated from the bone.

The skin, transparent and ground to bits, along with the meat scraps was added back to the strained pot of broth with salt, pepper, and vinegar for flavoring. After another, shorter cooking, the mixture was poured into flat pans where it would set up because of the gelatin from the bones and skin.

"Where should I put the headcheese, Mamma?"

"I think in the empty granary. The night breeze will cool it down quickly. Cover it with muslin to keep the flies off."

"I'll call Pappa and the boys to supper on my way back." Klara picked up the stack of headcheese pans. "Leave the dirty kettle. I'll wash it later."

By the time the sun finally dropped below the trees the whole household was sleeping the sleep of the exhausted. Another day of grindingly hard work awaited them in five short hours.

The next morning the women separated the meat from the bones as the men brought the sides and shoulders into the house. Everyone pitched in to cut the meat and fat into pieces small enough to run through the hand grinder.

The hams and side bacon were trimmed, then rubbed with salt and sugar. When the hams were finished, Anna sewed them up into bags of plain cloth. Per and Ivar carried them to the smoke house to hang above a slow, smoky fire which would burn for weeks.

The slabs of bacon were salted and placed in a wooden box whose bottom contained numerous small drainage holes. Its lid fit inside the box and a heavy weight was placed on it to press down on the stacked bacon slabs inside. The liquid worked from the meat by the salt would drain out the bottom. After several days the bacon would also be sewn into bags and hung in the smoke house.

The only pork that would escape the boiling, the sausage grinder, or the curing process would be the tenderloin, the thin roll of meat along the hog's back bone. The loin was sliced and fried with potatoes, a feast for the weary butchers.

Per appeared in the doorway with a long cascade of white fat in each hand.

"Here is the leaf fat, Mamma. Will you render it today?"

"Such a lot."

Klara brought a clean enamel pan and held it for the sheaves of fat. They made a sharp rustling sound as Per folded the foul smelling membrane holding the gut fat into the pan. Klara always wondered how the most desirable lard could be rendered from such a stinking part of the hog.

"I'll find a cool place for it. We'll try to wait till later to work it."

"Please."

Anna turned to Per. "Will you be staying to crank the sausage grinder?"

She had the bowl of salted casings ready on the table alongside the huge mound of grinding size pieces of pork and fat. Ivar was busy fastening the grinder to the edge of the bare plank table, while James struggled to assemble the cast iron contraption used to force the ground pork into the narrow casings. The sausage stuffer was a fat cylinder with a top that spiraled down inside when the crank was turned, forcing the ground meat out the spout at the bottom. The casing would be placed over the spout and held there as the ground meat squinched out in a tight finger of sausage.

"A nice mess of sausages to trade," said Anna.

"I hope it turns off cool in the morning," answered Per. "Would be a shame if the lot spoiled."

And so went the time of the first butchering. In a month or so they would go through much of the same process with the three goats, but since that meat would be for the family's use, they would wait for cooler weather to keep the meat from spoiling as long as possible.

When the wagon was loaded for the trip to town, Klara stood with her father assessing their chances of having enough to trade for everything they needed.

"You have the list, Papa?"

"It seems long. What should I leave off if the trading doesn't go well?"

"It's hard to know. Just do the best you can."

Klara hesitated, then knowing her mother would come outside at any minute, made a request of her father.

"Could you try to get a bottle of balsam tonic for Mamma? Don't tell her, but please try. I'm worried about her."

She pressed a scrap of paper, an old label with the name of the patent medicine, into his hand and quickly kissed him on the cheek. "Thank you, Papa."

Ivar, his hair slicked back and wearing his best shirt, appeared, ready to go. Anna followed him with a more instructions on how to behave and being careful. Father and son climbed into the wagon and set off down the winding track to the main road.

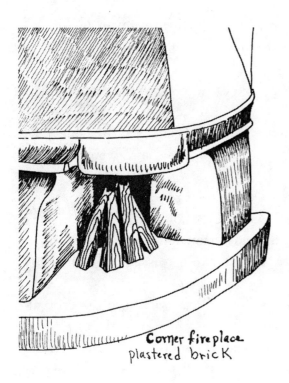

Corner fireplace
plastered brick

The Little Foxes Spoil the Vine.

Per stomped into the kitchen and sat down to wait for his supper to be placed before him. He leaned his elbows on the table and rested his forehead on his knuckles.

"Otto Lof is cutting his barley. First the rye, now the barley," he said. "It's not good."

Ivar finished drying his hands and joined his father at the table. The family dog, a brown creature with matted coat and whippish tail, sprawled at his feet.

"The chickens are already huddled on their roost," he said.

"The stars are close tonight. No clouds to hold the heat."

Ivar reached down and ran his hands through the dog's rough hair.

"Look at the coat on Fenrye. Seems like he just finished shedding out from last winter."

"I expect we're in for an early frost. I fear we'll lose the crop all together if we don't harvest now."

Anna brought the kettle of yellow pea soup to the table, while Klara broke a round of flat rye bread into hand-sized pieces. Dishes of pickled beets, slabs of cabbage, and boiled eggs had already been placed on the table.

"It's barely September. I wish we could hold off longer," said Anna.

She ladled out soup and returned the kettle to the stove. A high pitched wail from the corner by the loom interrupted her before she could sit down. Five-year-old Moochie was tormenting the baby, again. Anna hurried to pry Moochie's fingers from the baby's scalp.

She called to Stina, "Come get Moochie," then returned to the table.

She didn't watch as eleven-year-old Stina bent down to take Moochie in her arms. The screaming child was almost too heavy and Stina staggered as she put her arms around Moochie's waist and lifted her off the floor. Moochie protested by screaming louder and beating on Stina's face with her clenched fists. Like a little mother Stina jiggled the child and covered her face with kisses in an attempt to soothe her, while she paced up and down the room.

Anna spooned up her soup, crumbled hard bread into it, but ate little. The baby sat alone in the loom corner, crying.

"Shut them up, now," said Per. "Please."

He seldom paid the younger children any mind, but the racket was greater than usual. The load of worry, heavier.

"Klara, get the baby."

Klara scooped up the baby and sat down to finish her supper. She knew her father was on edge. His short fuse, his demand for quiet, the way he rubbed his eyes, all signaled his anxiety. I need to try harder, she thought. Keep Moochie out of trouble. Remind Stina to watch, too. Her father's next comment startled her from her musing.

"I should take her to the Charity Asylum," said Per.

Anna stood up quickly, her bowl of soup skittered across the table leaving a wet trail.

"Take her away? You can't take her away."

"She'll be wandering the countryside like the Olden's idiot before long. The parish board will censure us, maybe levy a fine, and then, where will we be?"

Klara shared her father's fear, but hadn't even begun to think of a solution to Moochie's future.

"I thought they only accepted orphans. Our Moochie hardly qualifies."

"I expect they'll take any child in need. I'll ask next time I'm in town."

Anna didn't answer him this time, didn't cry out in protest, didn't nod in agreement. She just stood staring at Moochie. Stina held the child by her upper arms, supporting most of her weight because Moochie was being uncooperative by refusing to stand up. The two of them bumped awkwardly around the room in a kind of macabre dance. Moochie's feet just brushed the floor, her hands flailed aimlessly, ripping at anything in reach, her sister's hair, dress, her own face. Her cheeks flushed red and her nose dripped. Long strings of saliva dropped from the corners of her mouth. Before Anna could speak, Stina danced the screaming child into the back bedroom.

Klara held up the baby and spoke into the sudden stillness.

"We really need to name this baby and have her baptized before the snow comes."

No one answered her.

~~~

Great flocks of migrating birds began their twice yearly fly over the next day. That evening Per brought the wooden handled swathing scythes down from their place under the eaves of the storage building. He spent several hours bracing each curved blade against his knee with one hand, while he meticulously sharpened its cutting edge with a whetstone. Klara tried to build the fire higher so he could work on the blades without straining his eyes in the semi-darkness of the room.

She sat across the room from her parents, shelling out beans, slicing cabbage for pickling, or carding wool from one of the large bags piled under the washstand. It was picky, time consuming work, but something she could do mostly by feel in the long evenings.

Her mother sat spinning the carded wool or just gazing off into space. Stina and Will knelt on the floor in the shadows, where they played with Moochie and the baby. Per had not mentioned sending Moochie away, again. James and Ivar had taken advantage of the brief time without work to build a sled. They had the box finished and the steering yoke roughed out. Tonight they were thinning and smoothing the long, curved runners.

Watching Stina and Will, Klara wondered if anyone would remember the baby's first birthday. Surly they would name the child then. She was a bright, quick, happy child and deserved a name. She was already talking and copying the simple finger games the children showed her. Teaching her enchanted them as much as trying to teach Moochie frustrated them. No matter how hard they tried, Moochie failed to respond to their songs and games.

Stina was careful to stay between the baby and Moochie as they sat together on the rag rug. Past experience had taught them that Moochie would dig her finger nails into an unsuspecting person's hair or cheek and there would be a battle to detach her. She grew larger and stronger each day, but showed little awareness of the world around her.

When the *nisse* child was quiet and seemingly content, she looked like a pretty, rosie-cheeked little girl except for the strands of drool on her chin and the unfocused look in her eyes. A closer look revealed the scars of old scratches on her face and the uneven pale hair that seemed to always be trying to grow back in the bare spots on her head.

Moochie could walk, run even, but would crash into the furniture or pitch over on her face at unexpected times. Except for occasions like this evening when someone could find the time to supervise her, she spent her time tied to a bed post or some other heavy piece of furniture with a long strip of old bed sheet. Like a huge puppy needing a romp, James or Stina would take her outside and let her run herself to exhaustion once or twice a day.

Klara wondered how they would manage when winter bound them to the house for weeks on end. And what would happen to Moochie as she grew older? Older and stronger. She was almost as tall and as heavy as seven year old Will. The Olden child had wandered the countryside from the time he was six, sleeping in barns, eating from garbage heaps, frightening livestock. No one had paid him much attention until he torched a barn in the next parish. It was just before his twelfth birthday. The sheriff had taken him to the asylum in Borlange the next day.

From worrying over Moochie's future Klara's thoughts wandered to the harvest that would begin in the morning. The family grain fields were really just stony plots of cleared ground scattered in the few level places across the hill's spine and down along the river. The Larsson farm was like a wrinkled rag stuffed into some huge pocket on the earth with the river twisting through the bottom. The land went either uphill or downhill, but never really level. On the highest part grew wind-stunted fir that merged into thicker groves of pine and birch at the lower boundary of the narrow farm that angled over the steep hillside. Rocks, gray monsters of every size, thrust up the thin soil of the fields. Though many hours of stoop labor had been expended digging them out and piling them around the edges of the fields, a new crop emerged with each spring rain in never ending profusion.

Some of the cleared plots were too small to swing the scythe through and had to be cut with a sickle. Cutting grain with the hand sickle was a job hated by all but the very young, as it meant hours of bending to cut and bind the grain in those small plots. James would probably get the job this year, if Per thought he could be trusted to work with so sharp a tool.

The harvest would begin with the rye in the small fields on the other side of the ridge. Those plots were the farthest away, but had the best stand of grain. The day promised to be clear, so after a hurried breakfast Per, Ivar, and Stina loaded the wagon with the scythes, water crocks, hanks of binding cord made from wheat straw, the whetstone, and an extra blade.

In families with more resources, families where the husband worked away from home, cutting and sheaving the grain was considered women's work, but Anna had been unable to wield the heavy scythe since the birthing of Moochie. The last several years Klara had insisted on staying at home to help her mother with the unloading, the threshing, the winnowing. Now she helped Ivar hitch the bay mare to the wagon.

"Is the hired man from the Lof place coming to help?" said Klara. She held the single tree, so Ivar could fasten the traces.

"No, he's busy with the threshing. It'll be the Hansson boys."

"Too bad. It's more work, trading with the Hanssons." The Hanssons, a father and two sons, rented a piece of mountain land for their sheep, but lived in town. It was a long walk to their holdings.

"They'll meet us there," said Ivar. "I wish you would come, too."

Klara remembered other years, years when she had gone to the fields. The bundled grain would form sheaves so big that nine-year old James could not wrap his arms around them. They were bound with twisted wheat straw and carried from the hilly fields to the wagon waiting below on the steep path. When the wagon was loaded so high it threatened to topple over, Per would send James to lead the patient horse back to the farmstead.

~~~

When James arrived back at the farm yard, Klara met him and helped him tie the horse to the iron ring set in the wall of the granary. The two story square granary, whose second story overhung the first by several feet, was constructed of peeled and varnished logs. The windowless lower section was floored with slabs of stone and chinked tight to keep the grain after it had been threshed. The tight room could also be used as a threshing floor, though most years the area outside the granary was used.

The yard was a hard-packed earthen oval, stamped out by countless feet over the years. Here, when the grain was dry and fully ripe, the sheaves were trampled to separate the grain from the straw and chaff. This year the threshing would be done on the stone floor of the granary to be sure none was lost. The straw, along with dried grass hay and feed, was stored in the second story out of reach of rats and mice.

Klara and her mother unloaded the grain, while James fed and watered the horse and filled the water crocks to take back to the workers.

"Will we make horn bread from the rye, Mamma?"

Klara knew the green grain would quickly mold if stored in its raw form, but the thick rounds of sour rye bread would keep all winter if they were dried properly. At least, she thought they would keep all winter. She had no memory of the loaves' keeping properties being put to the ultimate test, since even in good years the horn bread would all be eaten by spring.

Horn bread was made from the new ground rye in the usual way, but before baking in the brick oven the loaves were punched through with a curved cow horn to give each one a hole in the middle. When the loaves cooled, they would be threaded on a long pole and hung near the ceiling of the kitchen to dry. With time the loaves would become hard as stone,

until they had to be soaked before they could be eaten.

"Horn bread from the rye, *tinbrod* from the wheat and barley. *Lefse* from whatever potatoes are left from the brewing."

Anna worked quickly, reaching to take the sheaves from Klara as she tossed them down from the wagon. She stacked the bundles against the whitewashed inner wall to await the threshing.

Klara stopped to brush the chaff from her forehead and catch her breath. Also to give her mother a rest.

"Do you think there will be enough food to get us through the winter?"

"There's always a way to get by, Klara. When I was a girl, I remember making bark bread when we ran out of food in mid winter. We stripped the pine and spruce trees of their inner bark and shredded it, mixed it with water, patted it into cakes, and baked it on the embers of the fire."

"How did it taste?"

Klara wrinkled her nose in disgust. Wouldn't that be a treat, she thought, bark bread and rotten small fish. She remembered how her granpappa told of trying to preserve the year's run of small fish when they were unable to buy salt. They had buried the silvery fish in the ground, hoping the even temperature of the earth would keep the fish from spoiling. The fish fermented, but hungry people ate it anyway and eventually developed a taste for the earth-soured small fish.

"What did bark bread taste like, Mamma?"

"It went well with Granpappa's rotten small fish," said Anna with a laugh. "That's what you were thinking about, wasn't it? Don't worry so much, Klara. We'll survive. We always have, haven't we?"

"It's always feast or famine for us isn't it?"

At least, she thought, Mamma is having a good day. Maybe she thought the talk about sending Moochie away was over or maybe her teeth didn't ache so much today. She couldn't understand why her mother was ever content with her life. Klara wondered if this was all she could hope for her own future. Sofia had escaped, hadn't she? Escaped from a situation far worse than her own. A clattering outside interrupted her musings.

James appeared in the doorway of the granary. His mother and sister had the wagon unloaded and the sheaves of grain almost all stacked in neat rows.

"I fed the horse. Water crocks are full. Is the food ready? Pappa and Stina said they was starving."

"At the house you'll find the pasties in the warming box over the stove. There's a basket on the table. Ask Will to help you."

Anna brushed the hank of straw blond hair back from James's eyes in an uncharacteristic gesture of affection.

"You need a haircut, again. Maybe your pappa can get around to it when the grain is in."

By the time the sheaves were stacked, James was back with the woven basket over his arm.

"See if we got everything, Mamma."

Klara reached past her mother to take the basket from James. She counted the onion and potato filled crusts called pasties and made sure he had included a jar of sour pickles and another of spiced beet relish to garnish them. A crock of butter milk and a dozen salt fish wrapped in oiled paper completed the meal.

"That'll do," she said and handed the basket back to James.

"Mamma, Will wants to come along and help out," said James.

He had already stuffed half a pastie into his mouth and would have the rest of his dinner eaten by the time he drove the horse out of the yard. A trail of crumbs rained down his shirt front as he spoke.

"He says he's old enough to work at loading sheaves. At least he could mind the horse. Please, let him come."

"And who will be minding the babies if I let Will go with you?"

Anna reached down and brushed the flakes from James's mouth and shirt.

"He's only seven, and we'll be threshing and winnowing here all afternoon."

"Why can't we bring the kiddels over here, so you can watch them while you work?"

"Don't be silly, James. We'd never get the job done, and besides, breathing this dust and chaff isn't good for them."

"Moochie and baby are asleep. You can check on them once in awhile."

"No. Hook up the horse and get going, now."

Without answering James left the granary, slamming the door behind him.

"Getting independent, isn't he?" said Anna.

Klara wondered if her mother was angry at James. He was only nine and a boy at that. She swept the stone floor of the threshing room and laid down the heavy cloth on which they placed the grain. Anna brought the thrashing flails and laid the first bundles of rye on the floor. They worked side-by-side, beating the piles of cut grain with the jointed, long-handled flails. The noise and the dust made conversation impossible.

Several hours later they had most of the grain shelled out on the floor. Anna motioned to Klara that it was time to stop and scoop up the finished grain. When the flails fell silent, it was a moment before Klara's hearing returned to normal.

"Do you hear something, Mamma?" Klara stood straighter and tried to listen. "From the direction of the house."

"Do you think it's the baby?"

She dropped her flail at the same time Klara dropped hers and they hurried out of the granary. The noise became frustrated howls punctuated with coughs and hiccups of exhaustion. The crying had been going on for a long time, masked by the noise and confinement of the threshing room.

They ran across the yard to find the door hanging ajar and the wash stand turned over. The baby sat in the puddle crying and hiccuping loudly. Klara scooped up the soaked child and pulled off her wet shirt. She ran her hands over the baby's head and body, but found nothing wrong.

"Just wet and a little scared, I think."

"Will. Will. Where are you?"

Anna quickly searched the main room, then went into the dugout bedroom, but found no sign of Will or Moochie.

"Where can they be? He wouldn't go off and leave the baby."

"Will might if he thought she was sleeping," said Klara. "He must have gone with James to the field, after all."

She held the child close against her shoulder and tried to soothe her by rubbing the back of her head. Jiggling the baby, Klara paced back and forth. She looked out across the yard all the while, hoping Will and Moochie would suddenly come into view.

"Where could they be?" Anna raised her hands to her throat. "Go to the field and see if they're with your father."

"No, Mamma. You go. I'll dry off the baby, then look through the barn and other buildings."

Klara knew going to the fields would be easier than searching the area around the house and barn toting the baby on one hip. Fear of what she might find also prompted Klara to send her mother to the harvesters. What if the children had fallen into the cistern or met with some wild animal? There were deep sink holes on the slope below the house. She thought about the goat they had pulled from one of the steep-sided pits last summer, its neck broken.

The roar of the river, running full this time of year, sent her fears careening off in a whole different direction. She watched her mother hurry out of the yard in the direction of the hilly fields. A wave of gray despair washed over her. Her knees were suddenly so weak she had to sit down for fear of dropping the baby. Her heart racing, she sat cradling the sobbing child.

Frantic to gain control of her own thoughts and desperate to distract the sobbing child, Klara stared at the chocolate set on its high shelf. She got up and laid the baby on the bed, her steps sure again. She went to the cupboard and brought down one of the bright cups. She held it out to the child and made soft mewing sounds to tempt her to look at it.

The baby reached for the pretty thing and finally stopped crying.

Klara felt a measure of relief and, for a moment, a sense of joy as she watched the expression of pain and frustration on the baby's face replaced by a sweet smile. She stripped off the rest of the baby's wet clothing and dressed her in a warm wrapper. She put on her own coat and scarf, then found a strip of cloth which she threaded through the handle of the small cup. Just before she left the house, she looped the strip of cloth around the baby's neck so the cup rested on her chest where she could finger it and suck on it. Maybe it would bring a measure of protection, too, like some ancient amulet. With a new sense of resolution she hefted the child on her shoulder and began hunting for Will and Moochie.

Klara started by methodically going through the attached stable, outhouse, and storage building. She looked through the boxes, the fish barrels, any place a small child could hide. From the outbuildings she began a slow series of sweeps across the slope below the farmstead until she reached the spruce grove that marked the southern most boundary of the Larsson farm. The river made further progress in that direction impossible.

Klara stood staring at the expanse of muddy bank while she shifted the baby to her other shoulder. The bank was churned and rutted by the feet of the animals, but she saw nothing odd or out of the ordinary that might indicate the struggle of a child in trouble. A hopeful sign, she thought and turned her back on the river to search the spruce grove. Thick underbrush filled the space between the trees and made her progress tedious.

When she stooped to free her long skirt from some briars, she saw a small mound of rocks at the base of a towering tree. Startled, she realized it was a grave mound. It must be baby Karl, the baby born to her mother even before she had married Per Larsson. Maybe it would be better for all of them if they were soon to pile a grave mound for Moochie, here. Klara turned away with a weary heart and made her way back to the house. Darkness would fall quickly now that the sun had dropped below the tree tops. The baby was fussing again, too.

Klara lifted the chocolate cup from around the baby's neck and placed it on the table before she carried the child to the back bedroom. Just after sundown Per and Anna, followed by Ivar, Stina, and a very frightened Will, hurried to the house.

James brought up the rear with the horse and wagon and a half load of rye. He tied the horse to the granary wall and started to unload. Klara held the door for them and called to James.

"Just take care of the horse and come in."

She wanted to hug Will, tell him she was so glad he was alive and well. She also wanted to shake him until he told her where Moochie was and what had he been thinking when he left the babies. She did neither.

"She's not with you?" said Klara.

"Did you find Moochie?" asked Ivar.

He looked worried and angry, more angry than worried, thought Klara.

"We had only cut and loaded the little plots of rye near the spruce grove when Mamma came looking for Will and Moochie."

"How's the baby?" asked Stina. "A fine thing it would be if she caught a chill in all this mess."

For all their questions no one needed an answer to know that Moochie was still missing.

"The baby's sleeping. No harm done, but I've found no trace of Moochie, yet."

Klara put her arms around her mother and led her to a chair near the fire.

"You're cold. Let me get you some tea."

"No. No, I must go look for her." Though she protested, Anna sat down and leaned her head back, eyes closed. "I should have checked them sooner."

Per looked anxiously at his wife, then went to the wood box and started gathering up a sack of pine knots. "I'm afraid it will be slow work searching in the dark."

Anna sat up straight and stared into the fire. Her eyes reflected the licking flame, her cheek bones and chin stood out from the shadows furrowing her forehead and deep lines around her mouth. When she spoke, it was with the firmness of an oracle.

"It's because we talked about sending Astrid away. We are being punished."

Her use of Moochie's real name sounded ominous in the dim room lighted only by the firelight. Klara felt a renewed sense of fear, but it was now fear for her mother. She tried to interject something encouraging for her mother's benefit.

"The dog is missing, too. I expect they're together somewhere. If this wind would just die down we could probably hear them."

She brought down the iron holder that would enable them to use the pine knots as a torch and handed it to her father.

"I don't think it will rain tonight. James and Will, stay here and look after Mamma and the baby. See that they get some supper. Keep the fire up."

Per, Ivar, Stina, and Klara put on their coats and stuffed caps and mittens in their pockets along with some bread so they could eat as they went. No one seemed to notice the delicate cup perched on the end of the table. The last thing Per did before leaving the room was to light the first pine knot from the fireplace and drop it into the iron basket of the torch. Once outside he turned to Klara.

"The Hansson boys left work early, even before James got back with the empty wagon. They thought a storm was brewing. They wanted to get on home to put their sheep under cover."

"I hope they're wrong. For Mamma's sake they have to be wrong."

Klara put on her scarf and tried to tie it under her chin. The wind nearly whipped it from her head and she had to turn her back before she could tie it.

They searched in ever widening circles from the house to the river bank. Twice Klara held the torch, while Per lowered Ivar into a sink hole to better see the bottom. They called and whistled until they were hoarse, though the desperate notes were flung back in their faces by the wind. No trace of the missing child was found by the time the last pine knot sputtered out. The searchers stumbled back to the house in the dark, wet, muddy, and chilled through.

With a few hours sleep Klara, Ivar, and Per were up before the sun to be ready to go out at first light. They moved quietly so they would not disturb Anna and the younger children who had finally fallen into an exhausted sleep.

It had rained hard in the night, but the dawn seemed to promise a clear day. Just before she left the house, Klara looked in on her mother. She lay sleeping with the baby cuddled on one side and Stina on the other. Her skin had a gray tinge and dark circles framed her eyes.

James and Will slept on the straw pallet nearby, twined together like two puppies. I hope Pappa won't punish them too harshly, she thought. A shudder of remembrance troubled the skin at the nape of her neck. Her thoughts went back, back to a time before Moochie was born, before her granpappa died, before Hulda and Sonja left for the city.

It was a day she had left her chores and ran off for a swim. Though her older step-sisters, Hulda and Sonja, bore the punishment, Klara always blamed herself, for the willow switch licking her sisters received, and for the more severe punishment meted out to her friend, Sofia.

It was the day the Russian saw sharpeners had frightened them. Sick in bed with a high fever after their escapade, Klara hadn't known about Sofia's punishment for months. Britz Varm had nearly killed her daughter that day. She beat Sofia with the strap, but, when the girl refused to repent, refused to cry, Mrs. Varm attacked her with the iron fire tongs. Only the intervention of Mrs. Lof saved her. Mrs. Varm was hauled off to jail for several months. Sofia had a concussion, a broken arm, and a new resolve to find a better life. Mrs. Lof set her arm and put the girl to bed, but Sofia vowed to leave as soon as she could find a way.

When Klara followed her father and Ivar out the door, she noticed the chocolate cup on the table. I must remember to put it away when I return, she thought.

They split up to cover more ground and agreed to ring the big yard bell if they found anything. In any case they would meet back at the house when the sun topped the spruce grove. While Ivar and Per elected to search the rough downhill slope and the river bank, Klara stood at the edge of the yard trying to decide which way Moochie might have gone when she escaped from the house. The smoothest, straightest path lay around the curve of the hill away from the farmstead. Except to chase down an errant goat, Klara normally had no reason to go that way because the smooth path quickly petered out and became a waste land of head-high boulders and tough, clothes shredding greenbriar vines. It was a rough, inhospitable piece of land. Today she took the dim path in that direction.

After she had walked a few minutes, Klara realized the curve of the hill muffled the shouts of those searching on the downhill slope by the river. No matter how loud she had yelled last night, no one here could have heard her. And in return, no one here could be heard. If the dog barked or Moochie cried, the sound would have been muffled completely by the hill and the wind.

With renewed hope Klara started calling every few minutes as she angled across the slope towards the tangle of rocks and briars. When she reached the first rock ridge, she called vigorously, held her breath and listened. Faint bird song and the moaning of birch leaves reached her ears over the pounding of her own heart, but nothing that suggested a child or a dog. She continued walking, stopping to call, and trying to listen. By the time she came to a second ridge of gray rock she was out of breath.

After a few more hoarse shouts Klara sat down on a rocky ledge to rest. When she finally caught her breath, she decided to sit just a little longer to think about where to go next.

No longer holding her breath and trying to hear over the beating of her own heart, Klara gradually became aware of faint sounds among the harsh voices of the red birds and chickadees. She shut her eyes and listened hard. Was the sound coming from beyond that wall of boulders? It seemed like faint barking and a thin high pitched wail, but maybe she imagined what she wanted so badly to hear. Still unsure of the sounds, Klara stood up and pivoted slowly, listening intently, afraid to even breath. She was sure it was barking, accompanied by the sound of snapping twigs in the underbrush on the uphill side of the natural wall of stone.

"Moochie, Fenrye. Is it you, Moochie? Please answer me."

Klara shouted again, with all her strength. Then muttered to herself, "Don't be so stupid, Klara. When has Moochie ever answered anybody?"

Convinced, now, that she had found Moochie and the dog, Klara worked her way along the piled rocks trying to find a way to climb up through the tangle. In the mass of vines at the base of the boulders she found a flat rock she could use as a step. She pulled herself up the slope by stepping on the flat rock and using a tangle of vines to haul herself up to the next ridge of rock. When she finally lay balanced on her stomach over the top most rock, she looked into the shallow pit of an abandoned mine, collapsed with age, time, weather. A huge mass of blackberry briar dominated the long neglected acreage with a few stunted trees covered with vine here and there.

"Moochie, Fenrye," she called. "Where are you?"

A faint barking came from the rocks piled along the inner side of pit.

"Fenrye, Fenrye," yelled Klara.

A flurry of barking and a great cracking of dead limbs drew her eye to a shadowy hole to her left. There she saw the dog trying to push his way through the brambles towards her. He managed to thrust his head up through the underbrush, but that was as far as he could get. The longthorned greenbriars caught in his ragged coat and kept him prisoner as effectively as chains. Klara's first impulse had been to climb down the wall and hurry to his aid, but seeing the danger of the briars she changed her mind.

"I'm going back for help. If I climb down there, we'll all be stuck. Hang on, Fenrye."

She wished the dog could talk. She would ask him if Moochie was with him, was she alive, how did they get into such a mess?

"Be quiet, Fenrye. You'll be out of there soon."

Klara hated the thought of leaving the terrified dog, but she knew she needed help.

"I'll be right back with Pappa and Ivar. Don't move. Promise? There I go again, talking to a dog as if he could understand me."

She climbed back down the slippery rock, then stopped and took off her apron, to tie to an overhanging branch. It would be stupid if she couldn't find this place when she returned with help. She gathered her long skirt up around her knees and headed down the slope for home. She slipped on the stony path several times, but recovered her balance before she sprawled in the dirt.

By the time Klara reached the house, the sun was over the spruce grove and her father was just coming up the hill.

She shouted to him. "I think I've found them, Pappa. Ring the bell for Ivar. We need rope and a sharp knife."

By the time Per found the rope and knife, Klara had told her mother the hopeful news and dug an old blanket out of the storeroom. Ivar ran into the yard and without giving him a chance to catch his breath, they followed Klara up the slope towards the rock ridge. The white apron fluttering against the trees near the top of the hill guided their mad scramble over the rocks.

At the wall Per boosted Ivar up the rock, then followed him into the old pit. Klara waited below. With the sound of her father's labored breathing in her ears, she could imagine his struggle to cut a path through the briars. Soon wild barking told her they were in the right place. A few minutes later Ivar stuck his head over the top of the rock.

"Heads up," he warned her.

A rough squirming bundle bumped down at the end of the rope. When the bundle revealed itself as the dog, Fenrye, wrapped in Ivar's jacket, Klara grinned and untied the animal. His coat was matted with mud and dried blood. He rolled over on his back, whining and slobbering before he settled down to lick his bleeding paws.

A shout drew her attention from the dog. Ivar scrambled down the face of the rock gripping the rope to steady himself. When he was firmly on the ground, Per lowered another bundle down to Ivar.

It was Moochie, a limp, still Moochie. Per had cocooned her in the blanket to drag her out of the briars and lower her down the rock. Now she lay on the ground between Ivar and Klara.

"Moochie, Moochie. Are you all right?"

Klara bent over and peeled the blanket back from the child's dirt blackened face and gently slapped her cheeks. She pulled the child close, listened to her chest.

"She's breathing."

She hadn't known her own hope for the outcome of Moochie's disappearance until now, but now she knew that this was best. Moochie had to be all right.

"She's cold and muddy, but who can say with one like this."

Per wrapped his coat around the child. He picked her up, folded the coat back from her face, then shifted her to his shoulder.

"I didn't realize how heavy she was getting."

Klara brushed the dirt from Moochie's forehead. The child's eyes were still closed and her mouth hung slightly open.

"We better get her back to the house."

"I'll see to Fenrye," said Ivar.

He tried urging the dog to head home under his own power, but soon gave up. The dog insisted on lying down to lick his feet. With bleeding paws and numerous deep scratches on his head and shoulders Fenrye seemed unable to clamber down the slope by himself, so Ivar picked him up. With the dog cradled in his arms, he scrambled to catch up to Klara and Per. They picked their way down the slope with great care.

~~~

Anna and Stina were waiting in the yard when they returned.

"She's alive, Anna," called Per.

He carried Moochie into the house over Anna's protest that she should take the child.

"Let me take her."

"She's too heavy for you, Anna. I don't want you carrying her."

"I'll heat some water," said Klara. "She's covered with mud."

Stina interrupted, "It's all ready, Klara. Let me take care of her, while you rest and have something to eat."

It was then that Klara realized it was way past noon and she was gnawingly hungry. It was too late to go to work in the fields. The harvest would have to wait another day. They ate, rested, and scraped the mud from their boots.

The bath revived Moochie. She came to her senses angry and ravenously hungry. They stuffed her full of bread and pickled beets and tried to calm her. Her head banging screams finally tapered off to a monotonous rocking. When Klara and Stina swaddled her in a blanket to stop her from picking at the cuts on her face, Moochie relaxed and fell asleep.

The dog needed attention, too. The boys washed Fenrye's cuts and scratches and plied him with fish heads and milk-soaked bread. In the urgency of the moment Klara failed to notice the wash of pain that periodically seized her mother. The harvest, though delayed, was not forgotten. Fear of winter and the need to gather as much food as possible lay uppermost in almost everyone's mind.

By morning it became apparent that Anna was in labor and would lose the baby she had carried a scant six months. Unable to lie down with any comfort, hit with cramps that doubled her over when she got up, she called Klara to help.

"Should I get Mrs. Lof, Mamma?"

Memories of the last time she ran for Mrs. Lof, when Moochie was born, flooded Klara's mind. She felt a knot of anxious fear in her stomach. What should she do?

Aloud she said, "Pappa could go for the doctor."

"No, nobody can do anything. It would be a waste."

"Just tell me what to do, then," said Klara.

"Get your father to go to the fields. He can't do anything here."

Klara returned to the table to assure her father there was nothing he could do. Stina packed a basket with salt fish and flat bread, then shooed her father, Ivar, James, and Will out of the house. The four of them would work in the barley fields all day Stina stayed to look after Moochie and the baby, to run errands for Klara.

When Anna reached a stage where she could no longer muffle her screams in the feather pillow, Klara sent Stina with the children to the granary to pick up stray heads of rye. By the time James and Will had brought the full wagon in twice to unload, it was over. Anna could finally relax and immediately went to sleep.

Klara cleaned up, then got a meal on the table. While the harvesters were unloading the last of the grain and tending the horse, Klara washed the tiny body of the child come too soon. She wrapped the dead baby in a linen napkin and carried it to the mound of stones under the tall spruce tree, intending to bury it there beside baby Karl.

"Can I help?" Ivar suddenly appeared through the screen of birch trees. "Sorry. I didn't mean to startle you."

"There are so many rocks, I don't know where to dig." Klara stood facing her brother, the setting sun through the yellow birch leaves outlined her thin figure.

"Let's move a few of these bigger ones covering the old grave."

"Won't that disturb things, too much?" Klara had been afraid of digging in the wrong place, afraid of disturbing old ghosts.

"No. I think there must be good clear soil above the old grave."

He took the spade from Klara. While she stood cradling the dead baby, he used the spade handle to lever out several of the large rocks. Finished with that, he scraped a shallow trench in the soft dirt.

"That should be deep enough. We won't risk disturbing the dead, either."

Klara knelt and placed her small bundle in Ivar's trench.

"Shouldn't we say a prayer or something? Can you remember the funeral service?"

Ivar looked doubtful, as if he was thinking through a hard puzzle, then he straightened his shoulders and began to speak.

"O Lord God. Thou Who for the sake of sin lettest people die and return to the earth again, teach us to remember that we must die. Teach us to remember so we will gain understanding of how to live. Dust thou art, to dust thou shalt return. Jesus Christ shall awaken thee on the Day of Judgment."

"Are you sure it was all right to say that about awakening at the Judgment?" Klara felt confused listening to her brother's words. "The babe never drew breath. It wasn't baptized."

"What can it hurt? How can an unborn baby be sinful?" Ivar scooped dirt over the little bundle. "It's sin that separates us from God."

"Did you learn that at school?"

Klara saw her younger brother as an adult for the first time. He was growing up and she hadn't noticed because she was so intent on her own troubles.

"Does the new pastor teach such things?"

"No. I've been reading the scriptures for myself." Ivar hefted the stones onto the new grave, twisting them down into the soil to make them harder to move.

"Making your own interpretation? Won't that get you into trouble?"

"I don't care."

When they returned to the house, she saw the chocolate cup on the table where she had left it the day before. At least it was safe. It seemed like she had left it there such a long time ago. Klara retrieved the cup and placed it on the high shelf.

That night a hard, killing frost laid the hope of a good harvest to rest. The remaining grain, the uncut wheat and barley, the oats growing in the low places, would not mature now. In the garden the potato plants lay wilted and black; the bean vines slumped flat in their rows.

A Candle For All Soul's Day.

That same night, the night of the season's first killing frost, Klara dreamed a dream so bleak, so cold, she shuddered each time she remembered it. In her dream time had swept ahead to November. Clad only in her summer dress, she found herself in the forest by the river. As she stood barefoot in the snow, she saw a bird drop down from the sky. It was a snowbird, slate gray with a lighter colored breast. She followed the swooping flight of the snowbird to the tree where she and Ivar had buried the stillborn baby. A pile of granite stone marked the tiny grave at the foot of the spruce tree.

From the grave two babies, the long dead Karl and the unnamed stillborn, watched the progress of their sister as she lifted her skirt above the drifted snow and picked her way toward them. Denied even a single breath of earth's good air, the stillborn now inhaled the atmosphere of the strange purgatory of the never-lived. Swaddled in their grave below the towering forest, they found solace in one-another. There, below the tall evergreens, time stood still and two souls waited for the last trumpet call.

Klara found the marker stones, brushed the snow back from the gray granite, and stood silent for a moment, listening for a word from the souls below. She thought about the day the second babe slipped from womb to grave without a pause between. Her mamma, the babes' mother, worn through with work and child bearing and some nameless ailment, had no energy left to grieve these small souls. Klara thought to pray for the eternal peace of the children, but found she lacked the words.

"I'm so sorry," she said to the small ones. "So sorry I can't light a candle on an alter, so sorry I can't pray you across the Jordan, hold your hands, wipe your tears."

Hot tears of her own ran down her cheeks. She didn't know she cried for herself.

"Sister, sister," called the oldest. "Don't cry, Sister, for you were not yet born when I came into the screams of this world."

"Klara, Klara," called the younger. "Cry. Cry for the times you could have worked a little harder, carried Mother's burden, held her hand, learned to pray."

"Don't cry."

"Cry she must."

"Hush, little one," murmured the elder. "Our Klara does her best. We must send her on her way with earth's blessing. Go in peace, Klara."

And Klara went, comforted rather than comforting. But before she went, she lit a candle and held it to drip on the largest rock. When a pool of melted wax formed, she stuck the candle there to lend its tiny light to push the darkness away for a little while.

In the Name of the Father.

Weeks passed and the snow accumulated. It piled higher and higher, first in the sheltered places, then on the open fields. The nights lengthened. The weak winter sun toiled just above the horizon to provide a few hours of daylight. The routine chores of feeding the animals, chopping wood, and bringing water to the house, were done mostly in the dark with the few daylight hours used for less mundane chores like repairing and chinking walls, scouring the woods for fallen branches and dead trees, and keeping the chimney clean.

At first the children reveled in the snow packed hills and the ice road of the frozen river. By moonlight they skated the river as far as the weirs at Hagge. Fewer chores gave James and Will time to test their new sled until they could maneuver around trees and boulders on the long hill to the river with ease. Ivar joined them occasionally, but since he was now allowed to attend school at a neighboring farm, he only lived at home on weekends. In the long evenings Per repaired harness, made shoes, and peeled logs, logs intended for a pig pen he wanted to build in the spring. Most important was the job of preserving the grain and potatoes.

In the dim morning light the family worked at turning the precious grain and potatoes into bread and *brannvin*. Per had hauled the grain to the mill at Hagge to be ground on the last possible day. The mill closed soon after because of inadequate water power. Twice a year, spring and fall, the water flow was right for grinding grain. Too little water in the late fall and too much in the summer demanded that grain be ground in the short periods of mid-fall and late spring.

But even ground into flour, the grain was too fragile to keep and must be made into bread.

The women had worked the previous week making the course, unleavened horn bread from the rye flour. The finished horn bread, threaded onto long poles hanging from brackets near the ceiling of the front room, was already hard enough to sound hollow when rapped with the knuckles. Per had appropriated several of the bread rounds to add to his brew of potato mash.

Though now illegal, nearly every country household had a *brannvin* still. *Brannvin* had provided a welcome source of income for farmers in earlier years, but the growing problem of alcoholism had spawned an influential temperance movement. The vodka-like drink was brewed from potatoes or rye, so the addition of a little rye bread was not unusual.

While Per tended the still, Anna, Stina, and Klara worked up the portion of the potato crop deemed to spoil first.

"I want to go to school, Mamma," said Stina.

She pounded the boiled potatoes in her wooden bowl with a vengeance, thumping an angry rhythm on the table top.

Anna continued to roll the already paper-thin sheet of dough without looking at her daughter.

"Klara, a little more flour, please."

She tested the thickness of the wheel-sized circle of dough by patting it gently. It had grown large enough to hang over the edges of the table.

"Stina, bring the oven stick, then check the fire."

Stina left off pounding the potatoes. She brought her mother the oven stick, a six foot hardwood wand about the size of a broom handle with a flat paddle on one end, then went to look to the fire that heated the brick oven in the wall next to the fireplace.

"The oven's hot enough."

Klara took over mixing the next batch of dough, while Stina and Anna rolled the finished *lefse* on the oven stick like a furled flag. Stina held the cast iron door open, while her mother thrust the *lefse* onto the bottom of the oven and unrolled it.

The thin, unleavened bread baked in the time it took Anna to wipe the sweat from her forehead, the flour from her hands, and reverse the oven stick to its paddle end. When she pulled the hot bread from the oven, it hung limply over the paddle. In a few hours it would become dry and leathery. She handed it to Stina, who quickly spread it flat on the table and vigorously brushed flour and ashes from it with a small whisk broom. When the bread was tidy, Stina folded it twice and draped it over a rack to cool and dry.

Klara shaped the new batch of dough into a rough cone, then dusted the table with a handful of flour and placed the dough on it. She thought about the two winters she had gone to school. She remembered how hard it was to struggle through the snow behind her older, taller stepsisters, then sit all day on a bench in the neighbor's hot living room. At first the heat felt good, but when the edge wore off her chill, she would become aware of her damp, itchy clothes. No matter how hard she tried to listen to the lessons given by the traveling schoolmaster, Klara would find it harder and harder to concentrate. After a cold lunch of bread and cheese, her stepsisters would find Klara curled up under the bench, sound asleep.

It was felt that only boys needed to learn writing and figures, so Klara learned to read *Luther's Small Catechism* and the *Bible*. Because that year's teacher had a special interest in travel, she also learned a little geography. With her new knowledge she had managed to teach Stina the bare bones of reading.

Klara felt that Stina had other motives for wanting to go to school, like gabbing with the Lof twins or flirting with Ivar's new friends who lived on the old Jansson place.

"Maybe you should let Stina go to school. In a few weeks the bread making will be finished. I can do Stina's chores during the week."

"Please, Mamma. Please let me go." Stina grabbed up the rolling pin and attacked the cone of dough. "You let Klara go to school when she was ten."

"I'll talk to your father about it, but no more now. You're giving me the headache."

Klara stopped mixing dough to look at her mother. Against the harsh winter light Anna seemed thinner, almost skeletal. She looked every minute and then some of her forty years. She wore an aura of pallor accented by the wisps of hair slipping from her usually neat crown of braids; her skin stretched almost transparent across her cheek bones. She had an oddly distracted air since she lost the baby. What was it that caused her mother so much pain? The dead baby? The worry of caring for Moochie? The toothache again?

Aloud, Klara said, "I'll get your medicine, Mamma, then you should rest. Stina and I can finish the *lefse*."

By supper time drying *lefse* hung from every rung of the rack and spread out on poles hanging swing-like the length of the room like wash on a clothes line. Since they couldn't get to the table without tangling in the *lefse*, Klara spread quarters of the fresh potato bread with butter, sprinkled them with sugar, and rolled them up for the children's meal. They could eat sitting on the floor by the stove. For her father she added a bowl of mashed potatoes with leftover bean soup spooned on it.

When the others were busy eating, Klara hastily choked down one of the bread rolls herself. Needs a little more salt, she thought. Well, they'll be better when they age a bit. She gathered up a dampened dish towel, a bowl of mashed potatoes, and some rolls of *lefse* for Moochie's supper and ducked into the back room.

Deep shadows fled before her when she opened the door to the dugout room, the back bedroom where Will, James, and Ivar shared one bed, Stina and Moochie the other. Klara called for Stina to bring a lamp, then placed the things she carried on a low stool next to the beds. Beds more like shelves, because, built-in, they lined the wall behind the fireplace for warmth, but had a floor to ceiling curtain instead of a set of doors to keep out the draft.

"Ah, Moochie, Moochie. What have you gone and done to yourself?" muttered Klara, looking down at Moochie. "Practicing to be a contortionist, are you?"

"Is she all right, Klara?"

Stina hung the oil lamp on a hook set in the wall beside the door. The light which flooded the small, low ceiled room, outlined Moochie's face with her fixed stare gazing up at them from under the edge of one of the beds. The strip of cloth binding her to the end of the bed had twisted her hands behind her back and now held her so tight she could scarcely breathe. Stina fumbled with the knots, but gave up and ran to find a knife.

Stina cut the child free, then picked her up and held her on the edge of the bed, while Klara washed her hands and face.

"Hold her while I feed her, would you, Stina?"

"She's more like a wild animal every day."

The child lunged towards the bowl of food Klara held, knocking the spoon to the floor.

"She's so strong."

Klara held the roll of bread out to Moochie, who ate it in two bites and howled for more. The second portion of bread followed the first.

"Hang on while I get the spoon," she warned Stina.

"What's going to happen to her, Klara?"

"I wish I knew. Maybe Pappa will take her to the orphan asylum."

"Will they take her if she has evil spirits?"

"Evil spirits? What are you talking about, Stina?"

"Evil spirits, invisible people who live under the ground. Mrs. Lof calls them *huldrer*. She says we did something wrong when Moochie was first born and we let a *huldrer* into the house. The *huldrer* traded its child, Moochie, for our Astrid."

"That's silly. Don't listen to that old woman. She's a foreigner from someplace over the mountains in Norway. They believe in trolls and all sorts of ugly spirits."

"She said we should have put a silver spoon or an iron knife in the baby's bed." Stina sounded less sure of herself, now. "Or if we didn't have a silver spoon, couldn't afford a silver spoon, we could have sewed a page from the scriptures or the hymn book into her swaddling clothes. She thought a page from the small catechism might have worked, too."

"That's absolute nonsense, Stina. Don't let Mamma hear you speak so."

"But what if the *huldrers* take the baby , too?"

Stina meant last years unnamed, unbaptized baby, not the new one who had died before its time.

Without answering her sister, Klara spooned the last bite of mashed potatoes into Moochie's grasping mouth and put the bowl on the stool.

"Now let's get her changed and ready for bed. It's been a long day."

She knew, too well, that the next morning would begin the whole process of feeding and cleaning Moochie again, and again, and again. Moochie, the changeling, the child who, in years past, would have been left to die in an open grave, a curse for some family weakness, some collective sin.

~~~

When Ivar returned home from school on Friday, he reported a traveling pastor would be at the Lof farm on Sunday to preach and hold a baptismal service. Since the weather was clear, the family decided to take the youngest child, the baby who had just had her first birthday, to be baptized and named. It would have been nice to be able to take the child to the Norrbarke Church in Smedjebacken, but it was hard to make the nine mile trip over a road deep with ruts and half-frozen mud for a ceremony.

Klara wondered if her father also intended to ask about finding a place for Moochie. She thought her mother was almost reconciled to placing the child in an orphanage or institution now, if only a place could be found for the child.

"Mr. Lof says the visiting pastor is a fine speaker, a real treat." Ivar made good use of his elevated status as news bearer.

Klara noticed her brother had taken to slicking his straight blond hair back tight to his head and seemed to be paying much more attention to washing his face and neck.

"Are the Lof sisters taking lessons with you and the boys?"

Per interrupted. "What are we going to name this kiddel?" He jiggled the wide-eyed child on his knee. "How about Carolina or Maria? We've not used our granmutters' names."

"Was Maria your mother's sister or your father's sister?" said Ivar.

"Your granpappa's wife was Maria."

"I think we should call her Gisele," said Stina. "It sounds modern and stylish."

"Stylish? What need does this baby have for stylish?" Anna spoke up for the first time. "All she has to look forward to is work and more work. She'll scrub and cook and look after the animals till some man comes along to wife her. Then she'll clean, cook, have babies, and wake one morning to discover she's a dried up old woman. She'd be better off dead under the spruce tree."

Klara felt a sharp pang of alarm grip her chest. She looked to her father for reassurance; surely he could say something to lay her mother's words in a less serious light. But when she saw the dismay and deep worry lines cross her father's face, she knew reassurance was impossible. The strained silence was finally broken by Ivar.

"I think we should call the baby, Naomi, a good Biblical name. It means pleasant, which suits this little one perfectly." Ivar took the baby from his father and held her up for inspection. "Little Naomi, the pleasant one."

"Naomi Maria, yes. A fine name for a fine babe." Per leaned back in his chair, obviously satisfied with the choice. "She'll be happy we waited so long."

"Enough talk. We have work to do if we're having a baptism on Sunday."

Klara got up and crossed the room to the wooden trunk where the family's good clothes were stored.

"Stina, get the flat irons heating."

Ivar handed the baby to his mother. "I'll go put the runners on the big wagon. You want to help me, James? Will?"

Friday evening and Saturday went quickly with the distraction of getting ready for the trip to the Lof farm. By Sunday morning only a few details remained before they could leave. At breakfast Per set the boys to their remaining chores.

"Clean out the wagon box and fill it with clean straw to sit on," he commanded. "I need to do some stitching on the double harness, then we'll brush the horses."

Per and the boys went outside to take care of the horses, while Anna disappeared into the back room with little Naomi. Klara and Stina inspected their good outfits, ankle length black skirts sewn from homespun wool, white blouses with long puffed sleeves of hand-woven linen, red vests which laced up the front, and store-bought white aprons of the thinnest gauze. This was the dress costume worn by all the women of the region on special occasions. Per and Ivar had dark woolen trousers to wear with their usual loose shirts and heavy jackets. James and Will would have to make do with a clean version of their everyday work clothes.

Stina sorted through the folded clothing, shaking out the skirts and carefully laying out the white blouses. In a corner of the chest she found the little satin caps that went with the outfits.

"I wish we could have new caps. These are almost threadbare and the ribbons are worn. I think the mice have been at them."

"I guess we haven't worn them since we had Will baptized at church. We made flower wreaths the last few times we dressed up." Klara found a length of red ribbon for Stina. "Here, you can put new ties on your cap."

"The flower wreaths were nice, weren't they? We looked just as fine as the town girls."

"Better, Stina. Now let's get to our ironing or we'll be showing up in our every day."

Klara left her sister checking the temperature of the irons, while she went to see if her mother needed any help. She wondered how they were going to deal with Moochie on this special day. Could they chance leaving her home by herself or would they take her along to scream her way through this most solemn of occasions?

The question was still unanswered when Ivar drove the horses up close to the front door. Klara could hear the pair of bays, mother and son, snorting and pawing.

"I'll go tell Pappa we'll be a little longer getting ready."

"No, Klara. I'll go speak to him." Anna balanced Naomi on her hip, though the child squirmed to get down. "Hold still. Mustn't spoil your christening outfit."

After Anna left the room Klara got Moochie washed up and pulled a clean dress over her head. Over Moochie's squeals of protest she could hear her parent's raised voices.

"You're not dressed, Anna?" Per sounded puzzled. "We need to be going."

"I'm staying here, Per."

Anna had not changed her clothes, though Stina had ironed her things and laid them out on the bed.

"Let me take the kiddel, so you can change." He reached out for Naomi. "Pretty baby."

And pretty she was. Anna had dressed her in the long christening robe handed down from generations of more prosperous ancestors. Heavy with lace, embroidery, and tiny seed pearls, the robe made the little girl seem a princess out-of-place. The rough fabric of Anna's dress and the dullness of the room were accented by the brightness of the little girl with her curling blond hair and clear blue eyes. Her father's hands, chapped and swollen with arthritis, on the rich dress made it seem that father and daughter were two unrelated species of being.

"Somebody has to stay here."

Anna watched Naomi and her husband, but made no move to gather up the clothing laid out for her.

"Klara and Ivar will stand as her Godparents, if the Lofs are unwilling. You and Stina can present her for the ceremony."

"No, Anna. I want you there. You need to get out, see people."

"Yes, Mamma," added Ivar. "We'll take turns with Moochie."

Will said, "We can leave Moochie. She stays tied to the bed all day, anyway."

Hearing this suggestion, Klara came into the room, lugging the newly clean Moochie. "She nearly strangled herself earlier this week. We can't leave her alone. I'll take care of her."

Per said, "Do you have to carry her? She's getting too big for you to lift."

Stina answered for Klara, "She won't walk when you want. She just flops down."

"She is getting pretty heavy," Klara admitted.

James spoke the words no one had been willing to voice: "I wish Moochie was dead."

"Hush, James," Klara objected. "You don't really mean that."

"I do too mean it."

"We must find a place for her, Anna. This gets harder month by month."

Per sat down with a grunt. The effort of such an important speech seemed to exhaust him. He sat cradling Naomi against his shoulder. Klara joined him on the bench. She tried to get Moochie to sit beside her, but the child slid off onto the floor. Klara bent to pick her up.

Per said, "Leave her be. What can it hurt?"

Klara turned away from Moochie and said, "You should be getting ready, Mamma."

"I said I wasn't going." Anna stared out the window. "Go now or you'll be late."

"Anna, you will come along. I insist." Per was firm. "We'll go see that the wagon is ready. You be dressed when I get back."

~~~

The family voice prevailed and Anna agreed to go to the baptism. Klara gave Moochie into Stina's care, picked up the fresh ironed clothes from the bed, and ushered her mother into the back room. While the rest of the family put on their winter outer clothing and went to settle themselves in the runnered wagon, Klara brushed her mother's long hair and braided it into a crown. She pinned the embroidered cap behind the tight braid, then helped her mother lace up the red vest.

She kissed her mother's dry cheek and helped her with the heavy coat and scarf.

"Leave me be, Klara."

"You look beautiful, Mamma. Just like a young girl."

"Stop fussing."

"Now hustle out to the wagon, while I get my coat. Don't forget your mittens."

Klara put her mother's hairbrush in the box that held her few personal things. She ran her fingers over the smooth surface of the Birchwood box with its worn moss green paint.

This was your marriage box, Mamma. Grandfather Eric Axel, himself, painted these faded red birds, these spindly roe deer. Granpappa, I'm sorry you can't be here to stand for your granddaughter, Naomi, today, hear her laughter and watch the smile light up her face. You would have loved to teach her your songs and stories and she would have loved you, too.

How silly you are, Klara. Talking to a man dead these ten long years.

When she reached inside to return the brush to its niche, something pricked her finger. With in-drawn breath Klara saw she had cut herself on a piece of broken china. It was the shards of the chocolate cup she had dropped the year she was five.

"Oh, Mamma, Mamma. You kept it all these years."

Klara wound a rag around her finger to stop the blood, then wrapped her cloak around her shoulders, and stooped to make a last check on the fire. When she straightened up, the chocolate set drew her eye and for a moment she allowed her gaze to follow the clean, stately lines of the tall pitcher and its seven dainty cups.

~~~

The trip to the Lof farm was postcard perfect, a family dressed in their holiday finery being carried over the new snow by a pair of heavy-maned horses. The children's singing and a well-placed scarf drowned out the breathy, hiccuping cries of Moochie, the changeling. Only a close-up view could reveal the worn, patched clothing, homemade shoes, and piecemeal harness of the mismatched plow-team, already winter thin beneath their thick coats.

Moochie's frantic squirming stopped when Klara propped her up so she could catch the wind full in her face. Klara glanced over at her mother holding James on her lap and saw she was smiling.

I wish we could ride like this, forever, she thought. If you were here, Granpappa, you would paint us flying across the snow, stroke us onto a slab of birch wood.

The answer came, no, Granddaughter. I would paint you onto the high gable of some fine building for all the countryside to see.

~~~

Klara hung back to let the rest of the family move ahead of her on the cobbled path to the Lof's front door. Settling Moochie more firmly against her shoulder, Klara pulled the blanket tighter around the dozing child. Now that the time had come, she wished she had accepted Ivar's offer to help her through the ordeal of speaking to the minister and walking into the house.

She watched the young minister greet each family member at the Lof's doorstep. He wore a new black suit and held his bowler hat in one hand, while he shook hands with the other. Klara noticed that Otto and Matilda Lof stood in the vestibule behind the minister. She thought the couple seemed unsure of how they should react to the ragged families filing into the front room with their unbaptized babies. These families were farmhands, copper workers, tree cutters, while the Lofs were landowners, important people in the community.

Mrs. Lof headed the Women's Temperance League and served as parish midwife, a position nearly as elevated as that of the local doctor and certainly more influential. Mr. Lof served as treasurer for the parish church in addition to holding office in several local societies.

The minister greeted each person with a firm handshake and a vigorous "Bless you." Klara relaxed a little when she saw him stoop to greet Will and James. He paused to speak further with Ivar, asking him about a point of catechism they had discussed during the week. When Per presented Naomi, the minister shook her small hand with solemn care. Gifting them with a divine smile, the minister told Mr. and Mrs. Larsson what a fine daughter they had.

Klara saw that smile disappear when her turn came to pass the minister and walk into the house. She was convinced he was looking at her and Moochie with disgust. Had he stepped back as she approached? And were the Lofs whispering about them? Mrs. Lof was saying something to her husband in her usual stiff-lipped fashion. Whatever she said, it caused a flush of red to creep up Mr. Lof's neck and spread over his ample cheeks. Klara could hear him reprimand her though he tried to keep his voice low.

Hurt and nearly ready to retreat back to the barn where the team and wagon were tied, Klara was surprised when Mr. Lof hurried to her, put his pudgy hand on her arm, and led her to a chair in the corner of the room.

"Sit here. If the child gets fussy, you can take her into the back bedroom." He indicated a door to Klara's left, then hurried back to take his place beside his wife.

Relief and a flood of affection for Mr. Lof came over Klara as she sat down with Moochie on her lap. God, please make her sleep through the service. Don't let us spoil Naomi's day. Through her own murmured prayer, she overheard the conversation between the minister and the Lofs.

"Why have the Larssons waited so long for the baptism their daughter? She must be at least a year old," said the minister. He looked to Mr. Lof for an answer.

Matilda Lof bent her head toward the two men. "Careless folk they are. Haven't been to service since Easter Tide."

"Nonsense, Matilda." Mr. Lof said, "They've had more than their share of trouble, much more."

His wife continued her tirade. "I'd be embarrassed to tears if I had to stand up with a year old child for baptism."

"Who will be God parents for the Larsson child?"

It was typical for the minister to obtain information from the householder where he held services, since he had no other way of knowing the members of his transient flock.

"I don't see relatives with the Larssons. Just the other children."

"They don't have any kin hereabouts. Mrs. Larsson was an only child and her parents are dead. The Mr. comes from Soderbarke parish," said Mrs. Lof.

Mr. Lof turned away from his wife. "We will stand for the Larsson child."

"We will not," said Mrs. Lof. "Why the very idea turns my stomach."

"Be still, Matilda. You talk too much."

After a hymn and a short sermon the other families brought their infants to the minister, one at a time. The three babies baptized were just a few weeks old and had a gaggle of aunts and grandmothers in attendance.

When the Larsson's turn came, Per with Naomi in his arms and his wife by his side, walked to the front of the room with Ivar and Stina following behind.

From her seat behind everyone else, Klara could see Mr. Lof's exertions to prompt his wife to join him at the makeshift alter. He whispered in her ear, his face earnest and beseeching. She rebuffed him with a black scowl and set her gaze on the birch tree outside the window. He stiffened, then with set jaw grasped her by the arm and nearly lifted her from the cushioned chair.

"'He that despiseth his neighbor sinneth.' Come along, Matilda."

"And 'the rich ruleth over the poor.' That's scripture, too."

Mrs. Lof stood up, but she continued muttering to the back of her husband's head as she followed him to stand beside the Larssons.

Mr. Lof answered, "'Whoso keepeth his mouth and his tongue keepeth his soul from troubles.'"

He stood at his wife's side and studied the varnished beam above his head with great care.

Red faced, lips pursed thin, Mrs. Lof held out her arms for Naomi. Klara was pleased to see that her baby sister played no favorites. The little girl laughed and smiled at old Mrs. Lof, patted her black satin bodice and reached to touch her crystal necklace. Mrs. Lof was, after all, first and foremost, a mother and grandmother. She could not resist such temptation and was soon crooning and clucking to Naomi.

"Are we ready?" said the minister. "Who will stand up for this child, agree to nurture and protect her if the need arises?"

"We agree," said Mr. and Mrs. Lof.

"Baptism is not simply water. It is the water comprehended in God's command, connected with God's Word. With the authority given to me by the Lutheran Church of Sweden and the Sacred Word of God I baptize you, Naomi Maria Larsson, in the name of the Father, the Son, and the Holy Ghost."

The minister dipped three fingers into the silver bowl on the alter and dabbed Naomi on the forehead.

"Know that baptism places this child under the protection of God Almighty. It works forgiveness of sin, delivers from death and the devil, and provides for the washing of regeneration in the Holy Spirit. Walk with God, Naomi."

Mrs. Lof was almost smiling. "I, Matilda Lof, return this child, Naomi, to you, her parents. Because of the ritual of baptism, I can say I hand over a Christian child rather than a heathen."

After the child was safely in her mother's arms, Mrs. Lof took off her necklace and placed it over Naomi's head.

"There, you have your first christening present."

Six Again.

After the benediction Klara watched her father stop the minister before he could slip away from the gathering.

"Sir. May I speak to you? In private."

The minister gestured Per through the bedroom door near where Klara sat with Moochie.

"What can I do for you?"

"Sir. I was wondering if you knew about the orphan asylum at Borlange. Do they take children other than orphans? Children whose parents can't do for them properly?"

"What are you saying? Speak clearly, man."

"The little girl there, sleeping on the arm of my oldest daughter. She isn't right in the head and we are worn out with her care. She's getting too big, too strong for us to deal with."

Per pointed to Klara where she sat with Moochie. Klara reddened with the attention, but tried to smile at the minister. She was so pleased with Moochie for sleeping through the service, she felt a glow of gratitude toward everyone.

"The child seems quiet and well behaved. She made no noise through the whole service."

"Only by God's blessing. Maybe the sacred word calms her," said Per.

"How old is she?"

"It is almost five years since she was born, but we cannot teach her. She is more a baby than the infants you baptized today."

"You know you must give her up, if she is committed to an asylum? How does your wife feel about it?"

"We cannot survive the winter with this child." Per seemed near tears. "Let me call my daughter in here. She can stand as a witness to my words."

When she heard her father's words, Klara with Moochie in her arms joined the men.

The minister pointed to a cot by the window.

"Put the child there. Rest yourself."

"She'll probably wake and start crying," said Klara. She laid Moochie on the cot. "That's a relief. My arms ache from holding her so long."

"Can the child speak or feed herself?" The minister did not look at Moochie. "There is a training school near Gayle that takes slow children as workers."

"No. No. She shows no inclination to learn. Klara and her sister, Stina, feed her, change her, clean her. She can do nothing."

"Please, sir. Can you find a place for Moochie?"

"I'll ask my superior when I return to town," the minister said.

"No, sir. We cannot wait longer. You must find a remedy for us, now."

At that moment Moochie awoke with an abrupt scream and rolled off the cot. Before Klara could reach her, the child had fought her way out of the blanket and ran howling from the room. By the time she reached the front door she had pulled off her wrapper and dress. She ran into the yard naked. Klara dodged through the crowded room after her.

"Stop her. Please, stop her."

Ivar held his arm across the door to keep Klara from running out into the snow.

"Calm yourself, sister. I'll get Moochie. You go back inside."

Per turned to the minister who was watching the transformation of Moochie with his jaw sagging.

"Now you see how we are suffer? My wife isn't well, either."

In a few minutes Ivar captured Moochie and brought her back to the house covered with his jacket. Klara wrapped the still screaming child in the blanket and carried her into the back room. The minister followed her.

"Now that I see the nature of the problem, I think I can help."

"How?" Per was, himself, a little shocked by the violence of Moochie's reaction. "Tell me, please."

"The almshouse at Borlange can give her a certificate of need, which will allow her to be institutionalized at the Asylum for the Feeble-minded. Maybe the doctors there can even help her."

Klara said, "When can she go?"

"We can go today, but one of you must come with her on the train."

"On the train?" Per seemed doubtful.

"I could go with her to Borlange. See that she was settled there," said Klara.

"Yes. I'm afraid you'll have to buy tickets. The child can probably ride half-fare, but Klara will need a regular ticket."

Klara's father and the minister talked about arrangements for the trip, the cost of the tickets, and legal matters. It was decided to postpone the trip until the next day so Klara could return home and collect needed items for an overnight journey. The minister would spend another night with the Lofs, so he could accompany Klara and Moochie to the almshouse. He was certain Klara could spend her night stopover in Borlange with the local pastor and his wife.

"I will write a letter detailing the case, then you can sign it," said the minister. "That just leaves the matter of the train tickets."

"Maybe Mr. Lof can buy one of our young goats. Surely it is worth that much. I'll go and ask him."

"Have you ever ridden the train before?" The minister seemed to want to get the disposition of the idiot child over with as quickly as possible now that he had committed himself.

"No, never." Klara was suddenly afraid, not for herself, but for Moochie. "Will they take good care of her?"

"As good as you can expect, I would say. You can visit as often as you like."

A hopeless idea, thought Klara. If it costs the price of a goat to visit the asylum, we'll never see Moochie again. She realized then, this young minister was only trying to give her a measure of comfort.

"Thank you, sir."

~~~

The trip home and the flurry of preparation blurred in Klara's mind. Her mother was strangely silent, her father feverishly busy with refurbishing a small trunk to hold food and clothing for the trip. The boys had a boiling, bickering fight over the choice of the goat they would take to Mr. Lof. But when they settled on the older of the two tan does, they were quick to get the animal fed and brushed. Stina heated the flat irons and pressed Klara's dress and cloak, then gathered up the things she would need for Moochie's care on the trip.

Klara suffered through a night of dark nightmares, where she ran and ran to catch up with Moochie. Each time she reached for the child, she caught only the edge of her floating dress. When the phantom child pulled away, Klara was left holding a wad of thin gauzy fabric. Then they were falling through a long tunnel, spiraling ever downward, falling, running. When Klara found herself flat on the ground, she looked over the edge of a high cliff to see Moochie below, flying through the air, swooping and turning like a bird.

Come back, come back, Klara felt herself speak, but no words came.

Klara, Klara, Moochie called. Come fly with me, sister.

Come back, shouted Klara. Don't leave.

Farther way, now, Moochie called again, but Klara could hear only her own voice. She woke with start to remember today was the day she was to take Moochie to the asylum, the day she was to ride the train for the first time, the day she was to see the world.

Somehow the Larssons struggled through breakfast, though Klara felt too agitated to eat. Anna ate nothing, said nothing.

When it came time to leave, James and Will loaded Klara's little trunk into the back of the runnered wagon. They stood in the snow with the tan goat, while Klara hugged her mother and settled herself on the seat beside her father. Ivar handed Moochie up to her, while the boys lifted the goat into the back and jumped in beside her.

The boys obviously thought it a treat to ride to the Lof farm, even as goat tenders. With a final wave they were off through the early morning chill. No one noticed the silent scream that contorted Anna's face, the clenched hands, the spasms of pain radiating through her body. Only sheer willpower kept her on her feet. Kept her from throwing herself on the wagon to drag her child back.

~~~

"I wish we could go with you, Klara," said Per. "Please be careful."

"Hurry back to Mamma." Klara stood ready to climb into the minister's rented buggy. "Stay close to home. She needs you right now."

Per handed Klara an envelope.

"Here are the papers and the money for the fare. There may be a little extra because Mr. Lof thought you might need it. Use it however you see fit."

At the station the minister found he could buy Klara a discounted ticket because she was still two months shy of her sixteenth birthday.

"Hold out your hand," he said to Klara, when he returned from the ticket window. "Did you ever see so much money before?"

"Never," said Klara. "Pappa has always kept the money, what little there was."

"These little silver coins are twenty-five *ore*. They're the most valuable." He poked around in the heap of money in Klara's hand. "These bigger copper coins are five *ore*. Five of them are the same as one silver coin."

"What about all the small coppers?"

"Those are one and two *ore* coins. This one looks different because it has the likeness of old King Oscar." He squinted to see the coin better. "It's dated 1858, so it's forty-two years old."

"Is it any good?"

"Yes, of course. The same as the others. One hundred *ore* make one *riksdaler*."

"Thank you."

She put the coins in the small bag at her waist. She only hoped it would be enough if the pastor at Borlange asked her to pay for her lodging.

By the time they boarded the train, Klara was weak with excitement. There was so much to see. She sat next to the window with Moochie on her lap facing the scenery moving past. The throbbing of the train or perhaps, the movement of the countryside past the window, lulled the child into silence. She relaxed against Klara's shoulder and put her thumb and first finger into her mouth to suck.

The car was nearly full of passengers. Most were men in suits with stiff collars and gold watch chains, but her traveling companion identified several of the more casually dressed fellows as managers at the iron works. One of them seemed to be the husband of one of the two women traveling in the car.

The other woman, dressed in a tight-fitted gown of some smooth, shiny material, attracted Klara's attention. When she asked the minister about her, he refused to answer except to comment on the impropriety of a woman traveling alone. Whenever Klara managed to take her eyes off the panorama of rocks and trees, mine housings, equipment sheds, farms with all their buildings painted a fine red ochre with white trim, she found herself staring at the woman in the tight dress. She had never seen anyone with such long finger nails, and painted red, besides. Almost as strange was the woman's feather boa which undulated with the movement of the train.

When train entered a particularly barren stretch of countryside, Klara dared examine the woman even more closely. She noticed the heavy sweep of black over her eyes, the oddly flat eyebrows that flared like wings back along the woman's temples, the two red spots on either cheek which matched the vermilion of her dress, the little black spot next to her full red mouth. She leaned over to the minister.

"She looks painted."

"She's a working girl," said the minister, but when Klara didn't respond, he amended his comment. "A hussy, a round heel."

Later, when Klara remembered her first train ride it would be with a mixture of pleasure, embarrassment, and guilt.

The minister stood up and tapped Klara on the shoulder. "We get off at the next stop. Gather up your things, so we can move to the door."

Klara put on her cloak and wrapped Moochie in the quilt her mother had insisted on sending with her. The minister had checked his own bags, so he lifted Klara's small trunk from the overhead rack. With a final whistle the train slowed to a stop. This is really happening, thought Klara. Sober thoughts replaced the taste of freedom the trip had given her. She was taking Moochie to live with strangers. How could she do that? She hardly saw the station or the fine houses along the street.

"The parsonage is close, so we'll take your trunk there first, then we'll go to the almshouse."

"What about your trunk?" said Klara.

She was nearly overwhelmed by the barrage of sounds from the crowded station. Iron-wheeled baggage wagons loaded high with mysterious parcels clattered along the cobbled walkway of the platform. Pushed by a crush of young boys shouting, "Make way, make way," the carts seemed a threat to the knots of people trying to sort out belongings, greet relatives, retrieve errant children. The porter's ear-piercing whistles and the urgency of the train's warning bell filled Klara's head. Moochie's screams failed to draw her attention until the minister, by a series of nervous gestures, indicated they should move out into the street.

In the relative quiet of the street the minister said, "Later, I'll come for my baggage later."

At the parsonage they found only the hired man at home, a strong fellow with a head of white-blond hair much in need of cutting. He found a place for Klara's trunk and told her the pastor was sure to welcome her, he always did, a right hospitable man he was. Much to Klara's surprise, the hired man then offered to go with them to the almshouse.

"I'll carry the child," he said. "She looks heavy."

Klara looked to the minister for guidance. He nodded and smiled at the hired man.

"Thank you, Knute. I'm sure the lady would appreciate that."

Klara and the minister followed the young man, who strode on ahead, jiggling Moochie on his shoulder and clucking to her.

"He's nice," said Klara. "Am I to pay him for his help?"

"Thank him again and give him a small copper. He'll feel well rewarded." The minister seemed to know the young man, perhaps from previous visits. "Knute probably feels more at home with your Moochie, than with us. He's from the training school at the idiot asylum."

"You mean he's a simpleton, an imbecile?"

"A high-grade imbecile, I think they refer to them as morons these days. The terminology seems to change every few years. Knute is one of Dr. Lectiky's success stories. I believe he presented his case history at the Geneva Conference on the Insane and Feeble-minded last year."

At the almshouse Klara was questioned about her family's financial situation. Satisfied, they gave her a certificate of need to present at the asylum. Knute seemed to know the procedure well because he was out of the room and on his way to the asylum before Klara realized they were finished with the first part of the admittance procedure.

By the time they walked through the park-like grounds surrounding the asylum, Moochie was screaming again. Knute's soothing failed to quiet her this time. At the asylum reception room they were given a long list of questions to answer, questions about Moochie, her family, her habits, her history.

"I'm not sure I can do this," said Klara. "There are two pages of questions."

"I'll read them aloud, one-by-one, and you can tell me the answer to write on the form."

The minister found a pencil and settled himself on the bench near the front of the room. He seemed at ease, much as though he admitted children to the asylum everyday. By now Moochie was stiff and red from her screaming, though her cries seemed less obtrusive in this gray, noisy place. Klara's ears were not attuned to the din of such a public place, so she was unable to distinguish the howls of the insane from the angry yelling of an inmate in search of food.

"The applicant's full name?" The minister began the questionnaire.

"Astrid Marie Larsson."

Thus went the usual questions about name, age, date and place of birth, name of parents, then the more searching questions were asked.

"At what age was any peculiarity first noticed?"

"At birth she wouldn't nurse. We fed her by hand. By four months she would have stiffening fits. After a few minutes her eyes would roll up into her head and she would go limp. We thought she was dead several times."

"At what age did she start to talk?"

"She has never spoken."

"No language," he wrote carefully. "We'll skip over the next group of questions, then. Does she understand spoken commands?"

"No. She understands nothing."

"Was she born at the full period of gestation?"

"I don't understand," said Klara. She wondered how anyone could work in such a noisy place. Her head was beginning to ache.

"Was the mother with child the usual length of time?"

"Yes. Maybe a little longer." Klara thought about the baby that came too soon. Was it possible for a baby to survive being born too soon?

"Were there any extraordinary circumstances attendant upon delivery, the baby's birthing?"

"It was a very hard birth. Mrs. Lof came as midwife. We dosed Mamma with pennyroyal and mugwort first, then we used berries from the bay tree."

"And that brought the baby?"

"Yes, very quickly"

"Bay tree is very poisonous. A medical doctor would never use such a powerful drug."

"My mother would have died otherwise. Mrs. Lof said so."

"What's done is done. Let's continue with the questions. What was the general health of the mother of the applicant? Strong and healthy, or the contrary?"

"As well as usual. Tired, but she worked hard."

"Was she scrofulous or ever subject to fits?"

"No, never."

"Was she always a temperate woman? Did she drink?"

"No. I mean yes. When her teeth ache she takes a bit for the pain."

"Umm. How long has this been going on?"

"As long as I can remember."

"How old was she when the applicant was born?"

"I'm not sure. Does it matter?"

"Was she subject to any extraordinary mental emotions or great fright or sorrow?"

"I don't think so. Oh. Granpappa had died a few months before."

"Was she related by blood to her husband?"

"Of course not. What has that to do with Moochie?" Klara was beginning to resent these strange questions.

"I'm sorry. They do seem to be impertinent, but doctors are trying to study these cases to determine what causes feeble-mindedness. I suppose they expect to find a remedy one day. Anyway, that was the last one. I'll read this over and you can sign it."

"I haven't learned to write."

"Then make your mark and I'll sign it as a witness."

After Klara made her mark on the paper, the minister took the papers to the clerk. He stamped them, then passed them to a man standing in the shadow at the back of the room. Klara wondered if he had been standing there watching all this time. After some moments of consultation, another man was called. The three of them crossed the room to where Knute stood rocking Moochie back and forth.

"Are they going to take her now?" She whispered her question to the minister, afraid of being heard.

"Yes. We'd best be going. Knute will take her to the ward. Parting from her will only be harder if we wait around."

Klara looked at Moochie. The child lay across Knute's arms, totally limp, eyes unfocused. No way to say goodbye, thought Klara. No way. She followed the minister from the room.

At the parsonage everyone treated Klara with extra consideration. She was given a fine supper, urged to take a second helping of dessert, and then was escorted to evening prayer service by the whole family. Klara tried hard to stay sad. It seemed to be the appropriate response to leaving Moochie at the asylum, but she couldn't remain glum in the middle of this happy family with its many children.

As the evening drew to a close, the young minister who had accompanied Klara on her journey stood to leave.

"May I have a word with Klara before I go?"

"You're leaving?" said Klara. She walked with him to the door.

"Yes. I have things to attend to before I go to my next meeting."

"Thank you for everything. I couldn't have gotten through today without your help."

"Someone here will see that you catch your train in the morning. You have your return ticket? I've asked Knute to take your trunk to the station."

"Yes, thank you." Klara hesitated, but knew she wouldn't feel comfortable inquiring of anyone else. "What time does the train go?"

"Just before noon. Your father knows when he must meet you at the station in Smedjebacken."

"Am I to pay the pastor for my board?"

"No. The almshouse has a fund to reimburse him for helping you. It's part of his job."

"Then the money is mine."

"Free and clear." He seemed to enjoy helping Klara sort out her small concerns. "The shops will be open in the morning. You might enjoy a little shopping with Christmas coming so soon." He didn't need to hear an answer from Klara because a look of pure pleasure lit up her face. "I'll tell Knute you want to go early and shop before you catch your train."

~~~

At exactly eleven minutes before the hour the express from Mora pulled into the station with its whistle screaming. Almost before the train came to a shuddering halt, Knute had hoisted Klara's trunk onto his shoulder and scrambled up the steps of the second class car. In the jostle of boarding and debarking passengers, he still managed to turn to give her a hand up the steps. Grateful, Klara followed him to her seat. She barely remembered to thank the young man and press a few copper coins into his hand before he placed her trunk in the overhead rack and raced back down the aisle. When she saw him appear on the platform below, she waved and called her thanks through the thick glass.

When the train jerked out of the station, Klara leaned back in her seat and thought about her morning. As the train picked up speed, she let her mind roam through the shops she had walked through that morning, the bag of treasures she carried home. With Christmas presents for everyone, she wondered if she could keep it a secret for so many days.

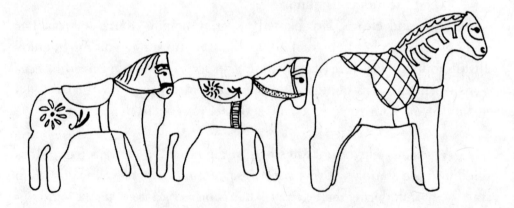

Weary People Need to Dance.

The Christmas Goat.

Klara pulled the wool coat tighter around her shoulders with mittened fingers. Its deep hood shielded her face from the sting of wind-driven snow until she turned to the north, but her old boots were hardly adequate protection against the wet and cold. She paced the narrow track from the farmyard to the main road, back and forth, stomping her feet and swinging her arms to keep warm. Ivar and Stina were late coming home from the Lof farm. Fear that the two would miss the turn off from the main road had prompted Klara into the storm to watch for them. The snow now filled her tracks almost before she turned around at the corner of the barn. Full dark will make it even harder to find the path, she thought. One more trip up and back, then I'll get a lantern. It was the shortest day of the year and the thin gray daylight faded quickly.

With the wind howling in her face Klara struggled towards the road again. Her eyes ran tears that froze on her cheeks, her nose felt like ice, and all the while sweat trailed between her breasts under the layers of wool clothing. She scrubbed a mittened hand across her face to clear her vision, then stood quiet beside the tall pine at the roadside and watched. Count to thirty, Klara told herself. Look at the snow so beautiful against the dark trees, so beautiful and so bitter. She tried not to think about the Jelking boy suffocated, frozen beneath a load of snow slipping from the branches of a fir tree. His family, his neighbors, had searched for him, but finally gave up with the hope he had run away to the city. It was a hope withdrawn when the snow melted in the spring.

Klara roused herself. The cold was creeping up her arms, stiffening her knees. She beat her hands against her body and struggled up the main road a few paces. Fear made her bolder and she ventured as far as the house-sized rock marking the overgrown path through the woods. At each step she screamed into the wind, screamed until her throat closed up and her voice dropped to a croak. She knew this was as far as she dared go. If she lost her sense of direction now, she would never find her way home.

Klara touched the rough surface of the stone, leaned into it for protection from the stinging snow. I'll rest a moment, then go back to the house, she thought. I can't do any more. Her back to the rock, Klara peered intently into the blowing whiteness. She could make out several mounds of snow among the trees, but the path became invisible after a few feet.

Were those mounds moving closer, she wondered? They grew darker against the snow, developed flapping appendages, which she recognized as beating arms, flowing scarves, pumping legs.

"Ivar, Stina," she screamed. Tears of relief crusted her cheeks as she threw her arms around her brother and sister. "This way. You're almost home."

With a great deal of shouting, stomping of snow rimed boots, and shaking of coats and mittens Ivar, Stina, and Klara ducked through the door into the warm front room of the house. The heat from the open fire folded around them and the heavy aroma of yellow pea soup and salt pork filled the air. A garland of lingonberry and pine branches on the door announced it was Christmas.

Bleary-eyed, Klara thought the colors swirled brighter than she remembered. The firelight, the candles, and the old lantern on the table alternately flared and flickered with the draft from the opened door. Klara realized her father had been about to come looking for them. The ready lantern, the boots beside his chair, and the anxious look on his usually placid face told the story.

A noise drew her gaze to her mother who stood in the shadows on the other side of the fireplace. A niggle of apprehension clawed at the back of Klara's throat when she saw her mother clenching and kneading something between her hands. A linen napkin, one of the good napkins passed down from great-grandmother, Maria, thought Klara.

What is she doing with it?

Anna's rough hands had worried the careful weave, her thin fingers had picked at the delicate embroidery until it was frayed. She stared back at Klara, silent and stone-faced.

"Mamma was worried about you," said Per. "Wanted me to get the team out to look for you."

"Sorry, Pappa," said Ivar. "We had a late start, so we took the short cut and missed the path. If Klara hadn't spied us through the trees and hailed us, we'd still be walking."

Klara removed her coat and crossed the room to her mother. When she tried to take the crumpled napkin from her, Anna jerked back, turned away.

"Mamma, Mamma, it's all right. Everyone is safe."

Anna looked down at the ruined napkin in her hands and seemed to see it for the first time. With a gasp she threw it into the fire, then, as if nothing had happened, took Klara's coat and spread it on the drying rack beside the stove.

Seeming to ignore her children, Anna gathered the other wet coats and scarves near the stove. Her fingers smoothed and straightened the woolen material as she draped the coats over the drying rack. When blasting heat from the fire licked at the wet wool, a damp animal stink filled the room. Finished with the coats, she turned and looked at Stina.

"Are you all right?"

"I'm fine, Mamma."

Stina sat down to take off her wet boots. Her pale hair had come unpinned and fell forward over her face as she bent to unlace her boots.

Anna leaned over and brushed the hair back from Stina's face, rubbed her thumb over the girl's cheek.

"You've got frostbite. I'll get some snow." Taking a pan from the rack, she stepped outside to scoop up a mound of clean snow.

"How do you know it's frost bite?" Stina, dry and wrapped in a blanket, now, sat on a stool by the fire. "It doesn't hurt."

"Would be better if it did."

Anna continued to press snow to the white patches on Stina's cheeks. Klara and Ivar dried off and changed their clothes.

Serious conversation came to an abrupt end with the appearance of Will and James from the back room. They were arguing and punching each other as they burst through the doorway, flushed and sweaty. Though close in age, the two boys were clearly developing in different directions. Nine-year old James, with a stubborn concern for right and wrong in other people's lives, had little sense of his own flaws and thought he was being picked on by everyone. Will, on the other hand, was easy going, quick to laugh, and delighted in games, practical jokes, and tormenting James.

"What are you two into, now?" said Ivar. "Come tell me about your week."

The pair ignored Ivar and stood facing their father.

James with his feet apart and his fists on his hips, said, "Will told Naomi that the *Jultomten* comes with presents on Christmas Day. He'll go to Hell for lying. Make him stop."

"He'll come, I know the *Jultomten* will come." Will held his ground before James's moral pronouncement, but unshed tears made his eyes bright. "He's got to bring presents this year."

"Who is this *Jultomten*? A Christmas elf, perhaps."

"Yes."

"He isn't real. We never get presents," said James.

Per put aside the strip of leather he had been working with an awl and hammer. A neat row of holes already lined one edge of the strip.

"I know the *Tomtens* are invisible little fellows who are supposed to guard the farm. Your mamma leaves them a bowl of oat porridge on Christmas night."

James argued with his father. "That's superstition. The preacher said it was a sin to believe in the forest spirits."

Ivar tried to soothe young James who looked as if he was about to explode with righteous indignation. "Don't be silly, James. It's only a harmless tradition."

James seemed not to hear and repeated his opinion. "I told Will it was wrong, not just wrong, a sin to tell Naomi lies."

Ivar tried another tack. "Everybody knows the Christmas goat brings the presents, but if Will wants to call him the *Jultomten*, what can it matter?"

"The Christmas goat never comes here, but I'll bet the *Jultomten* will come," said Will. He turned to James and grabbed him by the shirt front. "Did the goat ever bring you anything?"

Ivar gave up and turned to his father. "Will must have overheard the school teacher talking at Naomi's baptism. He was worried about a new fad in Stockholm. The German St. Nicholas as the bringer of Christmas presents is becoming very popular in the city, only they call him, *Jultomten*, the Christmas spirit. It's just a man dressed in a long red robe."

Stina had escaped her mother with her pan of snow and stood combing her long hair. "I expect the old Christmas goat will keep on making his rounds of farm houses. We don't get much from him and we don't expect much."

James refused to give up. "It's all lies. Why won't you listen?"

Ivar interrupted, "He'll come this year, whatever you want to call him. I'm sure of it."

"How can an old straw goat bring presents? He isn't even alive." James was at odds with everyone now.

Tired of the argument, Will dropped his chin to his chest, laid his hands alongside his head like horns, and stomped his feet. When James ignored this mocking, he lunged at him with a bellow.

"Stop it. Nobody will come if you boys keep fighting." Per separated the two boys. "Go get Naomi and help her wash up for supper."

"You never know about these goats and elves. This may be the year they decide to stop here," said Ivar.

He grinned at Stina and she giggled. Going to school together seemed to draw the brother and sister closer together, though three years separated them.

Anna leaned over the iron pot hanging in the open fire, large wooden spoon in hand. She said, "The soup is ready. Klara, can you help me dish up?"

Thursday pea soup, without the salt pork, of course, was a tradition dating back to before the Reformation, when the entire country observed Catholic fast days and feast days with a rigor worthy of Saint Peter, himself. The medieval Christmas fast had been a meatless fortnight before the season of over-eating that surrounded December 25th. Now it was merely the habit of yellow pea soup on Thursdays.

"What will we have for Christmas dinner?" said Stina. Her cheeks were now a mottled red. "The Lofs are having fresh pork. They saved back a piglet at butchering time and now they will have roast pork."

"They're putting on airs," said Anna. She reached for a round of flat bread from the rack above the table. "Fresh pig meat to celebrate the birth of Jesus Christ seems odd indeed."

Per nodded, then began a tale from his own youth.

"I remember we had fresh pork one Christmas, but it wasn't like we planned it that way. It happened when an old sow fell in a pit, a collapsed mine tunnel. We worked all day trying to pull her out, but in the end we had to butcher her. Right there in the pit with my mother and sister holding lanterns so we could see."

"That's different, since you didn't plan it." Ivar sat down next to his father and pulled his bowl closer. "Do you think there's any chance we can go to Christmas service at Smedjebacken this year?"

The Christmas service, *Julotta*, was always scheduled to conclude with the sunrise. The sleepy congregation would stand and sing their alleluias to the accompaniment of the rising sun. Christmas celebrated the birth of the Son, but it also celebrated the rebirth of the sun.

Stina interrupted, "Oh. That would be fun. Could we, Pappa?"

Per seemed to give the question a good mulling over before he answered. "If the snow stops in the next day or so, we might consider it. The wagon has the runners on and the horses are in pretty good shape. Ten miles over packed snow would be fairly easy. Better than trying to get there through the mud."

Later in the evening, Klara surprised Ivar and Stina whispering together. When she asked, they told her they were talking about a school assignment the teacher had left with them. A bit of determined teasing failed to pry out their secrets, so Klara left them to their plotting.

Too warm, now, Klara sat heavy-eyed by the fire thinking about the last few weeks. She savored her own Christmas surprise, a surprise made possible because of her journey to Borlange with Moochie. Somehow Christmas seemed so very important this year.

The atmosphere of the Larsson home had changed drastically after the baptism at the Lof farm. The decision to commit Moochie to the Custodial Asylum at Borlange had lifted a great weight from the household. Sadness mingled with huge relief gave Klara a giddy, lightheaded feeling. With Moochie gone, everyday life seemed so peaceful and orderly. Suddenly it was possible to plan for the future again. They could think about a trip to town for Christmas morning service, invite company to supper, or have a day skiing and sledding.

Even her mother had perked up a little, singing a bit of an old hymn as she worked the strip loom next to the fireplace. Her periods of odd behavior, brief fainting spells, flares of anger had become so much worse since her miscarriage. Maybe she was finally getting better.

Klara felt a sense of shame and guilt when she stopped to realize her new joy came at the expense of her sister, but the sure knowledge that they had done their best by Moochie was some solace. The relief of having the youngest child, Naomi, in the fold of the Church, her soul rescued from eternal fire, added to Klara's sense of well-being. And now, Ivar and

Stina were safely home from school.

Half asleep, she wondered if this winter could possibly be as bad as the old ones predicted. This was the longest night of the year, the winter solstice. Tomorrow the sun would stay above the horizon an instant longer.

Klara thought back to the week before, when a tradition dating into the dim past was celebrated. Under the mistaken notion that December 13th was the longest day of the year, people gathered to call for the return of the sun, to celebrate a festival of light called St. Lucia's Day. Days of growing darkness stirred a primitive longing for the light, a longing born of fear and depression.

With Stina and Ivar away at school and Moochie's departure still fresh in everyone's mind, the Larsson's celebration of St. Lucia's Day had been minimal. It had been Stina's turn to play the part of St. Lucia, but she was away. That left Klara, and little Naomi who was hardly big enough to carry the breakfast tray.

Sankta Lucia

Still, Klara decided she must make some effort to mark the holiday. She climbed out of bed while the rest of the family slept. To stop her shivering she wrapped her outdoor cloak around her shoulders and poked up the embers in the fireplace. As the fire took hold, she put water on to boil for coffee. On the painted tin tray she assembled spoons, cups, and napkins. She added a plate of *tinbrod*, a little butter and a piece of hard cheese. After much searching, she found her mother's hidden cache of loaf sugar and added a few of the precious lumps. By then the coffee aroma had permeated the house and she could hear the family stirring. She slipped off her coat and carried the tray to her parent's bedside, humming a little of the Sankta Lucia song.

"Good morning, Pappa, Mamma. I've come to dispel the curse of winter darkness. Well, at least I've come with breakfast."

"What? No candles in your hair? No long white robe?"

"Sorry, Pappa. I'm just a stand-in Lucia. Maybe Naomi will give you full measure next year."

Klara smiled at the thought of Naomi all grown-up and appearing in the morning darkness with candles in her hair, white gown graceful to the floor.

Anna frowned as she accepted the cup of coffee from Klara. "You used the store-bought coffee?"

"You deserve a good cup of coffee, Mamma, especially on Saint Lucia's Day."

Klara felt a twinge of guilt. She knew her mother had been brewing a mixture of roast grain to conserve the meager supply of coffee.

"What if company comes, Klara? What will they think if I serve them barley coffee?"

"I don't care what they think. You need to take care of yourself."

The memory of her mother's sharp words forced Klara back into the present. The coffee reminded her of the meager supplies laid in for the rest of the year. Though several storms had battered them already, winter was only just beginning. The hens would not lay without the sun; the cow was almost dry; her father would have no work at the mines until spring thaw.

~~~

Even with all the attention paid to the holidays, Klara found time to dream her old dream of going to America. One brief letter from Arvid and Sofia to announce their safe, but tumultuous arrival back in America had been all but forgotten in the struggle to save what they could of the grain crop.

Now on this dark afternoon, when everyone else was busy with their own chores and amusements, Klara lifted down the old tea box from the shelf above the table and carried the red painted box to a stool by the oil lamp. She savored the little thrill of discovery the tin box always gave her.

It had been years since the box had held tea, but its bright painted design of blue flowers and a black-suited lad bowing to a white-clad lass had assured the tea tin a perpetual place on the shelf. With her finger tips Klara opened the lid to look at the small collection of letters, a medal bearing the likeness of King Gustav, a few jet buttons from some long forgotten dress, and a faded bit of newspaper.

Klara removed the letter from America that lay on top. It was postmarked July 25, 1900. The letter had reached the Larsson farm in September. Klara remembered finding the Lof's hired hand, Jansson, in the yard when she returned from cutting rye on the strip of land beyond the river.

The postmaster had enlisted him to deliver the letter on his way back to the Lof farm and the fellow, not finding anyone at home, had seized the opportunity for a nap. By waiting to deliver the letter to one of the family face-to-face he assured himself of an excuse for his late return to work. Klara found the heavy shouldered fellow sacked out on a pile of birch bark intended for roof repair. He had jumped up and thrust the letter at her before bolting down the path.

Now Klara held the letter to the light to read the return address, examine the stamp, and turn the envelope over to see the short note on the back.

PS Please, please consider coming to us before summer. Just one word and we will send your ticket.

You don't know what you ask, Sofia. It was easy for you to leave because you had no family to cling to. Klara thought about the Lindblad's visit last summer, thought about Arvid's greasy mouth hot against her own. Maybe it would all work out if she went. Maybe she had over-reacted to Arvid's drunken advances at the going away party. Things might be different there in Arvid and Sofia's home. She wouldn't have to stay with them that long, just until she had learned the language, found a job and a place to stay. She was sure she could get through what other emigrants called the "dog year" in a much shorter time. The "dog year" was that first difficult period after they arrived in America, when they didn't speak the language, have a job, money, or a home.

Klara slipped the pink, scented letter from its worn envelope and unfolded it.

Dearest Clara,

I must apologize for not having written to you before, but I have hardly had a quiet moment since I reached home. Arvid was dreadfully seasick on the return trip. I thought this very odd because I am usually the one who is sick. The rolling of the ship never bothered Arvid before. Even after we reached home he was obviously sick. When we finally called the doctor, he said it was appendicitis and that Arvid was very lucky it hadn't burst. To make a long story short, he had to have an operation to remove the affected part. The procedure is very new and we were lucky that the surgeon who invented it, practices at Boston Hospital. Arvid is recovering, but doesn't take to being an invalid. He calls on me constantly to bring him a drink, a book, or just to talk to him. I hardly have time to tend Lillian and prepare meals. We haven't been home long enough to hire another girl for the heavy work either. That little fool, Adie, found another job while we were away. That's the Irish for you.

I hope you will consider coming to Boston in the spring. The sea journey is not so bad at that time of year. Arvid says we will send you a ticket on the Swedish-America Line, as well as the train fare to Karlstad. Just let us know when you want to come. It will only take you about a year to work off the price of your passage. I will find some sweet ruffled curtains for the maid's room, so you can be sure of your comfort.

Yours Sincerely,
Sophia Lindblad

With a sigh Klara folded the letter and slipped it into its envelope. Ivar had written a letter of answer for her and mailed it months ago. No reply came, nor did Klara really expect one because she had spurned Sofia's offer once again. But after her trip to Borlange, Klara had thought more and more about going to America. The trip that seemed so impossible last summer was somehow easier, closer. She felt empowered by mastering her fear of traveling on the train. She felt confident in her ability to deal with ticket sellers, conductors, new people, baggage. That she'd had the help of an experienced traveling companion seemed to recede to the back of her memory.

"Klara, the gingerbreads need to come out of the oven." Stina's voice brought her back to earth with a jolt. "Hurry or they'll burn."

"Sorry," muttered Klara. She put down the letter and ran to lift the flat pan of gingermen from the brick oven with the long-handled paddle. With a crash she plunked it down on the table. "I was thinking about Sofia. Do you remember when her baby is due?"

"Be careful. You've broken the head off one of them."

Stina stirred a bowl of butter frosting. A dish of dried currents sat on the table to use for eyes and buttons.

"Did you put salve on your face this morning?" Stina's frost bitten cheeks had scabbed over and looked quite awful. Klara put her hand to her sister's face. "Maybe lard would help or a poltice."

Stina turned away from Klara's touch. "I wish we had some candied fruit for decoration. The cookies would be so pretty with orange buttons and red mouths."

"They look nice just the way you're doing them. The frosting hair is a nice touch." With a sigh Klara cut another batch of gingermen using an old wooden cookie pattern to cut around. "Why don't we ever make gingerwomen?"

"I don't see why we can't make gingerbread girls. Let me try."

She took the pattern and the knife from Klara and began by making light strokes on the cookie dough. When the design seemed to suit her, she made the cuts to free a line of ginger girls from the dough. With a deft flick of the fingers she laid the long-skirted cookies on the baking flat.

"There you are. Put them in the oven and we'll see how they turn out."

Soon a row of ginger girls joined the row of gingerbread men cooling on the long table. Stina went down the line decorating each one with a smear of frosting and a handful of currents.

Klara inspected the handiwork. "They're lovely, Stina. Almost too nice to eat. You have Grandfather's artistic touch."

"The boys will make short work of them." Though her words gave no hint, anyone could have seen that Stina was pleased to be thought artistic.

"Not until tomorrow, they won't, if they expect the Christmas goat to bring them anything."

Klara could see James watching from the doorway. It was hard to believe he was nine this year. Maybe it was because he still acted like a child or maybe it was his smallness. She stood at the wash stand scouring the bowls and pans they had used. The cold water made her hands ache, but it seemed silly to heat water for such a small washing up. Tomorrow was the big day, the day before Christmas. There would be presents and cookies; they would light the three-branched candles.

"Oh, Stina, I forgot the candles."

"I'll get the candles," said James. "Please let me get them."

"Do you know where they are?" Stina spoke sternly to the over-eager boy, but his fierce nodding indicated he did, indeed, know where the candles were stored. "Be careful with them."

By the time Per, Ivar, and Will came in from feeding the animals and chopping wood, Anna had milked the cow, strained the milk, and put it to cool in the well house. James, whose job had been to carry water to the house, was adjusting the three pronged candles in their holders in the center of the table, when the others came into the house.

Per looked at James. "Did you bring the water?"

"Old lazy bones, James," said Will. "He's doing women's work."

"Am not."

"Are too."

"I'm getting it now."

Bristling with rage barely held in check, James grabbed his coat and headed for the door. "I'm just getting the water now," he mumbled before he bolted through the door to the well house.

Klara thought about her brother. Many boys his age were already hired out as field hands with wages paid in meager food and a suit of clothes. If the family had money, they could buy him a commission in the military when he turned fifteen. Or they could pay to send him to seminary for the study of church doctrine which could lead to his becoming a pastor or teacher in a few years. Without the prospect of money and cursed with a hot-headed, impulsive nature, labeled lazy by the hard-working people around him, James had a rough road ahead of him. Mamma always said James was the child most like Granpappa. Was it this impulsive nature that had doomed Grandfather Erik Axel, led to the debts that had lost him the farm?

~~~

Late that night Klara slipped out of bed to wrap her Christmas presents, the presents she had bought in Borlange with the money left over from Moochie's train fare, from Mr. Lof's generosity.

From her sewing bag she selected some scraps of material. For Stina she had a hair brush and new ribbons, for Ivar a comb and a case with a mirror. She fervently hoped it would not embarrass him. James would get the paint set with its papers of dry pigment waiting to be mixed with linseed oil, egg yolk, or plain water. For Will there was the harmonica. Her parents would have coffee and a sack of hard candy they would undoubtedly pass out to the children.

Best of all was the tiny china tea set for Naomi. How she would have liked to have had such a present when she was Naomi's age.

On impulse she went to the shelf above the stove and brought down the treasured chocolate set handed through the family from Granpappa's brother, Andrew. She polished the dainty cups and put one at each place around the table set for the Christmas meal. Seven cups, enough for everyone except little Naomi.

She can sit on my lap and share with me, decided Klara. I'll serve the coffee from the chocolate pot tomorrow. It will be too late for Mamma to forbid it. Even the youngest of children were given a sip or two of coffee on special occasions.

She covered the readied table with a white cloth, hiding the gleaming cups from view. Then she piled the wrapped presents on the unused end under the window and went back to bed. In the morning the cookies would be divided and added to each person's Christmas pile. This year the Christmas goat would leave evidence of his visit.

~~~

Next morning Klara was awakened by shouting.

"*Julklapp*, Christmas knocks, Christmas insults."

"Merry Christmas."

The greeting was followed by something hard landing on her stomach. A large ball of straw tied round and round with string had been hurled across the room with wonderful aim. She looked over to see that Stina's bed was empty, but that the door of her parents' bed hung open and another *Julklapp* had been delivered there, two more Christmas knocks, in fact.

One present looked like a misshapen pillow casing tied up with a hank of rough-spun flax, the other package was smaller and wrapped in white tissue paper. She could hear shouts and giggles from the dugout room. The younger children must be receiving their knocks. It was the custom to open presents on the afternoon of December 24th, but the knocks could be opened when the whole family assembled for breakfast.

Half-dressed, James, Will, and Naomi came to the table clutching their variously wrapped knocks.

"Can we open them now, Mamma?" said Will. "Please, Mamma."

"You got to read the poem first. Out loud," said Ivar. "Then you may open it."

"What about Naomi?" said James. "She can't read."

"Neither can you, silly," said Stina.

James put his present on the table and looked at it with disapproval. "Mine is awful small. Look how big Klara's knock is."

"Naomi's package is very pretty," said Klara. "She can use the gold ribbon in her hair."

"Who will go first?" Per obviously wanted to get on with breakfast.

"Let Naomi begin. Who will read her verse?"

"I'll read it," said Klara.

She wondered what horrible little insults they would be bombarded with in the next few minutes. This must be what Stina and Ivar had been whispering about the last couple of weeks. She knew the custom of Christmas knocks or insults, but with no presents to exchange, it had not been a family tradition. She removed the bit of lined paper from the big paper-wrapped ball Naomi held and read:

> *Take a stool.*
> *Set you down.*
> *Wipe the drool*
> *From off your gown.*

Drool, how disgusting, thought Klara. Fortunately Naomi is too young to care.

"Now you can open your present, Naomi. Be careful with the ribbon."

Obediently Naomi sat down on the stool in front of the fireplace and unwrapped her present. Under the layers of paper she found a doll whittled from a piece of soft pine.

"Baba," she said and immediately lifted the doll's skirt to examine her drawers.

Stina jabbed Ivar with her elbow, hardly able to contain her giggling.

"See, I told you I had to sew undies for the baby doll."

"Klara, read your own knock," said Per.

Klara pulled the strip of paper from the ratty ball of straw and read:

> *Your face is cold as a winter day,*
> *Blue and purple if I may say.*
> *Take this scarf of knitted wool.*
> *Wrap your head and look the fool.*

She quickly stripped the layers of straw away to reveal a soft parcel wrapped in paper. Inside she found a fuzzy wisp of a scarf long enough to wrap around her head and tuck into her collar.

"Did you make this, Stina? It's beautiful."

"It's made in the Russian style," replied Stina. "Supposedly it can be passed through the eye of large needle. Ivar got the wool from Mrs. Lof's angora goats in return for plucking wool for her."

"She sure got her money's worth," said Ivar. "You don't shear those critters, you pull out the long hairs a few at a time."

"Thank you, both, then." Klara turned to her mother. "What does your knock say?"

"Hey, what about me," said James. He was bouncing on the bench picking at his package. "Let me be next."

"All right," said Ivar. "You and Will have the same verse. I'll read it and you both can unwrap your presents." He read:

> *Little knocks for little boys*
> *Whose hands are deep in mischief.*
> *Hope these toys will bring you joys*
> *And from your pranks bring us relief.*

They hurried to rip through the rags and straw, layer after layer the balls became smaller and smaller.

"There's nothing in here," screamed James. "I've been cheated."

"Shut up, James. There's a note."

Will plucked the bit of paper from the wreckage of James's knock and handed it to Klara.

"Read it, please."

"Your note, too," said Klara. "It says James is to search the hollow in the old spruce tree by the well house and Will is to go to the box under the wagon seat."

The two boys were off and running before she finished reading.

"This is taking far too long. I'll say the prayer and we can finish the other presents while we eat."

Because the table was set for Christmas dinner, they would eat breakfast by the fire, their bowls balanced on their knees. Per completed his grace before the front door slammed behind Will and James. While he emptied his bowl of oat porridge, Klara and Stina urged their mother to read her knock. She gave in and read:

> *Mamma dear, we have no guile*
> *Just love and kisses to make you smile.*
> *And this fine knock to give you style.*

"Well then. What is it?"

"Open it. Hurry."

Per spread his *lefse* with a little sugared honey and rolled it up.

"I hope you two don't expect to make a living as poets."

Anna opened her package with careful fingers. She wound the bit of ribbon into a neat twist and smoothed the paper. When she was good and ready, she lifted the silver-colored brooch from its bed of cotton to show the others.

"It's beautiful. Where on earth did you get the money for a store-bought gift?"

"Do you like it?" Stina hovered over her mother. "I thought the bird was the prettiest. Let me help you pin it on your collar."

"Stina helped with the younger children at the school and we helped Mrs. Lof in the kitchen to earn the money. Pappa gave us the rest, so it's from him, too. The school teacher bought the brooch when he went to Borlange one weekend."

The front door banged again and a red-faced James came tearing into the room. He tracked great clouts of wet snow from the door to the table.

"There wasn't anything there. Just this old piece of wood."

Per grabbed the angry James and sat him down at his side.

"Let me see it, boy. I'll be glad when you learn to read for yourself." He squinted at the flat side of the slab of wood. "It says you are to go to the rhune stone, then walk backwards twenty steps. You can count to twenty can't you?"

"Of course," said James. "What else?"

"Dig, it says dig there and you will find a sign."

James went out again and Stina and Ivar urged Per to read his verse now that he was finished with his breakfast. He read:

A knock for you, Father, dear.
Insults come but once a year.
These slippers of straw woven so gaily
Will bring you comfort almost daily.

The slippers weren't really made of straw. Rather they were woven of birch, veneered along the grain to make strong strips of wood about an inch wide and thin enough to be pliable.

"Aha, just what I needed," said Per.

And, indeed, he had reason to appreciate his gift. It was a great relief to shuck wet leather boots after work outside was complete. The wet boots would be placed over the stove along with endless rows of drying socks. This necessary chore gave even the best of households a winter aroma that permeated the very walls. The bone-aching cold of the plank-over-stone floor made it a great misery to go around in stocking feet and it would be unthinkable to wear one's Sunday shoes for everyday, so various slippers of straw, wood, or felt were made to wear in the house.

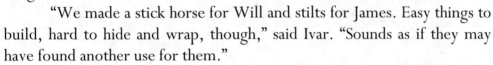

Woven slippers
(birch bark)

James and Will must have finally solved the riddle of their knocks thought Klara. She felt she could have heard them coming a mile away.

"What have you given those two ruffians?" she asked Ivar. "They sound dangerous."

"We made a stick horse for Will and stilts for James. Easy things to build, hard to hide and wrap, though," said Ivar. "Sounds as if they may have found another use for them."

A great clashing and banging could be heard in the yard outside.

"I think they are about to clout each others' brains to mush," said Klara. "They're bashing each other silly."

"This was your doing, Ivar. You go break them up," said Per.

He prepared to go to his morning chores. Horses, cows, and goats had to be fed, milked, watered, doctored for lice or whatever winter ills beset them. Stables and barns had to be cleaned, manure scraped up and hauled to the dung heap out back. Wood had to be split, then stacked or carried to the house. Ashes had to be shoveled from the stove and fireplace and carried outside. Work on a farm, even a tiny plot of rock and worn-out soil, had no end.

Sticks And Stones.

As time for Christmas dinner approached, Klara felt a tight anxiety in her stomach. She had been so sure her mother would have noticed the chocolate set absent from its usual place by now. She had pictured a reasonable conversation where she quietly persuaded her mother it was a good idea to use the chocolate set, good to use the extra special things to decorate the table on Christmas.

Now Klara was fearful of an angry outburst at mealtime. She was torn. Should she go to her mother to explain or should she just replace the cups and pitcher on the shelf? She paced back and forth across the room arguing with herself.

Why shouldn't we use the nice things once-in-a-while? We work hard to make things special. Look at the decorated cookies, the candles, the embroidered table cloth.

You fool, Klara. You can't disguise the fact we're eating hardbread, pickled salt fish, and beets again. The ham and egg pie seems special, but it's made with the last of the season's eggs, eggs hoarded all month, eggs mixed with the last of the milk, the last slice of ham chopped into tiny bits. You know this is a dish calculated to stretch meager ingredients enough to fill eight growling bellies. No celebration here, unless it's the celebration of the empty larder. With a frustrated sigh Klara removed the cloth covering the table.

She stood by the table with the cloth in her hands. While her fingers searched for the crease marking the center fold of the cloth, she watched the light play over the bowls of red beets, the pewter knives and forks polished almost silver for the occasion, the porcelain cups, the white candles in their holders made from split birch logs decorated with pine cones and greenery.

She laid the cloth aside and went to the fireplace for a burning splinter to light the candles. The flame wavered and went out when her father threw open the front door. With a scattering of snow and a draft of cold air he stomped into the warm, glowing house, followed by Ivar,

James, and Will.

With perfect timing, Anna brought the ham pie hot from the oven where she had been huddled with Stina for the last half hour, turning and probing the bubbling dish. Stina followed close behind with a stack of hot pads.

"Dinner is almost ready," said Anna. "Get those wet clothes off. Hang them by the fire."

Klara watched the two younger boys with their stilts and stick horse straggle in behind their father and Ivar.

"Leave those sticks outside, James, Will."

Per turned to the boys. "Do as you're told."

"We're playing a game."

"I'm the black knight," announced Will. He pounded his stick horse on the floor and pulled down his pretend visor.

James was trying to shuck his coat without dropping his stilts. He stopped to face Will.

"No you're not. I'm oldest, so I'm the black knight." One stilt slipped from his grasp and clattered to the floor. "Don't touch my lance, Will. I'm warnin you."

With a snort Will tossed his shorter stick horse in the corner and made a dive for the stilt. He gripped it near the top end with both hands and looked up at James from where he crouched on the floor.

"Got it," he said. "The black knight says prepare to die."

Still clutching the smoking sliver of pine intended for lighting the candles, Klara watched the two boys with growing apprehension.

From his position on the floor, Will swung the stick at James. The thick end of the stilt moved in a wide arc toward the older boy. The heavy clod of icy mud on the foot of the stilt came loose and flew past James's ear. It bumped and skidded across the table before it crashed into one of the fragile chocolate cups.

As the cup teetered a brief moment, Klara willed her muscles to intervene, to reach out and rescue the cup. Nothing happened. Her arms felt frozen, her cry came out a hoarse croak.

The cup catapulted over the edge of the table to shatter on the floor. The stilt, itself, smacked James alongside the neck and knocked him down. Scarf and coat collar kept him from injury, but the surprise of it all stunned everyone to silence.

Anna was the first to find her voice. "You did this, Klara. On purpose."

"No, Mamma. I...."

"A stake through my heart. You ungrateful...."

"I'm sorry. Please...."

"I do my best for you and this is how you repay me?"

Per tried to silence her. "Hush, Anna. It was an accident."

"Devil's spawn, all of you. Nothing but pain and trouble."

~~~

Christmas dinner was solemn and uncomfortable. Will was still smarting from the whipping Anna had insisted Per administer. Klara had escaped a like fate only because her father insisted she was too old to whip.

Her eyes were red and puffy as she took her place at the table. She had just finished putting the chocolate set away on its shelf and brought out the chipped stoneware mugs. She felt confused and disoriented, glad Stina had cleaned up the mud and the broken cup. Though she had expected her mother to be upset, to fret and complain, she had not expected the emotional tirade, the deep anger.

"It's only a cup, Anna." Per dunked his ginger cookie in his coffee before taking a small bite. "It's Christmas. Don't spoil it." His voice sounded tired and his hands trembled a little.

"I'm sorry, Per." Anna rubbed her eyes with rough, broken-nailed fingers. "I'm sorry, Klara. I shouldn't have said such ugly things to you. I don't know what got into me."

"Maybe we could open Klara's presents now," said Stina. "Before Naomi and Will fall asleep."

"Here, James. Your box is on top." Ivar passed a square box down the table to James.

James accepted the box and carefully unwrapped it. His face glowed and the stubborn set of his mouth softened when he saw the paint set with its brushes and colors.

"Thank you, Klara. It's wonderful."

Ivar handed a tiny bundle to Naomi who sat on Stina's lap holding her doll. With a little help she unwrapped the tea set. As each piece emerged from its paper, Stina placed it on the table until the set was complete. Before the little girl could even try to pinch the tiny cups between thumb and fingers and wave it in the direction of the doll's painted nose, Anna gathered up the new tea set and placed it on the shelf out of reach.

"Let her play with it, Mamma," said Klara. "It's only a toy."

"When she's old enough, she can have it," said Anna.

"When, Mamma?"

To herself she thought, old enough, good enough, special enough. Does that time ever come? Klara leaned back and closed her eyes, her shoulders slumped.

Ivar and Stina opened their gifts and thanked Klara, then slipped their new combs and brushes out of sight. Now they sat together on the bench staring into the fire, mesmerized by its flickering patterns. Will sat on the floor by the loom and picked out a few listless tunes on his harmonica. Naomi was already asleep on the rag rug with the dog. Per and Anna had parceled out some of the hard candy and everyone sat quiet, savoring the sweetness of the candy and the heat of the fireplace.

When the last of the sweetness faded, they argued briefly about brewing another pot of coffee, but decided it would be wasteful. Weariness made Klara feel thick, heavy, unwilling to move. What a long day, she murmured to herself.

She let her thoughts follow her eyes around the room, resting for a time on each face. Too bad we can't take James's brushes and paint this moment. Did any artist have the talent to catch Will's quirky off-center grin or the serious belligerence that often creased James's forehead? How hard it would be to stroke the lines of new maturity on Ivar's face, the determined set of his shoulders, the little forward tilt of his chin when he tried to puzzle out something new. And Stina, could anyone capture her subtle resemblance to Mamma, particularly, when she bent over the stew pot or dressed Naomi? Surely, no brush could trace the soft lines of Naomi's cheek and soft shoulder as she lay curled against the rough coated dog on the old rug?

Letting her thoughts run, she wondered about Sofia so far from her homeland. Klara felt guilty because she hadn't thought about her friend for days and days. Did they have Christmas in America, she wondered? How strange it would be to celebrate without her brothers and sisters, her crotchety old mamma, her kind pappa.

Per finally roused himself. "We'd best be off to bed if we're going to get an early start in the morning."

James and the Dragon.

The trip through the darkness behind the team of horses was like riding in a capsule of fierce air with only a slide, a skid, a bump to break the silent motion. By the time they reached the church their vaporous breath had frozen white beards on scarves wrapped around their chilled faces. Cold-clumsy they hoisted themselves out of the wagon.

Following her mother, Klara guided the younger children up the narrow walkway to the church vestibule, while her father and Ivar tied the horses to the long hitch rail outside. A worn blanket provided the only cover for the animals.

A blast of heat greeted them on entering the church. The caretaker had anticipated the bitter cold of the early morning and had had the two coke-fired stoves cranking out heat since midnight. The stoves also produced an acrid smoke which added to the discomfort of the worshipers.

By the time the sermon reached its climax Klara noted the nodding heads and drooping eyes of those around her. Her father must be asleep, she thought. His closed eyes, chin resting on his chest, mouth slightly ajar gave him away. She expected him to start snoring any minute, now. Only James seemed alert, awake and interested.

While she watched him, she realized it was the church, itself, that held his attention. He gave no indication of hearing a word of the service. When the worshippers stood to sing the final anthem, she saw him slip from his place at the end of the pew and disappear down the side aisle toward the front of the church. While she watched James, she noticed the pale shadings of the morning's first light creep over the window sills.

With the sun about to appear through the window behind the altar, Klara forgot about James and turned her attention to the prayerful singing, the expectant waiting for the dawn of Christmas Day. As the sunlight played over the walls and high-vaulted ceiling of the church, it drowned out the feeble light of the scattered candles and oil lamps ensconced on the walls. The natural light flooding the church drove away the darkness, the deep shadows in the upper reaches of the building to reveal the blue-painted ceiling with its scatter of gold stars. In the dazzle of sun light the upper walls arching over the long nave seemed like heaven itself.

A sharp screech pulled her attention from heaven to the side aisle. She saw James, almost out of sight behind a pillar, wrestling a huge chair into place beneath the painting which decorated the side wall.

Before she could figure out his intention, he had climbed up into the chair, then, holding its back for balance, stepped onto chair's arm. In view of most of the congregation, now, he stood balanced on one of the carved armrests of the throne-like chair, the bishop's chair. Totally oblivious to the church full of people, James stretched as far as he could towards the painting of the young dragon slayer, George, on his white horse. His finger traced the line of the coiled beast attacking the ready spear of the saint. The winter sun played over the faces of boy and saint to give each a pale glow of rapt concentration.

"Get him down from there, Klara," said Anna in a tiny whisper. "Please, before he makes a fuss."

Klara pushed her way past the other people in the pew and hurried to warn James to behave. When she reached the wall painting of Saint George, she found the young pastor who had accompanied her to Borlange with Moochie. He was already lifting the reluctant boy from his perch on the bishop's throne.

"Looking for this one, Klara?" He whispered to her. He kept a firm grip on James's arm, but seemed to have forgotten the child. "You know, I don't think we were ever properly introduced, which is pretty odd considering we rode all the way to the city together."

"You are Pastor Theilgurd, of course." Klara wondered what he wanted her to say.

"Actually, I'm just a pastor in training. My name is Karl."

He smiled and Klara forgot about the cold, the dull sermon, her pesky brother. It gave her an unexpected feeling of warmth to have a young man take an interest in her.

"Why is he so interested in the wall painting?"

"Who?" Klara blushed.

"Your brother, silly." Pastor Karl bent to James's level. "You want to see the paintings? Are you interested in horses, maybe?"

James must have decided it was safe to speak.

"No, I want to see how the paint is put on the wall."

"James fancies himself an artist. He got a paint box for Christmas. He has his grandfather's old painting things, too."

"Your grandfather was an artist?"

"Sort of. He did simple wall paintings in his room at our house. Before that he painted the manor house, where the Lofs live now."

"Well, then, my boy, I'll show you some real paintings," said Karl.

He let go of James's arm and led them down a hallway to a door in the paneled wall. He produced a ring of large brass keys and selected one to unlock the padlock on the door hasp.

"You might like to see this, too, Klara."

The trio found themselves in a narrow passageway leading to an older part of the church, a part of the church where the confessional booths had stood in pre-reformation times. Like most of the churches in Sweden, the Norrbarke church had once been Roman Catholic. Karl pulled back a curtain covering most of one wall to reveal a series of old pictures, vivid with vermilion, cobalt blue, earth green, and slashes of chrome yellow. The life-size images were bright as the day they had been laid on the plaster wall by hands long turned to dust.

"Here's Elijah carried into heaven by a chariot of fire and this fine fellow with his hide full of arrows is Saint Sebastian."

From the panels of Old Testament heroes and early saints Karl moved to Saint Anne, mother of the Virgin Mary, herself.

"Folks believed Anne, and the Virgin, too, didn't die like regular people. Instead they were translated directly to heaven. That's what the painter imagined in this painting. See the cloud of angels holding the edges of Anne's robe? And here they are at the heavenly throne with more angels. We Lutherans don't put much store in saints, but we feel it's a crime to destroy the work of an artist, unlike the barbaric English."

Neither Klara, nor Karl noticed the rapt way James examined the paintings. What he couldn't reach to trace with his finger, he traced with his eye, memorizing the shapes and colors, the dramatic line defining robes and hair and fierce Old Testament gazes. In a small alcove at the back of the room he found another Saint George. Prominent in this painting was a golden-haired maiden with her hands clasped in fear and consternation.

"Tell me the story," James demanded of Karl. "Are there dragons in Sweden?"

~~~

Two days after Christmas the Lof's hired man, Jansson, again played the role of mailman, when he came huffing and sweating through the snow with a package for Klara. It was from Sofia.

When she unwrapped the flat parcel, Klara found an English/Swedish dictionary with a gray cloth cover and red-stamped title. She traced the fancy script with her finger, *"Engelsk-Svensk och Svensk-Engelsk, Ordbok Med Fullstandig Uttalsbeteckning, English-Swedish and Swedish-English, A wordbook With Complete Pronunciation Guide."* She couldn't tell if the pang in her stomach was joy or dread. She hugged the book tight against her chest and vowed to learn a new word every day.

When she was finally able to open the book by the light of the evening fire, her simple hope of a word a day was dashed by the complexity of the book's contents. She tried to read through the material in the front of the book, introduction, table of contents, rules of pronunciation and equivalencies. If she couldn't even understand the parts of the book written in Swedish, how could she learn the foreign parts? Maybe it would be easier in the morning when she was less tired. Klara turned to the main section of the book and read aloud the first few entries.

"'Abaft meaning at the stern.' What is that all about?"

Ivar looked up from his work. "Something about ships, I think. Nothing very useful."

"At least there are some pictures." Klara flipped through the pages until she came to a photograph of harvesters in a wheat field. "Look at this farm, Ivar."

"It must be enormous, if those tiny figures are men and horses."

"Teams of four horses pulling something. Do you think it's hay they're cutting?"

"Wheat, I think. Look up the words in the caption. What a tremendous amount of food that would be."

~~~

A week later, just after the new year, the impact of the church paintings on James became apparent. Heavy clouds and darkening skies indicated an approaching blizzard. While the rest of the family labored to bank the foundations of the house and attached stable with pine boughs and rock, James slipped back inside. He spread his painting kit on the table and set to work. With a piece of charcoal he outlined a picture of

Elijah and a span of horses on the wall next to the iron cook stove.

When he had that picture sketched out, he turned to the white wall next to the door and started a picture of the dragon slayer with the long curling tail of the dragon undulating around the side-wall to the bed closet.

He was kneeling on the bench, concentrating on the creature's scale-crusted eyelid when the family came in, tired and cold. Per threw off his coat and mittens, his jaw clenched and the vein by his eye throbbed visibly.

"What are you doing in here, boy?"

Anna burst into tears and bent to pick up her husband's coat.

"How could you?" She turned on Klara who was coming in the door behind her. "It's your fault. You gave him paints."

"What are you talking about, Mamma?"

Klara pushed past her mother into the room where she saw a defiant James staring at her.

"Oh. James. I thought you were gathering pine branches with Stina."

James held the lump of charcoal in mid-stroke, almost afraid to breathe.

That one suspended moment was shattered when Per strode across the room and grabbed James by the back of his shirt.

"Shirker. We work in the cold and you're in here playing."

He cuffed James on the ear, not once, but twice, then the boy's howls penetrated his anger and he let go.

Until they realized how upset their parents were, Ivar and Stina had acted like James had pulled off a fine practical joke to get back at his little brother, Will, who stood staring at the pictures with his mouth open.

"He's ruined the walls," said Anna. She followed the sweep of the drawing around the room. "Like Granpappa. Always into something."

Per came up and put his arms around his wife.

"He draws good. If he wasn't so lazy, it wouldn't matter."

"I'm not lazy, Pappa. Let me finish the picture, please." Holding his charcoal in one hand, James absently rubbed his ear with the other. "I'll do my chores first."

"Make him clean it off." Anna reached to touch the hatching of black lines on the wall.

"It'll smear, Mamma," said James. "Don't touch, please."

"Maybe he'll work harder, if he has the painting to fool with afterward," said Per. "Whipping him hasn't helped."

"I'll work hard, Pappa. I promise."

"No painting until you have the wood box filled, the animals fed and watered. Do you understand?"

"Yes, Pappa."

~~~

As the days passed, the rest of the family continued to bicker about the painting, but James seemed impervious to it all. He filled in the black outlines with color brushed on with vigorous strokes. He seemed most to enjoy the reds and oranges of the flaming chariot and the dragon's breath. Those colors now dominated the room.

Klara tried to stop the arguing. It was hard enough living in the cramped house when everyone was at peace.

"He's used up most of his red pigment. At least he won't be able to paint hell on the other wall."

"It's one thing to live in a room with flowers, blue leaves, and

birds, but these wild men, horses, flames, and this ugly snake with wings,
I don't know."

"It's a dragon, Pappa." Klara smiled at her father and put his supper
on the table under the dragon's chin. "Maybe it will help keep us warm."

"Too bad we can't eat the beast," he said.

~~~

Another storm roared down from the mountains in the early hours
of morning. Unusually high winds blew fine dry snow through every
crack, under a loose section of birch bark roofing, around the windows
and door, down the chimney, nearly smothering the fire that remained in
the stove and fireplace.

Klara woke with a layer of snow on the feather tick she had pulled
over her head sometime in the night. She could hear the snapping of the
coals in the stove, but she could see nothing in the total darkness. Outside
the wind howled like a captured animal. She knew she should move, but
she was reluctant to climb out of the small capsule of warmth provided by
the wrapping of quilts under the feather tick. Then a few drops of cold
water from the snow melted by her body heat, trickled down her neck.

She squirmed around under the covers to pull on the extra pair of thick wool socks, then she threw back the quilts and stood up.

The assault of cold air took her breath away. How could it be so cold in the house? Wrapped in her cloak, she felt around by the fireplace for the dry kindling. Carefully, carefully she added splinters of pine to the bed of hissing coals and blew on them. Tiny flicks of flame ate up the pine and she added bigger pieces.

With relief she watched the birch log catch fire and send out the beginning of warmth. When the fire was crackling strong against the bitter cold, Klara felt it was safe to leave it long enough to find the oil lamp and light it with a long pine splint from the fire. In the lantern's light she could see the snow drifted across the floor and around the windows. She dressed quickly, then started a fire in the iron cook stove, too. The water in the bucket was frozen solid, so she set it on the back of the stove to thaw. Still numb with cold, she crept back to bed, telling herself she must not go back to sleep or the fire would go out.

All that day the wind screamed snow against the house. The feeble few hours of light were blotted to dim gray. Unable to work outside or even move far from the stove, the family concentrated on keeping the house warm and the animals comfortable.

"Can't you do something about this snow blowing in?"

Anna was about to slice a few shriveled parsnips into the soup pot. Throwing down the knife, she walked to the window and flicked a mist of snow off the sill.

"I can't stand this The cold pains me."

Stina picked up the knife and took the parsnip from her mother. "Maybe we could stuff flax in the cracks." She bent over the soup pot.

"I doubt it would help," said Per. "There is something we could try. Ivar, James, get your coats on and fill some buckets with snow. Pack it in because there won't be as much when it's thawed."

"Snow? Keep the snow out with more snow?" James didn't move to obey. He sat cross-legged on the floor with a paint brush. He stroked globs of dark paint onto the back hoof of George's horse with growing frustration. "We need to go back to church so I can see how to fix this leg."

Klara stood over him to look at the problem. "After you bring in the snow you can go look at the horses in the stable. They have legs and hooves, too."

James reluctantly put away his paints and got up. "It's not the same, real horses."

After the buckets of snow melted, Per and the boys bundled up in all their clothes and carried the buckets of water into the yard. He took the first bucket from Ivar.

"Get back or you'll get doused."

He threw the water over the window, where it froze almost instantly. A second wetting finished the job. Ice covered the window and the area around the sill, sealed it against the wind. A few more buckets of water took care of the other windows.

"Still think your old pappa crazy, boys?"

"Too bad we can't seal the door, too," said Ivar.

"Get the threshing cloth from the storage shed. We'll hang it up as a second door inside."

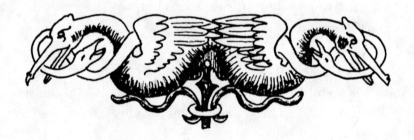

Trouble To Spare.

Storm followed storm; each blast from the mountains seemed to be colder and last longer than its predecessor. Ice and snow gripped the Larsson household tighter and tighter. Only the fact that the stable attached to the house saved the livestock. The milk cow, two nanny goats, and the team of horses, were no longer turned out at mid-day for air and exercise. The stable grew daily smaller with the manure mounded around the walls of the stable. It gave warmth and no one wanted to face the cold and wind to haul it outside.

The remaining chickens lived in a wicker coop under the family table next to the place where the dog, Fenrye, slept the days away. The chamber pots were emptied nearer and nearer to the downwind side of the front door. The stinking stew froze immediately into a growing arc of brindle ice that would haunt the family long after spring thaw began.

The level in the salt fish barrels dropped each day; empty spaces appeared among the rounds of bread spitted on the ceiling poles; the remaining potatoes softened and grew black spots; many of the pickling crocks, crocks of beets, parsnip, and cabbage, were empty, scrubbed clean and turned upside down on the shelf for next year.

The snares and rabbit traps set along the river were empty the few days when the boys could check them. The small game they did catch was often so thin and diseased, it was fit only for the dog.

Ivar came in from the stable where he had been feeding the animals, trying to make them as comfortable as possible. The cow had been dry since Christmas, but she appeared to be pregnant, a result of a visit to the Lof's bull in early fall.

"Pappa, come look at the cow," said Ivar.

"What's wrong?" said Per.

"She won't get up."

Per and Klara followed Ivar through the dark passage into the stable. The close air was thick with the stink of ammonia from the animals' urine. Stark shadows from the flickering lantern patterned the low ceiling. The walls were invisible in the blackness, a blackness echoed in the animals' eyes.

With her handkerchief over her mouth to keep back the choking fumes, Klara squinted at the cow. The big animal slumped listlessly on her breast bone, her muzzle resting on the ground. Thin strands of saliva drooled from her mouth and her steaming breath smelled rank and bitter.

"I wonder if she's lost her cud," said Ivar. "She seems so still."

"Worse than that, I think."

He probed the soft area under the cow's jaw, then ran his hands down her spine to her hip bones.

"She's starving to death. There's just not enough nourishment in this feed for her and the calf she's carrying."

"What can we do?" Ivar prodded at the animal's ribs. "She has to get up or she'll die."

Per nodded. "She'll get lung fever, if she stays down."

"Maybe we ought to kill her while we can still use the meat." Ivar watched his father's probing hands.

"And what would we do for a cow come summer?" Per stood up and wiped his palms on the seat of his pants. "Got to get her up."

"And think about the calf." Klara felt a desperate anxiety in her gut. "There must be something we can do. We lose twice if we butcher her now."

"It's chancy either way." Ivar kicked at the frozen dirt. "If we wait we may lose all together. Lose the meat, the calf, everything."

"Got to get her up."

Per seemed to have forgotten the rest of them. He put his shoulder to the cow's rib cage and tried to heave her up with brute strength. She let out a low groan, but did not move.

"We need a rope, Ivar. And a strip of cloth to put under her chest. Something strong."

Klara followed Ivar back into the kitchen. "What can we use?"

"Find something. I'll get the rope."

Klara searched through the sewing bag, through the bits and pieces of half-finished weaving near the loom. She thought about tearing up a quilt or blanket and rejected that notion, then she saw the linen funeral towels on their shelf by the door. Woven double for strength, the strips were more like canvas than cloth. They were made long enough pass under the coffin and still give the pallbearer on each side enough towel end to place over his shoulders for a better grip. There was no doubt that the funeral towels would fit around the biggest animal. Still, Klara hesitated. Would it be sacrilege to use the accouterments of death on a cow? Stilling her fears, she grabbed the four linen strips and went back to the stable.

"Do you think these will work, Pappa?" said Klara.

Ivar interrupted, "Those strips can't be strong enough. We should use the rope."

"The rope will tear up her skin." To Klara he said, "They don't need to hold the cow's entire weight. We just want to steady her, keep her from going down again. She'll carry most of her weight on her own legs."

They threaded the rope over one of the roof poles, a pole made from a birch tree to support that part of the heavy bark and earth roof. By digging out a little of the roofing and sawing the rope back and forth, they were able to position it over the cow's back. Ivar and Per stood on either side of the cow. They held either end of the two funeral cloths they had knotted together.

funeral towels

"Now, we got to get this under her," said Per. He was breathing hard.

"Can we roll her over?" Ivar held the linen strip gingerly. "She can't weigh all that much."

"Dig a trench under her. Maybe."

Klara knew it was time she went to help her mother with supper, but she lingered in the cow stable.

Ivar flipped his end of the cloth strip to his father.

"That might work, Klara. I'll get the shovel and a hand trowel."

"Better get something to kneel on, too."

When Ivar returned, Klara hung the lantern on a hook and joined him beside the cow. She helped her brother spread the tattered blanket over the black stable muck, then rolled up her sleeves and pulled her long skirt up. She got down beside the cow with Ivar and began working the linen strip under the cow as Ivar made way for it through the wet ooze. By the time they had the strip as far as the cow's breast bone, Klara was resting her head on the cow's hairy side in order to reach far enough.

"Push it a little farther," said Ivar. He was sweating, though the stable was cold.

"That's as far as I can reach."

"I'll dig alongside her and maybe we can flop her over on her side."

In a few minutes he had a shallow trench the length of the cow's body. Per squeezed in beside them.

"Now we'll give her a pull and see if anything happens."

The three of them reached over the cow's body to try for a grip on her other side. Ivar had the easiest job at the head end because he could wrap his arms around her neck. Klara in the middle tried to wedge her hands over the cow's rib cage, but ended up gripping the poor old creature by the loose skin behind her forearm. Per simply put an elbow over her angular hip and grabbed her tail with his other hand.

On the count of three they gave a heave and the cow toppled over onto the strip of linen. Before she could struggle away, Ivar made a dive for the end of the strip which he could see sticking out from beneath her breast bone.

"Got it," he shouted.

They pulled the linen strip under the cow and secured it around her body just behind her front legs. Once they had made a loop in the cloth and knotted it to the rope over the beam, they rolled the cow back onto her breast bone. With a great deal of shouting and pushing they moved the animal closer to an upright position.

Klara maneuvered the rope over the pole and secured it with a half-hitch which she could use to take up the slack as Ivar and Per were able, little by little, to hoist the cow to her feet. With the cow upright Per made a hard knot in the rope to keep the her on her feet.

"There. At least the old thing won't get lung fever. Now we need to scrounge up some better feed. If she's this far gone, the horses won't be far behind."

Klara stood looking at the cow. "The grass is covered with snow and ice and the willow shoots are all dried up."

Ivar stared at the cow, then down at his filthy shirt.

He said, "Can cows eat bread?"

"We need all the bread we have or we'll be starving next," said Klara. "We better try to do a laundry before this filth sets. Let's go change."

"Jenks said one of his steers died before Christmas. When they cut it open, its stomach was full of sticks."

Per picked up the shovel and trowel and wiped them off.

"I'm going to have to try and find some work. Maybe the Lofs will have something for me, if they know I'm willing to take my pay in feed for the animals."

Ivar turned away from the cow. "Me too. We ought to be able to earn enough to get the livestock through until things green up."

Klara picked up the two remaining funeral towels and folded them into a neat rectangle. She silently begged forgiveness from some unseen power for their desecration.

"I'll take James and Will out and hunt for dry grass, twigs, maybe some bark."

They went back through the narrow passageway connecting the cow stable to the house. When they stepped into the warm room, Anna stopped her pacing.

Klara thought she must have been picking and pulling at her hair because it straggled down around her face in lank disarray. She looked at her mother, really looked at her. Could her hair possibly be that gray? She remembered combing and braiding it for the baptism just a few months ago. The lines around her mouth seemed deeper, her lips dry and crusted. And her eyes, Klara thought, her mother's eyes burned flinty in their wrinkled sockets.

"You spoil everything." Anna spoke to the whole family, but her eyes and voice bored into Klara. "Did you have to use the funeral towels?"

"You would rather the cow died, Anna?" Per went to a locked trunk in the corner and took out a stoneware jug of spirits. "Can you find me an empty bottle, Stina? Please." While he waited for Stina, he swirled the liquor in the jug, trying to gauge the amount left.

"You have *brannvin*?" said Anna.

Her question came out as an accusation rather than a query. She leaned toward her husband with her eyes on the jug of alcohol.

"What are you doing with it?"

Per held out his hand to take the bottle Stina offered him.

"Thank you, Stina. Help me hold it steady."

He poured a careful inch of the potent liquor into the empty bottle, then corked and returned the almost full jug to the trunk. Looking at his wife, he replaced the lock on the hasp and snapped it shut.

"Now, add enough water to fill the bottle half-way, please." While waiting for Stina, he said, "Ivar, Klara, why don't you move the trunk to the storeroom?"

"Out of sight, out of mind," murmured Klara as she went to help Ivar with the trunk.

Anna stood by the table watching Stina dip water into the long-necked bottle.

"It's a waste to give good drink to a cow," she whispered.

She raised her hand to her swollen jaw, but nobody seemed to notice. She stepped back into the shadows and sat down on the bench.

Per took the bottle with its dilute mixture of water and alcohol from Stina. "We can eat after I drench the cow."

Next morning was clear and still and very cold. Per and Ivar bundled up enough things to tide them over for a few days, then left to walk over the ridge to the Lof farm. Surely if they came prepared to work, Oscar Lof would not turn them away. It was hard to find help willing to work outside in the bitter cold.

After checking the snares for game and finding only the paw pads and gallbladder of an eaten animal, Klara, James, and Will spent the daylight hours stripping bark from the trees along the river. Stina stayed in the house to tend the fire, watch Naomi, and keep an eye on her mother.

Anna had had a fainting spell after breakfast and had gone back to bed. She had begged Klara to get the *brannvin* from the box in the storeroom. Klara answered she had no key, then went to hurry the boys into their coats and boots.

When Klara and the boys slogged up the path to the house that afternoon, James broke the silence. "Will Pappa be home?" He stooped under his load of sticks and bark.

"We better hope not," said Klara.

Though the bundles of twigs and bark were not heavy, her knees and back ached from walking up hill through the deep snow. The strain of keeping track of the two boys and urging them to keep working added to her weariness.

"If they get work, we won't see them this week."

"What do I do with this stuff?" Will could hardly be heard through the thick scarf wrapped around his face.

Klara stopped and shrugged her load to the ground. "Take your bundles to the store house. We'll feed my bundle tonight."

"Tonight? You mean they'll eat all this in three days?"

"We'll be lucky if it lasts three days," said Klara.

"Who's going to feed?" said James.

"I'll feed. You two start hauling water after you stow your bundles."

When Klara saw the boys headed to the store house, she picked up her own bundle and ducked through the door. Keeping the animals watered was a major chore. It never ceased to amaze her how much a grown horse or cow would drink in a day. Even hauling two buckets at a time with the shoulder yoke, it would take the two boys a dozen trips apiece from the well house to the stable before the animals had had enough. With the thought of water on her mind, Klara wondered if this would be a good time to do a washing. With fewer people in the house they could bring the heated water inside and scrub clothes in the relative comfort of the house. More room to hang the drying clothes, too.

Anxious to ask her mother about doing a laundry, Klara decided to take her bark bundle through the house to the stable. Her mother could be thinking over her answer while Klara fed the animals. Maybe the old cow would find something palatable in her offering.

Odd, she thought when she got inside. The room doesn't feel very warm. No cooking smells, just an aroma out of place and unidentifiable. The lamp isn't burning, either. No candles. It's so dark. She dropped her bundle, threw off her mittens without noticing where they fell, and peered around the dim room. She could hear whimpering from the back room, but no other sound reached her.

"Mamma, Stina."

When no one answered, Klara fumbled her way to the stove and found a few embers in the far corner. With a practiced touch she fed small shavings and bits of dry bark to the coals until a thin ring of flame crowned the lengths of birch wood she had laid in a loose pyramid. While she waited for the flames to catch, she flexed her stiff fingers, rubbed her numb cheeks.

When the flames grew steady, she found the candles and brought them to the stove to light. Her shaking hands sent the candle-light wavering against the shadows. Able to see now, Klara inspected the room. The ruins of breakfast still cluttered the table, a pile of quilts lay in a heap, the beds were unmade, kitchen utensils had been dropped on the floor, the loom was quiet, the hens untended, no yellow bean soup simmered in the cast iron kettle hanging on the fireplace hook.

Without taking off her coat she walked around the room touching things, tidying small objects, scattering the crumbs she brushed from the table into the hens' cage, almost expecting Stina to come popping out from behind the table or the back room, almost, but not quite. Finally, she took a deep breath and went to the far side of the room, where she saw the door to her parents' cupboard bed ajar. When she looked in, she saw her mother sprawled across the top quilt, breathing through her mouth.

Klara shook her, then realized the odor she had been sensing was *brannvin*. God, is Mamma drunk? How could she do this with Pappa gone? Where are Stina and Naomi?

"Stina, Christina. Where are you?"

Then she heard the whimper again. She had thought it was the dog when she first came in the house, but now she wasn't sure. Throwing a cover over her mother, Klara picked up a candle and went into the dugout bedroom. At first she didn't see anything out of the ordinary. Unlike the bed in the front room, the beds behind the chimney were neatly made. A rustling sound drew her attention to the corner farthest from the door. What she had taken for a pile of dirty laundry seemed to be moving, alternately heaving and sagging.

When Klara bent down to examine the pile, she realized it was the feather tick from her own bed in the other room. She lifted a corner of the stiff material and held the candle closer. There in the folds of the cover, Stina looked up at her. Her blond hair was plastered dark across her forehead and it looked like she had peeled the healing scabs from the old patches of frost bite on her cheeks. Smudges of dried blood streaked her face. A bit of motion caught Klara's eye before she could demand an explanation. It was Naomi's small hand picking at Stina's collar. She flipped the cover back to reveal Naomi cradled against Stina's shoulder.

"Are you all right?"

Klara nearly dropped the candle as she knelt on the floor.

"Oh, Klara." New tears tracked down Stina's face and she clutched Naomi tighter. "I'm so glad it's you."

Klara put the candle aside and hugged Stina and Naomi to her. "Naomi, Stina. Are you playing games? Let me look at you."

"So glad. I thought you were Mamma, when I heard you walking around."

"You must be freezing." Klara lifted Naomi away from the older girl. Her fierce wiggling and a demand to be put down reassured Klara. "Why are you here? What happened?"

"Is Naomi all right?" Stina got to her feet. The feather tick slipped to the floor.

"Come out by the stove." Klara led the girls into the front room. "Sit down. I'll make tea."

Stina sat down on the stool next to the stove and began rocking herself back and forth. Klara put the water on.

While the water heated, Klara went to the store room to see if her suspicions were true. She found the locked box in the center of the floor, its top hacked open. The ax lay nearby.

The cup of tea with a spoon of sugar seemed to revive Stina. Naomi chewed happily on a bit of flatbread. The effort it took to reassure them made Klara reluctant to explain the situation to James and Will. It was scary enough with their father away and their mother sick. Klara knew she only had a few minutes before the boys would burst into the kitchen.

"Tell me what happened. Please, before James and Will finish watering the animals."

"I'm sorry, Klara. I tried to stop her."

"Where's the jug? Surely she didn't drink it all."

Klara jumped up and began hunting for the stone-ware jug. It wasn't in the bed near her mother and she didn't find it on the table or by the stove.

Those are the sensible places to look, thought Klara. Drunk people aren't sensible, so where would she put it?

With a sigh she went back to the broken box in the storage area. There in the far corner was the *brannvin* jug, corked and wrapped in an old apron. When she lifted it up, she could tell it was empty.

How can that be? What did she do with the rest of the liquor. Pour it into a bottle, another jug? Pappa, Pappa, come home; tell me what to do. I must find it.

She heard James and Will at the door, so she tucked the jug back into the box and pushed it into the corner. She kicked the ax under a pile of birch bark roofing and went to meet the boys before they could barge in on Stina and their mother.

"Did you get all the animals watered?"

"Yes."

"I'm hungry. I could eat a bear."

"Did you bring water for us?"

"Forgot."

"We'll do it now. Come on, James."

Klara hurried back to Stina and Naomi. "Can you help me clean things up before the boys come back?"

Klara was already piling the breakfast mess in the wash basin. The boys wouldn't notice dirty dishes unless they were right under their noses. She wiped down the table, picked up the mittens, utensils, boots, and bed clothes strewn around the room. She tucked the quilt over her mother, checked to see if her breathing sounded normal, then closed the door on the bed closet.

Supper? What can I do about supper with nothing cooked. And Stina, her face and hair look a fright. No point in giving the boys too big of a shock. It's going to be bad enough when they find their mother sick in bed. Grabbing a damp rag, Klara scrubbed her sister's face as if she were a baby. While she was at it, she scrubbed Naomi, too.

"Now, Stina, take Naomi and go into the back room. Comb your hair, then comb Naomi's." She got Stina up off the stool by the fire and shoved her into the back room. "You can do that for me?" Stina nodded.

Now for supper, Klara thought. She put the flat griddle on the stove and added a little bacon grease. The smell of heating grease would cover the *brannvin* odor, anyway. In a large bowl she poured out a measure of flour. It was starting to smell of damp, so she didn't feel too bad about using it. She added soda, some salt and sugar, then beat in enough water to make a thin batter. It would be a poor excuse for griddle cakes. Now for something to go with the griddle cakes. She had put out a dish of beets, a small bowl of salt fish, when she heard Stina come back into the room. She looks almost normal. Thank heavens.

"Stina, are there any preserves in the store room?"

"Lingonberry or cloudberry?"

"Cloudberry, please."

Klara was relieved. The sticky sweet jam would keep the boys happy. She got the logs in the fireplace burning, added more wood to the stove, more water to the kettle, then she picked up the bundle of bark and twigs she had abandoned and hurried to the cow stable. Damnation, she muttered as she ducked through the door. I forgot the candle. She put down the feed and went back for a candle.

With the light held as far away as possible from the bundle of twigs and bark, Klara stepped into the dank stable. She was gratified to see that the ailing cow was still alive, suspended from the beam by the linen sling. She hurried around spreading small piles of bark and twigs in front of each of the animals. She paused to watch the cow pull a mouthful of willow twigs into her mouth with big rubbery lips. A good sign, she thought.

The animals fed, Klara tried to calm herself before she entered the front room. Standing in the doorway, she took off her coat and smoothed her dress. The room looked warm and bright. She could smell the aroma of sizzling bacon grease. Stina was setting the table, while Naomi played with her doll in front of the fire.

James and Will had filled the wash basin and were now using it with great vigor. She put down her candle and slipped past them to the front door where she hung her coat and scarf on one of the pegs. Returning to the room, she washed her hands and face in the cold water, then began pouring the batter onto the hot griddle. The boys sat banging their forks on the table, while she dished up the food.

"Oh boy. Hot cakes." Will seemed absorbed in the prospect of eating. "And jam, too."

"Where's Mamma?" James sat next to Naomi, helped her to a large spoon of jam when it was passed to him.

Klara signaled Stina with a finger to her lips. "Sleeping. She's not feeling well," she told James.

His mouth full, Will asked, "Is Pappa coming home tonight?"

"Not tonight. Leave some for the rest of us."

"Do we have to leave some for Mamma?"

Klara shook her head. "I'll make bean soup. She can have soup when she wakes up."

Will said, "I hate bean soup."

~~~

At bedtime Klara put Naomi in with the two boys. "That way I can share with Stina," she told them. They were too tired to object. After the three youngest children were asleep, Klara left them to check on her mother. Unable to rouse her mother, she went back to Stina.

"Stina, did anything else happen today? Did Mamma fall or hit her head?" she asked.

"No. She hollered and shoved me, scared me. She was so loud and she was throwing things, then she got the ax. I tried to stop her, but she pushed me away. Then she broke the box and found the *brannvin*. After that she danced around and laughed and laughed."

"I'm sorry I wasn't here."

"There is something else, Klara. When she brought the ax in from the chopping block, she held it up against her throat. Said she would get rid of all her troubles. I was afraid for her. And I was afraid she would hurt me. And Naomi."

Klara wanted to take her sister in her arms and hold her, but this kind of talk was too frightening and she worried about encouraging it.

"Stina, Stina hush. You're tired. It's been a hard day."

"I didn't know what to do, Klara."

"You did right. You kept Naomi safe."

"Should I have come looking for you?"

"No. It's always best to stay where it's warm and dry. Now we need to get some sleep."

"What's going to happen? When Mamma wakes up?"

"I'm not going to leave you again. Don't worry. If Mamma is angry, she can be angry with me."

"What if she wakes up in the night?"

"I'll stay awake and listen for her. Things will be better in the morning."

"I can help you listen."

"All right, but climb into bed and rest. You can listen and rest at the same time."

"Where are you going, Klara? Don't leave us."

"I need to check the door and put more wood on the fire."

Still dressed, Klara went to put the bolt in the door. What if Mamma gets up in the middle of the night? She tried to imagine how it would feel to wake in the dark, alone, sick. I can't leave a lantern burning, it gets too hot. It might catch the house on fire or Mamma might blunder around and knock it over.

She decided to leave a candle burning. She put it in a thick stoneware bowl and placed it on a shelf out of easy reach. She built the fire higher than usual, determined to stay awake to keep an eye on it. Though the house felt warm now, the walls and floor were cold from being unheated all day and that cold would seep out and chill them in their sleep.

When Klara returned to the back bedroom, Stina was asleep, whimpering softly in her dream world. Klara took off her shoes, but did not undress before she slipped into bed next to her sister. But, as hard as she tried to keep her eyes open, it was impossible.

She struggled from her cocoon of sleep at the usual time, stiff and cold. It took her a few minutes to remember why she was sleeping in the back room with Stina. When it hit her, she jumped out of bed and went out to see if her mother was awake.

Anna had the coffee water boiling and the oat porridge steaming on the back of the stove. She looked haggard, gray faced, but her eyes were bright and her voice strong and steady. She had brushed and braided her hair, twisting it into a double cornet over the top of her head.

"Good morning, Mamma." Klara felt relieved, but oddly shy approaching her mother after last night. "Are you all right?"

"Of course. Are the boys up yet?"

Klara tried to detect evidence that her mother had been nipping at the *brannvin* again, but found no trace in her action or demeanor. She returned to the back room to roust her siblings from their beds. She cautioned Stina to keep quiet about yesterday and went back to wash up and help her mother.

"We could wash clothes today, Mamma."

"I've mixed an ointment for Stina. Her face isn't healing."

"She needs to stop picking at it."

When Klara got the mugs and bowls from the shelf, she noticed the candle she had left burning there last night. It was barely burned, its wick carefully trimmed.

While the boys did morning chores, Klara, Stina, and Anna moved the furniture out of the way and sorted the dirty clothes into piles of wools and linens. Klara went outside to lay a fire under the cast iron laundry tubs. When the boys had finished feeding the animals, they were set to hauling water to fill them and mind the fire. They would do the scrubbing outside, the rinsing and wringing inside.

By the time the house filled with drying shirts, trousers, dresses, aprons, towels, everyone was complaining of aching backs, raw hands.

Klara had watched her mother throughout the day, but had observed only her growing exhaustion and her swollen jaw. For awhile, Klara suspected her mother had hidden the *brannvin* in the outhouse, but she could see no change in her behavior when she returned from sporadic visits. By supper time Klara was almost convinced all was well. Perhaps she was wrong about the level of liquor in the *brannvin* jug. Maybe it had been nearly empty.

~~~

Klara gave in to Stina's pleading and slept in the back room again. It is warmer, she thought. I'll be black and blue from Stina's elbows, though. What a squirmer.

How long she had been asleep, she didn't know. A loud thumping sound pulled her awake. In total darkness, Klara lay cradled in the feather tick and listened, listened for a repetition of the sound.

Maybe she had dreamt it, but, no, there it was again. This time she could hear the soft rumbling voice of the cow and the wuffling of a horse startled from sleep. She sat up too quickly and cracked her head on the ceiling of the bed closet.

As she was wrapping a heavy shawl around her shoulders, James spoke, his voice thick with sleep, "What's wrong?"

"Something's bothering the animals."

"I'll come with you."

"Get dressed and get back into bed to keep warm. In case I need you." Klara realized she was whispering. "Don't wake the others."

Fumbling in the dark, she found a candle by the stove and held it to the coals. After a brief minute the wick caught a thin flame. She stifled a cry of fright when the flickering light illuminated the fierce-eyed Elijah painted on the wall. Waiting for her wildly pounding heart to calm, she held the candle high enough to see the rest of the picture. She let her eyes carry her thoughts over the details of the scene, the story of the old prophet taken up to heaven in the fiery chariot. It calmed her to imagine how it might feel to sail through the air behind those snorting beasts, travel to a new and unknown place. Shaking her head at the absurdity of her thoughts, Klara turned toward the stable.

As she approached the stable door, she could see a light inside and pinched the wick of her own candle between thumb and forefinger. Klara stood shivering in the darkness, the clean smell of the snuffed candle in her nostrils a moment before it was drowned by the acrid stable smell.

She could see that her mother, clad in a faded nightdress, had placed her lantern on the floor near the cow. Against the brightness of the flickering light, her mother looked bone-thin, angular and severe. She stood barefoot in the straw-clotted muck and clawed at the knot in the funeral towels that kept the starving cow on her feet.

As Klara watched, her mother lost her balance and pitched forward against the cow. The animal snorted, tossed her head, but did not move. Anna regained her feet and tried to grip the knot again. She missed and beat the air with her hands, nearly falling again. She must have thought she could get closer from the other side because she walked around the cow's head. She picked her feet up high in exaggerated steps, grabbing at the animal for support.

"Mamma." Klara called softly for fear of startling her mother, but she got no response.

"Mamma. Mamma."

"Not now, Klara. I have to finish the washing."

"Come back inside before you catch a chill."

She took off her shawl and tried to wrap it around her mother's shoulders. With a shriek Anna flung off the shawl and nearly sent Klara into the piled manure. Klara retrieved the shawl and wound it tighter around her mother. She half carried, half pushed her back into the house to a chair by the banked fire.

"Sit down, Mamma. I'll build up the fire."

"No. I'm too warm." Anna threw off the wrap and stood up.

"Then we'll move away from the fire," said Klara.

She took her mother by the hand and led her to the bench by the table.

"Sit here, Mamma. We need to get you cleaned up a little." How could her mother possibly be too hot when she felt so cold?

Klara went to warm a pan of water on the stove, then find a clean rag. By the time the water was heated, the fire was blazing. It sent wild patterns of light and shadow around the room.

When she knelt on the floor with the pan of warm water, she looked up to see the garish mouth of the painted dragon leering over her mother's head. In the harsh contrast of dark and bright, the two of them seemed cut from the same cloth of unreality.

Until her mother reached to pat her hair, Klara was unaware of her own whimpering, the hot tears staining her cheeks, her trembling fingers.

She wiped her eyes on her sleeve and dipped the rag in the pan of water. Wringing out the cloth, she tucked her mother's gown up out of the way and washed the muck from her feet and ankles.

When James came into the dim room, the first rush of flame from the fire was over and shadow was overtaking light once again. Klara was kneeling in front of her mother drying her feet.

"Is everything all right?"

"I think so. Can you get the lantern from the stable and see if the animals are settled?"

By the time James returned, she had her mother in bed. Klara was thankful she was so passive, so near sleep. She heated a flat stone and wrapped it in an old towel to put at her feet, tucked an extra quilt around her, brushed her hair back from her forehead.

"I think she's asleep."

"The animals are quiet. I wish Pappa were here."

"Be brave, James. You're the chief dragon slayer for now."

"What's going to happen, Klara?"

"Tomorrow will be better. Wait and see."

Broken Trees and Bruised Souls.

Sharp cracking sounds woke them early the next morning. Before Klara had time to react, Will and Naomi had piled into bed on top of her. James held back from trying to follow, but huddled close with his feather tick wrapped around him.

"Get off, get off," yelled Stina who was on the bottom.

James wrapped his arms around Will and pulled him away from Stina.

"What is it, Klara?"

"Let me go, James. They're shooting at us"

"Shooting? Who's shooting?"

Klara rolled out of bed and went to the main room. The fire was low, but not out. While she was wedging a large birch log into the stove, she heard another loud pop followed by a crash on the roof. She quickly checked and saw that her mother was deep asleep, then went back to the children.

"Get up and get dressed. No one is shooting at you."

"So, what's that noise?"

"Trees breaking. They sort of explode, then splinter and fall."

Klara sat on the edge of the bed to tie Naomi's shoes. To Will and James she said, "If you're about dressed, go out and put the kettle on the stove."

"Why are the trees breaking?" Stina shrugged her nightdress over her head and started dressing. "It's so loud."

"Must be really, really cold." Klara finished dressing and helped Stina button up the back of her dress. "Let's go fix some breakfast."

By the time they had eaten their oat porridge, the cracking sounds had increased and several limbs had thudded onto the roof. Bundled up in extra scarves and sweaters the boys ventured out to get water. Within a few minutes they were back.

"There's a tree down in the yard. We can't get past it to the well house."

"It's really cold out there." Will stomped and swung his arms in mimic of his brother.

Klara put on her coat and scarf and went to see if the tree was as big and obstructive as James reported. She was shocked to find it worse. Not only was the tree blocking the way to the well, it had collapsed the south wall of the storage building and now loomed over the house. The mass of branches fairly filled the space in front of the door. Though it was cold, the sky was crystal clear. Through the branches, she could see the softly glowing crescent moon and the stars sharp against the early morning darkness. The sun, just below the horizon, bled the sky pink. How small and alone she felt. She turned her back on it all and went back in the house, feeling numb, unable to think clearly.

"So what do we do, Klara?" said James. "We could melt snow for the animals."

"I'll get the ax and start chopping a path," said Will. Klara nodded.

"Are you going to let him use the ax?" said Stina.

"Do you have a better idea?" Klara tossed her coat on the bench. "I need to see about Mamma."

Anna was touchy and short tempered, when Klara woke her. She seemed slow and groggy as she sat eating her oat porridge.

"What's happening, Klara?"

"Finish your breakfast. There's nothing to worry about."

Anna pushed her bowl aside and got up.

"What? Don't lie to me."

She went to the front door and yanked it open. She ignored the blast of cold air and stepped outside. James, gathering a bucket of snow, tried to guide her back inside.

"Go in, Mamma. You'll freeze without a coat."

"Let go. I have to take care of something."

She tried to climb through the tangle of branches across the path, slipped in the snow, and fell to her knees.

"Klara, Stina. Come help," screamed James.

He put his arms around his struggling mother and tried to pull her back to the house. Her flailing arms knocked him down before Klara could intervene. Finally the three of them wrestled the screaming woman into the house. Even before they could catch their breath, she had shook them off and run out into the snow again.

"Catch her, James, Stina. I'll be right back." Klara ran for the house to get the linen funeral cloths. The two unused towels were still on the shelf above the door. With a breath of relief she reached for them.

With the long strips of linen in her hand, she hurried back to the yard. Stina, James, and Will had caught Anna, but were making little progress getting her back to the house. Remorse, more than cold, made Klara's hands shake as she wound the long strips of cloth around her mother, binding her arms to her sides, giving them enough of an advantage to drag her into the house.

Will slammed the door and dropped the bolt into its slot. Klara wrapped a quilt around her mother and bundled her into bed. It took all of her strength and resolve to bind her mother's hands and feet to the bed. Anna shrieked and babbled incoherently.

"What's wrong with her, Klara?"

Tears ran down Stina's scabby cheeks. Will and Naomi stood watching from a little distance. James had helped Klara tie the knots, now he stood nearby, rubbing a long scratch down the side of his face.

Klara wanted to cry, herself, but looking at the pale, frightened faces of her siblings, she knew she did not have that luxury.

"Put more wood on the fire, then get back to work."

Naomi, who was just beginning to speak sentences, surprised them to silence with her baby-thin voice.

"Why did Mamma run outside?"

"Maybe she wanted to get something," said Will. He was busy poking the fire back to life.

Klara surprised herself by speaking her thoughts aloud.

"The *brannvin*. She must have been looking for it. Maybe it's hidden with the laundry tubs."

James stroked his mother's hair back out of her eyes. "Her toothache must be terrible bad." When she focused on him, James patted her shoulder and said, "Can't we give her some?"

Klara answered sharply, "No. It's bad for her."

"She can't go on like this," said Stina.

James patted his mother again, then said, "We'll look for the medicine. After we move the branches."

They spent the rest of the day melting snow for the animals, hacking at the fallen tree, and keeping the house warm. They piled the smaller twigs and branches against the end of the stable to feed the animals and felt grateful for the unexpected bounty. A few dead branches among the live ones were hacked up for firewood. The rest they dragged to the edge of the yard, out of the path.

In this way they managed to remove all but the huge trunk of the fallen tree. That would have to wait for men with saws and axes. Cold and shaky, Klara let them stop work. They ate a supper of thin bean soup with bits of hard bread. They finished the meal with mugs of bark tea, except for Naomi, who was given a brew of crushed rose hips, pale pink and slightly sweet, a drink reserved for the youngest children.

Green Woodpecker

The Call for the Tooth Puller.

Klara dished out a portion of soup for her mother, while James and Will went out for water to use in the morning. While Stina washed up the dishes, she confided in Klara.

"Those boys are much too young to be carrying those heavy buckets of water."

"Why do you say that, Stina? James is nine and Will must be nearly seven."

"James has complained his legs ache, almost every night."

"Growing pains," said Klara.

"You sound like Mamma."

"Don't talk nonsense, Stina. And speaking of Mamma, I'd better get her soup."

She broke a piece of hard bread into the bowl to soften, then went to undo her mother's wrists and help her sit up. Stuffing a pillow behind her back, Klara held the soup bowl and handed a spoon to her mother.

"The soup will make you feel better, Mamma."

Anna refused to take the spoon, so Klara fed her, plunging the spoon into the crack-lipped mouth each time her mother opened it to protest. She was urging her mother to take a little more, when the boys clattered into the room.

"We found it."

"I did."

"Me too. I helped."

"A pot of gold, no doubt." Stina dried her hands and confronted the boys. "You two get slower every day."

"No. What you been hunting for." James was nearly shouting in his excitement.

"The *brannvin*, that's what," said Will. He pointed to the corked stoneware jug James had clasped in his arms. "You been looking for it, haven't you?"

Anna pushed the spoon away. "Thank God. Bring me some. Please." Her voice sounded thin, quarrelsome as that of a tired child.

"Mamma, no. Have some more soup."

"Leave me alone, Klara. You don't know what it's like." She covered her face with her hands, rocked back and forth in the bed. "That soup is slop fit only for pigs."

"It's what we have. At least eat the bread. It's soft now."

Anna snatched the bowl from Klara, fished the lumps of bread out with her fingers, and crammed them into her mouth and swallowed them in one gulp.

"Now bring me the *brannvin*."

Without looking at Klara, James got a mug from the shelf. With Stina's help he poured an inch of the brownish liqueur and brought it to his mother.

She hugged him to her and took the mug from him. Still holding him close, she swallowed the *brannvin* in one long slug.

"Thank you. You're a good boy. Bring me another."

"No, James. Don't."

"Let Mamma have it. Her mouth hurts."

Klara saw she was alone in her fear, so she said no more. When her mother finally fell asleep, she replaced the bindings on her arms. At least I won't have to worry about her coming to in the middle of the night and running out into the snow or burning the house down, she thought.

Aloud, she said, "Get to bed, now. We have another hard day waiting for us tomorrow."

In her heart she resolved to go to the Lofs for help if her father had not returned by mid-day.

When noon came with no sign of her father, Klara prepared to leave. With a last check to be sure there was enough wood stacked inside the front door, enough water for evening, she gave James and Stina a final admonition.

"Stay inside and keep the fire going. Don't untie Mamma, no matter how much she complains."

"Do you have to go?" Stina stood twisting her hands in her apron with little Naomi peeking out from behind her skirt.

"You'll be all right. I'll be back by supper time." Klara gave her sisters a hug, kissed Naomi on the forehead. "Be good now."

James stepped back to avoid the hugging and kissing. "What's going to happen to Mamma?"

"She'll probably sleep until I get back."

Klara had no desire to discuss her mother's possible future with anyone. She refused to dwell on the possibilities. Maybe it was only a minor bit of trouble. She remembered another time when her mother seemed sick almost to the point of death, unable to eat or sleep because of the pain that set her to beating her head against the walls, themselves.

Mrs. Lof had brought the tooth puller who worked the fair at Smedjebacken to the house. The stooped, gaunt man with hair bristling in all directions had wiped his hideous tongs on his blood-crusted apron, then stepped over to Anna.

"Open up now, madam."

Only the restraining hands of her husband and the hefty Mrs. Lof kept Anna from running off to the forest. They pried her mouth open and before anyone could comment, the tooth puller had the offending molar gripped in his vile instrument. One twist to the right, one to the left, and the rotted tooth was out. With the burst of blood and pus came instant relief.

Anna cried and laughed, then embraced the filthy man and proclaimed him her savior. How awful it had seemed at the time. How wonderful it would be if such simple measures would work to relieve her mother's distress now.

"Klara, are you all right?" Stina was waiting to help her with her coat. "Did you see a ghost?"

"Something like that. Stay inside. Take care of Naomi and your brothers, Stina."

With a last wave Klara made her way through the tangle of branches in the yard and disappeared from view.

The walk to the neighboring farm took longer than Klara had calculated. The snow was deep and she missed the turn onto the shortcut. Going around by the road was slower because of the deep icy ruts left by tree cutters hauling timbers for the mine. By the time she explained the situation to her father and the Lofs, it was nearly dark.

"Could it be the tooth ache?" Klara looked at Mrs. Lof with hope and pleading. "Can you find the tooth puller?"

"Not much we can do tonight," said Mr. Lof. "It's almost full dark."

Per motioned Klara aside. "Did you have to come here? We'd be home tomorrow."

"I'm sorry, Pappa."

Klara could sense her father was embarrassed. She wondered if she had made a mistake coming for help. Should she have tried to keep her mother's problems quiet? But how much could she endure? And what about the danger to the children? First she had angered her mother, now she felt a deepening gulf between herself and her father.

"The mister is right. You can sleep with our girls tonight, Klara." Mrs. Lof went to tell her twins they were having company.

"I should go back."

She thought about Stina and the children alone in that dark house with their mother, not knowing what to expect, what to do. She slept little that night with all the could haves and should haves running through her head. Sleeping in a strange bed, with the two girls who barely tolerated her presence, added little to her ease. She was well aware that she was an unwanted intrusion.

When Klara, Ivar, and Per returned from the Lof farm the next morning, they found the house in an uproar, hot, smoky, noisy. James had untied his mother. She had taken the *brannvin* from him and now sat hunched in the corner by the stove. She had been raving about someone trying to get her and now, she demanded they build the fire higher to warm her chilly bones. She was urging James to load more wood into the stove when Klara, Ivar, and Per came into the room.

Alarmed at the acrid fumes, the blast of heat, the slurred cries from the stove corner, Klara drew back.

"What's happening?" She threw off her coat and confronted James. "Where are the rest of the children?"

James dropped the birch log he had been about to shove into the stove.

"Don't worry. They're in the back room."

Not bothering to remove his coat, Per shoved James aside and hurried to the stove.

"The chimney will catch fire."

He scattered the wood with the poker, then went back outside to lower the flat stone damper controlling the amount of air to the fire. With the damper closed, the roar in the stove died down. Ivar and his father lifted Anna to her feet and guided her to a chair. Klara brought a quilt to wrap around her shoulders. Per looked at Klara, his hands shaking, voice hoarse.

"How could you let this happen, Klara?"

"There's no reasoning with her, Pappa."

James spoke up. "The *brannvin* helps Mamma's toothache, but it makes her awful strong."

"Is that it, Anna? Is it the toothache, again?"

Per pulled up a stool and sat down beside his wife. He pushed the quilt back from her face and gently probed her neck and jaw with his thick fingers. When his forefinger brushed the hair back from the angle of her cheek below the ear, she cried out in pain. He drew back his hand.

"Come look at this, Klara."

Almost reluctantly Klara came to stand beside her father. She had noticed the swelling on her mother's jaw weeks ago, but now it was much larger, bulging the side of her face double its normal size. The skin was tight and purple-red near the bone itself.

"It looks terrible."

To reassure his wife, he said, "Mrs. Lof is coming. Maybe she has a remedy."

At the mention of the Lofs, Anna let out a howl of protest, struggled to her feet, and lunged at Klara. She slapped her, hard.

"Why? Why are you doing this?"

"I want to help you, Mamma." Klara backed away from her mother, her hand to her reddening cheek.

"Help? You take my baby away; you smash my pretty things. Now you bring that evil old woman."

"Baby? Your baby was dead, Mamma."

"No. You took her away in the wagon. I saw you."

Per put his arms around his raving wife and tried to steer her to the bed in the corner.

"She's confused, Klara. She needs to rest."

"Yes, Pappa. I'll see to the children."

She went into the dugout bedroom, glad to be away from her mother. Her father could take care of her now.

When she entered the back bedroom, she found Stina, Will and Naomi playing jackstraws on a quilt spread on the floor.

"Are you all right?"

"I'm glad you're back, Klara," said Will. "Fix us pancakes, please."

Stina stood up, scattering the jackstraws and putting an end to the game.

"Why didn't you come last night?"

"It was too late."

"You promised."

She motioned Naomi and Will off the quilt, then gathered it up and folded it. Dark circles under her eyes made her skin look pale, more translucent.

"You said you would."

"I'm sorry. I couldn't."

Why does everyone blame me for this mess, wondered Klara. I'm supposed to fix everything, too. Bring dead babies to life, make idiots smart, and china cups strong as iron. I suppose I should be able to cure toothaches and drunkenness and starving cows, make the sun shine longer and keep the snow at bay.

"Get cleaned up. I'll go see about something to eat."

Stina and Klara were washing dishes when Mrs. Lof came bustling up the path. When she finally caught her breath, she said, "The mister had to drop me at the head of your lane. The horses couldn't make the turn with those downed trees in the way."

Her tone clearly placed the blame for the blocked road on the doorstep of the lazy, indolent Larssons.

Klara dried her hands and took Mrs. Lof's coat. "Did you bring the tooth pulling man?"

"The mister can go for the doctor in Smedjebacken if I need help."

Per laced on his outdoor boots and picked up his coat. "Ivar and I will go clear the road."

Klara looked at her father with dismay. Too little sleep, too much worry made her blurt out, "You're leaving? Stay. Mrs. Lof may need someone to help."

Per paused to look at his daughter. "You can handle this, Klara. You have Stina to help." He turned and walked out the door with Ivar behind him.

Mrs. Lof interrupted, "Don't stand there gawking, girl. Where's my patient?"

Klara led Mrs. Lof to the cupboard bed across the room. She was relieved to see her mother tied to the bed once again. At least her father realized it was the only way to deal with the incoherent woman. She leaned over and touched her mother's hand.

"Someone here to help you, Mamma."

Though her voice and manners were rough, old Mrs. Lof had a gentle, soothing touch. She carefully examined her patient.

"Dear, dear. The poison from her teeth has spread. See this swelling along her neck? It runs down to the soft places in her shoulder, maybe into her breast."

"Do something, please."

Klara felt a jabbing ache in her own body, a kind of sympathetic pain, which made her sick to her stomach. How can a body stand it?

"Get some pine gum, girl." The old midwife was already pulling packets of dried herbs from her bag. "Heat it until it's soft."

Klara was glad to retreat from her mother's presence, from the aura of pain and madness that flowed from the bed corner. She ran to throw on her coat and boots, then plunged out into the hard envelope of frigid air. In the wood shed she found a pine log, twisted with knots. Neither caring or noticing the log was near the bottom of the neatly stacked wood, she yanked at it without success. She discarded her mittens for a better grip and worked the log from its place with a series of short, hard pulls. The wood tore at her hands, sent splinters into her palms. With a last pull the entire pile toppled into disarray across the woodshed floor, but she managed to dislodge the fat pine from the tangle of birch logs and drag it to the house.

"Come help me, Will. Bring the ax."

The two of them managed to hack a fist-sized section from the log, though they left a mess of chips and bark on the floor. In a few minutes they had a wedge of gummy resin for Mrs. Lof.

"Ye gods, enough for a moose," she said. "Get a pan and heat it on the stove. Be careful or you'll be burning the house down."

When Klara brought the softened pine gum to Mrs. Lof, she complained about the bits of debris, bark, dirt, dead insects, sticking to the pitch. Still, she accepted it and began working a handful of dried willow bark and a half-cup of chopped rhubarb root into the gummy mess.

Satisfied, she applied the hot plaster to the side of Anna's face and neck. Before she wrapped her patient's jaw with a frayed woolen rag, the old midwife dabbed a small portion of the sticky stuff onto her little finger and rubbed it on Anna's gums. Her patient struggled and tried to spit out the bitter mix, but Mrs. Lof had her mouth wrapped shut before she could complete the act.

"Now we'll let the plaster work, while we make something to help her sleep."

Stina was sent to find a pestle and stoneware bowl in the storeroom, while Mrs. Lof sorted through her bag of dried roots, leaves, seeds, and flowers. She decided on a couple of the shriveled, gray-green pods and broke them into the bowl Stina brought for her. She mashed them to a fine dust, then asked for a pint of clean water, a little sugar and a small tinware pan. She stirred the gray dust into the sugar and water, then brought the mixture to a boil. When it had cooked down to a thick syrup, she took it off the stove and sent Will for a bucket of snow.

With the pan of syrup cooling in the snow, she went back to check on Anna, who, though still struggling against the restraints, was sweating profusely from the plaster.

"Ah, yes. You've raised a sweat, dearie." Mrs. Lof pressed the back of her hand to Anna's forehead. "Wipe her down with a cold cloth. We want to draw the poison, not kill her."

Klara and Stina took turns rinsing the cloths in snow water, wringing them out, and applying them to their mother's forehead, chest, and arms.

"Now we'll try the sleeping draught. It should dull the pain and give her some relief, let the plaster do its work."

Mrs. Lof had decanted the poppy syrup and was now approaching the bed with a spoon and bottle.

"Hold her up. That's right. Get your hands behind her. Undo the rag holding her jaw shut."

With a quick hand she fished the glob of pitch from Anna's slack mouth, then administered a hearty dose of the sweet syrup to her patient.

Within a few minutes Anna was asleep, though her eye-lids twitched spasmodically and her hands still jerked against the restraints.

Stina ventured her opinion, "Can we let her loose? She looks so uncomfortable."

"She'll hurt herself or pull off the plaster."

"What is this syrup?"

"Give her a spoonful every four hours, unless she's still asleep. No more, mind you, or you'll be planning a burial."

"Wouldn't the tooth puller do better? Get it over with?"

"He could pull them all and still not get the poison. Be patient."

~~~

While the women worked inside, Per and Ivar had cleared the road so Mr. Lof could drive his wagon into the yard. When Klara went outside again, she saw her father unloading bundles of grass hay and stacking it in the undamaged section of the storage shed. Mr. Lof had tied his team to the ring in the wall and was inspecting the remains of the tree that had crashed into the yard.

"This is one big tree, Miss Larsson."

"We were lucky it missed the house."

"It's going to be a job getting it out of here."

"Yes, sir."

"I'll bring a couple of men from the mine. Maybe we can saw it into sections."

Ivar joined them. "Klara, how's Mamma?"

"Sleeping. Finally."

"And the cow? Is she...?"

"Still alive? Yes. Stina said she seemed a little more alert."

~~~

The hay unloaded, they went back to the house to get warm. While the adults sat at the table and spoke together in low tones about the ailing Missus, Klara and Ivar herded the children into the back bedroom. They sat staring at each other until Ivar spoke.

"Have you thought anymore about going to America?"

What an odd thing to be asking, she thought, with so much to be done here at home. "Not really. Why do you ask?"

"Do you think I'd ever have a chance with Irena?"

Stina answered without waiting for Klara's opinion. "The Lof's daughter? When sparrows wear breeches, you ninny."

"I expect Stina is right. Even if Irena agreed, her parents would object."

James suddenly caught on to the topic of conversation and rolled over on the bed clutching his stomach. "Ivar has a girl friend. Ivar has a girl friend."

"I do not," said Ivar with all the dignity he could muster. "If we were in America, I could court any girl I wanted."

"But you're not," said Klara. "Irena is out of reach."

"Maybe not." Ivar swatted his brother who was having a fit of giggles. "If you accepted Sofia's offer, I could come later, when you were settled. You'd be my sponsor. I could send for Irena, later."

"And what would we be using for money?"

Klara wondered what had gone on at the Lof farm the last few days. Ivar certainly had a bee in his bonnet.

"I'd get a job. You could keep house and cook for me."

It was Klara's turn to swat Ivar. She hit him with a pillow. "Where do you get these ideas?"

"It's love, Klara. Love makes him stupid," said Stina. "I saw them kissing once."

"Did not," said Ivar.

"Did too. In the barn."

While Stina and Ivar picked at each other, Klara sat thinking about Sofia. If she was with child when she visited last summer, she must be about ready to deliver. Arvid would be no help and little Lillian must be old enough to be into everything. Without a mother or aunties to help out, Sofia must be getting frantic by now. She still marveled at how the tough, rebellious Sofia she knew as a child could grow into the cosseted princess who came to visit last summer. Was it America or marriage or maybe just Arvid with his heavy-handed ways forming, molding the ignorant country girl?

She felt guilty because she had been too busy, too preoccupied to think about Sofia's generous offer of train and ship passage to Boston, too worried about herself to consider Sofia's situation. Now Ivar wanted her to go to America so he might have a chance. And the money, she could earn money to send back to her family. Maybe she could do more for them by leaving. Her stepsisters had promised to send money when they became established in Stockholm, but it never happened. With a shake of her head Klara tried to focus on the conversation between Ivar and Stina.

"You can't expect someone like Irena to look twice at the likes of you."

"I'm not such a bad looking fellow."

"Says who?"

"I can work, get on at the mines this year."

"And buy Irena silk dresses on a miner's wage?"

"Enough," said Klara. "Time for chores."

~~~

The Lofs drove off a short time later, leaving directions for renewing the plaster on Anna's neck and jaw, warnings about over-dosing on the poppy syrup, and the hope that the remedy would be effective.

The family slept better that night and for several nights more.

By the morning of the third day, Anna seemed a little better. Her fever was down and she seemed calmer, more lucid. They untied her and Stina helped her clean up and dress. The residue from the plaster left a dark mark on her pale skin. The infection seemed to have retreated to the edge of her jaw which was swollen tight and fiercely purple. Though unable to eat, she managed to take a little thin oat gruel along with her medicine.

"It's a nice, clear day. Good day to take the team out," said Per.

He watched his wife closely, perhaps wondering if she would react. It would be easier if she cooperated with their plan to take her to the doctor in Smedjebacken. Mrs. Lof had been firm in her recommendation. When the swelling went down, Anna must see the doctor.

Ivar took the hint and said, "The horses need to get out and stretch their legs. The road's in fair shape. The wagon runners should glide well."

Klara added, "A work crew from the parish smoothed it with a dredge and ox team yesterday. We'll just skate along. We'll bundle up. It'll be fun."

Anna's silence was taken as agreement and they continued to plan the trip. Who would go, who would stay, what would they need, how long would it take, could they reasonably expect to make the trip over and back by evening? It was decided that Ivar should stay home with the children. With Stina's help he could be expected to manage everything. Without the chore of caring for the horses and worrying about their mother, the work and responsibility would be reduced many fold. Klara would make the trip to take care of her mother, while her father managed the team and wagon.

The only time Anna responded to their conversation was when they argued about how they would pay the doctor.

"Maybe he'll wait for his fee. I could hire out as housemaid when spring comes." Klara knew this was unrealistic, but could think of nothing else.

"Even in the mines I couldn't make enough," said Per.

"We'll make things to sell," said Stina. "Knitted caps, mittens, scarves."

"We could sell the chocolate set," said Will. "We never use it."

"Mrs. Lof might buy it," said Stina.

"I doubt it. She said it was old fashioned." Klara remembered the shelves and shelves of china dishes, copperware, and silver tea sets that filled the Lof home.

"It's so pretty, it should...."

In a voice muffled and unclear because of the pain and swelling in her mouth, Anna interrupted, "You can't sell the chocolate set. Not to that old woman. I'd rather throw it down the well." She leaned back, exhausted with the effort.

Klara patted her mother's arm. "We won't touch it, Mamma. Calm down."

They put one of the feather ticks in the wagon bed and settled Anna there, a quilt making a tent over her head. A basket with her mother's medicine, a few dried fish, hard bread, and the funeral towels, in case her mother became hard to control, were placed in the wagon. Klara walked alongside, until the horses thrashed their way onto the main road. When the going became easier, Per stopped the team so Klara could climb in. She tried not to think about the toll this trip would take on the half-starved horses.

A Larger World.

With the steeple of the parish church in view, Klara called to her father to stop the team.

"Mamma's getting agitated. I need to give her some medicine."

Though it was too soon for her dose of the poppy syrup, Klara decided she had no choice. When the wagon jolted to a stop, she knelt in the wagon bed and spooned the sweet liquid between her mother's lips, careful not to touch her teeth.

"You'll feel better in a few minutes."

"Take your time," said Per. "The horses need a rest. Standing in the stable all day is no preparation for work."

Klara climbed down to walk alongside when they were ready to start again. Her mother was asleep. She slept on as they drove by the railroad station, the mine maintenance shop, the deserted market square, the silent brown church with its tall spire. When they pulled up in front of the small building with the doctor's sign hanging above the street, she still slept.

"Stay with her, Klara. I'll go see if the doctor is in."

The team was blowing hard from the last uphill climb into town and the heavy lather seen only on horses in poor condition, rimed their necks and flanks.

Klara was trying to rouse her mother, when the doctor, followed by her father, came out of the building. The doctor examined his new patient.

"She's in a very deep sleep. That will make my work easier. Let's get her inside."

Between the three of them, they lifted Anna from the wagon and carried her inside where they stretched her out on the examination table. Klara unwrapped the quilt and removed her mother's coat, boots, and mittens.

"Thank you," said the doctor. "You can wait in the next room, young lady."

Per, too, seemed anxious to get out of the office with its strange smells, noises, and furniture.

"I'll go see to the horses."

"There's a barn in back. Give them some hay," said the doctor.

After a few minutes, the doctor came out to question Klara about her mother's condition. How long had she been ailing, what remedies had they tried, and who had given her the sleeping potion? He seemed most interested in the last question.

"Do you have any medicine left?"

Klara showed him the bottle of syrup Mrs. Lof had mixed. Only a small amount remained.

"This is interesting," he said. "Dangerous, but interesting."

"Can you give me more of this, for Mamma?"

"Probably not. I'll find something less potent."

He drummed his fingers on the bottle, perhaps thinking about how to proceed. He looked through the row of medicines on a high shelf, then selected a wicked looking set of instruments.

"I'm going to lance the swelling on her jaw. It will give her some relief, but she needs an operation."

"Can't you do it now?" Klara was thinking of the difficult trip into town, the weary horses. "Why wait?"

"She needs to see the doctor in Borlange."

"It's so far. Won't you do it?"

"I don't have the right equipment."

"Is it the money? We'll get it somehow. I give my word."

"I must lance her jaw now, before the opiate wears off. Get your father. I need his help."

~~~

Nervous and uncomfortable, Klara waited. An occasional moan, the clink of metal instruments, low muttered conversation were the only sounds that came from the examining room. Unable to stand it any longer, Klara leaped up and went outside where she paced up and down the board walkway in front of the office. When she approached the corner, someone called her name. She looked up to see a vaguely familiar figure hurrying across the street.

"Klara, Klara Larsson. You probably don't remember me. I'm the younger Hansson brother, Emil. I work at the post office now."

"Oh yes. You're Ivar's friend. Good to see you again."

"Lucky I noticed you here. I was going to send a man to your place with this."

He handed Klara a flat parcel nearly covered with stamps, cancel marks, customs seals and declarations.

"Looks important."

"Postmarked New York. It must be Sofia."

"She's a lucky one. I hope to emigrate when I save enough."

"Why would you want to leave? You have a good life here."

"That's what my father says. The farm is big enough to divide with my brother, but it's the new draft law I fear."

Though she would have preferred to wait, Klara decided to open the envelope while Emil Hansson watched. Give him some gossip to share, she thought.

"It is from Sofia, Sofia Varm. Do you remember her?"

"Of course. Every young man in the parish knew her, if you get what I mean."

Klara ignored his implication and pulled the papers from the envelope. A sheet of pink stationery folded around a thick set of official looking papers nearly fell from her hands.

"Oh dear. What is this?"

Emil took the papers from her.

"This is a train pass, one way to Karlstad, then on to Kristiania. That's in Norway. The other paper is a ticket for passage on the Swedish-Amerika Line. Lucky girl."

The young man's outward show of feeling embarrassed Klara. He seemed so like Ivar in his careless enthusiasm. She couldn't think of an answer, so she stood staring at him.

"I could help you learn English," he said.

"You speak English?"

"I'm learning. It would help me, too. The practice, I mean." It was Emil's turn to blush.

"Maybe we could. In the spring." Klara surprised herself with her daring reply. "I need to get back inside."

"See you then. Bye," said Emil.

Before the doctor finished treating Anna, Klara had said goodbye to the Hansson boy, hidden the tickets in her bag, and composed herself. She sat stiff, restrained on the bench in the waiting room when her father and the doctor came in.

"How is Mamma?"

"Resting. She'll be able to go home in about an hour. I want to be sure the bleeding has stopped before you take her."

The doctor busied himself with the bottles and jars lining the shelves in a closet-like space that opened just off the waiting area.

"I'm going to give you something for her pain. We'll mix it with the opiate she's been taking. Perhaps we can wean her from it that way."

Per put on his coat. "You wait with her, Klara. I'm going to the iron monger's shop."

When her father had gone, Klara went in to see her mother.

"Are you feeling better, Mamma?"

"She shouldn't try to speak for a while," said the doctor. He examined his patient's bandage. "Looks good. You'll be feeling better, soon."

"Will this new medicine work as good as the syrup Mrs. Lof gave her?"

"It won't make her sleep. I hope you realize it will be hard for her, not having the opium. People get dependent on it."

By the time her father returned, Klara had her mother ready to go. They helped her to the wagon and made her comfortable. The doctor agreed to wait for his fee, but again urged them to make arrangements to take Anna to Borlange.

They said they would do their best, but even the doctor knew how resistant these country people were to the idea of going to a doctor. He knew how desperate they must have been to come to him today. It wasn't just a lack of money, but, rather, a kind of strange, misplaced pride. How often had he heard the old men brag they had never seen a doctor their entire lives; the women shyly speak of the strength of their children in terms of the accidents and illness they had survived on their own. He watched the Larsson wagon groan its way down the street, then turned and went back into his office. He had done his best. The case was out of his hands now.

~~~

When they reached home, Stina and Ivar came out to help. Before long the team was stabled, the wagon dragged under cover, and Anna seated by the fire attended by the younger children. They patted her hands, brought a pillow for her back, and a shawl for her knees.

"Did you make soup, Stina?" Klara wondered why the trip to town was more tiring than a day's work in the fields. "And barley gruel?"

"Yes, but it's skimpy. I used the last of the beans."

"I'm going to kill the hens. Mamma has to have something to get her strength back."

"She won't be happy about that."

Stina dished up the soup, dividing it according to age, with her father getting the biggest portion, Naomi, the smallest. Klara broke the round of horn bread in pieces and filled the mugs with hot water.

"Don't give the hens anything to eat tonight. We'll do them in the morning."

"Probably just as well. The moldy grain I've been feeding them is almost gone."

"Three scrawny hens. We'll have to make them last."

Klara busiest herself thinking about how she would prepare the chicken. Don't mention it to the boys, though. To give them false hopes of fried chicken or savory stew would be too cruel.

Stina interrupted her thoughts. "Maybe Pappa could butcher one of the goats. Without a new baby in the house we can get along with one goat this summer."

"Goat meat. We can salt and dry it. Sliced thin, it will probably last until the spring fish run." Klara smiled and hugged Stina.

~~~

The next morning Klara had the boys fill one of the iron kettles with water and set it to heating in the yard. With her apron on over her coat she carried the wicker hen coop outside. She returned to the house for the ax.

Stina asked, "Where are we going to pluck and singe the birds?"

"Maybe the storage shed. It's out of the wind. If we stink up the house, Mamma will say she can't eat chicken because it tastes like burnt feathers."

"She didn't protest about killing them."

"I'm glad of that," said Klara. "She seemed to be feeling better this morning."

One at a time Klara chopped off the heads of the hens that had lived in the coop under the table since December. When the first chicken was dead, its blood splattered on the dirt floor of the storage shed, she ran out to the kettle of hot water to submerge the bird. In and out of the near boiling water, then she began plucking. As quickly as she could, she stripped the back and wings, grabbed the tail feathers and twisted the long feathers free. The wing feathers came off just as cleanly, but the smaller breast feathers slowed the job. She rubbed her fingers down the breast in the direction the feathers lay, rolling the wet gobs into her palm. When she was finished with the plucking, she carried the prickly looking carcass to Stina. With a torch of rough rags Stina singed off the pin feathers. While Klara killed the next hen, she gutted the first bird and rinsed it in a bowl of cold water. In an hour the job was finished and the birds were simmering on the stove.

~~~

A few days later the Hansson boy rode into the yard. He dismounted and was tying his horse to the fence when Klara came out to meet him.

"What brings you out here, Mr. Emil Hansson?" Klara dried her hands on her apron. "Shouldn't you be at work?"

"It's a postal holiday. No work. I thought we could study our English. If you're not too busy, that is." He opened the leather bag buckled to his saddle. "I brought my book."

"I don't know. I haven't told my family about the tickets." Klara made no move to walk him toward the house. She rubbed the horse's shaggy neck, inspected his muscular shoulders, sturdy legs. "What sort of horse is this?"

"I won't mention the tickets. We can still study, can't we?"

"He's a pretty dun color, but isn't he a bit small for you?"

"He's a Gotland, from the island, you know." Emil looked at the little horse as if he'd never seen him before. "Nice weather we're having this week."

"The snow will start melting if it keeps up."

Part of Klara wanted to beg Emil to stay, to help her learn English; another part of her wanted to demand he leave, immediately, and never come back. Time, she thought, I need time to think.

Aloud she said, "Spring will be a relief."

"It has been a hard winter, colder than usual, more snow and wind. The days are getting longer, though."

Emil handed Klara the book and put his arm through hers to steer her to the house.

"Last night I studied the section on how to greet someone, like when you meet them on the street. That might be a good place to start."

The two of them settled down at the end of the table nearest the window. Emil opened the book to a section near the back.

"You're that far into the book? I won't be able to keep up with you."

"Wait and see. The material in the front is mostly technical stuff, rules of grammar and spelling. This is the beginning of the useful material."

"The spelling didn't make much sense."

"I'll say the phrase and you repeat it. Good morning, Sir."

"Good morning, Sir."

"Good morning, Sir. How do you do?"

When Ivar came in from chopping wood, he joined the lesson. Stina brought the mending basket and heaped a tangle of worn socks on the table.

"We can sew and learn at the same time."

Almost automatically Klara threaded a needle and began weaving a patch across a monstrous hole in a wool sock.

Emil continued to read the lesson, "What did you say? Do you understand me? Are you done? Don't trouble yourself. It is no trouble at all."

They all repeated, "It is no trouble at all."

Stina was about to collapse with a fit of giggles. "It all sounds so silly."

"Here's a good one," said Emil. "It is a pity. Never mind."

"Never mind, never mind, never mind. That's enough for one day."

"How do you say, what's for supper?" Ivar got up and went to get his coat. "Time to water the animals."

"And time for me to get home," said Emil. "Maybe we can do this again soon."

"At least I know where to start now."

Klara knotted her stitch, cut the thread, and rolled the sock with its mate. She noticed Emil made no move to leave.

"Too bad we're not Akians."

"Not what?" Klara put her sewing scissors away in their little leather case. What a talkative fellow.

"Who, not what. The Akians are a religious sect. When my father heard I wanted to study English, he told me a strange story. Seems his cousin was an Akian. Most of them emigrated, about forty years ago, to escape being jailed for their odd beliefs. They thought they would speak perfect English when they stepped on America's shore."

"Without a book? Without studying? Where did they get that idea?"

"It happened to the apostles at the first Whitsuntide when they were filled with the Holy Ghost."

"What are you talking about?"

"Haven't you read the Book of Acts?"

"And did it happen? Did your father's cousin speak fluently when he reached America?"

"Father said he was never heard of again." Emil finally closed his book and stood up.

Klara escorted Emil to the front gate. "Thank you for the help."

Emil shut his book into his saddle bag, mounted the little horse, and saluted. "Good afternoon, Miss. Good bye," he said in solemn English.

"Never mind," Klara responded with the only phrase she could remember from the afternoon's lesson. She waved as Emil reined his horse around and out of the yard. She didn't feel like she had learned anything, but it had been fun.

Late because of the lesson, Stina and Klara had to hurry through their chores to be done in time for supper. James and Will stomped in, cold and hungry. They had checked the snares along the trail in the woods and by the frozen river, but had found nothing. Per came in a few minutes later. He had spent the day on the river with a long iron rod and a hatchet probing the thick ice. He hoped to find a deep hole where the ice was thinner, the fish accessible. He had found nothing, and now agreed it was time to butcher one of the nanny goats.

"We'll do it tomorrow," he said.

It was defeat worse than killing the hens. To eat the brood stock, like grinding the seed grain for bread, was the hallmark of a poor manager, an inept farmer. Klara felt like crying for her father. He sat with his shoulders slumped, his head bowed, chin almost touching his chest. When he finished the last of his chicken broth, the spoon clattered against the side of the bowl because of the tremor of his hand.

Spring at Last: Gullviva and Dandelion.

When the days grew longer, the snow began its slow melt. In mid-day little trickles of water ran from beneath the rough, dirty edges of the banked snow and the drifts grew visibly shorter. The night cold locked everything in place again, but each succeeding freeze found less and less of the icy riches.

At first it was only small trees and branches revealed by the melt, but one day Klara noticed the stiff finger tips of dried grass poking through the snow. The first day she could barely see them peppered over the glare of ice, but the next day the grass emerged enough to cast shadows on the crystal surface.

The noon meal finished, Klara began putting on her outdoor clothing. She called to Stina, "Get your coat and boots."

"I have to wash the dishes," said Stina.

"They can wait. Find the old broom, too."

Klara was tying a long scarf around her head. By the time Stina had finished pulling on her boots, Klara, broom and long handled hoe in hand, was out the door. Stina hurried to catch up. When they reached the long meadow by the river, Klara's mission became clear.

With broom and hoe the two girls beat the ice crust and snow from the dried grass. Long covered over, the stiff grass was well preserved with streaks of green on the thicker stems and leaf bases. They cut several large piles before Stina returned to the house for a square of sacking to wrap it in.

When they offered it to the animals later that day, they ate it voraciously and looked for more. The milk cow, still suspended in the sling, was given the bigger share. Thin as a wraith except for her calf-swollen belly, she was still too weak to stand on her own.

The calf was still alive, though. Later that evening their father showed them how to give the cow's belly a sudden push with their fist to shift the calf. They could feel the calf bump back, kicking, against their hand after they pushed against the cow's belly. It was almost as exciting as the bucket of fish Ivar had brought in that afternoon.

Small and sluggish, the bottom feeders would have been thrown back in the summer time, but now, fried in chicken fat, they seemed like the food of kings. With the craving for rich, fatty fare temporarily sated, the desire now was for something green, green and tender. It would become a contest of sorts, to see who would find the first gullviva, a yellow bell-shaped flower that announced spring. The gullviva wasn't edible, but the burdock, wild lettuce, and dandelion that came up soon after could be boiled up into a fine pot vegetable.

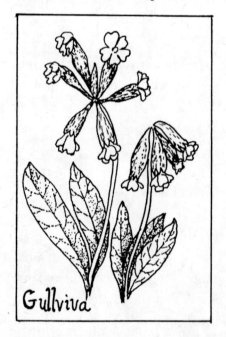

Gullviva

"Mamma, I need to talk to you," said Klara.

She dreaded talking to her mother about important things, but she had to tell her about the letter and tickets. She had to mention leaving home, speak about the possibility of going to America, and she knew she could put it off no longer. She waited until everyone was out and about with their various chores.

Ivar had gone with his father to try for more fish; James and Will were checking the snares. Stina had picked up a basket and announced she was off to look for greens and wild flowers. Klara doubted her sister would find much, but a bunch of gullviva, a few purple anemone would brighten the house. Naomi was in the back room playing with her Christmas doll.

"Mamma, I had another letter from Sofia a few weeks ago."

Klara watched her mother, wondering how she would respond. She seemed better since her visit to the doctor. At least the pain had subsided to the point where she could sleep and she no longer vacillated between violent frenzy and coma-like stupor. Mostly she sat working on bits of sewing or spinning. She had no energy for larger tasks and paid little attention to the comings and goings of the household.

"May I read it to you, Mamma?"

Klara decided her mother's silence was the most approval she was going to get. She unfolded the sheet of pink stationery and held it to the light streaming in the small diamond panes of the window over the table.

"She has such pretty writing paper and the ink even matches.

Something in what Klara said stirred her mother to speak.

"She probably has someone else write for her. A little hussy like that could never learn to write so nicely."

Klara ignored her mother's comment and read Sofia's letter aloud.

Dear Clara,

There is a June sailing of the steamer, Charlotta. Arvid will meet you at New York harbor and bring you to our home as I am indisposed. The baby is a little girl, very sweet and perfectly beautiful. This may be your last opportunity to come to us because Arvid is talking about moving west. The pamphlet with the tickets tells you what you need for the journey. Let us know as soon as possible

Sincerely,

Sophia Lindblad

"She actually sent tickets?" Anna sat up a little straighter, seemed to focus on her daughter for the first time in a long while.

"Yes, Mamma. For the train and the ship." Klara spread the tickets on the table.

"It must have cost a lot."

"Arvid makes good money." Klara's words seemed sure, but her tone held a question. What was it that Arvid did? She knew he was paid a certain amount by the various steamship companies to recruit passengers, but , surely, that wasn't enough of a job to finance the standard of living the Lindblads enjoyed.

"You'd best start making preparations. Don't let this chance pass you by."

"You'll let me go?"

"You're sixteen, Klara. I can't stop you."

"And Pappa? What will he say?"

"You should already have started a bride's box. Now you need an Amerika chest, instead."

"The list with the ticket says I need to bring a tin dish, knife, fork , and spoon, a water can and bed linen."

"You can take your granmutter's box."

"Thank you, Mamma."

Klara felt tired suddenly, deflated, unsure of her decision. She had expected an argument and received none. Maybe her mother wanted her to leave, wanted her out of the house, out of her life. She put the tickets away and went to heat water for scrubbing the floor.

~~~

"You're actually going? Which sailing?" Emil was sitting across the table, the language book open between them. "When do you leave?"

"I'm not sure. I hoped you might give me advice."

Klara found she had dropped a stitch and stopped to unravel her wool. "Sofia recommended the June sailing on the *Charlotta*."

"Let me see your ticket." He turned it over to read the instructions on the back. "I'll send them a letter to reserve space for you. I wonder if anyone else around here is traveling on that sailing?"

"It would certainly help, not going alone, I mean."

"I wish I could go."

"That would be very pleasant."

"Maybe next year."

Ivar came in before the conversation could go on. "Hello, Emil. I thought I saw your horse tied to the fence. Klara, we need your help."

"Coming."

"Is there something I can do?" said Emil.

"Sure thing, but you might dirty your hands a bit. We're about to move the old cow out of the stable. There's enough grass showing on the south facing bank to give her a square meal for a change."

Emil laughed and got up. "I helped the Jansson's with the same job, yesterday."

They had already led the horses, as well as the remaining goat, to the sheltered end of the field. The only animal remaining in the stable was the milk cow. By linking hands just above her hocks and pushing up and forward Ivar and Emil were able to get her moving. On either side Klara and her father held the linen strips wrapped around the cow's chest to steady her on her forced journey to the field. Though the cow settled down on her brisket when they released her, she immediately began eating the grass in front of her nose.

"Do you think we'll be able to get her up again?" said Klara.

"She'll be getting up on her own steam after she eats all the grass within reach," said Emil. "She may go down when she reaches a new patch of grass, but she'll get stronger each time."

"Yes, with a bit of coaxing she'll make it back to the stable. She'll be good as new in a week."

Per dusted the bits of straw and dander from his hands.

Klara doubted any of them would ever be good as new again, but she felt like a huge weight had lifted from her shoulders when they got the cow to pasture. Spring was in sight. New crops would soon green the black earth and they would plant peas, beans, potatoes, beets.

When she got back to the house, Stina was rinsing a bunch of wild lettuce, dandelion, and the slender gray-green shoots of *allium*, wild garlic. A quick dip in a pot of water boiling on the stove, a dressing of vinegar, and the greens were ready to eat.

~~~

With her father's help Klara refurbished the old bride box, the box her grandmother, Maria, had brought to her marriage with Erik Axel Norrling so many years before. While Per reinforced one of the box's corners with a piece of tin, Klara cut out a new lining from a worn sheet. She mitered the cloth to fit the box exactly, then glued it in place.

When she scrubbed the outside of the box with a bit of lye soap, the original pattern of interwoven stems and leaves showed through the grime of years. More rubbing revealed an old saying painted on the box in fancy script.

Klara read it aloud, "Marriage: the best method ever for getting acquainted."

In addition to the heavy box Klara also had a cloth satchel for the things she would need on her journey. She tried to figure out how many days she would be enroute. She knew the train to Kristiania would take a day and a half, but since the exact sailing date of the *Charlotta* would depend on her cargo and the amount of time necessary for loading and unloading, she could not be sure of the length of her stay in the harbor town. The sailing, itself, could take as few as ten days with another day or two in New York harbor depending on the number of ships landing passengers through Ellis Island at that particular time.

She looked up to see Ivar watching her. "How long have you been standing there?"

"Do you have things enough fill up that trunk?"

"Mamma says I need to take all my clothes and at least one quilt."

"I don't know if that's smart. Our things will look old fashioned, shabby, compared to the things city folk wear. You'll want to buy new stuff once you get there and get paid your first wages."

"I intend to send money home. I don't need new clothes."

"You'll soon change your mind. Did Sonja ever send money from Stockholm?"

"I'm not Sonja."

"We'll see," said Ivar. "Of course I do expect you to send me passage money."

"Do you know how much it is?"

"Emil said it was about forty dollars of American money."

"So much?"

~~~

Unlike the rousing party the Larssons had thrown for the Lindblad's leave taking, Klara's departure would hardly be noticed. Emil had found a local family with four small children booked on the same ship. He arranged for Klara to travel with them in return for her help with the children. It was a fine arrangement for everyone.

Klara burst into tears when Emil told her about the Ersson family. She had not realized how terrified she was at the thought of traveling alone. Now she had someone to talk to, someone to help with her heavy box, some one to distract her when she was afraid.

They decided to leave on the third Saturday of May. That would get them to Kristiania a few days early, but Mr. Ersson seemed to be a chronic worrier. What if they were delayed on the train? What if they had trouble finding a wagoneer to transport their boxes and trunks to the wharf? What if the *Charlotta* docked early, unloaded and loaded in record time? You just didn't know with these modern machines and gadgets they were using nowadays. His fretting made Klara's head spin. She would be very glad when they were safely on board and everyone could relax.

Emil told her there was an inn close by the harbor where passengers could get board and room while waiting their passage. When she protested that she had no money for lodging, he assured her that the Erssons would take care of it. Somewhat calmer, she continued her preparations.

"What on earth are you doing, Klara?" Stina had come in with an arm load of wood to find Klara sitting on the floor surrounded by all her things. "I thought you packed that box days ago."

"I was sure I had forgotten my winter stockings, the long black ones."

"Do you think it gets cold in America?"

"I don't have time to knit another pair."

"Here they are, you silly goose," said Stina. She held up the lumpy homemade stockings with their tops pulled out of shape by the garters used to hold them in place. "You had them packed all along."

Klara took the stockings from Stina and burst into tears.

"What's wrong, Klara? It's only a pair of stockings." When Klara said nothing, Stina though to change the subject. "You should take my good apron. It's much newer and nicer than yours."

She ran to get the gauzy apron, one of the few store bought things she owned. Made of imported cotton, her white apron was like those worn to church and on special occasions by all the women and girls of the parish. Just a few miles away, in the neighboring parish, the women wore aprons with vertical stripes of red and blue. Each region had its own color, its own pattern.

When Stina returned, she traded Klara's apron for her own crisp new one. "There you are."

Klara hugged her sister. "I'll think of you when I wear it."

"And this old ratty quilt? You're not taking this?"

"I didn't want to take a good one."

"Nonsense. You need something special."

"I suppose you think I should take Granmutter's wedding ring quilt?"

"No. Something better."

Stina grabbed Klara by the hand and pulled her into the storeroom. She pointed to a bundle perched on the highest shelf.

"Help me get that down. Mind the dust."

When they unwrapped the bundle, a brilliant mixture of colors and textures spilled out across the patch of sunshine on the floor. Bright as the day it was stitched, the crazy quilt dared Klara to touch it, pet it, rub it against her cheek, then make it a part of her journey to the new world.

"It's perfect, Klara. Mamma said she used it on her bed when she was a little girl. It's too small for a double bed. Just right for one person."

"Oh, Stina. It's too good, but I love it."

"It will fit in your box just right. You're all set."

"I'm going to miss you."

"You'll be back to visit before you know it."

~~~

A few weeks before the planned departure date another letter arrived. Klara slipped the single sheet of writing paper from the envelope, leaving the other papers for later.

Dear Klara,

> *Arvid says there is a new regulation that states you must have cash money when you come through Ellis Island. If you can find someone to loan you fifty dollars, it would make your entrance into the United States more certain. Everyone does this. The money can be returned immediately via one of the wire service offices at the docks. We look forward to seeing you soon.*

> > *Sincerely,*
> > *Sophia*

Klara was holding back tears of disappointment by the time she got to the end of the letter. Fifty dollars. How absurd. Sofia might as well be asking her to bring the moon. Then, through her tears, she saw that the letter had a handwritten postscript, a childish scrawl across the bottom of the pink paper.

When she read it, she could hear Sofia's voice and she knew then it was Arvid who wrote the polished, slightly formal letters she had been receiving. The strident tone, messy penmanship, and blatant misspellings of the postscript didn't bother Klara. It was Sofia through and through.

Der Klar,

> *I sen you $25 dolar Amerikan. It vas all I kud get. Arvid vatches me vith sharp eyes. I sav this from the food money. I snek out to sen this now. Come*

soon. Hurry! Hurry! Hurry! Luv, Sofy
When Klara examined the envelope, she found the papers were, indeed, money.

When Emil came for another lesson, she showed him the letter and the money. He explained that the worn bills were ones and fives. He showed her how five of the crumpled one dollar bills were equal to one of the five dollar bills, but he had a hard time trying to explain what it was worth in *riksdalers* and *ore*. It was more money than either of them had ever seen before.

"And do you think I will need so much money when I get to America?"

"You must find a safe way to carry it. There are thieves in the harbor towns, even on the ships."

"Mamma could use it for the doctor in Borlange."

"No, Klara. It's for you." Emil got up from the table and slammed the book shut. He began pacing up and down the narrow room. "Don't you remember the Nilsson family? Their father emigrated and sent them passage money. They spent it on seed grain and a cow. The next year the father sent pre-paid tickets because he couldn't trust them to use the money properly."

Klara was surprised at the passion in Emil's voice. Why does he care about how the money is spent? "You really want to emigrate, don't you?"

"I will. Soon."

"I wish you could come now. With me."

"You'll be fine, Klara. Don't worry so."

After Emil left, Klara found a strip of cloth, soft and faded by many washings. She stitched it double and sewed the money inside, all of the money except one of the dollar bills. Wrapping it around her middle, under her clothes, she tied the ends to form a secret belt. The dollar bill she placed in her waist purse.

~~~

With spring came work, hard, back-crunching work. Ivar and his father tilled the black soil to a velvet fine crumble, then put Will and Naomi to dredging rocks from the new plowing. The two children spent days criss-crossing the fields. Little Naomi, just learning to walk, piled rocks into her basket, then looked to Will to lug them to the old sink hole along with his own.

James and Stina worked up the garden plot and planted potatoes, onions, cabbage, and beets. The cow and goat had to be led to the woods, staked out to graze, moved every hour or so. Wood had to be cut, for the next winter as well as for the ever-present need for cooking and heating water. Ivar worked with his father in the fields, then helped with the harder jobs at home in the long evenings. The well had to be cleaned, the end of the storage shed rebuilt, birch bark stripped and dried for re-roofing a part of the house, the entire house had to be turned out, cleaned, aired, repaired. Spring was a time of frantic activity for everyone, everyone except Klara.

Because she was leaving, she was treated differently. It was almost as if her family was preparing for her leave taking by practicing life without her. No one asked her to help with the work or even with the normal household chores. She could join in if she chose, but no one made demands of her. Eventually she retreated to her own preparations.

She was alone in the house when, James came in for a drink of water and saw her fussing with the trunk again.

"Are you really going away, Klara?"

"You'll be going yourself in a few years."

He sat down on the floor and examined the wooden trunk closely. "I can paint better. There are only a few leaves on this side."

"It was done a long time ago. You can paint that side if you like."

"Yes. Then you won't forget me."

"Do it soon, so it will dry. I'll think of home whenever I look at it."

When James went back to work, Klara put on her coat and shawl and walked over to the Lof place. She found Mrs. Lof supervising the planting of her garden.

"Good afternoon, Mrs. Lof. May I have a minute, please?" Klara bobbed a slight curtsy to the old woman, then stood staring at the ground.

"What is it, girl? Don't stand there gawking. Speak up."

"I want some chickens, hens or pullets, if you please." Klara fumbled the dollar bill from her bag and held it out to Mrs. Lof. "Mamma has a craving for fresh eggs."

"Ye, gad. You can buy the coop full with that." She took the bill and examined it closely, smoothed it, smelled it. "Why do you need hens? Yours should be laying by now."

"We had to eat them."

There was no answer to that, so Mrs. Lof called one of the hired girls over. "Get one of the covered baskets and bring it along."

"Yes, Mum."

"Quick. Quick."

With Klara in tow she hustled down the path to the chicken pen. At the side of the chicken coop, an enclosure made of saplings woven together to form an almost solid fence, she stopped.

"Now what is it you need, child?"

"A couple of the red pullets. They have started laying, haven't they?"

"You probably ought to have some of the old hens, too. They'll be getting broody by summer, raise a batch of chicks for your mamma."

When the hired girl brought the basket, Mrs. Lof directed her to catch six of the young hens, the pullets. With dust and feathers flying the hired girl caught the birds and handed them to Klara, one at a time. Klara grasped each hen by its scaly feet and held it, head down, until the creature went quiet, then she could thrust it into the covered basket.

Mrs. Lof watched until the smaller chickens were loaded, then she sent the hired girl back to the garden work. To Klara she said, "The big hens won't fit. I'll send them over later this evening."

"Thank you." Klara picked up the basket. "They're heavy."

When the Lof's hired man brought the rest of the chickens that evening, Klara stood watching with her mouth open. He dumped five big hens, a rooster, and another four pullets into the chicken run. It was more chickens than the Larssons had ever owned before. Klara surreptitiously tied the cloth belt with the remaining money a little tighter.

A few days later Klara saw that James had painted the side panel of her Amerika box. He had painted a family in front of a house, her house, her family. In back stood Mamma and Pappa looking thin and gray. In front and at one side, he had depicted himself with a paint brush in hand alongside his brothers, Will and Ivar. Stina and Naomi stood on the other side holding big bunches of flowers. When she asked James why everyone was dressed in black, he told her it was because it was a funeral. Her funeral and her funeral flowers.

~~~

As leaving time came nearer, Klara startled herself with odd fits of crying over a bit of spoiled knitting, a dropped egg, a broken flower in the border by the door. Even the hasty scolding she gave James for slacking off on his morning chores, set her to remorseful weeping. She worried about what could possibly be wrong with her, but could barely begin the thought before something else caught her attention. The smallest of tasks seemed to take all of her will power to complete. Things she would normally do without a thought became great efforts. Her mother shrugged it off. School girl jitters, she called it and smiled a little.

~~~

Suddenly there was abundance. The hens were laying, the nanny goat produced twins, the cow had birthed a tiny black heifer calf and was now producing ample milk for her offspring and the family. Wild mushrooms carpeted the forest, the boys brought rabbits from the snares and fish from the river almost daily, and the first sweet morsels from the garden, slender green onions, tiny radishes, leaf lettuce, seemed fit for a king's table. The hills were shrouded with a cloak of tender green and wild flowers of yellow, lavender, and white painted the roadsides with their bloom.

Klara wondered how she could be leaving, when life here seemed so sweet, so dear, then Emil would ride up on his little dun Gotland and America would once again loom bright enough to pale the springtime, the homestead, the family.

All the dithering in the world could not hold back time and the day of Klara's departure loomed ever closer. Her box, packed and tied shut, sat by the door to remind her of the journey to come. She had been to the church at Smedjebacken for her examination of leaving. The church still controlled the coming in and the going out of the residents of the parish.

After questions about her baptism, confirmation, and education, she was examined for proof of small pox vaccination and for head lice. It was well known that passengers found with head lice would have their hair shaved off for immediate treatment and those without a visible vaccination scar would be sent to the ship's doctor. After the papers were filled out, she proudly added her signature to that of the official. Her lessons with Emil were bearing fruit.

Klara had thought she would feel reassured, calmer, after she had finished the ordeal of examination, but she was wrong. The questions raised more fears, more anxiety. Head lice. The very thought of having her long hair cut off, the thought of being made a public spectacle, made her shiver. What if she got lice at the inn at Kristiania? She had heard all sorts of things about people who stayed at public places. For days she suffered the agony of imagining creatures walking on her scalp. It was a fear that would return over and over until she finally reached her destination.

The evening before Klara was to leave, a few friends and neighbors dropped over to drink to her health and wish her well. Emil and his brother, Mr. Lof, his twin daughters, his hired hands, some of Ivar's friends sat around talking about the weather, the crops, the chance of a job at the mine, and the lure of America.

Nearly everyone in the parish had someone who had emigrated to the states. Some brought messages for her to pass on to those relatives. Because their absent kinsmen were so remiss in answering, they assumed their letters got lost along the way. A few toasts, a little quiet joking, good-byes, and promises to keep in touch, then they drifted away home, weary from a long day.

The next morning Klara was up before the rest of the family so she could have a little privacy for a bath in the old zinc tub. She had brought in water the night before, but decided not to take the time to warm it on the stove. With a shudder she stepped into the cold water and lathered herself with the harsh soap. After a quick rinse, she ducked her head under the water and washed her hair.

She dried off with piece of linen sacking, put on her good drawers, chemise, and long, knit stockings held up by garters. Before she put on her black skirt and long-sleeved white blouse, she gave her hair another toweling. As she rubbed her wet hair, she stood at the window to watch the pale pink morning creep across the countryside.

An eagle owl hooted in consort with a pair of willow-tits and a nearby tree-sparrow. With tentative strokes of her old tortoise shell comb, Klara untangled her damp hair. Listening to the birds, she thought about the green woodpecker she had stopped to watch the day before. The heavy-billed bird was sitting on the cone of a large ant-hill searching out choice morsels. The sun gleamed his feathers to a bronze glow that took her breath away. Would she ever see such beauty, experience this passionate joy ever again. She tried to imprint the scene on her mind.

Her hair free of tangles, she tied it back and finished dressing. Stina would braid it for her later. She tossed the bath water on the flower bed and put the tub away. By the time she got back to the house, the rest of the family was up and ready for breakfast.

"Sit down and eat a little, Klara." Stina had just settled Will and Naomi at the table with their plates heaped with fried eggs, milk pudding, horn bread, and cloudberry jam. "No telling when you'll get to eat again."

"I can't."

Anna brought a small parcel to the table.

"This will tide you over until you get to the inn."

"What is it, Mamma?" Klara examined the paper wrapped bundle tied with a bit of yarn.

"Hard boiled eggs, dried meat, some yeast bread."

"Where on earth did you get light bread, Mamma?" said Stina.

"Mrs. Hansson sent it."

"Thank you, Mamma."

Klara put her arms around her mother and held her close. How thin she is. And yielding, as if she had strength to move her limbs, hold up her head, but little else.

"You should eat it, yourself. How are you feeling today?"

Stina took her mother's arm and led her to the table. "I made some custard especially for you."

Klara poured the dandelion coffee into the mugs. The bitter brew was made from roots, roasted dry, then pulverized and boiled. She regretted not using another of her precious dollar bills to buy some coffee, sugar, a little flour, tea. How could she have been so selfish. In an attempt to make things right, she pulled Stina aside. She fumbled at the secret store of money at her waist and fished out another of the worn bills.

"Stina, take this. Next time you're in town get some things for Mamma. Some good coffee, sugar lumps, whatever you can think of she might like." Started now, the words poured out. "And claim some of the setting hens for yourself. Raise the chicks. Sell them at the fair. You can get yourself a new apron, a cap and ribbons, too. Please, Stina."

"I wish you didn't have to leave." Stina stood staring at her sister for a moment, then turned back to the table to serve up a plate of eggs to her father.

Klara decided she had to get out of the house for awhile, at least until breakfast was over. She wandered around the yard, seeing things with new eyes now that she was about to leave it all behind. The rude buildings, the garden, the animals spoke little to her, but the forest with its budding trees drew her.

Before long she was walking through the white fragrance of wild plum and cherry trees. The green of the stately old fir trees looked black against this pale beauty. Klara paused when she reached the largest of the trees, the fir where she had buried the stillborn baby in the fall. She sat down on the mossy ground and stared at the pile of granite rock.

"I've come to say goodbye little ones. I dare not think this when I'm with my family, but I fear I will never see this place again."

The dead babes answered, "Go, Klara, or your regret will sound like the keening of a bewildered crane on the autumn wind."

"I'm afraid, little ones."

"Rightly so, dear Klara," came the answer in untuned unison.

"I'm afraid."

"Listen to the peaceful beat of wave upon the shore. Hear this: our spirit sometimes hurries to a land we never see, where we lose the things that we have loved the best. Still, it is a wild and lasting yearning to see the land across the sea. You share this yearning."

Her voice, a cry on the morning breeze, repeated, "I am afraid."

"Go, Klara. Somewhere beyond the waters, you have a home."

A noise jarred her from her reverie. She twisted around and looked up to see Ivar walking towards her.

Ivar bent down to her. "Ground's cold. You'll catch a chill." He offered her a hand up and the two of them paused to remember the last time they had stood there together.

"You heard?"

"You'll be just fine, Klara."

NEW WAYS.

When Klara and Ivar returned to the house, a wagon loaded with trunks and boxes stood in the yard. A group of people clustered around, while several children skipped and ran about shouting, laughing.

"They're here," said Ivar.

"Already?" Klara could hardly speak.

She could see her father was rearranging the trunks in the wagon to make room for her small box. The Erssons certainly had a lot of baggage. She noticed Emil had ridden over with them. His horse was tied to the side of the wagon.

Emil walked over to intercept Klara. "I came to drive the wagon back," he said. "Let me introduce you to the rest of the Ersson family."

"In a minute. Please."

She had spoken only to the father, Mr. Ersson, but Klara felt too overwhelmed to face these strangers right now. She hurried into the house to get her satchel. She stuffed the food her mother had wrapped into it and looked around to see if she had forgotten anything. Oh yes, her tortoise shell comb and her Swedish-American word book. She found a space in her bag for them, straightened her skirt and hair, then closed her eyes and tried to gather her wits about her.

Emil burst in the doorway, intruding on her silence.

"Do you have your rail pass handy? You'll need it today."

"I think so."

"Not good enough."

He took her satchel and laid its contents out on the table.

"Comb, dictionary, unmentionables, stockings, mug, utensils, plate, water jar, pencil, examination certificate, and, yes, tickets."

He separated the train pass from the others, replaced things in her bag in the order he thought she might need them.

"Is this your dinner?" He held out the paper parcel.

"Yes." She watched him put the parcel into her bag.

"I was going to get you a going away present, but then I thought this might be more useful." He took her hand and filled it with silver *ore*. "It's not much, but I thought it might be a bit easier if you had some Swedish money. If you don't use it all, you can trade it for American money when you get there."

She put the coins into her waist purse, then reached out to Emil. They stood facing each other for a minute, then wrapped their arms around each other in a quick, self conscious hug.

"Thank you, Emil. Thank you for everything."

"I'll see you next spring, but you must let me know where you are."

"I gave you Sofia's address."

"You'll have to get someone to help you with a letter, in case you move."

"I will. I promise."

"One more thing before we go. I brought you this for luck."

He held up a long chain with a holed coin attached. He put it over her head, then took the coin between his thumb and forefinger.

"It's an English florin with Queen Victoria's portrait. My granny gave it to me for luck when I was confirmed. I figure you need it worse than me."

He slipped the coin down the neck of her blouse, then picked up her bag and gestured her past him to the door.

In the yard Klara hugged her siblings, then her mother. She waited to say her goodbye to her father last.

"I'll miss you, Pappa. Take care of Mamma."

Her tears prevented more words, so she gathered her skirt and climbed into the wagon box with the children she was to shepherd to the new world. Mrs. Ersson, her baby in her arms, sat with her husband on the narrow seat in front. Mr. Ersson whipped up the horses and they were off to the train station in Smedjebacken with Emil riding on ahead.

As they rattled along the dirt road, Mrs. Ersson turned to speak to Klara.

"I'm Maja and this is Katie. She's eight months old."

The young mother smiled broadly enough to reveal a gap in her front teeth when she mentioned little Katie. The chubby baby wore a long dress with rows of embroidery at the neck and hem. An odd choice for traveling, thought Klara.

"Very pretty," said Klara. "What about the other children?"

"Petter is the oldest. He's seven, almost eight. Matt is six and Lisa is nearly four."

The bouncing and shaking of the heavily laden wagon made conversation difficult, so Klara settled back to observe this family she was to be a part of for the next few weeks. Mr. Ersson, the perpetual worrier, always checking, always early, was tall and thin with quick hands and a permanent frown. She wondered if he was strong enough to handle the mountain of trunks and boxes crammed into the wagon bed with her and the three children. Her own box looked small and insignificant next to these leather trunks and iron shod boxes.

Mrs. Ersson, who asked to be called by her first name, was a small, round woman with soft hands and heavy blond hair which she wore in a thick braid down her back. She spoke little, smiled less, and seemed oblivious to the jouncing wagon. She fooled with her baby's wispy forelock, straightened her own dress or the baby's, and finally settled down to swaying rhythmically from side to side.

Emil had warned Klara to avoid asking the Erssons about their reason for leaving Sweden. She had thought little about it at the time, but now she sat speculating about the question. Surely these people weren't criminals running from some heinous act, nor did they appear so poor they were forced to seek a better life in America. In fact, they seemed fairly well off, at least to Klara's eyes. The children had new clothes, shoes even. The team and harness were in good condition and Mr. Ersson wore a store bought suit. Perhaps they had run up impossible debts or maybe Mr. Ersson was fleeing the draft. She knew that later idea could not be true. The military did not conscript family men. Boys like Ivar and Emil were the people they called.

The jolting wagon gradually over-powered her thoughts. She felt slightly sick. It's a good thing I didn't eat breakfast, she thought. The little boy, Matt, drew her attention. He takes after his mother, she thought. Soft and round, and right now he looks pinch-faced and a little green. Klara tapped Maja on the shoulder.

"Please. I think Matt is about to be sick. Can we stop a minute?"

"Hold him over the side," snapped Mr. Ersson. "He knows better than to be sick, now."

"Best do as he says."

Maja turned back to face front, leaving Klara to cope with the child. She crawled over to the boy and helped him to the sideboard of the rocking wagon. She held him up while he vomited, then cleaned him up with the handkerchief he dug out of his pocket. By the time the station at Smedjebacken was in sight they had repeated that scenario four times. How was this child going to survive the sea sickness everyone talked about? The other children, both blue-eyed and very blond, seemed unaffected by the rocking wagon.

At the station Klara helped the children from the wagon and led them to an out of the way place by the building. She watched as Emil dismounted and began hoisting the baggage from the wagon to the platform. After he had helped his wife and baby find a bench to sit on, Mr. Ersson went to help unload.

When the wagon was empty, Emil tied his horse to the back and climbed into the driver's seat. He clucked to the team, tipped his hat to the Erssons, and blew Klara a kiss. He wheeled the team around and was gone.

Emil's little horse trotting off behind the wagon seemed like the saddest thing she'd ever seen. Klara felt sorry for herself. Though the bored children were clamoring for attention, she felt light headed and alone. Her stomach hurt and her mouth was dry. How could she possibly make the train trip to Kristiania, much less cross the ocean.

Mr. Ersson, whose given name was Harald, disappeared into the station to buy tickets for his family. Maja, Klara, and the children tried to make themselves comfortable on the platform. The waiting room was for first class passengers only.

"When does the train come?" said Klara. She knew, but had trouble thinking of anything to say to Maja.

"Noon, I think. We have a bit of a wait."

"Mamma, Mamma, Matt hit Lisa." Petter, the older boy, was tugging at Maja's skirt. He was thin and gawky with pale hair and lashes that did little to give his long face character or definition. "He's bad."

Klara pulled herself from her bog of self pity. She wished she had something to offer these children. They've probably been up since before dawn, she thought. Tired and unhappy, they'll be picking at each other until they drop from exhaustion.

"Do they have any games, Maja?"

"No. Harald doesn't allow it."

How strange, thought Klara. "What do they normally do, then?"

"He had the boys learning leather work, when they weren't hoeing the garden or helping in the fields. Scraping, curing, tanning. Figured to have Petter learning to cut and stitch by year's end."

"They can't work all the time."

Klara thought about James and his paints, Will and Ivar with their sled, the jackstraws, the stilts and stick horses, Naomi and her doll. These children with their nice clothes and shoes were far poorer than her own family.

"They memorize scripture when they finish their quota of work each day."

"Quota? For such young children?"

"It was paid labor. For Harald's father. We needed every copper we could lay a hand on."

"But you seem to have everything you need."

"Oh, it's not for us, it's for the work."

"Work?"

"Didn't Emil tell you? We go to America to establish a new church."

"Church? Surely they have plenty of churches in America."

"It is for the Believer's Community at Albion, Minnesota. They sent us passage money, but Harald felt we should have cash to add to the communal goods."

None of this made any sense to Klara. No one had told her Mr. Ersson was a pastor. He certainly didn't look or act like any reverend she had ever seen. And wasn't money plentiful in America? Her head was beginning to ache and the children were tearing around in a frenzy. Mr. Ersson finally came out of the station, tickets in hand, and smirking a little.

He ignored the restless children and showed the tickets to his wife. "Saved fifteen *ore*. Just remember to say that Petter is under six."

"But he's not," said Maja.

"I'll tell him in case the conductor asks."

As the hour of waiting continued, Klara noticed people filling various containers with water from a pump near the station. She finally asked Maja about it and was told it was necessary to take water along on the train. The water on the trains was not safe for drinking, she said.

When Klara asked Maja about their water for the trip, she learned the Erssons had filled theirs at home. Klara jumped up and went to stand in line at the pump.

~~~

At precisely five minutes to twelve, the train pulled into the station with a flourish of steam and flying cinders. The knot of waiting passengers erupted into motion, scrambling for places at the doors of their respective first and second class cars. The porters churned along the platform to the baggage car with their loads of checked trunks and boxes.

With her satchel clutched to her chest Klara stumbled up the high metal step into the train, then followed the Erssons down the aisle to their seats. When the train sounded its ear-splitting whistle three minutes later, she was seated with Lisa at her side and the two boys facing her. Mr. and Mrs. Ersson had the two outside seats facing each other.

The trip soon settled into a restless monotony. They ate portions of their paper wrapped food soon after they got on the train and again before they were to change trains the first time. Klara was surprised when Mr. Ersson insisted they hold hands while he prayed over the food.

His words droned in her head, "Father God." She had never heard anyone address God in such familiar terms. "Father God, We thank Thee for this sustenance. Continue to work Your perfecting of our earthly souls and bodies with this food. Reveal Yourself to Your humble servants...."

Klara's eyes snapped open and she found herself staring into Mr. Ersson's light blue eyes. He had been watching her while he prayed. She gasped and shut her eyes. He continued with his prayer, "...that we might be Your prophets, priests in our own right in both name and deed."

What was he saying? Blasphemy, blasphemy, screamed through her mind. She put her hand over her mouth, fearful she had spoken aloud.

At the first change of trains everyone rushed to refill their water jars and cans before the next train hurtled into the station. When night came, Klara tried to make the weary children comfortable. Lisa stretched out across her lap and the boys curled like puppies in their seat. Klara thought she would be unable to sleep sitting in that cramped position. But when she awoke hours later, her neck stiff, her arms leaden from holding Lisa, she realized her body was more adaptive, resilient than she could have imagined. She looked over the head of the sleeping Lisa to see the country side speeding by the train window. The rocky woods had changed to broad fields with thin green lines of newly sprouted crops showing.

With her forehead against the cool glass she watched the farms stream by. As it grew lighter, she spied movement in the distant hedge row. When the train got closer she saw that it was a huge moose with a gawky calf at her side. The pair lifted their heads simultaneously, then floated out of sight with their long-legged, high stepping gait. The majestic animals, the rich black soil with its fuzz of green, and the soft mist of the new morning made Klara's heart sing.

The child on her lap whimpered. Klara stroked the little girl's hair back from her sweaty forehead and tried to make her more comfortable. The train was now running alongside a large lake with little clusters of houses and barns visible on the far shore. The conductor came through to announce a stop at Karlstad, a stop long enough for the passengers to stretch their legs, fill water jugs, buy food.

Klara reluctantly woke the sleeping children. When the train stopped, everyone filed out. After she got the children cleaned up at the hand pump, she washed her face in the icy cold water and tidied her hair as best she could. While the Erssons ate a hurried breakfast bought from a vendor, Klara washed down the last of her bread from home with a draught of cold water.

With another long ride ahead she knew she must part with some of her precious coins to buy something for the rest of the journey. She passed up the ham sandwiches garnished with pickled cabbage, the thin sliced smoked salmon arranged on buttered white bread, the tightly wrapped beef and onion rolls called *runde pulsa*, and settled for two thick slices of black bread with a slab of farmer's cheese between them. When she dropped the coins into the cupped palm of the bent old sandwich seller, she felt pain, actual physical pain at parting with the money.

Underway again, Klara saw the land was changing. As she watched, the plowed farmland gave way to rugged outcroppings of gray rock. The train slowed on the grade that would carry them over the mountains into Norway. On the down grade a stream appeared near the tracks, a rushing spume that eventually became a broad, placid river with groves of birch and willow reflected in its quiet surface.

Mr. Ersson interrupted her thoughts, "That's the River Glomma, the longest river in Norway. We'll travel beside it for many miles, almost all the way to Kristiania."

They finally arrived in the harbor town and climbed down from the train, stiff and tired. Though the station was only a few blocks from dockside, it was too far to carry a heavy box or trunk. For the first time on her trip Klara felt grateful to be traveling with the Erssons. Harald

Ersson found a porter with a handcart to unload their baggage and wheel it to the emigrant hotel near the place where the *Charlotta* would dock.

He went off with the porter, while Maja and Klara followed with the children. Even with Lisa and Matt pulling at either hand, Klara kept craning her neck to see the tall buildings on either side of the street. Horses and carts of every imaginable kind clattered up and down the cobbled Skiippergata, past the custom house, past the mercantile, on down the quay to Akershus Castle rising above the fjord.

By the time they reached the hotel, Klara was so dazed with the noise and the hustling people, the smells of roasting meat, rotting fish, and coal fumes, she hardly noticed the small, fourth floor room she was to share with the Ersson family. She would have a pallet on the floor with Lisa, while the boys had a second pallet close by. Maja and Harald, along with baby Katie, had the broken-backed bed. They were shown the communal washroom at the end of the hall and the privies in the courtyard at the back of the building. The breakfast room on the second floor was, by contrast, a spacious place flooded with light from floor to ceiling windows over-looking the water.

Though supper was included with the room, they had arrived too late for the meal the first day. The Erssons went off to visit an acquaintance and left Klara on her own for the evening. She decided she had to part with a little more of her money. She saw no street vendors or food shops in the neighborhood of the hotel, so she was forced to go into one of the many small eateries along the street.

The waiter brought her the day's special without bothering to try communicating with her. When the food was placed before her, she was, at first, confused that so much would be provided for one person. When the waiter's gestures convinced her it was all for her, she relaxed and began one of the more memorable feasts in her young life. The salt-cured mutton chops lay pink and pungent on a bed of peeled birch twigs with a mound of boiled rutabagas. A smaller dish held a slice of rust-colored goat cheese so strong she smelled it before the waiter crossed the room with it. Paper-thin flat bread was provided as a base for the cheese and a large glass of beer to wash it all down. Klara found the chops crisp, salty, the rutabagas buttery and slightly sweet. Never had food tasted so good.

Her meal finished and her purse a little lighter, Klara wandered down along the waterfront to watch the fishing boats before returning to the hotel. When she found the hotel almost deserted, she asked the woman behind the desk if it was possible to bathe and wash her hair. For one copper she was given hot water and a towel. In the washroom she hooked the door and hurried through her ablutions with a constant fear someone would come banging on the door. No knock, no footsteps in the hall interrupted her, though, and she dressed with a feeling of relief. It seemed a shame to waste the water, so she washed her drawers, stockings, and camisole, and hung them on a line in the courtyard. When the Erssons came back, she was sound asleep on her pallet.

Breakfast next morning was an array of food spread on a side table. Pickled herring, rye bread, black bread, cheese, butter and jam, fresh strawberries, boiled eggs, buttermilk, oat porridge, coffee, tea, and pitchers of milk, both sweet and sour, tempted even the children to overeat. Could kings and queens possibly eat better?

The only blot on the meal was Harald Ersson's demand that his family slip a few eggs, bread, and cheese from the communal table into their pockets when no one was looking. Klara assumed it was for their noon meal, but what was this man doing teaching his children to steal.

After breakfast she took the three older children to a grassy park near the hotel. Harald and Maja, with the baby, went to check on the expected arrival date of the *Charlotta*. She reluctantly shared the eggs and bread Matt and Lisa offered her at midday, then led the children back to the hotel for a nap before supper. Much to her surprise, Harald and Maja were still out.

"Did your folks say where they were going after they talked to the steamship people?" she said to Petter.

Matt answered instead, "Probably having a street meeting."

"I usually go with them. To take the offering," said Petter.

"Offering?"

This was a new idea to Klara. The church at home simply assessed each family a yearly tithe which was collected whenever possible. Poor families knew the system, but were not asked for a share.

"Sometimes we sing. Pappa says folks have looser pockets then." Matt was curled up on his blanket, almost asleep.

Petter flopped down beside him and was soon sound asleep.

Supper at the hotel was far more simple than breakfast. A plate was set for each guest with two slices of bread, jam and soft cheese. A serving girl came around with milk and tea, but no second helpings.

Harald pushed his chair back and addressed Klara, "We're going to meeting tonight. You're welcome to come."

"I'll stay here with the children," said Klara. She noticed Matt and Lisa brightened up considerably at her words and Petter actually smiled.

Their hopes crumbled when their father answered, "They'll come with us. We believe the family should worship together."

"They're awfully young for sermons."

"Never too young to hear the Word."

"Are you sure you won't come with us?" said Maja.

Jesus is sleeping, a great storm comes up, and waves roll over the ship.

God Hath Given His Children Travail.

The next two days followed the same pattern. Up early for breakfast, the day spent with the children sharing their stolen eggs and bread for dinner in the park, supper at the hotel, and the evening free when the Erssons went off to their meeting. Then the news came that the *Charlotta* was in port.

Klara and Maja spent the day washing clothes and bathing the children. Harald arranged to have the baggage transferred to the ship, then made sure the tickets were correct and in order. When he went to settle the hotel bill, he argued with the innkeeper, insisting the younger children ate next to nothing. In the end he paid the full tariff.

That evening Harald and Maja were much more insistent on Klara's attendance at their meeting. "It will be your last chance before we sail."

"Please come, Klara." Maja's voice had a pleading quaver to it. "The singing is very fine. All the old favorites."

"We need to do everything possible to gain God's favor for our journey."

Klara thought Harald seemed less forbidding tonight, more human. Was he afraid of sailing, afraid of the sea sickness they had been warned about, afraid of his future in America?

"Come and make your soul right with God."

"God will grant us safe passage if I come to church?"

Klara was having trouble keeping a sober face. She thought of the story of Jonah and wondered if Harald would want to heave her overboard if the ship floundered in a storm. In the end she gave in and went along. What could it hurt, she thought, and, besides, the children had told her there would be cookies and milk after the service.

~~~

The church wasn't a church at all. It was a narrow building near the docks that had once been a fish market. The stained plank floor still wafted the evidence to the noses of the worshipers as the temperature in the building rose. A row of smoking oil lamps added to the thick atmosphere and gave out a dingy orange light. Heat, fish smell, glaring lights faded into the background when the audience began to pray and sing.

No staid Lutheran congregation here. Klara saw first a heaving mass of bodies swaying from side-to-side, lifted hands, flying hair and scarves, stomping feet. She heard voices raised in rousing chorus, ringing shouts of "Alleluia" and "Praise God." As the music swelled, a young woman unpinned her long hair and began a gyrating dance up and down the aisle.

As her hair whipped about more and more violently, a high keening wail came from her lips. Except for shouts of "Amen, sister," and "Hallelujah," no one paid much attention to the agitated woman. Apparently her performance wasn't considered out of place or odd, except to Klara, who couldn't keep from staring at her. The mad dancer alternately bent forward with her hair sweeping the floor, then backwards until it seemed her spine would crack and she was staring at the ceiling. Klara realized that this was one of the dissenter churches, churches opposed to the control the state churches held over the lives of the people.

Groups like this had formed to urge congregants to involve themselves in politics, to beat the drum for temperance, to strike for the right to vote, and most radical of all, to further their belief that God still revealed Himself to his people through visions, voices, and prophets. Though she had heard about such people, she had never experienced them first hand.

She felt like running out the door. What was she doing among these outcasts, these lunatics. Only little Lisa tugging at her skirt, wanting to sit on her lap, kept her from leaving. She sat stone still, hardly hearing the sermon in her attempt to remain aloof from this heresy. The text was from the second chapter of the Book of Acts, obscure verses that exhorted believers to have "all things in common," sell "their possessions and goods" to share with "all men, as every man had need." No wonder the Erssons didn't feel that filling their pockets with breakfast eggs and bread was stealing. They were simply taking their share.

Klara was relieved when the last exhortation and the benediction rolled over the audience. Her relief was short lived, however, because a blur of men and women crowded around her with greetings, handshakes, and a few overly familiar hugs with kisses on both cheeks or forehead. Their words sounded stiff, learned from many repetitions.

"So glad to have you, Sister Larsson."

"Evenin, Sister. Good to see you amongst the blessed."

"Wonderful sermon tonight, wasn't it?"

Again one of the children rescued her. Matt wanted her to walk with him to the privy. "Please, Klara. It's dark out."

She took his hand and inched through the crowd at the back door of the building. She tried to clear her head while she stood in the dark waiting for Matt. Even the rank smell of the privies failed to quell the feeling of freedom that settled over her. Alone, just myself, me, no hot sweating bodies spouting platitudes.

Klara spread her arms to let the cool night air seep into every pore. She could almost touch the full moon above the building. She thought to make a wish on the crystal star sparkling in tandem with the moon, but all she could think of was home. Did Stina and Ivar, Will and James and Naomi, her mamma and pappa look up and see this marvelous sight in the heavens. Probably not, she decided. They would be sound asleep in their beds after a grueling hard day in the fields. She tried to stir the flicker of guilt in her heart, but the perils and excitement of her own new life were too great.

~~~

The morning was chaos. The Erssons insisted on wearing their very best clothes for the boarding of the ship. Baby Katie was dressed in her long gown with its many rows of embroidery and ruffles, Lisa had a navy blue sailor suit and shiny patent leather shoes with bows, Matt and Petter wore knee pants and pullovers with sailor collars and whistles on a cords around their necks.

Klara, in her homemade black skirt and white blouse, felt terribly out of place next to Maja who wore a dark gray skirt fitted over the waist and hips, then flared in a graceful curve to the floor. Her waist or blouse was lighter gray with thin maroon stripes. It had a high buttoned collar and fitted sleeves with lace cuffs. The Italian leghorn hat waiting on the dresser frothed with the same lace. The children's straw sailor hats lay next to it. Harald was probably the most splendid of all in his tweed sack suit and paisley print vest.

After the great enrobing was complete, a maelstrom of packing ensued, night clothes, sheets, Bibles, hymn books, everyday clothes, the small gifts pressed on the travelers by the members of the local congregation, letters and parcels intended for relatives in America, food enough to tide the seven of them over until their first meal on the boat. It all had to be stowed away in the satchels, baskets, and bundles they would carry onto the ship. The mass of trunks and boxes would be stored in the hold, inaccessible until they disembarked in New York.

In the confusion of dressing and packing and trying to stay clean, Lisa managed to lose her shoes. She ran into the room in her stocking feet at the very minute the porter came to carry their trunks and boxes to the dock. Klara and Maja got down on their knees to peer under the bed and dresser, while the boys ran up and down the hall searching the corners, the washroom, the stairway. Harald stood at the window, holding baby Katie and yelling at his family to get moving, then demanding the porter to wait just a little longer with the baggage.

Petter came down the hall with Matt behind him. "Here they are. Her shoes were behind the door."

"Thank heavens. It's her good pair," said Maja. She stood up and patted her skirt and hair into place. "Now we can go." She put on her hat and took the shoes from Petter.

Harald handed Katie to his wife and said, "It's about time. Gather up the hand luggage."

Klara took a quick look in the mirror over the dresser, then picked up her satchel.

"Where's Lisa?" Maja held the errant shoes in one hand, baby Katie on her other arm. "Lisa, Lisa."

"If you spent less time doting on the baby, you'd keep track of things." Harald was making a final check of the room before herding the family out into the hall. "She's not in here, so let's move along."

Klara tried to reassure Maja. "She's probably in the hallway. Did you see Lisa when you came in, Petter?"

She couldn't make out his answer. The bundle in his arms muffled his words. She tried to keep calm as she walked to the stairway. Where had the child gotten to. She couldn't help but think of Moochie's disappearance and the trouble that followed.

They searched the hallway and washroom without success, then decided to head downstairs. Maybe someone there had seen her. Harald sent the porter down the backstairs with the baggage and everyone else headed to the main stair.

With only a small bundle containing his everyday clothes to slow him down, Matt ran ahead. As they started down the stairs, they could hear him calling from the second floor landing.

"It's Lisa. Come quick. Hurry." His voice flattened out to a high pitched wail. "Hurry, hurry."

Harald dropped his satchel and the food basket and went racing down the stairs. Maja handed Katie to Klara and followed her husband still clutching the patent leather shoes. When Klara got to the second floor landing with Katie and Petter, Maja and Harald were kneeling on the floor with Lisa between them. Matt was sitting on the bottom step hugging his bundle, crying.

"Lisa, Lisa. Say something, speak to me." Maja pulled the child to her lap and stroked her hair back. Her fingers came away with blood on them. "Help me, Harald."

"Here, here, Maja. It's just a bump on the head. Don't panic."

He lifted Lisa away from his wife and patted the child on the cheek. When she didn't respond, he slapped her lightly.

"Wake up, Lisa. Come on. Wake up."

Maja sobbed, "She's dead, Harald. She's dead."

"Hush up. Go get a wet rag. It's just a scratch."

Lisa lay limp across his arms. He shook her a little, her arms flopped, but she did whimper, a little whisper of noise.

Klara fumbled a wash rag from one of the bundles on the stair and, still holding baby Katie, hurried back up to the washroom to soak the cloth. She delivered it to Maja and stepped back out of the way. Lisa moved a little, opened her eyes, and moaned. Though her response brought out a chorus of "Praise the Lord's" from her parents, Klara wondered about the unfocused look in the little girl's eyes.

"Shouldn't we get a doctor?" said Klara.

"Could we, Harald?" said Maja.

"Now, now, Maja. Calm yourself."

She washed the blood from the gash on Lisa's head, then wiped her own hands. She sent Petter to wash out the rag.

"Please, Harald? There's so much blood."

"These things always look worse than they really are."

Maja took Lisa from her husband's arms. "How do you feel, Lisa? Does your head hurt, baby?"

"Hurts, Mamma." Lisa rubbed her eyes with her knuckles, then stuck her thumb in her mouth.

"Let's take her to a doctor. Please, Harald?"

"We don't dare take the time. We'll miss our sailing."

Maja protested. "What if she's badly hurt?"

"If we miss our sailing, we lose our passage money and we don't have enough for train fare home."

"She could die." Tears were running down Maja's round cheeks.

"Klara, get me a quilt, a small one," said Harald.

He took Lisa and put her on the quilt Klara spread out on the floor. He carefully straightened the child's legs and folded her arms across her chest, then he swaddled her tightly.

"There, now, she can rest until we get under way. If it will make you feel better, we'll have the ship's doctor look at her."

"Maybe the ship's doctor can see her right away. If we told the officials, they might let us on first."

Harald spoke firmly, "If anyone asks, say she's sleeping."

Klara interrupted, "Why? Does it matter about Lisa?"

Harald said, "They won't let anyone sick on board the ship. It is of utmost importance to give the impression of health and vigor."

He picked up the swaddled child and placed her over his shoulder. Lisa squirmed a little and whimpered, then fell still.

Harald turned to the boys. "You'll have to take my share of the baggage."

~ ~ ~

When they reached the dock, they were caught up in a large crowd of people headed for the *Charlotta*. The porter dumped their baggage with the other luggage waiting to be loaded into the hold of the ship. Klara stood in line with Maja and the boys. She still carried baby Katie, along with her satchel. Maja carried only the patent leather shoes and her handbag. Her plumed hat and fine gown gave her a cool, stylish air, but Klara saw her pluck at her lace cuffs, gnaw at her fingernails, saw her chest heave as if she was having trouble catching her breath.

Harald paid the porter, while the boxes and trunks were tagged with their names and ticket numbers. They wouldn't reappear until the ship docked in New York. With Lisa in his arms Harald joined them in the swelling line of people waiting to board. With her eyes on Lisa, Klara hardly noticed the huge ship waiting for them. From a distance the ocean steamer appeared small, toy-like, but now the upswept bow of the *Charlotta* towered high above their heads. Klara clutched Katie tightly until the baby protested by crying.

Maja seemed to wake up and reached for the baby. "Let me take her, Klara. I'm sorry."

Klara took the shoes and put them in her satchel, then took a closer look at Lisa. The little girl appeared to be sleeping; her eyes were closed and, though her skin was pale, her breathing was quiet and even. Maybe she is all right, thought Klara. Maybe our worries are for naught.

They were only a short way from the head of the line. She tried to see what was happening at the check point and soon deduced it was tickets and examination papers they wanted. She balanced her satchel on her hip and found hers, then helped Maja with hers. When it was their turn, they had their papers in order and were allowed through after one section of each ticket was torn off. They were told to keep them out for the next official, the man in the gold trimmed cap at the head of the gangplank.

Klara saw they would have to walk up a narrow gangway to the deck of the ship and for a moment felt panic. It seemed so steep, so narrow, and the handrail at one side was weak looking, just a few post with a cable strung between them. What if someone fell off. They would surely drown.

Then, a new crush of passengers came through the gate and pushed Klara and the Erssons up the gangplank and onto the deck before they could think about it any more. The officer tore the second coupon from their tickets and pointed them to the next station. Here four crew members assisted the first class passengers up the stairs to the right. Second class ticket holders were sent along an interior hall to find their cabins by themselves. Steerage passengers were ordered downstairs. Klara knew her own ticket was for steerage and assumed the Erssons would be traveling the same way. When she was abruptly separated from them, she realized they were sailing in the relative luxury of second class. She wondered why Harald, with his penchant for detail, hadn't thought to check the class of her ticket.

Harald reacted first. "Where are you going, Klara?" He took a few steps after her.

The crewman stopped him and explained the difference in the tickets. "She can't come with your party, sir. She hasn't paid for second class passage."

"We need her to help with the children." The children seemed much in need of a nanny at that moment because both Matt and baby Katie were bawling. Petter was racing back and forth, yelling and climbing onto coils of rope and canvas-covered machinery. Only Lisa was still.

"I can believe that, sir, but I can't allow it."

"Can I pay the difference in her fare?" Harald was trying to get his wallet from his pocket without disturbing Lisa. "It can't be all that much."

Klara looked across the deck at Maja. How small she seems, standing on the windy deck of this huge ship with her children. Katie was stiff and red-faced with her hiccupy crying. Matt was clinging to her skirt, his eyes squinched up, nose running, crying loud enough to draw attention.

Maja spoke to the crewman, "Please, please, let her stay with us."

"But I can't."

"We've booked two cabins," said Harald. "It's not like she would need more room."

The passengers in line behind the Erssons were getting impatient. They had been waiting for hours, questioned, examined, ordered about, and now this crewman was causing another bottle neck. One man stepped forward. "Let him pay the difference, man."

Another man spoke up. "Yes, what can it hurt."

The crewman finally accepted the money offered him by Harald. It was only the matter of a few dollars difference. Klara would travel second class instead of steerage. The crowd gave her a cheer and the assistant escorted her back to the family.

She gave Maja a quick hug and took Matt's hand. "Let's get Petter and go see our new room."

Matt stopped crying and wiped his nose on his sleeve. She could hear Maja give a sigh of relief as Petter appeared and they all proceeded down the passageway to find their cabins.

After a long walk through narrow passages, Harald stopped. "Here they are, numbers ten-sixteen and ten-eighteen."

He unhooked the first metal door and went inside, stooping a little to avoid banging his head on the door frame. Inside, he place Lisa on a lower bunk, then stepped back into the hall. The cabin had two bunks, upper and lower, on each side and a built-in storage cabinet with a wash basin on top between them at the far wall.

"This is the big cabin. The other one has two bunks. How do you want to divide up, Maja?"

Klara volunteered to share the bigger cabin with the children, but Maja objected, "I want Katie with me."

"Fine enough," said Harald. "You and me and Katie in the small cabin. Klara, Petter, Matt, and Lisa in the this one. Perfect."

"Can we get the doctor, now?" Maja was looking pale with dark smudges below her eyes, eyes red from crying. "Harald, you promised."

"Klara can take a good look at Lisa and get the boys settled, then we'll decide what to do." He steered Maja into her cabin. "You need to rest. Get Katie to sleep, anyway."

Klara watched Harald and Maja disappear into their cabin and shut the door. Another family coming through the passage needed to get by, so she told Matt and Petter to lug the bags and bundles inside. She followed them and dropped her satchel on the other lower bunk.

"You two get the top bunks. Climb on up and give me some room."

"Hurrah."

She passed their bundles up to them so she could have room to kneel beside Lisa's bunk.

She felt the little girl's forehead. She seemed cool, maybe too cool. Klara was unsure if that was good or bad. She knew about fevers because she had nursed her younger brothers and sisters through a number of feverish ailments. This seemed different. She loosened the blanket and rubbed Lisa's hands, parted her hair and checked the cut on her head. No more blood, but she certainly had a goose egg. It can't be good to be so cold.

"Wake up, Lisa." The child opened her eyes and Klara sat the child upright. "We're on the boat, now. Look at your new room."

When Lisa tugged the blanket away and tried to crawl out of the bunk, Klara told Petter to watch her and went to find her a drink of water. She met Harald in the passageway.

"How is she?" he asked.

"I woke her, but she seems awfully cold and dazed."

"I didn't want to scare Maja any more than she already was, but Lisa must have fallen down at least one, possibly two flights, of stairs."

"And landed on her head, probably. I don't see any other marks on her."

"I think there are some other believers on board. I'm going to find them and organize prayer for Lisa."

"What about the doctor?"

"I doubt there's anything he can do. I'll be back as soon as I can."

"What about Maja?" Klara was loathe to let this man, this father, go off and leave her with the ailing child. "Lisa needs her mother."

"Maja's asleep. She got no rest at all last night." He turned abruptly and disappeared down the passageway.

Klara took a deep breath and pulled her shoulders back. She found the water taps at the end of the row of identical metal doors and filled her bottle. She stood a moment and looked around. Everything was metal, some sort of plate steel painted a monotonous yellow ochre, ceiling, walls, floor, doors, and fittings, all the same. She reached to touch the projection that served as a doorway. The surface felt slick, slightly greasy. There must be dozens of coats of paint on this ship, she thought. As she walked back to her cabin on the roughened metal floor, she noticed a pipe handrail ran the entire length of the passage. Even docked, the ship had a constant uneasy movement and she could feel the vibration of the huge engines throb through the floor to the soles of her feet.

While she helped Lisa with her cup of water, Matt and Petter kept asking if they could go exploring. She finally sent them next door to their mother. Even if she was sleeping, Klara felt Maja should decide what the children would be allowed to do on the ship. She also wanted Maja to have a look at Lisa.

The boys were soon back with their mother behind them. They squeezed into the narrow room and sat down on the bunk opposite Lisa. Maja was pale except for her red eyes and nose. Klara asked how she was feeling and had she had a nap. Maja answered she was feeling sick to her stomach and she had not slept. She had left baby Katie sleeping next door and hoped she would be all right.

"I'm sure she is," said Klara. "The boys want to go look around."

"I guess it would be all right." Maja took Petter by both hands and made him look her in the eye. "Hold Matt's hand and stay out of the way. Promise me." Petter gave his solemn word and left with Matt.

When Harald returned, Lisa was sleeping again. He brought several strangers to pray over her and though he asked Klara to join them, she declined and went to find the boys. She found them with a young crewman who was explaining the mechanism that lowered the life boats.

"Petter, Matt, are you bothering this man?"

He answered for the boys. "No madam, they're no bother."

"Oh. Thank you for taking care of the boys."

Klara was glad to hear someone speak Swedish after so many days of listening to Norwegian and the babble of odd tongues spoken by the crush of dock workers, refugees, and immigrants on the streets of Kristiania. Though she could make out simple commands and demands in Norwegian, this was the first of the ship personnel who spoke her native language.

"Do you know when we'll be leaving?"

"All the passengers are aboard, but we're still taking on cargo."

"Baggage?"

"No, that's all loaded. Come on. I'll show you." The young man hoisted Matt to his shoulder and took off toward the stern of the ship. At the rail he stopped and gestured to an open hatch in the deck below. "It's Swedish iron. We used to carry grain, but America raises so much now, it doesn't pay to ship it."

Matt piped up from his perch on the man's shoulder, "It looks heavy. Will the ship sink?"

"Don't worry. The ship needs weight in the bottom for balance. It's called ballast." He turned to Klara. "Did you bring food? The first shipboard meal will be breakfast tomorrow."

"Yes. Will we leave before dark?"

"I'll show you where you can eat. You'll have a good view of the harbor, too." He led them back along the deck rail to a lounge with tables, benches, and windows on three sides. "I have to get back to work, but if you have questions or need anything ask for Izzy."

"Izzy? What sort of name is that?"

Izzy put Matt down and laughed. "It's really Isaac, but everyone calls me Izzy."

~~~

Klara and the boys sat at the big window in the second class lounge. They watched the sun set on the water, while they shared a cold supper of bread, jam, and a tin of sardines. Two small snub-nosed boats were maneuvering around the *Charlotta's* bow. Crewmen on the her deck were lowering thick lines to those waiting below. One of the small tow boats caught her line immediately, but the other had to make several passes before they snagged the thick rope. The huge, tar-stained ropes were threaded through a slotted wooden guide set in the center deck of each of the smaller boats and the slack taken up with a hand winch.

Mesmerized with the activity below, it was some minutes before Klara realized the *Charlotta* was moving away from her mooring place. It seemed like the water and the horizon were gliding silently past the ship's rail. The skyline of the city slid into view and Klara gasped at the beauty of the port against the deep green of the hills beyond. The sun hanging just above the water sparkled pink and orange on the myriad of glass windows and made the land one with the sea. She watched, hardly daring to breathe, until Matt tugged on her sleeve.

"I'm sleepy."

With reluctance Klara gathered up the remains of their meal and led the boys back to their cabin. Outside the door she paused to listen. Were the strangers come to pray still inside? She heard nothing, so she cracked the door and peered in. The cabin was dark, so she ushered the boys inside. She left the door ajar so she could use the flickering hall light to get the boys ready for sleep. When she tried to settle them in opposite bunks, they begged to sleep together. Klara shifted the bundles to one bunk and admonished Petter to be careful with his sharp elbows.

Before she pulled the door closed, she knelt beside Lisa, to feel her forehead, listen to her shallow breathing, tuck the blanket a little closer. Deep hollows seemed to have formed under the child's eyes and her cheeks looked sunken. Maybe it was just the harsh light, thought Klara. Surely Lisa would be better in the morning. The floor seemed to shudder beneath her knees and the room rocked, gently at first, then strongly enough to pitch Klara forward against the edge of the bunk. Her face hurt and she realized her nose was bleeding. She struggled to her feet and found her handkerchief. Holding it tight against her nose, she tried to keep Matt and Petter from sliding from their bunk. They half fell, half climbed from their perch and Klara helped them into the lower bunk.

"I'll be back in a minute," she whispered.

Still holding the handkerchief to her nose, she made her way to the washroom at the end of the passage. The ship's jerky motion had been replaced with a steady rhythm and Klara decided she needed some fresh air to clear her head. On deck she joined a small crowd of passengers lined against the rail watching land slip away. A familiar voice interrupted her musing.

"Look hard. It'll be the last land you see for a good many days."

Izzy stood at her side. "Where are the boys?"

"Shouldn't you be working?"

"Want to see something?"

"What?"

"Follow me." He headed for the stairs to first class. When Klara hung back, he said, "Come on. It's all right."

She followed the young man with trepidation, past signs in many languages warning, "First class only," then past signs reading, "Keep out, crew only. On her hurried trip along the first class deck she caught glimpses into splendid salons with crystal chandeliers and gilt chairs with spindly legs and tiny padded arm rests. The passageway, itself, was carpeted with a thick diamond-patterned material of deep maroon. Had she the time she would have gaped at the mahogany doors, the polished brass handrails, knobs, lamp brackets, and fittings that garnished this part of the ship, but she was having trouble keeping Izzy's dark head and narrow shoulders in sight.

When Izzy finally burst through a small door, Klara almost knocked him down before she realized he had stopped. They were standing on a small observation deck facing the fast disappearing city lights. They were high above the second class deck, above the first class deck, even. The night air billowed Klara's skirt and stung her eyes, but she stood, fascinated by the widening strip of water between the shore and the ship. They really were under way. She forgot the chill air, her sore nose, the ache of loneliness that had surprised her after she had put the children to bed. To her left the sea ran to the horizon, to her right the mountains of Norway lay like a pencil-thin line of gray, a mere smudge on the edge of her world. The sun had dropped below the horizon, but the sky still glowed with the after light.

As the *Charlotta* was towed through the mouth of the harbor, other ships came into view, ships anchored on the open sea outside. When they got closer to the tethered ships, Klara realized the *Charlotta* was relatively small by comparison. She barely heard Izzy explaining the various types of ship, their weight and class, the cargo they carried, the routes they plied.

~ ~ ~

It was full dark when she slipped into her cabin. The children were asleep. She undressed quickly and climbed into the upper bunk. There, alone in the dark with the throb of the ship's engine vibrating through her body, Klara finally let herself think of home and sobbed herself to sleep.

A loud banging on the door woke her some hours later. She bumped her head on the ceiling, then remembered where she was. She climbed out of the bunk to open the door a crack. The words, "Hush or you'll wake the children," were out of her mouth before she realized it was Harald in the passageway.

"Maja's sick. Can you tend to her?"

Klara found her wrapper and went next door. Maja was bent over the wash basin vomiting, while baby Katie lay on the bunk, crying.

"See to the baby, Mr. Ersson. She's probably cold." Klara got Maja cleaned up and back in bed. "It's probably the sea sickness. I don't know what else to do."

"Take the baby." Harald handed her the child. "Maja will probably sleep now."

Klara returned to her bunk with Katie in her arms, but she was unable to get back to sleep. She lay in the darkness with the baby warm on her chest and thought about home, about her own baby sister, Naomi.

Those who were able, dressed and went to breakfast in the large dining room. It was easy to tell the neophyte sailors among the passengers because they gripped the handrails and walked spraddle-legged along the passageways. Klara took the boys and baby Katie to breakfast. She had been unable to rouse Lisa enough to get her dressed, but Harald said he would stay with her and Maja until she came back.

Matt and Petter ran ahead to the dining room. They looked in every open doorway, every nook and cranny. The rails around the edges of the table elicited a barrage of questions and comments. Petter hoped for a huge storm, so he could watch the dishes sliding to the edges of the tables to be caught in the nick of time. The smell of fresh brewed coffee quickly settled them on their bench in anticipation. Even the youngest children drank coffee and the Ersson boys were no exception.

Breakfast was bowls of steaming oat porridge with wells of butter melting in the center. Pitchers of milk and cream, bowls of soft brown sugar, and heaping plates of toasted bread were lined up the length of the table. A waiter brought hot tea and strong coffee. Klara fed Katie from her own bowl and looked around for Izzy. Just what was his job on the ship, anyway. The dry toast settled her stomach and she decided to take some back to Maja. With a warning to behave and not fall overboard she left the boys to explore on their own.

When she got back to the cabin, Harald and a stout man in a white coat stood outside the open door.

"What's wrong?" she said to Harald.

Harald barely glanced at her. "Take Katie to her mother, please."

She hurried in to Maja and tried to place Katie in her arms. When Maja pushed the baby away, Klara settled her on the end of the bunk.

"A little dry toast, Maja. How does that sound? It'll help your stomach." When Maja groaned and turned her head, Klara put the plate on the wash stand within reach. "There, now. You have it when you're ready." She backed out of the narrow cabin which already had the sour smell of a sick room.

Harald spoke to the man in the white coat. "This is Miss Larsson, the children's nanny. If you would give her instructions for Lisa's care, I would appreciate it." To Klara he said, " I'm going to breakfast. Listen carefully to the doctor."

The doctor pushed his glasses up on his forehead and cleared his throat. "The child seems to have experienced a convulsion." When Klara didn't react, he rephrased his pronouncement. "A fit, the little girl had a fit a few minutes ago."

Alarmed, Klara tried to push past the stout man into the cabin. He restrained her with a pudgy hand on her arm. "I must see Lisa," she said.

"No need. She's sleeping now. I'll be back to bleed her this afternoon."

Klara stared at the man. Didn't Harald explain what had happened to Lisa.

"Why?"

"If she wakes up, you can give her a little dry toast, some thin gruel, but no milk. Do you understand?" He didn't wait for her answer, but hurried off to his next case.

~~~

Over the next few days Klara found her time filled with an endless round of tending the injured Lisa, cleaning up seasick Maja, and comforting baby Katie who was suffering from an abrupt weaning from her mother's breast. Lisa seemed a little more alert, but visibly weaker. Whether this was from her injury, the bleeding procedure, or the wretched diet ordered by the doctor, it was impossible to know. Maja left her bunk only to stagger down the passage to the toilet and spent the rest of her time vomiting into the basin or turned to the wall in total misery.

BANANAS AND BREAD PUDDING

Klara did her best to keep the two invalids clean, but it was a losing battle. On the third day Harald moved out to stay with one of his new acquaintances, leaving the stinking cabin to his wife and children. To make her own work easier Klara moved Maja in with Lisa and gave the smaller cabin to Matt and Petter. She, herself, felt only minor queasiness now and then and the boys were not bothered by the rolling ship at all. Izzy, who helped her clean up the smaller cabin for the boys, said it was because they were active, running around the decks, chasing up and down the stairs. They had got their sea legs, he said, and urged Klara to get on deck as often as possible.

Her schedule was further complicated by Matt's fear of going to the toilet by himself. Since he had never seen a convenience other than a dark-holed privy, he was convinced great sea monsters lurked in the water of the ship's toilets. At times Klara wondered if the child might not be right, though she felt large fish more likely than monsters.

Even with so many onerous chores, Klara found much to gladden her heart. The food was plentiful and though the treat of fresh milk, fruit, and vegetables was replaced by more staple foods as the days passed, there was still wonderful surprises at each meal.

For a few days they were served bananas, something neither Klara, nor the boys had ever seen before. Matt let out a terrific howl when he bit into his. Izzy came to the rescue and showed them how to peel the yellow fruit. Still, many of the passengers did not like this new food and tossed theirs down to the steerage passengers. When the milk began to sour and fewer people eating because of the sea sickness left large quantities of leftover bread, a new dish appeared at both dinner and supper. This was bread pudding, a lush mix of stale bread, sour milk, eggs, sugar, raisins, and cinnamon, baked in the huge ovens below deck. Klara loved it at first bite and could hardly get enough of the sweet stuff. She promised herself she would learn the recipe and make it every day of her new life. A few days after they had bananas, the bread pudding took on a new flavor as the over-ripe fruit was added to the mixture.

Molasses sweetened Boston baked beans and macaroni with cheese were favored by Matt and Petter until the day they were served spaghetti and meatballs. For the rest of the trip they argued about who liked spaghetti best and raced to the dining room to see if it was on the menu again.

Izzy entertained Matt and Petter whenever he had the time and taught Klara a few new English phrases. She was confused at first because Izzy pronounced the words she thought she had learned in such a strange manner. It took a great deal of persuasion to convince her Izzy was right and Emil wrong. By the fifth day at sea Klara worried Izzy was spending so much time with her, he would get in trouble. He insisted he didn't care, said he was going to jump ship in New York. When he saw how uneasy Klara felt at his words, he explained he was only teasing her.

"I'm the ship's translator," he said. "Important work, but not very demanding."

She also felt uneasy about Lisa. The doctor had pronounced her fit after the third treatment and Harald acted as if nothing was amiss, but Klara saw the child was weak, barely able to walk. Klara was certain Lisa could speak quite normally for her age before the accident, but now seemed unable to say anything more than unconnected words. She sat staring at nothing for hours on end, her mouth slightly open. Klara brought a bowl of oatmeal or soup from the dining room and spoon-fed her. With baby Katie to look after it was too much to carry Lisa down to the dining room, too.

By the morning of the seventh day experienced passengers were looking forward to landfall. Many had packed up their belongings and had taken to standing at the rail searching for signs of land, floating debris, logs, twigs, leaves, birds, but they were disappointed. This was not to be the hoped for near record breaking crossing some of them anticipated.

As the day wore on black clouds gathered on the horizon and the wind made standing on the open deck uncomfortable. By supper the ship was rolling too hard for the cooks to prepare hot meals. Late in the evening the storm showed no sign of slacking off, so the crew passed out bread and sliced ham, apples and jugs of tea for the passengers to eat in their cabins or in the enclosed lounges. Only crew members were allowed on the open decks and access doors were locked, chains barred the way to areas without doors.

Klara sat Matt and Petter on their bunks and gave them a share of the meat and bread.

"When you finish, come next door. I'll slice your apples, then bed time."

They asserted they could manage their apples without her so she left to feed Lisa and Katie. With outward patience she sopped the bread in the cold tea and tried to make a game of getting it into their open mouths. The rolling ship caused several mishaps and Klara was damp and out of sorts by the time the girls were ready for their small bites of peeled apple. She wiped faces and hands with a damp rag, walked Lisa to the toilet and changed Katie, then declared them set for bed.

Hungry and tried she noticed Maja had not touched her food. She wondered if Maja was really as sick as she made out to be. How could anyone be seasick for so long. How could she survive on the few bites of bread Klara had seen her eat over the last five or six days.

"Eat something, Maja," she begged. "The children need you."

"How is Katie?"

"Fine. She's ready for bed."

"Let me hold her, please." She reached for little Katie and held her close. "Poor baby. Your mamma loves you."

Katie started to fuss, so Klara took her back and put her to bed with Lisa, head to foot in the narrow bunk. Finished with the children, Klara turned her attention to Maja, again.

"Let's get you cleaned up and maybe you'll feel better."

Klara treated her much like the children, washed her hands and face, brushed her hair, and straightened her night dress. With her hair fanned out on the pillow Maja seemed content, willing to let Klara tend to everything.

Klara convinced Maja to take a little tea and a few mouthfuls of bread. After she helped Maja down the passage to the toilet, Klara sat down to her own supper. Even in the cramped, smelly cabin, sitting on the hard bunk, she enjoyed the soft bread, fresh, slightly yeasty, with crunchy brown crusts. The cold butter and salty pink ham went perfectly with the bread. She ate ravenously, then stretched out on her bunk.

The storm made other evening activities impossible. The tossing of the ship had almost lulled her to sleep when Matt shook her.

"Klara, Klara, I can't find Petter."

Half asleep she tried to figure out what was wrong. "Is he in the top bunk?" She knew the two boys slept together in the narrow lower bunk, but maybe Petter tired of his little brother at times.

"He's gone."

She sat up and tried to clear her head. "Go back to bed."

In the wedge of light from the open door she could see Lisa stirring in the bunk below and across from her. She was sure to wake baby Katie asleep at the other end of the bed. Below her Maja was groaning. The ship seemed to be churning along in a furor, snapping back and forth in a series of harsh side slips. Even standing up would be difficult.

"Can I stay with you?" Matt was climbing into her bunk.

While he settled himself, Lisa stiffened, cried out some muffled plea. Klara slid out of her nest of blankets and bent to pick up Katie. Before she could huddle the baby in with Matt on the upper bunk, Lisa's body contorted and her eyes rolled back in her skull. Klara dumped baby Katie on top of the covers and demanded Matt see to her. An instant later she was yelling for him to go find his father, Izzy, the doctor, anybody.

Matt scrambled out the open door and disappeared down the corridor. Klara threw herself on the bed alongside Lisa to hold her safe, keep her from hammering her fists and feet and head against the steel walls, then she remembered Katie on the top bunk. She let go of Lisa to lift Katie down. She put the baby across Maja's stomach and grabbed Lisa again. The child convulsed so violently Klara feared she would snap her spine with the backward thrust of her head and shoulders. She beat her hands against the rough wall until her fingers bled. When the convulsion let go, Lisa relaxed and began to whimper, then sob. In the darkness nearby Katie was crying, too, louder and louder until she was screaming, almost drowning out a new sound, the sound of Maja gasping and retching.

"Maja, Maja, get hold of yourself. I need you."

"Help me, Klara." Maja seemed not to hear the screaming of her own baby. "Please."

While she lay trying to protect and comfort Lisa, Klara was almost overwhelmed by the sour stink of vomit. Maja hadn't managed to reach the jar she had been using to keep her noxious out pouring from offending her cabin-mates. The thought of trying to wash sheets, quilts, and night clothes in the small basin with cold water invaded Klara's thoughts for a moment before Lisa's thrashing and gasping reminded her of the real problem.

"Dear God, the child is turning blue." Klara spoke aloud to herself, trying to keep control of her own feelings. Loosen her collar, rub her wrists and chest. Where is Matt. He should be back. Oh no. The man in the next cabin is banging on the wall. Katie's screaming must have angered him. Maybe he'll call the purser. Or come over himself. Anybody would be a help.

Just when she thought the situation could get no worse, the ship caught a particularly big wave and lurched hard enough to slam baby Katie out of the bunk onto the floor. The flickering light from the passageway went out and they were left in darkness. Klara pulled the screaming Katie onto the bed with Lisa and tried to quiet her. Lisa coughed and struggled to get her breath. Near collapse, herself, Klara shook Lisa, turned her over and pounded her back, begged her to breathe. She was holding the limp child over her knees, when she heard voices in the passage.

Light flooded the cabin. Someone must have brought an oil lamp. Klara could see the color come back into Lisa's pale cheeks, see her chest heave with each gasping breath. She slid the child onto the bunk and picked up Katie, tried to quiet her. When she brushed Katie's damp hair back from her face, she felt wetness and then realized it was blood on her fingers. Before she could figure out that Katie just had a scrape on her forehead, Klara burst into tears.

Izzy found her standing between the bunks sobbing into Katie's baby-soft hair, muttering, "Poor baby, poor, poor baby."

Izzy took her by the shoulders. "Have you found Petter?"

Klara looked at the young man as if she had never seen him before. "Petter?"

"Yes, Petter. Matt came caterwauling into the day room screaming about Petter being lost."

Matt stuck his head in the doorway. "Phew. What a stink. I found him for you, Klara. Now we can look for Petter."

Klara handed Katie to Izzy, then collapsed on the bunk with Lisa. Izzy passed the child to her father, Harald, who was standing in the passageway with the stout doctor.

Izzy took Matt's hand. "Looks like we'll have to search for Petter by ourselves. Let's get out of here and make room for the doc." They lurched down the hall together.

Harald stepped back from the doorway to let the doctor pass.

"Hokay, Ladies. What seems to be the problem?"

He ignored Klara since he had seen her standing with Izzy the moment before. He gave the seasick Maja a cursory glance.

"A case of the vapors," he muttered to himself. He probably saw thousands of cases like hers and knew it to be a nuisance rather than a disease. He could sit in the sailor's day room playing gin rummy most of the trip if it weren't for seasick passengers.

Lisa's case was different. She had seemed to be on the way to recovery and now she was having convulsions. Even as he turned to speak to Mr. Ersson, Lisa stiffened and threw back her head, flailed her arms. The doctor took a handkerchief from his pocket, rolled it and placed it between Lisa's teeth. He held her until she was quiet again, then opened a vial of smelling salts to hold under her nose. He gave Klara a whiff, too.

When the sharp, turpentine odor of the smelling salts flicked up Klara's nostrils, she came to herself, coughed and sneezed until her eyes were spilling tears. She sat up and pulled her hanky from her sleeve.

"Oh, that smells bad. Like the tar we pack in the horses feet in winter."

"It works, so don't complain." The doctor put Lisa back on the bed. "I think the child is better." He stepped outside to speak to Harald.

Klara followed him. "Have they found Petter?"

"Not yet," said Harald. "I can't think where he could be."

"Well, I have a broken leg to attend in steerage."

The doctor hurried off. The ship seemed to toss less violently and the ship's boy had lit the gas lights along the passageway once more.

Baby Katie seemed content in her father's arms, so Klara asked if she might go look for Petter. "I can check his hideouts," she said. She was desperate to get out of the dank cabin with its reek of vomit.

"Go. I'll see to Maja and the girls," said Harald.

Klara had remembered Petter's fascination with the table tops and their protective railings. Maybe he had found a way into the closed dining room. On her way down the hall she met up with Izzy and Matt.

"Did you find him?"

"No, nothing. He's not in any of the lounges and the sailors insist he couldn't have gotten on deck."

"Thank God for that. Is there any way he could get into the dining room?"

"They locked the main doors at the first sign of high seas." Izzy frowned. "Maybe through the kitchen. Let's check."

As Izzy had said, they found the public doors of the dining room shut tight. They continued down the hall to a small door which opened once Izzy removed the bar that held it shut. In the narrow galley the light was dim. Klara bumped into drawers that had slid open and barely missed cracking her head on a cabinet door that suddenly swung out. The kitchen staff had not secured the place properly. She heard Izzy swearing up ahead. When she reached him, he was getting to his feet.

"Careful. Something slippery on the floor here."

"We could use a light," said Klara. She stepped around the puddle that had tripped up Izzy.

"Should be better in the next room." He pushed through the swinging half-door. "Yikes. What a mess."

Klara followed to stand next to him. She called, "Petter. Come out, Petter." Her feet crunched the broken crockery on the floor as she walked between the tables. Without conscious thought she stooped and picked unbroken salt cellars and several knives and forks from the rubble. She placed them on the nearest table and walked on down the room. The floor no longer heaved and jumped under foot and the constant roar of the wind had stopped. She could hear Izzy opening and closing the doors of the long row of storage cabinets lining the room. Somehow it didn't seem like a place where Petter would hide.

At the far end of the room a double door opened out on a small viewing deck. Klara remembered taking the boys there to watch a last flock of gulls sweep down on the trail of garbage left in the ship's wake. When the next garbage was pitched out, the ship was far at sea, out of the birds' range. Matt had enjoyed the sweeping flight of the white birds, but Petter seemed not to notice for he wandered off before the gulls had finished their battle over the bread crusts and vegetable peelings floating on the water. Now she wondered if something else on the deck had drawn his attention.

The doors were neither locked, nor barred. Passengers would not be expected to have access to this area with the dining room closed. Unless, of course, someone crept in through the kitchen or slipped into a storage cabinet while the crew went about their storm preparations. Klara pushed through the heavy doors. The wind still held the power to whip her hair from its tight coil at the nape of her neck and lift her skirt above her knees. The waves no longer sloshed over the rail onto the floor, but the pooled water told her the sea had battered this area during the storm. The sky had cleared and a full moon etched the details in its path sharp, while casting impenetrable shadows everywhere else. Klara stepped to the rail, mesmerized by the moonlight tracing the patterns of the churning water.

"It's beautiful," she said to herself.

"I never get tired of watching the ocean." Izzy was there beside her, suddenly, startling her with his silent approach. "Be careful. The deck is slippery."

He put his arm around her waist. They stood together, close enough for Klara's hair to flow dark across Izzy's shoulder. The moment was shattered by a scuffling noise. Klara tensed, started to pull away, but Izzy tightened his hold.

"Rats probably." He drew Klara close again.

"Maybe it's Petter."

"Maybe."

She jerked away and stumbled towards the shadowed end of the deck. Izzy mumbled a curse and followed her.

"The lifeboat, the noise is coming from the lifeboat."

She stood on her tiptoes to peer into the small craft slung from a pair of metal stanchions. The damp canvas cover flapped against her cheek.

"It's so dark. Petter, Petter." She thought the sound was moving toward her. "Petter, come here."

"I'll get a light," said Izzy. She heard the dining room door slam.

"Petter. Come out. No one is mad at you, just worried."

She was certain Petter was in the lifeboat, now. When Izzy returned with the lantern, he handed it to Klara.

"It's Petter. I'm sure of it."

"Hold it high."

He scrambled up the stanchion and dropped into the boat. His shoes squished in water and the canvas left dark smudges on his white trousers.

"All right, Petter. The game is up. Either you come out or I'll come in."

He began removing the canvas cover, rolling it away from him, but before he reached the midsection of the lifeboat, Petter crawled out. Izzy picked him up and hoisted him over the side where Klara helped him slide down to the deck. Petter wrapped his arms around her and buried his face in her skirt.

"I'm hungry."

"We were worried about you," she answered. "Why did you run off?"

"To see the plates slide across the tables."

"What?"

"It didn't work, Klara. They all fell down and broke. I got scared and hid in the little boat."

Izzy stooped down. "How about a piggyback ride to your cabin. We'll grab some bread and jam as we go through the galley. Wouldn't want a sailor to go hungry."

Klara followed Izzy and Petter through the deserted lounge. She stumbled over a bench cushion on the floor and realized she was shaking; her knees felt like jelly. She pulled her shawl closer about her shoulders. A splash of bright color caught her attention as she picked her way through the mess between the dining room tables.

She stopped and bent to examine the gleam of rose and gold that burned against the dull gray of the floor, against the shards of rough brown stoneware littering the room. It was a china cup, chipped and cracked. Perhaps it had belonged to one of the ship's officers or maybe a kitchen worker had stolen it from first class. Klara knelt in the rubble, picked up the cup, held it to her cheek.

"Mamma, Mamma, I'm so sorry. I didn't mean to break it."

When Izzy returned to look for her, Klara was sitting on the floor holding the broken cup, hot tears tracing down her face. He lifted her up and took the broken cup from her hands. Though his motions were careful, slow and gentle, the raw edge of the porcelain caught on Klara's cheek and pulled a thin red scratch across her tender skin.

"I'm sorry, Klara." He dabbed the scratch with his handkerchief. "Does it hurt?"

"No. I'm fine, thank you." She pulled away from him. "I need to get Petter to bed. Thanks for all your help."

~~~

With Petter safely in bed, Klara went to fill the wash basin. Katie and Lisa were bedded down in the boys' cabin. She helped Maja wash up and climb into her own bunk. How lucky it was Maja had so many nightgowns, she thought. It was nearly dawn before she had the bed things washed and the cabin cleaned up. Too tired to go to breakfast, she climbed into the other top bunk and fell asleep immediately.

While Klara slept, the ship steamed into harbor. Izzy came to show her the Statue of Liberty, but Maja answered his knock at the door.

"She had a long night," she told him. "Best let her sleep."

Recovered from her seasickness, Maja went back to combing her long hair. Izzy escorted Matt and Petter to the observation deck and Klara missed her chance to see the famous statue.

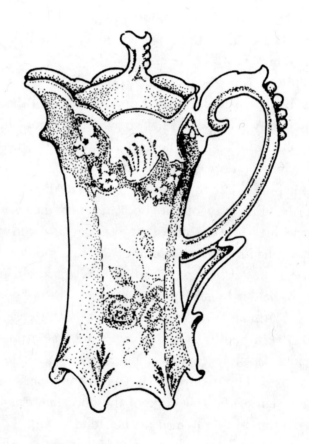

Separation Unto a New Day.

As the ship docked at one of the West Side Manhattan piers, the first and second class passengers were called on deck for inspection prior to disembarkation. Klara stood with Harald, Maja, and the children at their place on deck. A stiff breeze ruffled their hair and threatened to send Maja's picture hat sailing over the rail. Klara felt light-headed, confused from lack of sleep, and anxiety.

She had overslept and missed breakfast. She had rushed to dress and pack up her things with the call to appear on deck blasting her ears. The last thing she did was to double-check the money sewn into the belt under her clothes. When she finally arrived on deck, she found most of the passengers assembled in ragged groups awaiting inspection. Tight lipped with embarrassment, she searched until she found Maja and Harald with the children near the first examination station.

"You're late," said Harald when he saw her. "Take Lisa."

"Isn't it a beautiful day?" said Maja. "I feel like singing."

Klara felt more like crying, but she did think Maja looked especially attractive in the morning light. Except for the dark circles that showed through the layer of face powder she had applied a few hours earlier, Maja showed no sign of her weeks of seasickness. She wore a traveling suit of navy blue, fitted at the waist and flared over her hips. She carried Katie who was done up in her best outfit, the scrape on her forehead from her fall from the bunk already scabbed over. The boys wore their sailor suits and huddled close to their father.

Lisa held onto Klara's skirt with both hands, held on so tightly her knuckles showed white. Barely aware of the child, Klara rubbed her fingers over a stain on her white cuff, scraped at it with a finger nail rough and cracked from hours of washing up in cold water. She noticed patches of lint clinging to her black skirt, noticed the toes of her shoes scuffed gray from kneeling over the wash basin or the children's bunks. Unable to spare the time to braid her hair and put it up, she had tied it back and covered it with a scarf.

She patted Lisa on the head and tried to concentrate on her surroundings. A white-coated man and an elderly nurse were engaged in checking each traveler for eye disease or defect. Klara had read that any passenger found with cataracts, conjunctivitis, or trachoma, whatever those things were, would be sent home on the next ship. What was it the doctors saw, she wondered.

Watching them made Klara terribly conscious of her own eyes. They felt so itchy this morning. Though the day was overcast with a fine mist of fog hovering over the smoke stacks of the ship, everything seemed too bright and the glare from the water made her eyes tear up. Gulls screamed beside the ship, occasionally making a pass over the deck. Klara found a place in line behind Harald and Maja and settled in to wait. She could see the passengers from steerage filing onto a ferry for the trip to Ellis Island. Piles and piles of baggage disgorged from the hold cluttered the deck. Harald had to speak to her several times before she realized she was being addressed.

"Make her stand up. The examiner is coming this way."

Klara finally understood he was referring to Lisa. The little girl had sat down on the deck and was playing with a bit of waste paper, a thin line of saliva trailed off her chin onto her ruffled dress. Klara muttered an apology and stooped to lift the child to her feet, wiped her face and tried to clean the smudges of dirt from her hands. Lisa whimpered, but didn't cry.

The examiner gave Harald and his family a cursory check, looked at their papers, saw that they had a fat wad of cash, then motioned them forward, closer to the gangway. Fortunately he spoke Swedish.

"Your papers will be stamped at the next table, then you will be free to debark. Welcome to America."

"Thank you, sir," said Harald. He took the family's papers and guided Matt and Petter to the foredeck with Maja and Katie close behind. Klara took Lisa's hand and turned to follow, but the examiner stopped her with a hand on her elbow.

"The child is cleared, but I need to see your papers." To Harald he called, "Come get your daughter, sir."

Harald came back across the deck. "What's wrong?"

"He says you must take charge of Lisa until he's looked at my papers," said Klara. She pushed Lisa towards her father.

Harald swung Lisa to his shoulder and said to the examiner, "Miss Larsson is with us. Can you move things along?"

"Sorry, sir. She's steerage and must go through processing on the island." To Klara he said, "To your left, miss, then down the stairs to the ferry. Pick up your baggage on the way."

Harald said, "Nonsense. She traveled second class with us. We paid the extra fare."

The examiner ignored him and urged Klara to hurry. "You'll have a long wait if you miss this ferry. Find your luggage and get aboard." He pointed to the mound of bundles and trunks unloaded from the hold.

Klara looked to Harald, but saw that he was already following his family to the last processing station. No help would come from that quarter. She made one attempt to ask the examiner if he could find Izzy, but his only response was a shove in the direction of the ferry. With a sob Klara joined the steerage passengers lined up to claim their belongings. Three or four officials with lists of names and numbers made sure each match was correct.

Klara was at first delighted to see her own box with its painted decorations in among the heap of luggage. Several times on the journey she had wondered if she would ever see it again. After trying to pick it up she wondered how it could have gotten so much heavier. A red-faced man with a thick sheaf of papers had checked her name against his list and was waving her on to the line for the ferry. With a desperate effort she wrestled her box to the gang plank, then slid it down the narrow slope to the dock and her place at the end of the line. Momentarily relieved, she sat down on her box to catch her breath.

As the line edged forward, she slid her box along the worn planking of the dock. A group of INS men walked up and down the line of immigrants to make sure no one bolted for freedom prematurely. The INS directed them onto the ferry, but made no move to help any of the over-burdened travelers with their trunks and bundles. The much smaller boat rose and fell with the water's incessant movement, but Klara hardly noticed. She managed to haul her box onto the ferry and find a place near the rail with several women traveling alone. Packed shoulder to shoulder with hundreds of strangers, she had never felt so alone in her entire life.

The ride across to the island was short, but Klara felt the old nausea of seasickness she had experienced weeks earlier begin to come back. Despite the tales she had heard of the horrors of the place, she was very glad when the ferry bumped up against the dock at Ellis Island.

When they struggled off the ferry, each person was tagged with their name and the name of the ship on which they had traveled. With a great deal of shouting and gesturing the mass of people was split into two groups, men to the left, women and children to the right. Bewildered at this unexpected development, they formed two ragged lines at the entrance doors.

Officials rechecked name tags and baggage labels with long lists from the manifests of the several ships that had landed that day. Though it was a hot summer day, they wore heavy blue coats with a plethora of brass buttons and stiff-billed caps. Several times Klara saw them stop to wipe the sweat from their necks and faces. Every ten or fifteen minutes the processing would halt while the officials retired to the shade for a drink of water and a rest. No such relief was available to the travelers who stood waiting to enter the building.

The heat was almost over-powering and Klara tried to focus on her surroundings to blot out her misery. The Main Building was built of brick and gray limestone. Four copper-roofed turrets marked the corners and three glass-filled arches spanned the front, a double door in each arch. As they got closer to the building, a porch extended the luxury of shade to the waiting people. Though thousands of immigrants had passed through the building since it opened in December, it still looked new, its copper gleaming, its stone work clean and untouched.

It was unfortunate that families were separated before the baggage check. It often left women already overwhelmed with small children faced with the added burden of heavy boxes or trunks. With the other women Klara tried to lug her box up the shallow steps into the Main Building. She struggled to lift the box, then gave up and pushed it, end over end, up the steps until she caught up with the line. With a sigh she sat down on her box. Her head throbbed and she felt weak and hot. The ground floor room was a swirl of noise and people. The head of the line seemed to be the source of the terrible uproar.

A bent old woman was shrilling at two young men, uniformed workers. They were trying to take the woman's bundle and she was resisting with loud cries, pulling her poor belongings away from the man and throwing herself on her baggage. No one seemed to speak her language and the worker kept shouting louder and louder in his attempt at making her understand. The other worker copied information from the woman's name tag onto a square of cardboard. When the other young man finally wrestled the bundle from the old woman, he tore the cardboard in half, tied one part to the bundle and pressed the other part into the woman's hand. The old woman stood working her mouth, the tears flowing down her crumpled cheeks, while the men moved down the line to the next person.

Klara watched them approach the next person in line with trembling hands. She wanted to reach inside her blouse to feel her money, but Izzy had warned her against betraying the hiding place of her small nest egg. This time it was a meek child about her own age who surrendered her trunk without protest. A new group from the next ferry crowded into the room and Klara lost sight of the baggage checkers.

She settled down on her box to wait for the line to move forward. The mass of people in the hall seemed to swell, she felt light-headed, dizzy. Her neck ached and her stomach hurt. If only she had had some breakfast, more sleep. Why had she ever left home. Would she ever manage to pass the medical inspectors, how was she going to manage her heavy box. Maybe it would be better if they took it from her. How would she survive if she was sent home, survive the humiliation, the shame of failure. Were Sofia and Arvid coming to meet her. How would they even find her in this mess. Her thoughts seemed about to pound through her skull and escape to the high, tiled ceiling of the room.

As the hour wore on new worries crowded into her tired mind. The line seemed totally stalled; the young men with the cardboard squares had disappeared. She felt so weak and hot. Was she going to vomit or faint in front of all these strange people. In invisible waves the noise and heat washed over her and over the huddled families around her. Now and then an official would call a family or a single man from the lines, hurry them out a side door, leaving those behind to rush forward to fill the gap.

When the family just ahead was called out, Klara struggled her box across the gap, dragging, pushing, half lifting the clumsy thing, afraid of losing her place in line. She sat down on her box to catch her breath and surreptitiously slip her hand under her blouse to feel her money.

After she calmed a little she noticed the family now in front of her. The dark-haired woman looked like her own mother, thin and leathery from years of hard work. A number of small children crowded around her and she held a tiny baby to her breast. They were all barefoot and wore shapeless clothing cut down from old adult garments. They had no boxes or trunks, only lumpish gray bundles tied up with string and rags. The oldest, a girl of six or seven, drew Klara's attention. The pinch-faced, dirty child held a large antique bowl in her arms.

A terrible wave of homesickness caught Klara while she watched the child struggle to keep the family heirloom, a bowl of thinnest porcelain, safe. She had it clasped tight to her skinny chest. When she had to walk forward to keep up with her mother, she craned her neck to see the floor where she was to step. It was remarkable that the family had been able to carry this fragile bowl from whatever hamlet they had called home to the ship, then clear across the ocean to Ellis Island.

It must be a beloved treasure, thought Klara.

The pattern of roses twined with gold-edged leaves was so much like the pattern on the chocolate set at home. The pitcher and seven cups, no six cups, she amended, that stood on the shelf above the stove. The memory of that seventh cup, and the eighth, filled her with remorse and guilt.

Could she do nothing right. Here she was, watching a mere babe caretaking her family's treasure, when she, herself, had managed to break two of her mother's chocolate cups. Klara swallowed the sobs that gathered in her throat. Thoughts swirled and beat through her mind. Flashes of broken cups, fallen trees, leering tramps, her own dear mother screaming, distraught.

Klara tried to clear her head, concentrate on the task of getting through the inspection. She looked away from the tattered child, the fragile bowl, tried to see what was happening to the line of people ahead. They must be getting close by now.

When Klara could finally see the head of the line again, she nearly swooned. The line made a sharp turn and wound up a long staircase to the second floor. At the head of the stairs she could see tables and many people, men dressed in suits and ties, doctors in their white coats carrying stethoscopes and charts, nurses dressed in white with starched caps.

Did she have to wrestle her box up those many steps. Was this why the two young men were taking the passengers' luggage. Before she could puzzle this out, they were back, moving quickly down the line trading the cardboard squares for trunks and boxes. They ignored the rag-wrapped bundles and the porcelain bowl, but took Klara's box. She put the cardboard square into her waist pouch after she saw it had the same numbers as her name tag. Her only regret was she had lost her seat and had to stand now.

A tall young orderly, a black man, approached, checking name tags and asking questions through an interpreter. For a few minutes the waiting travelers roused themselves from their apathy, some pulled back in surprise, others crossed themselves. Klara was only mildly interested in the man's deep brown skin and tightly curled black hair because she had seen Africans on the wharf in Kristiania.

The child with the rose-painted bowl, however, seemed terrified. She's probably never seen a black person before, thought Klara.

The little girl screamed, then jerked away when he tried to read her name tag. She caught her toes in the uneven hem of her long dress and fell forward, then caught herself. Though she tried to protect the bowl, it slipped from her weary fingers and crashed to the floor to fracture into a dozen pieces. Before Klara could expel her indrawn breath the mother reached out and clouted the child on the ear. The little girl was unable to regain her balance this time and fell in the mess of the broken bowl.

Though the language was different, Klara's voice joined with the child's scream.

"Mamma, I'm sorry, Mamma," before she fainted.

Days later she would remember many hands lifting her to a gurney, bumping her along to another building, placing her on a bed with cool rough sheets. Mostly she let her mind wander back to her home, her brothers and sisters, her grandfather and the stories he told of the early years. She tried to avoid thinking about the child with the bowl, the broken chocolate cups, and her mother's harsh words. It was Granpappa's voice that soothed and entertained her as she drifted in and out of the hectic sleep of fever.

In a few days the fever abated and Klara was able to sit up, to take note of her surroundings. She discovered she was in the hospital building on Ellis Island. A smiling nurse, accompanied by a translator, came in to take her temperature and relay a message from Sofia and Arvid.

"They will come to get you as soon as the doctor signs your

release."

"I'm not being sent back?" Klara said. "When can I go?"

"In a day or two. You don't want a relapse."

"My box, my clothes. Where are they."

Klara tried to climb out of bed, then reached for the Queen Victoria coin around her neck. At least that was still there, she thought.

The nurse pushed her back and smoothed the sheet.

"Your box is safe in the baggage check. You can get it when you leave. Your other things are right here." She bent down and pulled a box from under the bed. "See, there's nothing to worry about."

Klara lay back on the newly fluffed pillow. Relieved, but still apprehensive, she decided she would look for her money when the nurse left. A constant stream of people in and out of the ward soon convinced her she would have to wait.

When breakfast came, Klara downed the glass of milk and bowl of oatmeal before the aide had left her bedside. How long had she been here she wondered. The aide serving breakfast interrupted her.

"My, my. Somebody has their appetite back."

Klara looked at the plump woman and tried to figure out what she had said. The aide decided Klara was still hungry and gave her an extra bowl of cereal and a plate of rubbery buttered toast. When Klara continued to stare at her, she added a small dish of strawberry jam, patted Klara on the shoulder, and went on about her serving.

Later in the morning Klara crept out of bed to look through her belongings. She knelt on the tile floor with her back to the curious eyes of the other women on the ward. When she found her money belt with its American five and one dollar bills intact, she was greatly relieved. She wadded the tattered rag belt under her hospital gown and climbed back into bed, knees trembling with the exertion.

On Friday the doctor gave Klara a clean bill of health, signed her medical certificate, and sent the nurse in to help her dress and find her way to the main building. The nurse ordered her to the shower room before allowing her to dress.

The shower was one of the most amazing things Klara had ever experienced. The hard stream of hot water made her eyes tear with pleasure and though the soap had a faint medicinal smell, it worked into mounds of soothing lather. She washed her hair and stood under the spray until impatient knocking on the door told her it was time to finish. She dried on the towel she found on the hook outside, then dressed quickly.

She decided the shower was even more enjoyable than the banana pudding she had eaten on the ship. Was it possible to have one at home. A hot water shower and banana pudding would be heaven itself.

Dressed and walking to the main building, Klara felt a bit wobbly, but the fresh air lifted her spirits, made her feel like singing, shouting. She had made it. She was in America, the promised land. Arvid and Sofia were waiting to take her home. A few more formalities in the Main Hall and her new life would begin.

ISBN 1-41205030-8

9 781412 050302